Praise for *Sister Mary Baruch: The Early Years*

Sister Mary Baruch shows how ordinary struggles become the stuff of a divine life of grace. Through the imaginative eyes of Sr. Mary Baruch, Fr. Jacob has given us a look into the mystery of the Dominican cloistered nun and captured the intersection of the human with the divine.

> —Fr. Basil Cole, O.P., Professor of Moral Theology, Dominican House of Studies, Washington, D.C.

I would thoroughly encourage anyone to read this book. It is truly an abundant presentation of Monastic life yesterday and today. We had the opportunity of having Fr. Jacob as our chaplain for six years, and during his homilies at Mass we heard many of the stories that make up the foundation of this book. Once you start reading this book, you won't be able to put it down, believe me!

> —Sr. Theresa Marie, O.P., *Monastery of the Mother of God, West Springfield, MA*

Such a blessing, this book. Fr Jacob is a gifted storyteller who can be hilariously funny and yet pierce the heart. His years of experience as a monastery chaplain give him authentic insights into the trials and the profundity of cloistered life, and he skillfully balances a story of delightful simplicity with profound insights into human nature and the mystery of the monastic life.

—Sr. Mary Dominic, O.P., *Monastery of Our Lady of the Rosary, Buffalo, NY*

Father Restrick's novel offers characters, settings, and life situations that are realistic and recognizable to a wide-range of readers. One is easily drawn into sharing the ups and downs, joys and sorrows of Rebecca's life and spiritual journey while experiencing the pulse and culture of New York City living. Readers will smile, chuckle, and knowingly nod as they are unexpectedly lead to gentle reflections of God's providential impact in their own lives. A delightful story that begs to be continued!

—Marianne T. Jablonski, O.P., *Dominican Laity*

Fr. Jacob's attention to detail is what makes everything come alive for the reader. At times he made me laugh, at other times weep, and at times he made me pray. He weaves truths about the Catholic faith into the story's fabric, educating even as he entertains the reader.

—Darillyn Paterson, *Dominican Laity*

Sister Mary Baruch

SISTER MARY BARUCH

The Early Years

Fr. Jacob Restrick, O.P.

TAN Books
Charlotte, North Carolina

Cover design by Caroline K. Green

Cover image: The Ceiling of a Gothic Church. Photo by kombattle/Shutterstock

ISBN: 978-1-5051-1455-3

Published in the United States by
TAN Books
PO Box 410487
Charlotte, NC 28241
www.TANBooks.com

Printed in the United States of America

This humble work is dedicated to today's cloistered daughters of St. Dominic who walk this road less traveled, and to the sons of our Holy Father Dominic who serve them and depend on their prayers.

Two roads diverged in a wood, and I—
I took the one less traveled by,
And that has made all the difference.

—Robert Frost

FOREWORD

THIS IS THE story of Sister Mary Baruch's deep loves. As we come to know Becky Feinstein (her name "in the world" before becoming a contemplative Dominican nun), we learn about her love for warm bagels and good chocolate, for Broadway theater and good books, for her good friends and her close-knit family, and, of course, for New York City itself. But it is another love—one that comes upon her quite unexpectedly—that gives her story its power: the love of Jesus himself.

This is a story of conversion, acknowledging all of the crises and consolations, both small and large, that come from that. We follow Becky as she first comes to hear the Lord in that "still, quiet place" in her heart and then as she follows that newfound love and encounters its (sometimes bittersweet) consequences.

This book is the fruit of the contemplation and the rich experience of a wise and gifted preacher. Fr. Jacob Restrick's long service as a chaplain to different communities of Dominican nuns has given him a privileged insight into the experience of this form of intimate friendship with Jesus, and its moments both sublime and ordinary. The reader who accompanies Sr. Mary Baruch on her odyssey is receiving not only the story of a soul but a profound lesson about the spiritual life itself.

—Jonah Teller, O.P.

PREFACE

The nuns of the Order of Preachers came into being when our Holy Father Dominic gathered women converts to the Catholic faith in the monastery of Blessed Mary of Prouille. These women, free for God alone, he associated with his "holy preaching" by their prayer and penance. Our Holy Father drew up a rule to be followed and constantly showed a father's love and care for these nuns and for others established later in the same way of life. In fact, "they had no other master to instruct them about the Order." Finally, he entrusted them as part of the same Order to the fraternal concern of his sons.

—Fundamental Constitution of the Nuns 1.1

I WAS PREACHING AN Advent retreat at one of our cloistered monasteries and the readings at Mass for the Monday of the Second Week are from Isaiah and the Gospel of Luke. I wondered how a cloistered nun would reflect on these reading and how they pertain to the life of a cloistered nun. And so Sr. Mary Baruch of the Advent Heart was born. I "discovered" a journal she had written with her own reflections on these readings and shared them in my homily. The nuns seemed to identify with her, and so she would appear in homilies thereafter. Through her journals, we eventually got to know her family and the story of her own conversion from Judaism. Here the full story can be told.

Sr. Mary Baruch was originally written for Dominican nuns, as I had been chaplain to two of our cloistered monasteries, and familiar with most of the others. But her story has entertained, and I hope, inspired, many beyond the cloister walls: Dominican laity, priests, Sisters, Brothers, Catholic and non-Catholic friends alike.

We welcome a new and revised edition of Sr. Mary Baruch, O.P. The Early Years. There have been a few factual errors in the original which have been corrected, while the storyline remains the same.

I am especially grateful to two of my Dominican brothers, Jonah Teller and Henry Stephan, for their editorial expertise, desire, and diligence in editing and reformatting the entire novel. I am also grateful to the many Sisters who have come to know Sr. Mary Baruch and welcomed her into their hearts, and have offered their personal reflections.

Sr. Mary Baruch is completely fictitious, as is her monastery of Our Lady Queen of Hope in Brooklyn Heights, New York. The Sisters, priests, family, and friends of Sr. Mary Baruch are also completely fictitious, while the churches and places in New York are factual (except for Tea on Thames).

If you have not met Sister Mary Baruch before, the early chapters will introduce you to her and her family and friends, and her coming into the Faith of the Holy Catholic Church. If you are reacquainting yourself with her, you will follow her again into the monastery and the grace-filled life of a Dominican nun. Whether you are reading for the first time or renewing the acquaintance, may you be moved to laughter, to tears, and, most of all, to prayer. May you find something of yourself in Sr. Mary Baruch, who has found that loving God with all one's heart is "such a blessing."

Fr. Jacob Restrick, O.P.
October 31, 2015
Vigil of All Saints

One

MY NAME IS Baruch; I know, it's not a girl's name, but it's *my* name…Mary Baruch, actually, which gives it a nice feminine flavor, yes? Sister Mary Baruch to be exact, but *Sister* is a title that we nuns are all called by. I did not choose Mary Baruch as my name when I became a nun; it was chosen for me. It was a day I'll never forget. In my journal I have written right after the date, November 1, 1970, *My Wedding Day.*

It was a crisp, autumn-in-New-York kind of day. The community had just chanted Lauds before the Solemn High Mass for All Saints' Day. I had come into the choir, the nuns' part of the chapel, dressed in an eggshell white Chantilly lace wedding dress. It was a used dress; I don't know how many nuns before me had worn it, probably not too many, as it came off the extra-large rack and even then had to be let out some. Most of the more portly nuns don't acquire their portliness till many years after their wedding day, but I came in as a size 18 and a half. Some of the nuns had even worn their own mothers' wedding dresses, if they passed the inspection of the prioress; they couldn't be too exquisite, but plain and not tight-fitting.

Mine was not my dear mother's, who would have been horrified at the thought of her gown being worn by a Catholic nun, even if—or especially if—it was her own daughter.

She wasn't even in our lovely chapel that All Saints' Day to see me in Chantilly lace with the little pillbox lace veil. I may have looked like a chubby old gal making her First Holy Communion, but I couldn't have been happier. My wearing the wedding dress was an exception to the rule, as the custom had been let go some years before. "Letting go is always difficult," Mother John Dominic, the prioress, would often say; we seemed to be more reluctant than others. Mother also had another reason to make this exception in my case, which I'll explain later.

Like all the nuns that came before me, I was dying to know what *name* I would receive. When I entered and officially became a postulant, I was called Sister Rebecca; Rebecca was my "name in the world." As a postulant, just entering the cloister, I wore a 1930s style schoolgirl's jumper and white blouse with a black caplet and a shoulder length black veil. We were three postulants in 1970. I was the third from that group to receive the habit. We entered the chapel as brides on our vestition day, the day we were married to Christ, although we didn't take our vows then, but were clothed in the habit of the Order. Our hair was cut for the first time, and we were given our new names.

I had never heard of a Sr. Mary Baruch before and doubt that Baruch is even counted as a saint. I was hoping for the name of one of the Apostles, or one of our Dominican Saints. Well, I confess, I thought Mother John Dominic would probably name me after Thomas Aquinas; I think he may have worn a size 18 and a half tunic too. But I learned later that Mother wanted something from the Hebrew Scriptures, or the Old Testament, as we Catholics called them. Rachel or Ruth would have been nice, even Judith, as there's a bit of the old warrior in me. Of course, I would have been thrilled to have been given the name Hannah, my dear old mother's name. I called her Hannah of a Thousand Silver Hairs. And Ruth is the name of my younger sister; she would have been thrilled to no end. So it was to my surprise that I was to be called Mary Baruch of the Advent Heart. *Baruch?* I didn't know the Hebrew Scriptures all that well, and Baruch, for me, was the name of the college on Lexington Avenue and 24th Street where my cousin Esther went to get her teaching degree.

Mother John Dominic no doubt thought she was being clever naming me Baruch, as the Old Testament Baruch was the personal secretary to the Prophet Jeremiah. Actually, "Jeremiah" would have fit me better as I was often given to jeremiads, even before we were encouraged to speak up at community meetings. I've grown to love my name, however, as I know it means "Blessed." And I have certainly been blessed. Hannah, I hope, loved it too, as Mama used to say that we, her children, were each a blessing. Even when we'd make awful or dumb mistakes, or have accidents, she could see the blessing in everything. "Such a blessing for you," Mama would say, usually while remedying the situation.

Before all that, I was just a nice Jewish girl from the Upper West Side of Manhattan. I grew up on West 79th Street between Columbus and Amsterdam, in the shadow of the Museum of Natural History and the wonderful Hayden's Planetarium. How I loved that mysterious place; I think it made us kids both awestruck and giddy with joy. They could make the whole night sky—the Big Dipper and everything—shine and move on the ceiling-dome above us. My older brother, David, always wanted to go see the dinosaur remains, but my sisters and I loved the Planetarium. Actually, we didn't go to the Museum of Natural History very much, even though it was just a half block away.

Across the street was a synagogue where we went. I would like to say that we went every Friday night or Saturday morning, but we didn't. I did go to Hebrew School, along with my sisters Sally and Ruthie and my brothers David and Joshua, so we *got the basics*, as Mama would say. "Such a blessing you should have to know a little Hebrew!"

We were not the most devout of Jewish families, but we did keep Shabbat every week; that was probably the strictest...or at least the most self-conscious part of growing up Jewish; and it was one of the nicest too. I have emblazoned on my memory Mama lighting the Shabbat candles on the dining room table, which was always covered with a special lace tablecloth only used on Shabbat. I can still see her covering her eyes while she prayed aloud in a voice that I will always remember; it was somehow different from her normal voice the rest of the week. The Hebrew words seemed to roll off her tongue like a quiet brook flowing in the woods.

Barukh atah Adonai,	Blessed are you, Lord,
Eloheinu, melekh ha'olam	our God, sovereign of the
asher kidishanu b'mitz'vo-	universe, Who has sancti-
tav v'tzivanu l'had'lik neir	fied us with His command-
shel Shabbat. Amein	ments and commanded
	us to light the lights of
	Shabbat. Amen

The house was always quieter after the candles were lit, or so it seemed.

My full family name was Rebecca Abigail Feinstein. My initials were thus shared with the British Royal Air Force. I was called Becky by everyone except Papa who always called me either Rebecca or Raf; I thought it was for the R.A.F. but Papa said it was short for Raphael and that I was his little angel. Papa's name was Ruben, but people called him Ben; not Benny, but Ben. When I got a little older and Papa would call me "Raf, my little angel," I would say, "What is it, Ruben, my little corned-beef sandwich?" And Papa would laugh and give me a hug.

"Becky, Becky, my little side of coleslaw, why are you being such a sour pickle today? So serious you are, for sixteen years old."

And I would laugh too; Papa could always make me laugh...funny, huh? It makes me almost weep today when I remember it and how I thought I broke his heart, and he never showed it. But that was a few years after my sixteenth birthday. I don't know what broke my father's heart more... when my brother, Josh, at nineteen years old was killed in Vietnam, or when I became a Christian when I was twenty. These are not totally unrelated as I think about it all now. Funny how time changes the way we see things. Time is capable of putting things in a context, in a setting, like a fine piece of jewelry.

I *was* a serious child, as Papa teased, at least compared to my sisters. Sally, or Sarah, was the oldest girl, just four years older than me. She was also serious, but in an academic way. She was the smartest daughter of the three Feinstein girls, or so I believed because I heard it said once by Mrs. Melbourne at Max the Butcher's. She was discussing something about lamb chops with her spinster sister, when Sally and I rushed past them with our newly butchered, but neatly wrapped, chickens. They were not wrapped tightly, and chicken blood dripped out from the brown paper and down my seersucker jumper. I, of course, gave out a scream of horror, causing the old ladies to jump three feet in the air and clutch their chests. Sally very calmly explained that our chickens were apparently leaking a bit and perhaps Max could double wrap them for us, and would he have a washcloth for Becky's jumper? It wasn't a highly intelligent explanation of the situation, but Mrs. Melbourne squeaked out, "Oh, my dear, look at your poor dress, all covered with blood. You mustn't grasp the packages too close to yourself, dear, carry them straight down away from yourself. Oh my."

We were scurrying past the two commentators, now fussing over the wrapping of their lamb chops, when I heard Mrs. Melbourne nonchalantly say to her sister, "The older girl, Sarah, should be charge of the packages; after all, she's older, *and* she's the brightest of the Feinstein girls."

I never questioned anyone how Mrs. Melbourne came to that bit of knowledge, but it was true. Sally was always on the Honor Roll at school, and dumb ole Becky was just schlepping her bag of books around and letting chicken blood drip all over her dress.

I did okay in school; Sally was already at Barnard, the women's college at Columbia University, when I was a high school sophomore. She was going to be a teacher someday. I wanted to go to Barnard too, and study law or English

Literature or creative writing and be a journalist for the *New York Times*! I wanted to write for the *Sunday Times Art and Entertainment* section and get free tickets to all the Broadway shows and be invited to movie premieres. Sally wound up being the journalist, not for the *New York Times*, but the *Philadelphia Inquirer*. She relocated, as we say today, to Philly which I would have found to be the greatest sacrifice in the world. I wouldn't leave New York City for a million bucks. Why would anyone, I thought, ever want to live anywhere else? I wanted to visit all the grand cities in Europe, but not to stay, and not till all the wars were over.

I wanted to see London's Broadway, which I knew they called the West End; and Amsterdam, which I pictured with windmills on every corner, and people walking around in wooden shoes, and pointed hats looking like nurses' caps, with embroidered pink and blue and yellow tulips growing around even more windmills. All the boys looking like the little Dutch boy on Dutch Boy Paints.

Mama had a single Dutch wooden shoe, painted white with little windmills and tulips painted on it. She had gotten it in the mail all the way from Holland, from Berta, her pen-pal for many years, ever since World War II, I think. They never met, but would write almost every month to each other.

Mama would always remember Berta's birthday, and of course, we kids always made fun of the tongue twisting alliteration: *Better buy Berta's Birthday Box*. Mama's wooden shoe was a real Dutch wooden shoe, sent to her from Berta for one of Mama's "berte-days." She kept it on a shelf in the front parlor, and sometimes we'd find things in it, like rock

candy and sour balls. I used to hold it and imagine everybody clopping around the sidewalks of Amsterdam in those
clodhoppers. When I was older I read that one could visit
the house in Amsterdam where Anne Frank had been hidden and wrote her diary. I saw the Broadway show when it
first came out, and afterwards I wanted more than anything
to write stories that would hold people spellbound, like I
experienced that night on Broadway.

I had two papier-mâché theatrical masks, the Comedy and
Tragedy faces. They were hanging in my corner of the bedroom I shared with Ruthie. I understood what they meant
and how spiritual it was to *touch people's souls*, as Mama
would say. Mama would say that her greatest spiritual experience, besides lighting the Shabbat candles, was listening
to the cantor, especially on Yom Kippur. I knew what she
meant. His voice carried you to another place inside of you.
I liked that place. It wasn't the same as the Broadway theater, but something akin to it. I was fascinated by it; I wasn't
afraid of it like I was afraid of buses and delivery boys on
bikes, swerving and weaving in and out of New York traffic.
I wasn't afraid of it like sometimes I was afraid of the dark.
Ruthie and I kept the Venetian blinds in our bedroom window slightly open, enough so we could see the street light.
We were afraid if the light went out that it was an air-raid
and we were going to be bombed, right on West 79th Street.

We were all afraid of air-raids and even rehearsed them
in school. We'd have to crouch down next to our desks with
our heads almost on the floor. It was a most unladylike position, and once acquired, it caused giggles and fits of laughter
among the girls. Once, Nola Finley, probably the smartest

(and fattest) girl in our class, tried getting in "air-raid-position," which was most difficult for her size, and she broke wind. Tommy Schultz shouted, "We've been bombed!" The whole class got hysterical laughing, even Mrs. Peterson, our second grade teacher. It makes me laugh today to think of it, but I also feel sorry for poor Nola Finley; nobody thought about how humiliated she must've felt, but I think she ended up laughing too. The next day, Tommy Schultz's bike tires were mysteriously flat, and he had to walk home pushing his bike. I wonder what ever happened to Nola?

When I was afraid, I could escape to my secret hiding place, like Anne Frank, but mine was inside. I could feel it on the other side of my rib cage. I think Mama escaped to her hiding place too when she prayed and closed her eyes and her voice became all mellow. Sometimes, it seemed I could find that place inside of me more at a Broadway play than at Temple—I could get all teary-eyed during a curtain call, more than the saddest lamentation on Yom Kippur. I didn't think about it, but I knew those tears sprang up because something was touched in that secret hiding place. I didn't analyze it when I was a kid, but that secret place, surrounding my heart, behind my sternum, I just knew it was always there, and I was safe there…it was my inner space.

Ruthie shared my interest in show biz news, and we loved to go to the movies together, and if we were down around 57th Street, we'd go into Horn and Hardart's for a piece of pie from the automat, and tea. We called it our afternoon high tea; we would both be "her ladyship" and addressed each other rather formally with our amateur British accents, but we were sure we were fooling the tourists who goggled at us British girls. We, of course, were dressed as properly as we could be for a matinee and high tea. We always remembered our white linen gloves, even when indoors, and I would pour as I was the elder, even if I was not as smart as Sally. I was a better "pourer" than Ruthie, who was too full of antsy energy to pour a decent cup of tea.

If she were going to become the grand actress in the Feinstein family, of course she would have to change her name, so she informed us, every time she came up with a new one. For several months she was Edith Friend or Edie Stein...and that's when she discovered a story in the *New Amsterdam Jewish Press*, about a German Jewish girl who was a Catholic nun, a Carmelite, who died at Auschwitz. It was a fascinating story which we knew we couldn't talk about at home, at the dinner table, but Edith Stein was welcomed at our imaginary high teas at Horn's. "Little steins" became our secret code word for "caramels"...the little brown square ones which were so chewy they could almost pull out your fillings, not the caramel in all its creamy thickness, hidden in Snicker bars or poured over vanilla ice cream, which was often served at our high teas, along with lady fingers. Ruthie loved lady fingers. We used to joke that if we ever became nuns we would be "caramelites," like Edith Stein. Ruthie was my sister, but also my best friend, and the keeper of secrets. We also planned on being each other's maids of honor when we got married under the white and gold brocade canopy at Temple.

It seemed to all change overnight when we were both in high school, and boys became more interesting than afternoon tea parties. *Fiddler on the Roof* was all the rage on Broadway, and David, the eldest and firstborn son of Ruben and Hannah Feinstein, had the most brilliant idea for a gift to celebrate Mama and Papa's twenty-fifth wedding anniversary: Broadway tickets to *Fiddler* for the whole family—except Josh, of course, who was in Vietnam. We had already gotten the Broadway album and knew the songs almost by heart. Papa was no Zero Mostel, of course, but he did have three daughters, like Tevye, who had five. Mama and Papa knew all the words to *Sunrise, Sunset*, and would sing out loud with the album, but they wouldn't splurge and go see the show. David really paid for the tickets, but we each contributed something from our "Broadway Fund."

Ruthie and I had a joint fund. It was an empty Maxwell House Coffee tin, which we kept on the bookshelf under my Comedy/Tragedy masks. We would save quarters and dimes whenever we could. We still got allowances for the little chores we did around the apartment, and sometimes we could put half our allowance in our Theater Tin. We'd save and save for months, and sometimes cheated and used the savings for movies rather than the theater. But David accepted our contribution, which I don't think paid for one ticket. Sally was coming up from Philadelphia and probably paid more than David, but let us think David did; he had come up with the idea. It was perfect—Tevye and his three daughters, off to break tradition, which we did...off to the theater on a Friday night. We ate before sunset so we wouldn't be late for the theater, arriving in two cabs, which was a treat in itself. Hannah of a Thousand Silver Hairs looked so elegant in her powder blue dress and the pearls she wore on her wedding day. It had been years since she went to a Broadway musical, and I caught her getting all teary-eyed when the house lights went down, and the overture began. She and Papa held hands like lovesick newlyweds. David, always the proper one among us, leaned over me and Ruthie and whispered to them, "Now you two behave yourselves." Mama blushed a little, but it made her face youthful and almost regal. I know when Tevye and Golda sang their love song together near the end, we were all holding back the tears. Such a blessing, I thought, to have my own Golda and her milkman.

After the theater we took two more taxis home, and when we got in it was almost eleven o'clock, but Mama lit the candles for Shabbat, and we all ate cake and drank Mogen David's Elderberry Wine, Mama's favorite. David had another surprise which had been hidden all night in the soup tureen on the dining room buffet table. It was neatly wrapped in silver metallic paper, which fascinated everyone, as metallic paper was not a common wrapping paper. It didn't have a ribbon or bow on it; it didn't need one, the paper itself was so pretty—very fancy for David, we all thought.

Well, it wasn't from David at all; he was just the delivery boy. It was from Josh, sent to David weeks before from Manila, where Josh had been deployed before going to Vietnam. Inside the box were two other smaller boxes, marked M and P. That was for Mama and Papa, not Military Police. Papa opened his first. It was a gold Timex watch with a Speidel expandable band. Papa was quite taken by it, as his old Bulova watch was always "on the blink." He had actually taken to going watch-less for the last month, thinking maybe Santa would bring him a new one for Chanukah. We had a Jewish Santa, you see.

And Mama's gift was an exquisite brooch, which she said must have cost Josh six months' wages. It was silver, appropriately, but an old, antique, burnished kind of silver, with ruby and sapphire chips set in a lace-like spread of tiny leaves with five tiny flowers in the center. She touched the silver flowers very gently and lisped through a tiny flood of tears rolling down her cheek, "How thoughtful of Josh, my five children."

Papa squeezed her shoulders and gently took the brooch in his hands and pinned it on her dress below her left shoulder. It looked even more beautiful with a powder-blue backdrop. Almost on cue, she took Papa's new watch and slipped it onto his left wrist, "*Mazel Tov*, my Ruben." And the Feinstein Family Singers shouted back, "*Mazel Tov*," and sang "Happy Anniversary to You."

David opened another bottle of Mogen David, in honor of Josh. Of course, we put *Fiddler* on the hi-fi and sang most of the score to our hearts' content, talked about how wonderful everybody was in the show, and wondered if we had a fiddler on our roof. Papa had us all in stitches pretending Fred, our Super, was Fred our Fiddler. Everyone in our building called him "Fred Mertz" (for Fred from *I Love Lucy*) because he could have been William Frawley's understudy: Fred the Fiddler on the Roof.

We needed a "fiddler on the roof," without realizing it, that happy September evening in 1964. Two days later "Tevye and Golda" received the telegram every parent with a son or daughter in the army dreads to receive. Josh had been killed in action. Sally came up from Philly again that same night, and David with his three sisters surrounded them with love and grief. We were not conservative Jews, but we covered the mirrors, and rent our garments and Mama and Papa went without shoes…sitting Shiva and saying Kaddish. It just seemed to be the right thing to do. How poor we become when we lose the life of a loved one. How much Josh would have been moved.

My brother, Joshua Hiram Feinstein, was only two years older than me. I was his first baby sister, he would like to remind me. I think he did that on purpose so I wouldn't be jealous of Ruthie when she came along and I lost the position. Nonetheless, Josh was probably the most religious of the Feinstein kids. We always thought if there was going to be a rabbi in the family, it would be Joshua. He had a voice which was a cantor in the making, and a sense of humor like a stand-up comic at Grossinger's.

However, he wasn't given too much to school work and didn't want to go to college. Maybe he felt inferior to David, who was the eldest and the shining star. "My Star of David" Papa would call him. So if it wasn't rabbinical school, Baruch College, or Grossinger's—what would it be? Mama was always afraid he'd run off to a kibbutz in Israel and get married over there and we'd never see him again. Ruthie and I wanted him to audition for Broadway; he had the talent, and the looks, but not the ambition. And to everyone's surprise, he enlisted in the army. David had beat the draft because he had flat feet and was partially blind in one eye. ("Such a blessing, your feet," Mama said when he was rejected by the draft board.) Josh enlisted before he could be drafted, even if it was for a longer time, it would be better…he would be an officer.

I think Josh's death touched something different in each of us. We never played our *Fiddler on the Roof* album after that, although they are not really related except by the association of time. I don't think Mama and Papa really celebrated their anniversary afterwards, except in a quiet private way. Papa never took his watch off, and Mama's brooch, well, I don't remember her ever wearing it, but she kept it in its box, with the tissue paper and metallic wrapping, in the top drawer of her dresser, where she had Josh's photo in his uniform framed.

David lost himself in his studies. He didn't seem to come home as often. Sally came home more often, it seemed, and filled the house with her chatter and news, which was usually more annoying than informative. Ruthie became a distracted teenager who screamed over rock stars and got lost in her school activities, which weren't always so savory.

I graduated high school that next year and planned to go to Barnard College. Josh's death affected me in ways that I couldn't talk about. I still went to the movies, but took to going by myself and liked the escape into the darkness of the theater and my "hiding place." That interior place I would go to became more like a second home. I was going to live at home, of course, and since David and Josh's room was empty now, it became my room, for which I was very grateful. Ruthie was playing her music all the time and wanted an extension phone in the bedroom, which she got for Chanukah. I even gave her my theater masks as a "room departing gift," and she gave me the Theater Tin. The family was still close, but it was different. Or maybe I was just different. Something was stirring inside me, which I didn't know at the time.

I loved walking in New York, at all times of the year. There are always a million people out walking, it seemed, but one could always be alone. My friend, Gracie, was probably my best friend from school. We graduated from high school together and had been good friends all during school, ever since we were on the *Banner* together. That was our school newspaper, which came out every two weeks. She was a reporter for the *Banner* and I was an editor. She was lots of fun to talk to, and wasn't boy crazy like so many of the other girls in school. If we weren't going to the movies, we'd go for long walks on Saturdays and Sundays.

During the day it was pretty safe to walk through Central Park, and it was really like another world. For one thing, it could be very entertaining; you never knew what you'd see or hear. And the show was for free! Gracie and I would make up stories about the people we observed, like the bird-watchers going by with their binoculars and tweed jackets. I suppose Gracie took the place of Ruthie when we'd do things like go for coffee at the Boathouse Café and pretend we were actresses taking a break between takes. Gracie loved to ride the carousel. We'd jump on with all the kids and ride on a painted pony which moved up and down with the music. Sometimes when I'm feeling sad or lonely, I close my eyes, and I can feel myself riding the carousel; the warm air of Central Park blowing through my hair; and I can almost hear the carousel music and hear Gracie's laughter. It can still make me smile.

But I also enjoyed going for solitary walks. I found it very easy to think and get everything in focus. Living near the Park was "such a blessing, the Park," as Mama would say. I think it must've been good for me too, in dealing with the stress of living in the city and all that meant, but I didn't think about that and didn't think I was under stress. I liked to think about more serious things. And I liked to read, which is not unusual, of course, but I didn't read fashion magazines or romance novels or the more spicy novels the girls passed around at school.

I liked biographies and what today we would call the "classics." English Lit had become my favorite subject in school, which again, was not unusual. I always liked a good story; that's why the movies and the theater were my second homes. But books! It's a whole universe to explore, and everybody has a story. Every single life is a story in the making. That realization is probably what helped me get through the sad years after my brother's death, my sisters' running off to other worlds, and my own—well, how should I put it? My own "falling in love."

It was a Saturday morning in early autumn when I had taken a crosstown bus to the East Side. Gracie had called me at daybreak to tell me she was in Mt. Sinai Hospital. She had been running around the Reservoir in Central Park the night before and became very weak and nauseous, and before she knew it she was being rushed by ambulance to Mt. Sinai. Apparently she had passed out, and another jogger ran to get the Park police, who called the ambulance. They kept her overnight, and she was feeling okay, but she was scared, and *could I come over?* I wasn't sure they'd let me visit her this early in the morning, on the Sabbath yet, but I would try. I'd tell them I was her sister.

Well, maybe that wouldn't be the best thing, to lie. They wouldn't believe me anyway. Gracie was thin, blonde, had blue eyes, and would never be hidden in an attic with Anne Frank. But even if we didn't look like sisters, she was my friend, so I bundled off the crosstown bus at Madison Avenue and 98th Street. There was an entrance to the Guggenheim Pavilion on Madison and 100th Street, but I like the Fifth Avenue entrance. So I walked a block over. I remember it being rather chilly. My light jacket had a large collar which I raised up; I donned a pair of sunglasses, more to protect my eyes from the cold than the sun, and covered my head with the silk scarf that Ruthie had given me for my birthday. It came from Bloomingdale's and looked very smart with light autumn jackets. Ruthie had one too, and thought they made us look older. She called them our *scarves*, but Mama called them *bandannas*. I thought I looked rather Broadway star-ish as I made my grand and confident entrance into the Guggenheim Pavilion.

There was a matronly-looking volunteer (probably) at the reception desk where one obtains a visitor's pass. Trying my best to appear like a Guggenheim Girl, I requested the room number of Grace Darling Price, and I was politely told visiting hours were not until 11:00. It was only around 9:45. Even removing the sunglasses and giving my best smile didn't change her mind.

I silently turned away, wanting to put on my best Tallulah Bankhead: "*Thank you, Dahling,*" but it came out sounding like a hurt little girl wearing a bandanna.

"I know," I said to myself, "I'll have a nice stroll down Fifth Avenue, get a bagel and coffee, and peoplewatch the crowd." Besides, I needed some quiet time to think. And so I did. Autumn in New York. There was a deli coffee shop across the street from the Metropolitan Museum, just a few blocks, really, down from Mt. Sinai. I nursed a pot of tea and a cinnamon-raisin bagel, sitting at a tiny little table in the front window, where I could watch the people going by. I loved those in-between times when one's thinking moves above the mundane thoughts that occupy the mind.

I thought about Gracie…Grace Darling Price, my gentile friend. She was much more popular in high school than I ever was. She was a cheerleader our junior and senior year, and she went out with Malcolm Linton, the big quarterback star, till he twisted his ankle one fateful Saturday afternoon in October, and his stardom faded for the rest of the year. He became sullen and rather crude in his conversational skills, to put it nicely. He also dropped Gracie…he would snicker, "The Price wasn't right." That got handed in by the senior student-gossip columnist to the *Banner*, and Gracie let it be printed. I always liked her because of that, and that she never whined and cried and became all maudlin over a broken love-affair. Well, not really a "love-affair" in the Hollywood sense of that; they were high school sweethearts for a few months. I think Malcolm's interest was more in showing off his girlfriend as part of his claim to fame. Lord knows he didn't excel in the academic hall of fame. Sometimes I think I was more angry at him than Gracie was; Gracie never said a bad thing about him. She once told me in the *Banner* Office, when I was going off about him, that I shouldn't be angry with him, but to "pray for him; it's the best thing. I lit a candle for him at

church." She took me a little aback because she didn't—*we*
didn't—talk about religious things, let alone engage in them.
I think I muttered something like, "Yeah, I'll pray Kaddish
for him," but it went over her blonde head. (Kaddish is our
Jewish Prayer for the dead.)

She didn't get the Kaddish part. She was no dumb blonde,
but very smart, popular—and I discovered, apparently
prayerful, too! So I sat with my teapot, gazing out on Fifth
Avenue, wondering what could possibly be wrong with her.
She wasn't attacked; she didn't say she tripped and fell or
had a Charley horse or "hit the wall" as they say. But here
she was, overnight at Mt. Sinai. I decided to myself that I
should get her something. Here I was like a real schmuck,
coming to visit her in the hospital empty handed. Flowers
would be nice, but they were also expensive, and I only had a
little over seven dollars when I left home; minus bus fare and
my bagel and tea, I could probably get one yellow rose; she
liked yellow roses (she called them "blonde roses")…but one
rose seemed so Saint-Exupery, and it wouldn't last too long.
I would get her a couple magazines instead— something
to read. So I gulped the rest of my Earl Grey and headed
east to Lexington Avenue. I could get her a fashion magazine and put it in a Bloomingdale's bag. That would impress
her. I walked quickly down Park Avenue to 72nd Street and
over to Lexington Avenue and went south on Lexington.
It had warmed up a bit, or I had, thanks to Earl Grey
and the athletic strides I was making. I was perspiring on
my forehead and the back of my neck, so I whipped off my
Bloomingdale's scarf and made it a neck-scarf again.

Growing up on the West Side of Manhattan, the East Side always seemed so much more fashionable and somehow quieter; even the passers-by seemed more reserved and pensive. People on the West Side were always kibitzing down the street and made more noise. As I was crossing 66th Street right in front of me was the massive stone church of St. Vincent Ferrer. I had never been inside a Catholic Church, but there was a lady coming out the doors and down the stairs—and it was Saturday morning. I don't know what made me stop, right there, in front of the steps, but I had the instant inspiration to go inside. *I could light a candle for Gracie.* I wasn't quite sure what that meant or how you'd do it, but I'd seen it more than once in a movie. So there I was making my way up the stairs of St. Vincent's on my Sabbath day, which I wasn't keeping very well running around the East Side. I covered my head again with my scarf; I knew girls were supposed to have their heads covered like men covered theirs in the synagogue. There was a nice entry way, which I later learned was called a vestibule. It had several racks of pamphlets and Catholic magazines and newspapers for sale. There's the ticket. That would save me going all the way to Bloomingdale's—I'd get her a Catholic magazine and a lit candle to boot. The vestibule doors were a little heavy to push open, but I managed easily enough, not without some trepidation. I didn't think the ceiling would fall in on me, or anyone would yell, "A Jewess! Get her out!" It was more a quiet fear of walking into an unknown territory, and even feeling somehow naughty for it. What would Papa say if he could see me now? Little did I know that, for my poor soul, it was a sunrise…sunset.

Two

I STOOD IN UTTER silence in the back of the church, immobile, not from my supposed fear, which vanished in an instant, but enthralled by the beauty of the place, the smell of it, the peacefulness which seemed to settle over me instantly. The stained-glass windows which filled both sides of the nave (a word I didn't know then) caused the morning sun to spill into the church in a multitude of hues: yellows and reds and blues like I'd never seen before. All of this cast onto gray stone and dark wood. The sounds of the city outside were muted and nearly disappeared, and one could truly *listen to the sound of silence* as the song put it. I was bowled over by it, something I was not expecting at all. I just wanted to pop in, light a candle for Gracie, pop out and be merrily on my way back to Mt. Sinai.

I stood very quiet in the back, watching what people were doing, and saw that it was okay to walk around, so I looked around me. Directly on my right was a shrine, almost like a church within the church. One passed through a laced wooden archway, and there were three statues each on the three different sides, with a flood of little burning candles in red holders. There were two women on wooden padded kneelers. I didn't want to interrupt them, so I walked slowly around to the far right aisle which had other side shrines. One such shrine had a life-size statue of St. Vincent Ferrer, for whom this church was named. I wouldn't have known that, of course, except there was a prayer printed in front of the statue with his name on it. I had never even heard of him, nor was I sure I was pronouncing his last name correctly...it kind of got lost behind my front teeth.

Next to the prayer, embedded in the kneeler in front of the statue, was a glass about the size of a silver dollar. I wasn't sure what was behind the glass, and I as afraid to look. There was also a bell on the pillar next to St. Vincent which didn't have a cord or a button, I guessed so no one would ring it? There were racks of little red candles there too. He was dressed in white robes with a black cape, he had his hand raised like he was giving an emotional speech, and there was a peculiar thing right over his head, which I think was supposed to be a flame of fire. It was all very interesting...they named this whole beautiful church after this man with fire coming out of his head. Maybe the bell was a fire alarm? I knew that Catholics had all kinds of saints and named them as patrons of different things. Maybe St. Vincent Ferrer was the patron of firemen.

Just past St. Vincent was another, smaller than life-size, but very beautiful, statue of Christ, but unlike any I had ever seen before—not that my repertoire of Catholic statues was very extensive! He didn't really have the Jewish robes you usually see in pictures of him, but something more formal, looking rather rich and embroidered. The statue was all enameled wood. His heart was exposed in the middle of his chest, and his left hand was pointing to it, his right hand raised in blessing. But it was his face that almost moved me to tears. It was as if he knew me, and knew that I was feeling sad because of Gracie's accident, and that I didn't know what to do or what it all meant. I thought to myself, "This is just a little bit spooky. Why would I even think the Christian Jesus knew me?" But it was uncanny; that may be a better word than spooky. The heart was enameled red with a brown crown of thorns around it. It was all too fascinating.

I watched other people around me, and saw how you go about lighting a candle: quite easy actually, taking the flame from an already burning one, using a thin wooden stick that went into the sandbox afterwards. I waited till no one was nearby, and took the fire from in front of St. Vincent (appropriate, I thought) and lit a candle in front of Jesus with the beautiful face. I think I must've whispered something like, "This is for Gracie. Please make her better." And I prayed the candle lighting prayer Mama prayed every Friday night; it was the Sabbath.

I was feeling a little lightheaded, I remember, and thought I'd better sit down; "I hope I'm not going to pass out. Wouldn't that be awful," I thought. Headline in the *New York Times*: *Great-granddaughter of Rabbi Feinstein from Vienna Passes Out in Catholic Church.* So I moved quickly up towards the front and moved into a pew. Others were seated throughout the body of the church, so I figured that was acceptable to do. It didn't appear like there was a division between men and women, like in some synagogues. I put my head in my hands for a moment and breathed deeply. And when I looked up, I was dazed by the beauty of the high altar and what I would come to know as a *reredos*. It was unlike anything I had ever seen in pictures, movies, or certainly in the synagogues, some of which were quite magnificent, too.

There were small statues and paintings of lots of saints; most of them, I noticed, were wearing the same uniform as St. Vincent, and at the very top there was his picture, at least I think it was he. He looked heavier and older than the good-looking Vincent back by the entrance, but there was that same flame of fire coming out of his head. And above him, a most enthralling carved image of Jesus crowned like a king. This huge wooden backdrop filled the whole back wall and, interestingly, directed one's eyes to a large brass "circular box" right in the middle, draped with a lovely green cover etched with gold thread. Hanging from the ceiling in front of it were seven or eight wrought iron candle holders with large candles in them, also in red globes like the smaller ones. Over the draped box was a crucifix, flanked on either side by candles in huge brass or silver candlesticks. This was all elevated from the section before it, which was also elevated from the body of the church where I sat. Both sections were divided by a marble railing running the length of the section. The middle section was all wooden pews, facing each other, but each place was also separated from the one next to it. There were three rows on each side, each a step higher than the row in front. The floor was all gray slate stones with different emblems on them, including what I thought looked like shields. Again, the light from the windows high above flooded the floors with a warm bluish hue. Beyond the railing that separated that section from the back section were three stone or marble steps going to the marble altar which held the draped box. The coverlet hid most of it, but one could see the front panel.

I didn't know for sure what I was looking at, but I couldn't pull my gaze away from it. The face of the Christ statue, where I lit my candle, was still present to me, and *I knew at that moment, that Jesus was real.* There were no voices, no visions, no ethereal music, but a deep peace. It was as if my secret hiding place was full of warmth and peace, and I had come home. Before I realized it, I was weeping ever so quietly, and I wasn't thinking of Gracie, but of my brother Joshua. And there was a heavy weight lifted from me about him and his death, and I knew he was all right. I knew he was with God. I had never felt this before in the nearly two years since his passing. And I kept seeing that face of Christ, and I knew He was not a long-dead prophet from two thousand years ago, but was alive, and I knew He was here... although I couldn't put any of that into words or clear concepts at the time. And I wasn't afraid.

I think I may have dozed off for a bit, although I don't really remember. All I remember is the peacefulness I found myself in, and a realization that everything was going to be okay. I also felt a presence, but I wouldn't have said that then; it would take time for me to realize that the presence was indeed there, and emanating from the draped box. I would come to know that this whole magnificent edifice, its gorgeous architecture, the exquisite glass windows, the smell and sight of candles and incense which permeated the wood, that it all was for the One in that draped, golden box, who showed me for the first time that autumn morning His Sacred Heart.

I rested in the peacefulness for what I thought was probably twenty minutes. When I eventually roused myself and looked at my watch, it was almost two o'clock. I had been here for nearly three hours!

I knew I needed to get to Mt. Sinai, but I also knew I would return here and explore all the other side chapels. I watched carefully before bounding out of the pew. There were always a handful of people kneeling and praying, some holding their rosary beads. I knew what rosary beads were; Gracie had actually shown me hers once, but I wasn't sure how they "worked." Passing by my candle, I checked that it was still burning; it was. I paused at the younger-looking St. Vincent, and whispered, "Thank you, St. Vincent for welcoming this little Jewish girl into your beautiful house. I'm off to see my friend, Gracie, but I hope I can come back someday." I had to smile to myself. I wasn't sounding much like a sophisticated sophomore at Barnard College. Oy vey.

Nearing the vestibule doors again, I noticed that everyone coming in or leaving a pew would go down on one knee, and some would make the sign of the cross at the same time. And everyone dipped their fingers in a stone pillar by the entrance, hollowed out in the middle and filled with water. They would make the sign of the cross on themselves with the water. This didn't seem strange to me; of course, Jews were used to sprinkling water and washing their hands. I didn't do it myself— this first time—but I did stop for a minute and look over the literature rack in the vestibule. It had many pamphlets and booklets, a few newspapers, a magazine or two, and even some prayer books. I didn't know if they were for sale or free, but I took about five of the pamphlets and a Catholic newspaper and one magazine, for Gracie. The magazine was called *SIGN* and had a lovely picture of a nun praying on the cover. She looked so beautiful and peaceful; I knew Gracie would love it. She once told me that she had "played nun" as a little girl. Her pretend name was Sr. Clare, and she taught third grade. She said that she was very strict, but all the children loved her because she was so pretty.

I looked at my watch and almost flew through the doors and made my way up Lexington Avenue to Mt. Sinai. My scarf came off and was tied around my neck at the first red light. It was remarkably warmer than this morning. I turned left at 74th Street, not for any reason, except the traffic and lights allowed it, and I wanted to eventually go west to Fifth Avenue. I passed another huge Catholic church called St. Jean Baptiste. It was a French-speaking church, apparently, and I made a mental note that I must pop in there someday, but I knew that the beauty I had experienced at St. Vincent's would not be found anywhere else. I was still feeling quite light and happy as Mt. Sinai Hospital came into view.

I entered this time without a problem, stopped to get my visitor's pass, and took the elevator to the fifth floor, to Room 543. I suddenly wished I had a handful of flowers with me, but there I was schlepping in with my Catholic pamphlets and magazine, and full of questions for my Catholic girlfriend, the jogger.

Gracie looked very pale; her normally twinkling blue eyes seemed a little dull and sunken. She was sitting up in her bed. Her mother was there, and her younger brother, Skip.

"Hello, Mrs. Price, I'm sorry I'm late. I was here earlier, but they wouldn't let me in...Gracie!" I turned to the patient, who was all smiles now at my arrival and who didn't seem surprised by my disheveled hair. I leaned over the bed and kissed her on the cheek and gave her a little hug. "Look at you, all wrapped up in a very smart hospital gown."

She held her arms out in a modeling pose. "My modeling career may be over before I hit the runway." Gracie looked like a model, and I knew she secretly wanted to do that rather than teach elementary school. So much for Sr. Clare! She was an Education Major at New York University, but was flirting with fashion design at Parson's.

"What do you mean?" I chimed in. "Did you break something when you fell running?" Gracie was an avid runner before that became a national pastime. If anything, she always looked a bit anorexic to me, but then everybody looked a bit anorexic to me, especially blonde Gentile girls. I was always a bit on the chunky side, not "fat," but "full-bodied." I figured Gracie was obsessed with being thin; part of the would-be model regime, and so the compulsion to run.

I had tried jogging once with Gracie, in a moment of exasperation. My spring wardrobe uncannily shrunk during the winter, and I wanted to lose the "excess winter baggage," as my complimentary brother, David, called it. So Gracie invited me to run with her around the reservoir in Central Park. Of course, I freaked out before that even happened. What should I wear? I didn't have a jogger's wardrobe, like Gracie did. I didn't even have sweat pants. My brothers did, but then, they were allowed to sweat. Ruthie and I had decided years before, at one of our proper tea parties, that it was unbecoming for ladies to perspire. So we vowed not to, ever, as we finished off the crumpets.

Gracie said a comfortable pair of baggy old jeans would be fine…I think we may have called them dungarees then. I did have a hand-me-down pair from David, which fit me loosely enough. It was still sweatshirt weather, and I did have one, not to sweat in, but to wear to football games. I also had a pair of old sneakers, which were reliable footwear to the library or Zabar's on Broadway. They would have to withstand their maiden voyage around the reservoir.

It was a Sunday morning. I told Gracie I couldn't jog on Saturday: it was forbidden by the Law of Moses. She accepted that without question, and seemed to have no qualms about running on the Christian Sabbath.

"I'll go to the 6:30 Mass and meet you in your lobby at 9:00."

Even earlier would have been fine with me, as I would have to go through the interrogation by my siblings as to why I was dressed for a hayride in April. They wouldn't have believed me, I'm sure, if I had told them that I was going for a morning jog, or however experienced joggers referred to it.

I had a quick breakfast—two banana nut muffins and a cheese Danish, with a cup of sweet coffee, which was mostly milk. The boys weren't even up yet, and Ruthie was engrossed in a Sunday morning cartoon on TV which she never seemed to outgrow. Mama was deep into the *Sunday Times*, and told me to eat more if I was going to the Park. I had mentioned the night before that I was going running with Gracie, but I don't think it registered in Mama's head. A Sunday morning stroll in the Park was a New York tradition and one of the benefits of living so close to the Park. Three minutes to nine the doorbell buzzed, signaling that Gracie had arrived. I grabbed my spring jacket, kissed Mama on the top of the head, and scurried off to meet my Olympic partner.

She was very instructive and knew about ten different warm-up stretches, which made me grateful I had had an extra banana nut muffin; the warm-up wore me out. But we began at a slow pace, chatting with each other on the soft gravel path which looked to me like a ten-mile track around the lake. Other runners, much more into it than we apparently were, passed us. It took less time than I thought, but we were coming up to the starting point, and I thought that would be it.

"Well, that was good!" I boasted to Gracie, slowing down and ready to stop.

"Come on, Becky, we're just getting started." She picked up the pace, and I'm proud to say I was able to keep up with her, although I was panting a little more heavily than she seemed to be, and I suddenly felt a slight chill in the wind at the back of my neck. I put my hand back there, and was shocked to find my hair wet with perspiration—not just damp, mind you, but wet. There was also a growing ache in my calves which I usually only felt if I was walking uphill for any length. My conversational skills were also becoming more and more difficult, but I managed to tell Gracie to go ahead of me, and I'd catch up with her at the starting point. And Gracie took off, leaving me to pant and sweat by myself. I got that infamous stitch in my side, which I blamed on the cheese Danish.

Gracie had nearly passed out of sight, so I felt free to bring it down to a walk, which I did. The spring jacket was almost too much now, but I couldn't leave it anywhere, and besides, I had stashed three Milky Ways in the pockets. When I was sure Gracie was beyond the pale, I unwrapped the first Milky Way and devoured it in three generous bites. The caramel and nougat never tasted so good in all my life. Besides, it gave me some immediate energy to run again, which I planned to do when I turned the last bend before the starting point, fully expecting Gracie to be there stretching or whatever she did when this torture was over. But she was not there. I couldn't believe it; she must've been off for a third time round. So I turned around and walked against the running traffic in the other direction. This was met with a few scowls and frowns by the serious Olympians. I waited in the corner of the last turn, off the track, behind a tree where I could see who was coming. Two young girls about my age were riding past me on the horse path. They were all decked out like they were going to a Virginia Hunt, and I kind of envied them at the moment. Neither of them appeared to be sweating.

When I saw Gracie prancing down the path like an antelope in heat, I moved onto the track, and jogged ever so laboriously till Gracie caught up with me.

"I can't go another round," I panted to her. "You've done really well, Feinstein, for your first time…I'll make a fast final lap and meet you at the starting place."

And she took off. "Feinstein?" I said out loud. "Feinstein?" She'd never called me by my last name. She must've morphed into her Phys-Ed teacher mode. Sr. Brunhilda. This running stuff was not healthy, I concluded, as I reached the beginning, which was my ending, thank God. I did a couple of the stretches we had done in the beginning, which felt much better this time than before. I was also able to devour another Milky Way before Gracie arrived home, her thin face glistening with perspiration.

If I wasn't convinced that my Olympic training was over that Sunday morning, I was doubly convinced on Monday morning when I tried getting out of my bed. Jogging wasn't for me, but I admired Gracie for her stamina.

And now here *she* was sitting up in a bed at Mt. Sinai, looking very pale and weak. "They're taking tests, and have taken gallons of blood from me, so I guess we won't be able to run this Sunday." She smiled her great smile and waited for my reaction.

"What a shame," I retorted, "and I just bought a dozen Milky Ways for, uh, energy." We both laughed. Mother and brother, not getting the private joke at all, were looking rather serious and grim.

A nurse came in, almost as if on cue, and announced that visitors should make it short right now, that Gracie needed to rest. They could come back this evening. I picked up the cue, and gave Gracie the *SIGN* magazine with the lovely nun on the cover, and told her, "I stopped into St. Vincent's and lit a candle for you." She seemed very pleased with both.

"Thanks, Miss Feinstein. I could always count on you."

"I would've been here sooner, but I fell asleep in the church, can you imagine!" I quickly kissed her on the cheek, and slipped something into her hand. "For later," I whispered. "Oh, here's the Catholic paper too. Goodbye, Mrs. Price, I'll be back tomorrow." And I slipped out quickly. I didn't know why I was overcome with emotion all of a sudden, but I sensed that there was more going on than anyone knew, or wanted to talk about. And I hoped Gracie wouldn't give her brother that Milky Way.

I thought about going back to St. Vincent's Church; or I could walk across the Park to 81st Street, or take the crosstown bus. The bus won. The ride through the Park was quick, once we got to the Park. I had a seat near the back, and I took out one of the pamphlets I had taken from the church. It had a picture on the front of a young nun holding an armful of roses. It read *The Little Way of the Little Flower*. I liked that thought. I like little ways, little jogs, little flowers, little Danishes. Something buried in my memory seemed to recognize this nun or someone like her, but I couldn't put my finger on it. The bus was stuck momentarily in a traffic jam on Fifth Avenue and 77th Street, and I was immersed in a little village in Normandy, France, named Lisieux, with a little flower whom they called Thérèse.

Thanks to the traffic jam, I was able to read the entire pamphlet. This young French girl was quite remarkable. She grew up in a pretty well-to-do family, with four other sisters and no brothers. Her mother died when she was just a child and the oldest sister became her "mother" until she left for Carmel. I figured out that Carmel was the name of the convent, and those who entered there were called Carmelites. I remembered Ruthie and I had met them years ago during one of our trips to Horn and Hardart's. Carmel, I read, was a strictly cloistered convent, which meant the nuns could never go out, or go on vacation, or visit their homes. Even their visitors talked to them through a double grate in the "speak room." It was hard to imagine anyone wanting to live like that, and this Thérèse wanted to be a Carmelite when she was 15! She even went to Rome to ask the Pope to let her!

I noted several references to her autobiography, *The Story of a Soul*. I made a mental note of it…maybe they would have it at the library. I realized that she wanted to do what most of us would find abhorrent because she loved Christ, and His Mother. There was even a kind of miracle when she was sick as a child and a statue of the Virgin Mary smiled at her. Funny, but I didn't find that ridiculous, not after my visit to St. Vincent's and the statue of Christ with His heart wrapped in thorns. I think it was there on the crosstown bus that autumn afternoon in New York, that I decided I wanted to get to know this Jesus. I could never ever say that at home, of course; my father would have a coronary on the spot, and my mother would put her head in the oven. Even if they… we…weren't the most devout Jews, we were descended from a great rabbinical family in Austria.

I closed the pamphlet in the middle of the ride through the park, and His face came back to my mind. Who *was* this Jesus? Little did I know that that "little way" through Central Park would change the course of my entire life.

Three

LIFE AT BARNARD College in the late 1960s could warrant a few volumes in itself. Not living on campus had its advantages, but also its disadvantages. I was certainly not anti-social by any means, but I was more serious about my studies, it seemed, than about time to socialize. I loved college for its rich diversity of people, both students and faculty. This was the Sixties, and many were involved in protesting the war; it was the age of the Beatles and the *flower children*. It was the time of folk songs, and "Abraham, Martin, and John" dominated the airwaves and the consciousness of many of us. It was like our whole country and our whole lives were being turned upside down. I guess I was glad to be somewhat removed from all that went on around campus. It's different when you've had a loved one die in the war.

I also knew it was good for Mama and Papa to have me at home, although I seemed to be out a lot. It gave me a stabilizing point of reference, a focus, in my life. David and Sally had moved out, and Josh had left us for Eternal Life; only Ruthie and I filled the almost empty nest. She was absorbed in being popular at school: singing in the All Girls' Chorus, acting, building sets, or helping direct in the Drama Department, and all the while balancing two or three "gentlemen friends," as she called them—without a Tennessee Williams accent.

I was majoring in English Lit with the intention of teaching, and perhaps doing something with the dramatic arts, still a great love in my life. I also thought about Law School and probably would have given that a try if my life hadn't been turned around so dramatically. And the worst part was that nobody, at least nobody in my family, knew what I was doing those many hours in the libraries on campus. There must be something like twenty-five libraries around the Columbia University campus alone. Maybe Mama thought I was seeing someone, and, in a way, I was. Only once did Mama hint at that suspicion.

"I just hope when you meet someone, he'll be Jewish."

I wanted to say, "He *is*, Mama, he is!" But I just smiled, thinking of that fateful trip to the East Side!

That same evening I had arrived home for supper, having visited St. Vincent's and Gracie at Mt. Sinai, I took the bus up Broadway to my favorite library. I also had a book due, which gave me a legitimate excuse. In all my born days, I had never opened a Christian Bible. Snatches of it would come up in the anthologies as literature, along with the Hebrew Scriptures, but I had never read a single gospel with the intent of getting to know Jesus. I would say I was almost stunned at the number of books written about Him, which I hadn't really noticed until then, but that was true of most religious founders. One would probably be stunned by the volume of books on Buddhism and Judaism at Columbia!

I was more than curious, as any Jewish person eventually is. I wanted to know more about why people, like the little French nun, could give her whole life to this man. And why I was so moved by a wooden statue in a fourteenth-century

French gothic church on Lexington Avenue. So I checked out my first New Testament. It was called the *Revised Standard Version*, and while I had no idea what that meant, I liked the leather-like cover and gold gilt edges on the paper, and that everything Jesus said was in red letters.

I also found a recent edition of *The Story of a Soul,* which I checked out. And it seemed like I made a thousand mental notes on other books that I would like to read, especially about the saints. They fascinated me in a way that movie stars and Broadway actors did…they were the best in their field. They were the Catholic stars, as it were. I had several used Columbia Bookstore book covers left over, and I neatly covered them; after all, I was going to bring them into the home of the descendants of Rabbi Feinstein from Vienna. I guess my classmates majoring in psychology would have immediately labeled me as paranoid and done a case study on me. Maybe I *was* a little paranoid. I was almost 20 years old, living at home, with my own bedroom with a lock on the door, and I was covering up my reading materials.

I remember clearing my desk of excess papers and books— not an easy chore to begin with—and taking the Bible out of my school bag and placing it on the desk. I opened it up to the first page of the first gospel, Matthew, and read: *The book of the genealogy of Jesus Christ, the son of David, the son of Abraham.* My goodness, how very Jewish this was sounding, and how clearly Matthew placed Jesus in a historical context, reviewing, as it were, the events of my Hebrew past which I learned long ago in Hebrew class. It was easy reading, almost academic, I thought. Not really what I was expecting.

But then he began to tell the nativity story, which every-body knows something about, growing up in a Christian culture. And then it began. The Bible called it *The Sermon on the Mount.* Oh, it was so lovely. It went from Chapter Five to almost the end of Chapter Seven.

And that was the beginning of my love affair with the teachings of Jesus. I went to go to the kitchen for a cup of tea and something to nosh, and passed Mama and Papa dancing together in the living room, along with all the others on the Lawrence Welk show. If they only knew!

Over the next couple weeks a lot happened. The saddest news of all was that Gracie was diagnosed with leukemia, and would be undergoing bone marrow treatments. I felt so sorry for her. I tried to get over to Mt. Sinai as often as I could. She looked wretched, but still had a kind of spar-kle in her eye. She said the bone marrow treatments were painful, using this very long needle, but "I'm offering it all up to the Sacred Heart." She said it so matter-of-fact, but I knew she really meant what she said. And I knew what "the Sacred Heart" was. The good news is that I contin-ued to visit my Sacred Heart of Jesus at St. Vincent's, and I learned that the embroidered clothes were actually a priestly vestment, a chasuble. He was dressed in priestly vesture... Christ the Priest. That in itself gave me something to think about...I'm still thinking about it, fifty years later! I didn't know a single priest in those days, or any Protestant minis-ters for that matter, and I was barely conversant with Rabbi Liebermann across the street. He always seemed to be play-ing his role as "rabbi" very studiously. I met his wife once at a wedding shower I attended with my mother. She didn't put on any airs of being the wife of a rabbi, and she would often comment to the bride-to-be and anyone else close enough to hear her what a wonderful husband and father her Sol was to her and the father of her children. Mama once looked over at me with her glasses pushed down her nose: "May my Becky be so blessed."

"Thanks, Ma," I returned, "such a blessing!" And I matched her overly benevolent smile. The point is, I knew rabbis and ministers all got married and had "such a blessing" as a devoted wife and children to fulfill their lives. But a Catholic priest didn't get married. It was all rather mystifying. A few years before that, I might have thought it was quite unnatural or weird, or a pity. Everybody loved Bing Crosby as a priest…and to think, he never got married. And here was Jesus Himself dressed up like a priest. It was probably the first time I ever realized that Jesus didn't get married either. And yet He praised marriage, as He did the Law of Moses and all the precepts of the Torah. And from what I read, the chosen twelve apostles left their wives and children and jobs and lands to follow Him. There must be something about this Jesus which would lead men and women to follow Him so profoundly. I would always begin my visit at St. Vincent's at "my Sacred Heart of Jesus the Priest." So maybe I could say He was the first priest I came to know!

I was delighted to make my way around the entire Church in time, and got to know all the side-altar shrines. And I'll always remember the afternoon when, almost by accident, I think it was my third visit, I discovered St. Thérèse. It was a rather modernized statue, but very attractive, one might even say cute, if modern sculptors and saints can be cute.

And I began to talk to her a lot and always paid her a visit in the church. I got to calling her my secret little girlfriend. And I commended my big girlfriend, Gracie Price, to her special care. St. Thérèse promised she would do more for us in Heaven than she did on earth, and even on earth, she prayed for others most fervently, and her prayers were answered.

Funny, I had never read anything about the Communion of Saints or the practice of praying to the saints, nor did I know it was one of the huge bugaboos among some Protestants. I just started doing it. Maybe, with my years growing up and eating in the *succoth* with pictures of our dead relatives, it just came naturally…both to pray for the dead, and to pray to them, because they are not really dead—dead to this world, maybe—but not to the Eternal Life of God. Such thoughts began to come into my mind, not with an unsettling abruptness, but a happy fulfillment. So I talked to Thérèse, and Martin de Porres, and St. Joseph, and St. Vincent like they were my friends, but I spent most of my time in the front pew, staring at the draped box and the seven large candles all burning in front of its polished door.

One afternoon a priest, I presume, came in from a side entrance in the middle section. He was dressed like St. Vincent, except for the black cape. He went up the stairs to the draped box, knelt on one knee, and with a twist of his hand opened the door of the box. He knelt again and then took out a golden-looking cup with a lid on it (I'm telling this as I remembered it then. I didn't know the Catholic vocabulary for these things—this being a ciborium which held the consecrated hosts reserved in the tabernacle). He took the lid off, but I couldn't see what he was doing. He closed the door, knelt on one knee again, got up, and exited as silently and quickly as he entered.

Now, it wasn't long after that that I uncovered the veil to many of my puzzlements in a wonderful pamphlet I helped myself to in the back, which was entitled: *The Holy Sacrifice of the Mass Explained.* I think it may have been a child's booklet, but I was grateful for the simplicity of it and the diagrams and pictures. In the front, right after the Foreword, was a drawing of the altar set up for Mass, and everything was labeled: the altar stone that the priest kissed, which was embedded in the center of the altar and contained relics of the saints; the altar cards, the missal and the missal stand; and best of all—the tabernacle. It was then that I learned that the hosts consecrated at a Mass were reserved in a ciborium, which was placed in the tabernacle. A sanctuary lamp would always be burning near it to alert one that the *Real Presence* was here.

I had never heard that expression, Real Presence, but I came to believe that I was, in truth, touched that first Saturday afternoon when I wandered into St. Vincent's; I was touched by the Real Presence. I hadn't read about it, but I knew it. It filled in many other things I observed those first couple weeks…why the women always had their heads covered, even if it was a Kleenex; why they genuflected before entering their pew and when leaving it; why there was this palpable silence in the church with everything directed towards this central point—the heart—the sacred heart of the church—*the Real Presence.*

This helpful little pamphlet also had a picture of a priest in his vestments, which he only wore when offering Mass, and I recognized it immediately—these were the priestly vestments of my Sacred Heart statue. In a brief blurb given, I understood that these were not literally the clothes Jesus wore, but were adopted by priests years later; they were Roman garments, the tunic, and chasuble, maniple, and stole. What I also instinctively knew was that while Jesus didn't wear these garments, He did offer the First Mass—it was called the Last Supper. This would both thrill and overwhelm a practicing Jew who every year of her life ate the Passover Seder with her family, who knew the story of the Passover almost by heart! Who knew the deep significance of bread and wine—it still holds a place of profound significance, not just in the Seder, but at every Shabbat.

If there's one thing every Jewish child is ingrained with it is that we are People of the Covenant...sons and daughters of the Commandments. Bar Mitzvah, or in my case Bat Mitzvah. The pamphlet went through the directives of the Mass—dividing it into two sections: The Mass of the Catechumens and the Mass of the Faithful. Some of the prayers were mentioned, and there were also Scriptural references, which I took special note of. I could look these up in my new New Testament.

Now, I don't know when this happened. Again, it was not like an angel came down from Heaven and touched my soul with a magic wand; nor did it come as a result of any kind of research, much less arguing with anyone. (I hadn't breathed a word to anybody, not even Gracie.) It may have even been that first visit—but I began *to pray to Jesus*. I may not even have formalized it with such words—I just talked to Him, and I sat in His Real Presence, and I knew—I think this might be the hardest part to put into words—I knew that He knew me and loved me. And I can't tell you what peace and comfort that brought to my soul. There was awakened in me such a desire to know Him and love Him back; to know all about Him. I knew in my soul why men and women could give up everything to follow Him, including husband, wife, children, and family—before I knew how to express it.

And so Rebecca Feinstein became a daily visitor to the Real Presence, for once I realized He was really present in the tabernacle, and every Catholic Church had a tabernacle, I sought Him out. I was falling in love with Love and didn't know what to do about it. I knew I couldn't breathe a word of this to Mama or Papa, or David, Sally, or Ruthie, and certainly not to Rabbi Liebermann. Maybe I was losing my mind? Maybe Josh's death really snapped something in me and I was seduced by religious sentimentality and self-induced feel-good therapy. Maybe I should visit one of the nice Jewish psychologists—they were running rampant around Columbia College.

Mama noticed my bedroom light on late into the night—engrossed no doubt in the Romantic Literature of the Victorian Age. She never would believe I was engrossed for hours in the Scriptures, and I'm afraid she would have had a stroke if she knew it was the Christian Scriptures. I actually took to going to Shabbat services on Friday night, for the more I seemed to immerse myself in my beautiful Judaism, the more it unfolded for me the Christ, the Son of the Living

God. Mama became a little suspicious; I could tell by her
pained expression glancing over at me during supper. But if
she suspected anything, it was probably that I was seeing a
nice Jewish man, a rabbinical student, probably, and was just
waiting for the right time to spill the kosher beans.

To make matters worse, I *had* met a nice Jewish boy who
was a pre-med student, but it was not what you're thinking,
or what Mama would have been hoping for.

In the brisk autumn days of October, I loved to walk to
school—it was not really that far, directly uptown on Broadway. The sights and sounds and smells of the Upper West
Side are romantic poems in themselves, and people seem to
have a livelier bounce to their step when the weather changes.
I discovered another most wonderful church on 121st Street
just east of Broadway. It was called Corpus Christi. It was
actually about five blocks north of campus, but one often
explored in all directions, looking for bookstores, vegetar-
ian restaurants, and coffee shops. Perhaps every age thinks
they've invented the coffee shop!

I was at school one Tuesday for my 9:00 seminar and it
was cancelled. So I took advantage of the time to go in search
of an out-of-the-way coffee shop where I could settle into a
bagel and coffee and whatever book I was into. And I discovered Corpus Christi. So I decided to pop in for a visit to
the Real Presence, but I didn't get any further than the back
pew by the vestibule. A funeral Mass was going on. There
were a few stragglers like me who were not there to pay their
respects to the deceased, but who were praying in the back
pews, a few making the rounds of the side altars. I quietly
slipped into a back pew, tightened my bandanna, and before

I knew it, I was enthralled by the chant of perhaps only four or five men, coming from the organ loft, directly above me.

I always loved our Jewish chants and could detect something of the Hebrew angst in this dramatic rising and falling of the notes. The words were in Latin, of course, but the emotion was very Hebrew!

I watched the priest walking around the coffin incensing it with billows of smoke. He was wearing black and silver watered silk vestments which matched the covering over the coffin. He returned silently to the altar and intoned certain phrases which the cantors above responded to. And then there was the clamor of bells, and everyone was on their knees. A few minutes later, the priest was bent over the bread and wine that were on the altar, and held them up one after the other, again with bells resounding throughout the whole church. No one stirred, or coughed, or even wept. It was like time was suspended for ten seconds, even in the back pews.

I knew from my pamphlet that this was the Consecration of the Mass, when the bread and wine, Catholics believe, literally become the body and blood of Christ. I knew this is when the Real Presence was made present. It wasn't too long after that that the priest turned to the people showed them the "bread"…and after that they began to move out of their pews very slowly and kneel along the rail. Watching these people return to their pews and burying their faces in their hands while kneeling moved me very much. It was like they really really believed. The Real Presence was real!

While I was moved profoundly in a sentimental way, I soon realized that I was also being confronted by the truth of the matter. Is this really true? And how could Christ make this possible, and why would He? And why doesn't everyone believe this incredible gift to the world? Which of course, kept bringing me back to the same haunting question: *is Christ really true?* I knew that if He is all that Christianity, or at least, Catholicism, claims He is, why doesn't everyone believe it? Is it all the greatest hoax ever laid on the human race, or is it the Truth? I knew that Judaism was at least 2000 years older than Christianity, and Buddhism and Hinduism, for that matter, were older than Judaism. Are all religions equally true or equally false? Are they just cultural phenomena that develop out of people's ignorance and their need to have something to explain their lives? Just because one is born and raised in a particular religion doesn't mean it's more true than another, does it? Was the Enlightenment a freedom from the darkness of religious ignorance? Will science explain away everything men ponder and imagine beyond what science can explain? I suspected this was my brother David's philosophy of life.

I could feel myself beginning to break out in a sweat, and I wasn't even running, except in my head, and I hated feeling the sweat roll down the back of my neck…I wanted to stay longer, but instead I leapt up and scurried out of the church before anyone noticed the perspiring young woman having a panic attack in the back of the church. The chant still echoing in my head, I turned to go downtown again on Broadway.

Tea on Thames was a quiet, out of the way tea shop owned and operated by a lovely British lady named Gwendolyn. It was my favorite haunt closest to Barnard, and I think I headed right for it. Ten blocks were just enough to clear my head. My anxiety level was well under wraps when I made my way to the little table in the front window, and Gwendolyn greeted me, by name, in her marvelous Yorkshire English.

"Well, if 'tisn't Miss Rebecca on this lovely day." Gwendolyn was one of those women whose age was almost impossible to guess, but I suspected she was a bit older than she looked, and she looked about thirty...a Sixties feminist in her own right—no makeup, no perfectly coiffed hair, and a full-bodied woman, like me, she loved muumuus or comfortable blousy tops with colorful full-length print skirts. She once said she was too old to be a Flower Child, but maybe a Flower Lady, Eliza Doolittle...to which she added a little curtsy. "How's the little princess?" She meant Ruthie, not me. I had brought Ruthie here for her birthday, as I knew she would love the whole English Tea Shop thing. The tables were all small, but had white linen tablecloths and real napkins, and each table had a small vase of fresh flowers; today's was a single golden chrysanthemum. Lining the back wall near the cash register were shelves of fancy teapots, from the elegant to the kinky. One whole shelf was devoted to penguin teapots or porcelain figurines of penguins in various poses.

When I am upset, I take refuge in Twining's Earl Grey, so I ordered a pot along with two homemade scones with a little crock of real British orange marmalade. So the Earl and I gazed out the window, lost in my thoughts. I knew something was going on in me which I hadn't planned on or in any way induced. I thought of Josh and wished he were here with the Earl and me to sift through all these religious questions. He would have calmed my nerves and set me straight, if I indeed needed to be set straight. *O Lord*, I halfheartedly prayed, *if I only had someone to talk to.*

My Scripture "study," for lack of better word, had carried me through what I learned were called the Synoptic Gospels. The teachings and miracles of Jesus were truly amazing, and I could see why we were not encouraged to read them. It was perfectly clear from them alone, that Jesus was the Messiah, or claimed to be, and seemed to fulfill all the prophecies concerning him.

Looking back on all this now, I don't think I was aware of what the Lord was doing in me. I thought it was all about *me*. It was *my* curiosity, *my* bold inquisitiveness that even made me go into St. Vincent's just a month and a half ago. Maybe it was just an innate and newly awakened sensitivity to art that made me fascinated by the wooden enameled statue of the Sacred Heart.

But I knew there was more going on. I knew because I knew my secret hiding place—my soul—and what was going on was going on in my soul. I knew it wasn't a Feinstein version of the Age of Rebellion. I wasn't rebelling against my Jewish faith and upbringing. I loved my family and all our Jewish customs. But Yeshua, the Son of Miriam of Nazareth was fully Jewish and claimed to be the fulfillment of the Law and the Prophets. I couldn't argue and prove He was the Messiah, millions have advanced those arguments on both sides for centuries, but neither could I deny that I believed He was still alive, and that I was drawn into His Real Presence.

And I knew it had to do more with love than anything else; it wasn't about politics or the business of religion; it wasn't about a school of philosophy or any kind of social dynamic; it was about love. And it wasn't about the love-child movement. I was not caught up in such rebellion. The Hippie Movement kind of repulsed me because it was blan-keted in a haze of drug-induced emotion, and drugs fright-ened me.

Well, I think I scarfed down the scones before my pot was empty, so I ordered two more and another half pot of Earl Grey, none of which even raised an eyebrow of Gwendolyn. I wondered what she thought about Jesus; she was probably born and raised in the Church of England and may have gone to one of those marvelous-looking public schools, but I didn't ask. Lady Gwendolyn would just be Lady Gwen-dolyn. I didn't have to bring in everybody into my current dilemma, if it were a dilemma.

Staring out the window, I was startled for a moment as a young man stopped directly in front of me and smiled. I smiled back, not because I knew him, but just out of the incongruity of it. And the next thing I knew the door was opening and he was coming in, and saying, "Hi, Becky... Becky isn't it?"

"Yes, it is...and you...?"

"I'm Ezra Goldman. I was behind you at the checkout desk at the library the other day. That overly friendly librar-ian handed you your book: 'Here you are, Becky...Becky, (looking at the sign-out card) Fernstead,' And you said, 'Becky Feinstein.' When you turned to go, you rolled your eyes at me."

Laughing, I said, "I remember that; she's really very nice, I think, but she thinks she has to say your name when she hands you back your book."

"She called me 'Ezra Goodman.'" And we both laughed. "So, Ezra Goodman, would you like a good cup of tea?"

"That would be lovely," he said, with a bit of an Irish brogue.

As Her Ladyship was bringing another tea cup, I informed him, "My class was cancelled this morning, so I came here for tea and scones."

"It's my Aunt Sarah's birthday, and I ran off to Riverside and 110th Street to have a birthday breakfast with her. There'll be a party tonight at my cousin's apartment downtown, but Aunt Sarah loves our private breakfasts—she's a bit of a Yenta, if you know what I mean."

"Oh, I do, I have a Yenta or two in my family, too." And we both laughed.

"So you *are* Jewish? I thought you were, but then…" and he hesitated.

"But what?"

"Nothing…"

Gwendolyn had arrived by that time, and she said, "What's it to be, love?" looking down at him and over to me with a Lady Gwendolyn Seal of Approval.

"Just a pot of Earl Grey." He didn't know why Gwendolyn and I both burst out laughing.

"That's what I'm having."

"I know…I can see the tea bag tabs." We both laughed. He waited till Gwendolyn left.

"I was going to say, I thought you were Jewish, but then I thought I saw you this morning coming out of Corpus

Christi Church up around 121st Street. I had been to this little German deli to get some potato salad for tonight, and that's when I saw you."

So I explained that I *am* Jewish, Rebecca Abigail Feinstein the First, and I was taking a course in culture and art, and liked to pop into churches to see what they had.

"Oh, you should visit Blessed Sacrament on 71st and Broadway—it's my favorite church. The windows are exquisite, and there's a heaviness in the air inside, that I find very peaceful. Sometimes I just go there to be quiet, you know. Aunt Sarah used to think I'd go off to rabbinical school…" He hesitated again. "But I've become a Catholic…sixth months ago, and I just told her this morning—some birthday present, huh?"

"Gwendolyn!" I shouted. "Another pot of Earl Grey!"

Four

THAT NIGHT I was ensconced in my newly acquired rocking chair. I loved the cushioned seat and back, and the easy rocking motion except for a slight squeak in the right rocker. I had actually found the chair on the street on Amsterdam Avenue near 75th Street. I bought the cushions later at one of those country-kitchen boutiques on Lexington Avenue. It was my new reading rocker, and it sat in a cleared corner of my room, next to a side table which was large enough for a lamp, a book, and a cup of tea! I was looking forward to a snowy winter and many hours in my rocker; Ruthie thought I was off my rocker.

I reviewed the day's events, amazed at how God intervenes in our lives right when we least expect it. Ezra and I had sat for another hour and two pots of tea in Tea on Thames, and then we walked down Riverside Park and sat on a bench looking over the Hudson at New Jersey. I told him everything about my falling into St. Vincent's and falling in love with the Lord. It was so liberating to talk about it, and with someone who knew what I was talking about, and who in his own way still had some of the family issues I had. But mostly we talked about the Lord, and our favorite passages from the Gospels. He was more into the Epistles than I was, and he commented that St. Paul was also a Jewish convert.

He also suggested I read the Farewell Discourse in John. I had not gotten that far yet.

It was feeling rather surreal. I wasn't expecting this to happen in my life; I was never especially religious, although I believed in God. He was kind of removed from the warp and woof of my life, like a benevolent grandfather who came to visit on high holy days, and was the epitome of kindness and expected the best of me. Ezra helped me see this, I think, as he had moved from an even more agnostic worldview which was confirmed by the sophisticated world which viewed religion as quaint or delusional, or both. I didn't know why I was suddenly so attracted to images of Jesus, or what was meant by the Incarnation, Redemption, and Blessed Sacrament. These were foreign to my thinking and my everyday experience of life.

I was home in time for supper. I wanted to talk about Ezra to everyone at the table, but I knew that would not be the prudent thing to do. *Just keep him secret for now.* I hurried through some homework, realizing how much of my mindset was now influenced by this new exploration into the spiritual life, or maybe I should say, the Christian life.

I typed a short critique of William Ernest Henley's poem "Invictus," which was very popular and had first appeared in my high school freshman English class, but I now realized how much it reflected the subjective secular turn in peoples' declaration of independence from God.

> I am the master of my fate; I am the captain of my soul.

I didn't believe that anymore, and really don't think I ever did. I dared to say so in my paper, which I didn't think Professor Linden would like. But then maybe he would; he was always urging us to be free-thinkers. But that usually didn't wash when one thought differently from him.

Then I opened my New Testament to John's Gospel for the first time, and read:

> In the beginning was the Word, and the Word was
> with God, and the Word was God...
> and the Word became flesh and dwelt among us.

I don't know if Mama noticed my light was on till three in the morning that night. I read the entire Gospel. It was the night that convinced my heart of its longings; I knew I would become a Catholic.

Meeting Ezra Goldman was "such a blessing," as Mama would say, but for entirely different reasons! I've learned over the years that we make the spiritual journey to God alone, together...together with others whom God places in our lives at just the right time. Even the Carthusian monk or a Camaldolese hermit in reclusion from everyone else is not really alone, but joined to Christ. He is joined with others in the one Mystical Body of Christ, something which Jews and most Protestants can't understand. God loves us in all the times and events of our lives, but especially through the love of others. Sometimes this becomes as profound as nuptial love in marriage, which itself is an image of the union of Christ with His Church. Or it can be as ordinary and precious as friendship and family, and as subtle as authors of

books and composers of music lyrics—a painting in an art
gallery momentarily takes your breath away, and you want
someone else there to share the experience. Alone, together.
My experience of "alone" has always been a part of my spiritual journey, even as a child—coming to know that hidden
place within—and certainly now, coming to know the Lord
unlike anyone in the Feinstein family ever had. I felt very
much alone, but not lonely.

Ezra Goldman became my friend. We explored all the
churches in New York City (or so it seemed), and would
sit in silence before the tabernacles of New York and afterwards marvel to each other at the incomprehensible gift of
the Blessed Sacrament. He took me first to his Blessed Sacrament Church on West 71st, and indeed, it had a splendid
interior, luminous with the colors of stained glass, much
like St. Vincent's. And there were wonderful statues on
the façade, including St. Thomas Aquinas. Blessed Sacrament Church was very conducive to prayer; most Catholic
churches are, but some more than others. The marble and
wood and stained glass all together create the setting; the
million burning lamps and lingering smell of incense create
the atmosphere; and the Blessed Sacrament…ah, He creates
the union of souls with the Divine, in Divine and human
friendship and nuptial love. Sometimes, sitting silently in
the presence of the Blessed Sacrament in the tabernacle, I
lost all sense of time, and couldn't hear New York going on
outside. It was amazing. Years later, in the monastery, I realized this was all grace and, for my young soul, the first drawing to the contemplative life.

I showed Ezra my St. Vincent's for his first time, and he was more enthralled than I had hoped for. He was especially enthralled at what we learned was called the Friars' Chapel. It was up front to the far right of the choir, or the middle section where the choir stalls were. It was screened off from the church proper by a wooden screen, which did not obscure people from seeing or hearing the Dominican friars chant their office. It was from Ezra that I learned that St. Vincent was a Dominican, and that this was a Dominican parish staffed by the Dominican Friars. Dominican didn't mean they were from the Dominican Republic, but that they belonged to the Order founded by St. Dominic in the thirteenth century. He was actually a Spaniard, but the Order was founded in southern France.

I didn't know anything about the different orders, except what most people learn by osmosis and going to the movies! So I learned a little about the saints who founded the big religious orders which are still in existence. There was St. Ignatius of Loyola Church, up on Park Avenue and 83rd St., in the sixteenth century; they were popularly called the Jesuits. We visited the two Franciscan churches down by Penn Station, both magnificent churches with a constant flow of people going in and out all day long to pray or go to confession. I also liked Our Lady of Pompeii in the West Village which was run by the Scalabrini Fathers, which was not really an order but a congregation of religious. There was so much to learn!

And of course...how could I forget? There was St. Patrick's Cathedral. One is never quite ready for the size and splendor of the place. It was a bit distracting because of the flood of tourists that constantly flowed in and out, but at the far end, away from the main entrance and the noise, was the tabernacle where it was silent, and the Lady Chapel in the apse behind the high altar. It would be some time before I ever attended a High Mass at St. Patrick's, but I would always try to make a visit whenever I was in Midtown.

Ezra's parish again was Blessed Sacrament, where he had taken instruction in a small class of five or six people only. He said the others were all engaged to Catholics and were converting before the wedding. He was the only one who was a student and not engaged; he was also the only Jewish man. His Jewish upbringing was even less traditional than mine. He was from Williamsville, New York, near Buffalo, and his family didn't really attend temple at all, nor really observe Shabbat. He had started dating a girl whose family went to a Reformed Synagogue, and eventually Ezra went with them, and became interested in Judaism, and eventually Christianity.

The girlfriend's name, if I remember right, was Judy, or was it Trudy? She wanted to be an artist and went off to Paris after high school graduation. Meanwhile, Ezra had won a scholarship to Columbia and moved to New York. He roomed with two other guys in a two-family brownstone on West 83rd Street near Broadway. His roommates were both from New Haven, Connecticut, and were members of Opus Dei. Ezra joked, "I didn't have a chance." But he said they didn't really proselytize him, they just lived their faith so comfortably and seriously that he was naturally attracted to what they had. They introduced him eventually to Fr. Kelly at Blessed Sacrament, who Ezra said was a most gentlemanly old priest whose cassock was rather worn and shabby looking, and who carried a hint of cigar smoke. He had unruly, bushy white eyebrows and wire-rimmed glasses, but a face with a perpetual twinkle in the eye and a smile on his mouth. He had that gift, Ezra said, of making you feel immediately at home.

"He was most enthused about my desire to become a Catholic, and I was hoping he was going to instruct me, but he handed me over to Fr. Rayburne, who was only a priest for less than a year. He didn't look much older than me!"

Ezra was happy once things got going. Fr. Rayburne was most zealous and articulate and answered everyone's questions very thoroughly. Ezra chose June 13 as his baptismal day, the feast of St. Anthony of Padua, and was baptized Ezra Anthony. His mother came down from Williamsville, and his Aunt Sarah from uptown actually attended the baptism and the small reception given by his two roommates, one being his godfather. The best thing, Ezra said, was that Fr. Kelly baptized him.

"He remains my confessor and a real spiritual father," Ezra would humbly boast, like the devoted disciple of a Desert Father.

His story all sounded so wonderful and ideal, and easy because his family seemed so accepting. I was scared to even mention I was thinking about becoming a Christian. I knew I was a grown up and capable of making my own decisions, but it was not in my mind or soul to be disobedient to my parents. On the contrary, it was a mitzvah to honor them. How would I ever get around that? I also knew Mama would think Ezra was a perfect match, until she found out he had

gone down this road before me. And Papa? I was most afraid
of breaking Papa's heart and, maybe even more selfishly, losing his love and respect. I was his "royal princess," after all.

Winter came upon us that year with a fury. We had a
grand blanket of snow before Thanksgiving, which always
transforms the city into a winter wonderland. Ezra had been
encouraging me to begin my instructions; he wanted me to
meet Fr. Rayburne, but I hesitated. I told him I couldn't
make any decisions till after Christmas, till the new year perhaps. And I prayed about this every day. I didn't always have
the change or dollar bills to light candles, but I lit a few on
the house.

One can't keep a secret too long in a family with two sisters and an observant mother. I thought Ruthie was oblivious to my comings and goings. She ignored me for the most
part, thinking I was too studious and not at all fun like when
we were younger, as if we were old maids now! I did find her
a bit much, especially with all the screaming and carrying on
over a British rock group named the Beatles. She was also
taken up with her little circle of girlfriends who were nice
Gentile girls, and who, from what I could tell, were caught
up in Beatlemania too.

Ruthie and two of her girlfriends were doing a school
project on Modern Art and were making an afterschool field
trip to the Guggenheim; they wanted to see the Pollock. She
was leaving the museum, wrapped up in her winter parka
and knit hat and ran into me and Ezra. We laughed and
kissed each other quickly, and I simply said, "This is a friend
from Columbia, Ezra Goldman…my little sister, Ruth Feinstein." Ruthie's eyes were dancing from me to Ezra and back

again, and said she was happy to meet him, and introduced her friends, and ran off downtown. Ezra and I laughed about how awkward kids could be, as if we were the experts on adulthood.

"Well, you know what this means? You will have to meet my family, as Ruthie will have announced meeting you before she has her coat hung-up, and Mama will be beside herself and will call my father at work and then my sister in Philadelphia and interrogate my older brother, David, who she thought knew everything."

"I'd like to meet your family," Ezra came back without hesitating. "I only have my aunt here, and neither of my roommates are majoring in culinary arts, to say the least."

It also just happened that Ezra's parents were on a Caribbean cruise over Thanksgiving, and Ezra wasn't planning to go home to Buffalo. He said he would probably take his aunt out for dinner. I didn't respond there and then, but would give it some thought.

My predictions concerning the brief encounter with Ruthie all came true; I didn't have my coat off and in the hall closet before Mama's voice came wafting down the hallway from the kitchen. "Becky, *dahling*, is that you?"

"No, Ma, it's Golda Meier. Do you have the chicken soup on?"

Mama appeared wiping her hands on a linen tea towel, her house dress and apron were spotted with flour; she was making challah for Shabbat tomorrow night. "So, tell me, about this Ezra fella Ruthie met; she said he's a real good-looker. How long have you been friends with this Ezra?"

I laughed, trying not to sound too inauthentic. "He's just a friend, Mama…we have a couple classes together, and he's interesting to talk to. He's from Buffalo."

"Buffalo? Like Niagara Falls, Buffalo?"

"Like Buffalo, New York, Ma. Like the Buffalo Bills."

"So when are we going to meet this 'only a friend' of yours?"

I could've sworn she was humming "Sunrise, Sunset" from *Fiddler* when she returned to her kneading.

That night the table conversation gradually got around to the Thanksgiving dinner in less than a week. "Your brother David, may he not forget his family, is going to Philadelphia to spend Thanksgiving with his sister, Sally, who is working and fixing her first turkey, God have mercy on her." Mama had known about this plan of theirs since Labor Day, but never let it rest in peace. "They have to go to a football game in Philadelphia? They're going to cook a whole turkey just for themselves and whoever else they've invited whom they don't want their mother to know about."

I knew what grand scheme was being introduced. Ezra and his aunt could take David and Sally's places at the table, and Ezra would not think about the cruise with his parents.

I told Mama (and Papa when he got a word in edgewise, but he seemed more engrossed in the chicken breast), that Ezra was a "free-thinker," one of many that went to Columbia. While he was a "good-looker," to quote Ruthie, "you might not think his mind is so attractive."

Mama was quick to respond: "Whatever could you mean by that? Is he a Communist or something?"

I remember I didn't quite know how to put it and knew I should avoid the religious question entirely, yet that was what I meant. So I just said, "Of course not, Mama, he's very intelligent and kind of a free-thinker, but a deep thinker." I held my breath, hoping I wouldn't have to go any further.

"Well, I hope he likes my stuffing." And that was that.

As it turned out, Ezra loved Mama's stuffing, or was charming enough to rave about it, which of course won her heart forever. By time we got to the homemade pumpkin pie in which Mama added her secret ingredient, the discussion came around to religion. "T.T." Josh used to call it... temple talk.

Ezra was very direct and even unassuming. "I have found the study of the Torah the most enriching thing in my life. We were brought up in a rather progressive Jewish household; I really didn't know any Hebrew or the meanings behind the great holy days, until I was older and could study things on my own."

"Ah, our Becky said you had a keen mind, I can see why. More pie? It has a secret ingredient, handed down from my mother's mother." Mama was being the perfect hostess, while Papa was quiet and reflective, as he always was.

Ezra took a fork full of pumpkin dabbed with whipped cream (also homemade) and rolled right into it. "When I came to Columbia I had been reading the Christian Scriptures, thanks to a nice Jewish girl I had been dating, and discovered most emphatically that Jesus was no doubt the Messiah."

Mama stopped cutting the pie, and plopped down in her seat, just a bit stunned. "I was most fortunate to room with two chaps from a Catholic organization called Opus Dei, and they explained a lot of the Catholic teachings to me, and even showed me how Catholic worship is derived actually from Jewish festivals and temple practices. And so about seven months ago, I was baptized just down the street here at Blessed Sacrament Church."

I don't think I ever experienced silence around our dining room table as profoundly as that Thanksgiving night. How could one respond to that, really? It's not like we were orthodox Jews who would have been scandalized and turned him out. Papa always encouraged us to think for ourselves and to hold fast to what we believed.

The silence was broken after what seemed like an interminable couple minutes by Mama. "Nutmeg…the secret ingredient is nutmeg." And no one said anything; we didn't laugh or cry. It was Aunt Sarah who picked up the ball.

"I thought it was something like that; it's delicious, Mrs. Feinstein, you must give me the recipe. I always knew our Ezra had a secret ingredient, too—he always loved God in his own way. His father, my brother, and I never really practiced any religion; we were Jewish by heritage, more than tradition. We didn't know where Ezra got his love for God so strongly that he did crazy things, like becoming a Christian, but we also knew that if he were in any trouble, like with drugs, may God preserve him, we'd do everything we could to help him…so why stand in the way of something good that he wanted?"

Ezra again picked up the ball. "It wasn't all as easy as apple pie, you understand. It was more than wanting to be good and more than an intellectual conclusion…it was coming to a personal relationship with Jesus Christ that made all the difference in the world...that was the..." his voice slowed and became pensive.

"Nutmeg," exclaimed Ruthie. "That was the nutmeg. Mama, what about *my* pie?"

Five

As I RECALL, that Thanksgiving was the watershed moment
for me. I watched my family's reaction, both then and in
the months afterwards. Mama and Papa didn't talk openly
about their feelings. Like so many of their generation, they
didn't even have the vocabulary to do so, if they felt the
need. Mama, not surprisingly, seemed sad about it all, and
any private dreams about Ezra and me under the canopy disappeared. She never questioned our friendship after that, or
spoke disparagingly about Ezra, but nor did she ever suggest
inviting him for supper again.

Papa only once brought it up to me when we were alone.
We had gone for a walk down Fifth Avenue to look at the
store windows decorated for Christmas and over to see the
tree at Rockefeller Plaza and to smile on the ice skaters
swooshing past the grand figure of Prometheus. It was an
annual tradition, usually with one or two other of my siblings and Papa. Christmas in New York is an electric time
of year, even if you're Jewish, at least a kind of New York
secular Jew.

This year Papa just invited me. It was a brisk walk down
Broadway to Central Park South and across to Fifth Avenue.
If we were really in for a treat, we'd stop at Wolfie's on 57th
Street for a deli sandwich and their wonderful coleslaw and
kosher dills, served at every table. And so we did, almost by

unspoken tradition. The sandwiches at Wolfie's were too big for your mouth, but we always managed. It was at Wolfie's, with New York's Christmas winter wonderland going on outside the windows, that Papa asked me.

"Are you still seeing your friend Ezra? You aren't thinking of becoming a Christian too, are you?" He said it without any venom in his tone, staring me gently in the eyes, as only Papa could do.

"Ezra and I are just friends, Papa, we're not dating. To tell you the truth, I think he's thinking of becoming a priest or something." I tried to smile and hesitated before answering the second part of his question. "And yes, Papa, I'm thinking about Christianity…I was even before I met Ezra, he hasn't influenced me in that way. I'm just coming to know about Christ and His Church, and I find it all very…consoling… and very…what would you say? Very close to all the wonderful spiritual things about life you've taught me, Papa, and very beautiful. Yes, beautiful. It's a beautiful religion."

"Judaism is a beautiful religion too, but I think I understand what you mean, my little Rafkins." Papa hadn't called me that in ten years! "Let's just keep it our little secret for now, okay? We don't need to say anything to your mother about it, okay?"

I was so moved I couldn't eat another bite of my sandwich, and had to have it wrapped up to take home. I never felt closer to my father than I did that day in Wolfie's Restaurant, and a great weight seemed to be lifted. I knew I would be okay, that *it* would be okay. I didn't know how or when, but it would be okay.

I tucked my arm in Papa's arm, and we huddled our way over to Rockefeller Center. The tree never looked more beautiful, and the angels blowing on their trumpets were almost audible. I didn't remember seeing them in years past.

We didn't speak of it again, until it had all happened, or was about to. I knew that Mama would not be as understanding as Papa, and I remember walking past St. Patrick's that afternoon, squeezing Papa's arm and secretly thanking God for Papa and asking Him to show me the way to tell Mama, if this was all supposed to be. It was a little spiritual experience, I think. I was holding onto Papa's arm, and I could feel my mind and heart going into the cathedral and kneeling before the tabernacle way in the back, and the same peace came to me walking by the church as when I went inside. How strange this new world of faith would be…I had no idea.

I'll always remember New Year's Eve of 1965. There was no big New Year's Eve party to go to, although there were plenty being scheduled around campus, and even at the Feinstein residence a small party was in the offing…perhaps more of a family reunion. Sally was coming up from Philly, and David was coming over and spending the night. Ruthie was allowed to have a girlfriend from school over to stay, and my Aunt Ruth from south Jersey was coming up. I think she even came together with Sally on the train. Aunt Ruth was Mother's older sister who was married to a musician who at one time had played in the Atlanta Symphony Orchestra, but now was in a small band at a fancy hotel-restaurant in Cherry Hill, New Jersey. I guess he had to stay in town to play his saxophone, and Aunt Ruth wanted to come to the Big Apple.

For myself, I had been invited by the Prices to spend the evening at their apartment. It was a concession on their part, wanting to do all they could for their dying daughter. Gracie was home for the holidays, which had been wonderful and rather emotional for the family. Poor Gracie was so gaunt looking, beyond even what anorexic models would desire, but she still had her tremendous smile, although I was taken aback by how large her teeth looked to me, rather like a horse, God forgive me, I should be so cruel in my thoughts.

But I'm getting ahead of myself. New Year's Eve day I had a "date" to meet Ezra at Tea on Thames for a brunch-tea. He was leaving early that afternoon for a Passionist Monastery in Massachusetts along with his roommates. How weird was that? Not many college guys are off to a monastery for a New Year's Eve retreat, but then Ezra was not an ordinary college guy. Lady Gwendolyn was in a festive holiday mood; her little tea house looked like a gingerbread house set down in the middle of a Dickens novel. One was expecting Scrooge or Tiny Tim to walk in. Gwendolyn herself was not in costume, but decorated in Victorian Christmas ornaments, or so it seemed. She loved costume jewelry, especially anything with bangles and bobs. She was always so cheerful and welcoming, and was calling on Earl Grey to make his way to our table before we could even ask for him. Tea on Thames had become a regular watering hole for us and a few of our friends.

I had been to Christmas Midnight Mass with Ezra at Blessed Sacrament Church. It was such a moving experience for me that I couldn't keep the tears from flowing, especially at Holy Communion time. I wanted so much to receive the Lord in Holy Communion. I meditated on how incomprehensible the Incarnation is, and the utter humility of God to become a man. This was Ezra's first Christmas as a Christian, and he was almost aglow with joy. It was my first Solemn High Mass, and I guess I basked in his glow and in His glow.

Ezra's favorite priest, Fr. Kelly, gave an impassioned sermon which opened up for me the beginning of a deeper study into what they all called theology. Fr. Kelly said words to the effect that one cannot really understand the mystery and the splendor of Christmas outside of the context of the Blessed Trinity. That was so true. It was the Blessed Trinity or the Triune God—the Three Divine Persons in the One God—that really separated the Christian from the Jew, and the Moslem for that matter. Jesus was not just a prophet like our noted prophets: Moses, Isaiah, Jeremiah, Ezekiel… He was not just a Rabbi, a teacher of the Torah imparting a social and spiritual teaching, even the Golden Rule. He was truly the Second Person of the Triune God, the Word (the *Logos*, in Greek). And it was this Second Person, the Word, who became man. He didn't come in the *appearance* of a man; He didn't somehow come down and take over the body of a human being; He was conceived in a virgin's womb, and was born of her nine months later.

I've been pondering this probably every day since that Christmas Midnight Mass. Oh, I had read this, and even tried to argue it and refute it, but spoken that night surrounded by the lights and fir trees and poinsettias galore, it began to sink into my head and my soul. And I knew that either this was true or everything else in Christianity was false; but if this were really the truth, then everything that flowed from it was also true. I'm not sure I put it all into such words in my head way back then, but I knew that was the heart of it. All that Jesus said and did were the words and actions of a Divine Person, or just another rabbinical teacher of Israel, like a Hasidic Rebbe.

I also remember that the side altar dedicated to the Blessed Virgin Mary was especially beautiful for Christmas, and it was her image I thought of all the next day whenever I listened to a Christmas carol being sung and mentioning her. Jesus and I both had a Jewish mother.

Ezra and I saw each other every day after Christmas, visiting all our favorite Churches and visiting their crèche scenes, praying quietly before the figurines of the Christ Child, Mary, Joseph, the angels and shepherds, and knowing and believing all the time that the very same Jesus this plaster figurine represented was really present in the tabernacle on the altar. The red sanctuary lamp was a living flame keeping watch before the living presence—like the shepherds and Mary and Joseph. It was wonderful to think about the birth of God into our poor world.

Even Gwendolyn had a nativity set in the front bay window, with penguins rather than sheep, which I never understood, nor did I dare ask her why. It was all part of her penguin collection. She had stuffed penguins, glass figurines, trinkets, and even penguin earrings.

It was there at Tea on Thames that I gave Ezra my Christmas gift. I think it may have been the first "Christmas present" I ever really gave to someone, with the exception of

Gracie's gifts over the years, but even those I called Chanukah gifts. I wanted to give Ezra something really special for his first Christmas as a Catholic, but it was very difficult to come up with something he didn't already have. So I didn't get him anything religious, at least not tangibly so.

Instead, I got him two tickets to *The Sound of Music*, the movie which was currently playing, starring Julie Andrews as Maria. It was apparently a smash hit, and I knew he hadn't seen it. That's why I got two tickets! I got to Tea on Thames about 15 minutes early, and filled Gwendolyn in on my present, and she went along with my hiding the tickets in an empty teapot. It was one of her finest Christmas teapots which looked like a replica of Ye Old Curiosity Shop, covered in white enameled snow. Her cups never matched or came in sets; we had two of her finest stoneware mugs of different design, shape, and color.

When Ezra arrived, I was already having my usual Earl Grey with some sugar cookies. "More Earl Grey," I shouted while welcoming dear Ezra. Gwendolyn of course brought the Old Curiosity House teapot in a matter of minutes. I waited to let Ezra pour, as I only had a splash left in my cup.

"This is very light!" he exclaimed, and swished it around. Nothing swished. "There's no tea in here," he said, half laughing and half disturbed. He did hear something rattling inside, and when he opened it, there was a fancy red envelope. He confessed later that he just thought it was a Christmas card from Gwendolyn, but it turned out to be two movie tickets. He laughed with delight when he saw it, and promised that we—yes, *we*, must go when he got back from Massachusetts. The movie tickets included dinner first.

Ezra was going to be on retreat for five full days. He'd be back in time for school, and the *Sound of Music*. It was funny; I don't think I had had a male best friend ever before, but that's what he had become. Maybe I was so used to having two brothers that I could laugh and talk and enjoy doing things with Ezra. He had been very sweet and gave Mama a Chanukah gift: a beautiful punch bowl set he had bought at Bloomingdale's. Mama was a little overcome with emotion and thanked him very warmly, and even wished him a Merry Christmas without it getting stuck in her throat. He knew Mama and Papa were not comfortable with his being friends with me, but in his own little ways he tried to assure them that his intentions towards me were "most gentlemanly," as Gwendolyn put it when we told her about the incident. He was all excited about going away to this monastery, and I listened carefully, not quite understanding what it all meant… retreats and monasteries and all that.

I told him that I was spending the night with Gracie, whom he had met more than once, and of course Gracie knew all about him from me. He was glad for her sake that I would be with her. It was probably her last New Year's, and she should be with her friends as much as possible.

When we were leaving, Gwendolyn, who had obviously picked up bits and pieces of the conversation, gave me a box of cinnamon-raisin scones for Gracie and her family, which I thought was very thoughtful of her, but more surprisingly, she gave Ezra a bag of Christmas cookies with the request that he remember her in his prayers while on retreat.

"God bless you," she said, not quite as poignantly as Tiny Tim, but it struck us both, as she had never said that before.

I think I saw her eyes watering up as she waved, her Victorian Father Christmas earrings bobbing up and down.

Walking down Broadway to the subway, we commented to each other that we really didn't know anything about Gwendolyn. She never really talked about her family. We didn't think she wore a wedding ring because she wore several rings on several fingers, but we would ask her about herself next time—"next year." Ezra said he would pray especially for me, and Gracie, and my family...and he would pray that the new year would be my year.

"My year?" I tried to make it humorous, but I knew what he meant. I decided to walk down Broadway instead of taking the subway, but Ezra needed to get home quickly to grab his bag and his roommates. They were taking a bus to Springfield. We hugged each other at the subway stairs.

"Happy New Year...see you next year..." his voice echoing down into the cavernous subway entrance.

I wanted to walk home to clear my head a little and window shop for something for Gracie. I was tempted to go back to Tea on Thames to see if Gwendolyn was okay, but got distracted by an ambulance siren careening very near me. When I looked up, I saw a crowd just ahead of me, across 86th Street. As I got closer, I could see that someone was lying on the pavement, and the medics were soon attending to her. No one seemed to know what happened, whether it was a heart attack, a stroke, or if she fell over something... or was shot or knifed. She was quickly put on a gurney, an oxygen mask placed on her mouth and nose, and was lifted up into the back of the ambulance. And off they went.

It's not unusual to see such things in New York; we see life and death right before our eyes every day, or so it seems. I mention it here only because it stuck in my mind for an entirely different—self-centered—reason. I stood there with the little crowd that had stopped for a moment, and I said a prayer for the lady—something very simple and short and spontaneous. I don't even remember what I said, but something like, "God take care of this old lady, please help her." And I made the sign of the cross over myself. That was first time I ever did that. I had thought about doing it. I had practiced doing it at home but felt awkward and self-conscious about it anywhere else, even in church. Now it happened almost without my thinking about it; it was almost a natural reaction to a crisis moment, for someone else, not for me.

I passed Westside Records, a favorite place of Gracie's, who had been much more into the Beatles, Elvis, and even Bob Dylan than I was. I thought of getting her a record, but it wasn't personal enough. Then I thought of the perfect gift for her, and hurried on home to change and go over to her apartment.

Aunt Ruth and Sally had arrived and were filling the kitchen with laughter and stories. Mogen David had also arrived by the sounds of it, brought no doubt by Aunt Ruth who had a special affection for ole Mogen. She was excited to see me, as always, commenting on everything from my hair to my shoes.

"A college student, and you're wearing a ponytail?" At least she didn't comment on my weight, which was probably because she couldn't talk; she was a "full-bodied woman" too, and then some...as Uncle Max would say.

Sally seemed happy to see me, and I was certainly glad to see her. She was the only one really interested in what courses I was taking, and what papers I was writing, and who was I dating, and what Broadway shows had I seen... sister talk. Apparently Mama hadn't reported to the reporter about my friend Ezra. She (Mama) probably decided to leave that to Ruthie. David, Papa, and Ruthie weren't at home, so I missed giving them all an early New Year's kiss, but I would see them all tomorrow night for supper.

I grabbed my overnight bag, wished Mama, Aunt Ruth, and Sally a Happy New Year, and took off for 68th Street. The Prices lived in a high-rise apartment on West 68th near Central Park West. Their living room had a picture window which looked out towards the Park. Mr. Price is some kind of producer for NBC. They only had two children, a boy nearly seven years older than Gracie, named William, but they called him "Skip," and Gracie "Darling." Mr. Price always seemed very friendly and welcoming, which probably comes from his work in television, while Gracie's mother seemed more formal and a bit chilly, as I remember. I don't think she really liked me or approved of me. I thought it was probably because I was Jewish and Mrs. Price didn't like Jews, but that's all conjecture. I guess sometimes we come to our own faulty ideas about people without really knowing the truth. Our prejudices or our projecting prejudice onto others can be very subjective.

Hector, their doorman, was very nice, as most doormen are. He's known me for years as I would meet Gracie in her lobby. He used to tease us about being careful of the wolves "out there." Gracie once whispered to me sardonically that his "literary acumen never advanced beyond *Little Red Riding Hood.*"

"Good afternoon, Miss Feinstein," I was greeted politely by Hector.

"Hi, Hector, I'm here to see in the new year with Gracie Price."

"I know," Hector smiled, holding the door for me, and walking with me towards the bank of elevators. "Miss Price informed me you'd be arriving." His literary acumen may not have advanced much, but his English was excellent, I thought, as I pushed the button for the 43rd floor.

"Happy New Year, Hector." The door closed, and I was on my way, hoping my ears wouldn't pop.

Mr. and Mrs. Price couldn't have been nicer, and welcomed me most cordially. I said hello to Skip, whom I hadn't seen since that Saturday at Mt. Sinai. I hadn't really noticed how grown up and handsome he looked. He also worked for NBC as an assistant set decorator. He had graduated from Rhode Island School of Design and had worked for a year at an interior design company in Boston before coming back to New York and working for NBC. He lived on the Upper East Side, I think around 73rd Street. He was just here for supper and would be off to a party on the East Side.

Gracie was in her bedroom, in a hospital bed actually, but would be coming out for supper. She was very pale and her luxurious blonde hair was now just flat and wispy, but she was sitting up and excited to see me. I would sleep in the same room in her former twin bed, and best of all, she

had her own color TV. There was her usual dresser with a
statue of Mary standing on a lace doily. Cluttered around
the Blessed Virgin were Christmas cards, and ribbons, a couple bottles of Jean Naté Eau de Toilette, a half-burned-down
vigil candle, and a framed photo of the family at our graduation. There was also a small vanity table near the window,
and a small desk, both of which were cluttered with papers,
magazines, books, and hospital paraphernalia. Between the
hospital bed and the twin bed was a night table with a
ballerina lamp, and an overstuffed living room chair which I
didn't remember being in her room before. I gave her a big
hug and she said, "Wanna go to Times Square tonight?"
I stuck my finger in my mouth like I was gagging, and we
laughed like silly high school girls again.

"I have a little present for you, but not till later; and it's
not wrapped up in anything…oh, Gwendolyn says 'Happy
New Year' and sent a whole box of cinnamon-raisin scones.
They look delicious." And Gracie laughed at me. I was tick-
led I could still make her laugh, she looked so pathetic. It
was all so sad, her being in that ugly hospital bed.

Supper was very nice: baked breaded flounder with wild
rice, acorn squash and asparagus spears done perfectly. We
had a non-kosher Pinot Grigio, which had been brought by
Skip, who informed us that he was now "William." Gracie
only had half a glass and whispered to me that she was saving
room for the champagne later tonight. Dessert was lady fingers smothered in peach preserves and whipped cream and
sprinkled with powdered sugar. (I thought to myself, "Aunt
Ruth would gag over this one.") But I smiled and cleaned
my plate as I had been taught, for the starving children in

China, which somewhere along the way became the hungry children on a kibbutz in Israel. Clean your plate for Israel.

We made up a divan in the living room for Gracie, who sat smothered in quilts and throw pillows, but sitting up like the queen of the ball. We all watched TV for a couple hours and then switched to the television coverage at Times Square. William left shortly after 9:00, and Mr. Price fell asleep in his easy chair sometime around 11:00, but Mrs. Price shook him and kicked his shoes and woke him up in time to watch the Ball drop in Times Square and the crowd going wild welcoming in 1966. Gracie wasn't kidding about the champagne. We had a glass or two, while singing "Auld Lang Syne" with the TV crowd and kissing each other, "Happy New Year." It was only then that poor Mrs. Price broke down and cried and quietly left the room. I felt for her and cried inside. But it was Gracie who said, "Let's say a decade of the Rosary."

Mrs. Price had returned from the kitchen with a handful of Kleenex. "Do you think we should, dear?" Her eyes indicated my Jewish presence.

"Oh course," I said, "The Virgin Mary was a nice Jewish girl too." And that broke the ice. We all laughed and hugged again, and got settled in our seats. Mrs. Price turned down the lights, and we all faced a beautiful icon of Our Mother of Perpetual Help, which was on the wall opposite the TV. Mr. Price didn't turn the TV off but turned the sound completely down. And it was he who led the Rosary. They all had rosary beads in their hands, and Gracie very unceremoniously handed me hers. They were lovely white beads with little gold "shoulder pads" around each one. From her bathrobe pocket, she pulled out another, less pretty, pair of brown beads, and closed her eyes. I knew the Hail Mary, but I had only prayed it quietly to myself. I was very content to begin the new year this way, in this apartment, with my best friend, and her rosary. We actually prayed five decades, not one, after which Gracie was very tired and wanted to go to her room. While mother and daughter took care of her medicine and getting into bed, I called home and wished Happy New Year to everyone. David scolded me for not being there, Mama was weepy, and I think a little too friendly with Mogen David, as was Aunt Ruth, whose wish was that Sally find herself a husband this year, and Sally whispered she wished Aunt Ruth would stay in Cherry Hill. Ruthie giggled something to me, and Papa got on the phone last. "The Lord bless you and keep you, may He make His face to shine upon you, and give you peace, my Raf-kins. Happy New Year."

I hung up the phone and said goodnight to Mr. and Mrs. Price and went into Gracie's room; changed into my PJ's and sat in the chair next to her bed. She turned over on her side, smiling at me. "So, what's your gift for me? I know, you're engaged to Ezra, and want me to be the maid of honor?"

"No, no, no…silly." I got closer and softly said, "I'm going to become a Catholic, and I want you to be my godmother."

Six

GRACIE WAS THRILLED with my New Year's Gift Announcement. We talked for nearly a half hour till Gracie couldn't keep her eyes open anymore. I told her it all began the day I went to visit her in the hospital and I went into St. Vincent's to light a candle for her. I told her about meeting Ezra and what a blessing he'd been in learning about the Catholic Faith. I talked about the Blessed Sacrament, the Blessed Virgin, St. Thérèse, the sermon on Christmas Eve and lots of things, and made her promise not to tell anyone, not even her parents. I confessed that I hadn't told my folks and didn't know how to go about it…my father knew I was interested in Christianity, and he had as much as told me he would support whatever decisions I made in life. But Mama and the others were another story.

Gracie never got to be my godmother, however. By the end of January she was back in the hospital and would have fewer good days. I'll never forget the last time we were actually alone. I went over to Mt. Sinai nearly every day then, and it was the last Friday in January. Mrs. Price was there when I arrived, and took advantage of my visit to go get a bit of lunch and some coffee. Gracie was very weak and speaking was difficult. "Well, I don't think I'm going to be your godmother after all, at least not on this side of heaven." She smiled. Her eyes were quite large and sparkling, which

I found unusual for someone dying of leukemia. I realized looking at her that there was a life in Grace Darling Price which leukemia and weakness and death itself could not take from her. Gracie was indeed "full of grace."

And I told her so: "Gracie, you're absolutely beautiful at this moment; I think you're very full of grace. I know you will be present when I am baptized and will be forever my honorary godmother. I'm going to miss you so much; you've always been my very best friend, you know." My own eyes were full of tears as they spilled down my cheeks.

Gracie raised her left arm and patted my cheeks. "I love you too, Becky Feinstein. I don't have the strength to tell you all I want to tell you, but I'm so proud of you…" Her voice faded quickly. I kissed her gently on the cheek and sat down in the bedside chair. Her brown rosary was on the night stand. I picked it up and noticed it had the scent of roses, and I quietly prayed the Hail Marys and Our Fathers which were now part of my newfound prayers. *Pray for us sinners now and at the hour of our death.* It never stops touching my soul.

Mrs. Price returned with William and some coffee for me, which I drank with them and then took my leave, saying, "I should be home before Shabbat begins," but I assured them that I would be praying for Gracie. I had felt rather close to Mrs. Price the last weeks, since New Year's, when we all prayed the Rosary.

Early the next morning, on the Jewish Sabbath, Grace Darling Price passed away. William was kind enough to call me around 6:30 a.m. to tell me. It was Papa who answered the phone and got the news, and he came to my room and

gently woke me. Just looking at his face, so kind and sympathetic, I knew it was Gracie.

Later in the day, I simply announced that I would be going to Gracie's funeral Mass with Ezra and some friends. Mama and Papa didn't say anything but nodded their approval. Late that same afternoon I met Ezra at Tea on Thames, and let Gwendolyn know, who surprisingly said she would like to go to the funeral Mass with us, if she could. I remember she sat down at our table and had a cup of tea with us. She had never done that before. Death can create intimacy among the living.

I don't think I had ever been to a Gentile funeral before. I knew it would be very different than the couple Jewish funerals I had attended. I dreaded going into the place where the wake was. Ortiz Funeral Parlor was on West 72nd Street. It was almost incongruent with the surroundings, although I remember it was a street Gracie liked to explore…lots of clothes and handmade jewelry; bargain places and restaurants, even a few which had kosher menus. So maybe there was something normal about being waked on West 72nd Street. Sounds like an off-Broadway Show.

Ezra was very attentive and said he would go with me. Ruthie asked to go, and of course I said *yes*. The three of us went together into the strange world of funeral parlors, and only then was I overcome with a fear of seeing Gracie in her coffin, and at the same time, a sadness and anguish that she was really dead. We were early, and there were not too many people mulling around. My hand was shaking a little as I signed the guest book and took a holy card; it was the same picture of Our Mother of Perpetual Help which the Prices had in their living room. There was just a hint of being in church; there was a kneeler by the side of the coffin, and red-globed candles in floor candlesticks at the head and the foot of the coffin. The holy card had her name and dates of birth and death, and a prayer which I had heard before: *Eternal rest grant unto her, O Lord, and let perpetual light shine upon her.*

I moved slowly into the light surrounding the coffin. There she was. She was so thin in death, but her hair seemed full and beautiful; it may have been a wig, I thought, but didn't think Gentiles would do that sort of thing. Her lips were obviously glued shut, and her smile was not her smile. But there was a peacefulness in her face. She was laid out in a beautiful and conservative cocktail dress/gown. I think she may have worn a version of it to our Senior Prom. In her folded hands was the brown rosary which smelled like roses. In the lid of the coffin there was a white wooden and bronze crucifix.

I knelt on the kneeler and tried to say a prayer. I felt like I was frozen to the kneeler and maybe wouldn't be able to get up. "Why, God, why? Why would you let Gracie suffer so much? Why was her life ended before it really got started? She wanted to teach special-ed children, did you know that, Lord? See what you've done!" I knew I had to get up before I completely lost it and told God what I really thought, like He didn't already know.

I got up, and went over to the Prices standing there, already looking very weary from it all. We didn't have to exchange words; and I couldn't speak at that point anyway; there was a hard lump stuck in my throat, but my face said it all. Mr. Price hugged me and thanked me for coming.

Mrs. Price actually kissed me on the cheek and told me to wait; she turned and left the room and disappeared through a door leading into an interior room. The saddest of all was William. He couldn't talk either, but let himself weep unabashedly; he grabbed me and hugged me tight; I heard him sob into my shoulder.

Mrs. Price returned holding a little blue felt box. "Grace wanted you to have this, dear, and I promised her I would give it to you." I thanked her and made my escape to one of the padded chairs arranged like for an audience. I didn't open the blue felt box yet. I knew I had to get to my inner space and calm myself down. I couldn't pray. I was suddenly angry at God for doing this, for taking away my best friend; how could He be a loving God if He let this happen? Didn't He know how talented and needed Gracie was?

I half-watched Ezra and Ruthie following my lead and speaking with Gracie's family. It was the first crisis moment I remember having since I fell into St. Vincent's on my way to see Gracie. For a cold, numb couple of minutes, I didn't believe in anything or anyone, especially a God. It was all self-hypnosis and delusion. What am I doing thinking I want to be a Catholic? How arrogant and misguided I must be to let some statue and church architecture influence my freedom. Most of my classmates were breaking away from the established old ways of their parents and their parents' parents. We were the generation that was going to change everything: no more war, no more deaths, and no more antiquated pious guilt. I thought of my brother and his life wiped out instantly in a jungle halfway around the world. For what? Religion was just a pious antidote to assuage the meaninglessness and emptiness of life. We live and we die, that's all there is.

I slipped the box into my jacket pocket. I felt an urge to tear up my holy card in little pieces and throw it up into the air like confetti. Ruthie slipped in next to me, pulling her chair smack next to mine. "Take a deep breath, Becky, you look like you're going to pass out. Do you want some water or something?" Her soft voice brought me around surprisingly

"I'm okay, Ruthie, I'm just a little overwhelmed by it all… maybe I do need some fresh air. Tell Ezra I'm going outside, would you?" And I bolted for the door.

The fresh air did feel cool, and the noise and smells of 72nd Street were like a pair of old slippers. It brought me back to reality, whatever that was. A lady with matted bleached hair and too much rouge and the reddest of red lipstick was sitting on the curb picking cigarette butts out of the gutter. She lit one, holding it in her right hand which had a huge turquoise ring on the middle finger. She let out an exhaling sigh of relief from stress. Real life. I was still angry with God and decided then and there that I would never talk to Him again, that this "becoming a Catholic thing" was sheer delusion and emotionalism, and a betrayal of my family heritage. I didn't even want to talk to Ezra right now or maybe ever again, and before he and Ruthie could come looking for me, I took off, heading west towards Riverside Drive.

I was feeling a little dizzy and almost got hit by a cab turning onto 72nd Street. He yelled obscenities at me and I yelled back and walked on. I decided to walk up to the 79th Street Boat Basin and sit on a park bench and pull myself together. I had to get a grip for Gracie; she would die if she knew I was carrying on like a newborn Nietzschean agnostic. But I felt so empty.

Of course, when one falls into such a mental and emotional state it affects everything else. This search for religious truth in Christianity and the Catholic Church hit me more than anything. But really, one momentarily experiences the fruitlessness of all life; the total aloneness. Is Ruthie any more authentic for worshipping the Beatles and Elvis Presley? Was Mama less real for mourning the death of Helena Rubenstein, someone she never met, but talked to people like she had? They were friends, for Heaven's sake! What does any of it matter in the end? David's knocking himself out to be a doctor to make people healthy or to make lots of money for himself? And Sally! She hasn't even called to send her condolences. She's too busy chasing after an inane story. For what?

I suddenly felt very hungry and remembered a cookie jar full of cookies from Zabar's. So I made my way east on 79th to home. "Evening, Miss," peeped the new doorman who seemed too young to me to be a doorman, but what did I know? My world was becoming very black, indeed. I didn't know anything.

Ruthie was home and exasperated with me. "Ezra and I waited for you and couldn't find you anywhere, so I left. I think he's probably still there looking for you…where did you go?"

I cut her off: "I don't want to talk about it right now." I grabbed a handful of cookies, darted off to my room, locked the door; and sat in my rocker and inhaled the cookies. Blessed be oatmeal raisin cookies.

What should I do? I felt so empty and alone, like I didn't or couldn't believe in anything...my own poor Jewish faith, all the prayers and reading about Christ and the Catholic Church, all the hours of talking with Ezra, praying with Gracie...and I broke down and sobbed right there. It was Gracie. Why was God doing this? Where is she now? What if it's not all true? What if there isn't a Heaven and a life after this? Is death just the annihilation of life and we just don't exist anymore? Even oatmeal raisin cookies couldn't restore any hope in me.

There was a light rapping on my bedroom door. I wiped my eyes and blew my nose and managed to get out a "Who is it?"

"It's your mother; who else would it be?" "Go away, Ma, I can't talk right now."

"Open this door, Rebecca, I'm not going away till you do!" So I did, and ten seconds later, fell into the arms of my Mama, who let me cry it all out. I hadn't cried like that since I could remember, not even when Josh died.

"It was awful, Mama, seeing her in the coffin." "May I sit in this nice rocker you have in your room?" Mama asked as she was literally sitting in it, not really expecting an answer because it wasn't really a question. "The cushions don't really match the bedspread like they could, you know." I sat on the side of my bed; I can't really sit on the floor and be comfortable. I looked at Mama, rocking back and forth, taking in my room like it was the first time she'd ever been in there.

"I don't think I can go to the funeral Mass tomorrow. It's too painful...besides, it's not right."

Mama looked at me and smiled. "What's not right about it? She was your friend and you should be there to pray for her and to say goodbye. Just think of it as Catholic Kaddish." Coming from Mama that struck my funny bone.

"Catholic Kaddish?" I repeated, and started to giggle.

"It's such a blessing to have a friend; you should pray Catholic Kaddish for her." My giggle turned into a laugh.

"Oh, Mama," I said and burst out laughing, and Mama joined me.

"A little bit of this, a little bit of that." I don't know what she was referring to, or if she was just quoting *Fiddler on the Roof.* "So you cry a little, what's wrong with a few tears? God counts the tears of women, so I've been told." Mama was off and running. "When I went to Helena Rubenstein's funeral, may she rest in peace and cosmetic heaven, I cried a little bit of this, a little bit of that. She certainly made a beautiful corpse, that Helena."

I laughed some more and went over and knelt next to her and put my head on her lap, and she stroked my hair like she'd done when I was a little girl. We stayed like that for at least ten minutes, lost in our thoughts.

"Your father will be home in a half hour. Such a blessing that man, but he always expects his supper on time." She started to get up. "Get yourself washed up and come help me in the kitchen; we're having company."

"Okay, Mama," I said, "I'll try. I'll be there in a few minutes." I did feel better having gotten all those tears out; that was a lot for God to count, I figured. Who could be coming for supper, of all nights? Well, I could eat and be excused to come to my room. I wondered if Mama had photocopied my bookshelf in her head. It was growing with Catholic books like the lives of the saints, the *Confessions* of St. Augustine, which Gracie had given me after I told her my news, and of course, there was the Christian Bible in full view. I changed into what Mama would call a "house dress," making me rather frumpy looking for my age, but it was loose and comfortable; I washed my face, held the cold washcloth to my eyes for a minute, took a deep breath, and headed to the kitchen.

Mama was up to her elbows in flour and bread dough, pointing out the carrots and potatoes that needed to be peeled. I could smell chicken roasting in the oven. "Who's coming to dinner that you're making such a fuss?"

"It's a surprise," said Mama with a glint in her eye. An hour later, everything was ready. Papa was home and washed up, buried for the moment in the evening paper.

Mama made me change out of the house dress to a skirt and blouse, and the doorman buzzed up that our guest was on his way. *His* way? Mama told me to answer the door, which I did, and there was Ezra. I must've given out a little gasp. "Ezra!" And he whispered, "Your mother invited me this afternoon."

I was grateful after all, and surprised at Mama's delicate compassion. It was a pleasant supper. "What's not to like about roasted chicken?" as Mama would say. We were able to actually talk about Gracie and how sad and unfortunate these times are. I was quite composed, I realized, and actually sounded like a grown up talking in a detached mood about it all. After supper Ezra insisted the two of us go out for a walk. That's when he explained that he came by when he couldn't find me and was concerned. Mama told him I was crying in my bedroom and should have some time to get it all out. She invited him to dinner. "You can talk to her better than we do, so come by for supper at quarter to five."

He seemed to be walking with a destination. "Where are we going?" I hoped it wasn't back to Ortiz's Funeral Home. I knew they were having the wake until 9:30 or 10:00 and that there would be the Rosary sometime this evening. I didn't think I could handle the Rosary right now.

"Your mother invited me to supper; now I'm taking you to see my mother." Ezra loved to talk that way—always leaving one to have to guess whatever he could mean.

"Your mother's here from Buffalo? I didn't know that."

"No, not that mother, my *other* mother." There he was again, talking in mysterious prose. "We'd better get a cab." And with that he was in the street with his arm waving, and before I could make any response, a yellow taxi was pulling up next to us. I figured this mysterious "other mother" must be in a fancy hotel in Midtown…I was hoping either the Plaza or the Waldorf. I could go for another dessert right about now. "East 61st Street between Second and First," Ezra told the cabbie. Well, that shot either of my choices.

As it turned out, it was not a hotel, but a church, Our Mother of Perpetual Help, run by the Redemptorist Fathers. I had never been there before. I wasn't so sure I wanted to "go to Church" right now. "I think I'd rather have a hot fudge sundae and a cup of tea," I informed my kidnapper. Ezra laughed.

"Maybe later, huh? I want you to see and hear this novena. It goes on every Tuesday night."

When I walked in, the smell of candles and lingering incense brought a sudden peace to my distraught soul. I was still full of darkness and doubts, probably more than when I first wandered into St. Vincent's, but there was a strange comfort in the candles and statues. Ezra is not a "back of the bus Catholic," so he walked me up to the third pew from the front, on the side of the beautiful shrine altar with the icon of Mary, Mother of Perpetual Help…the very image the Prices had in their living-room. It was the image on Gracie's holy card. I was impressed by the number of people there on a Tuesday night, of all ages and costumes. There were booklets available for us, and after about fifteen minutes the priest came out from the sacristy with a surplice and stole over what Ezra later told me was the Redemptorist habit. Everyone knelt and prayed together the first prayer of the novena:

> O Mother of Perpetual Help, thou art the dispenser of all the gifts which God grants to us, miserable sinners. He has made thee so powerful, so rich and so bountiful, that thou mayest succor us in our misery. Thou art the advocate of the most wretched and abandoned sinners who have recourse to thee. Come to my help; I commend myself to thee. In thy hands I place my eternal salvation. To thee I entrust my soul. Count me among thy most devoted servants. Take me under thy protection, and it is enough for me. If thou protect me, I fear nothing; not from my sins, because thou wilt obtain for me the pardon of them; not from the devils, because thou art more powerful than all hell

together; not even from Jesus, my Judge, because by
one prayer of thine He will be appeased. But one thing
I fear, that, in the hour of temptation, I may, through
negligence, fail to have recourse to thee, and thus per-
ish miserably. Obtain for me the pardon of my sins,
love for Jesus, final perseverance, and the grace ever to
have recourse to thee, O Mother of Perpetual Help.

The words were powerful, almost too much to take in
the first time. But a wonderful peace came over me, and I
knew that I had a Mother in Heaven too, who would always
be my perpetual help, in all things, at all times. I turned
over my dear friend Gracie to her, for she was her Mother
too, and every day of her life, Gracie had looked upon her
picture. How dear and comforting Mama was to me this
afternoon, stroking my hair, and making everything better;
she even ignored her own little prejudices and maybe fears,
and invited Ezra to dinner because *she wanted to help*. She's
such a blessing. And now I know whom she takes after in her
own little way—the Mother of Jesus.

I missed what was said for a few minutes, and the hymn
they sang is all blurred, but I came to as we prayed for all
our needs and sufferings. I put my hand in my jacket pocket
and felt the blue felt box Gracie's mother had given me. I
opened it quietly, and there was Gracie's beautiful white
rosary beads, her best pair. I held onto them.

And then everyone started to move out of their pews
and go to the altar rail like at Holy Communion time, but
instead, the priest presented a small icon of Mary, Mother
of Perpetual Help for each person to kiss. Ezra said it was

okay for me to do that too…so I knelt at the rail for the first time ever, and kissed the icon when she came to me, and holding her rosary, I prayed for Gracie and her soul… *Catholic Kaddish.*

Seven

THE NOVENA TO Our Mother of Perpetual Help and Benediction of the Blessed Sacrament the night before restored my soul to peace. I don't know why that was, but I tried not to analyze it and just accept it. Maybe that's the key—acceptance. When I'm struggling with something and unable to accept something, I can get myself all upset. I guess I hadn't really accepted that Gracie was gone and somehow, which I can't begin to understand, that it was God's will. Acceptance...boy! I did accept an ice-cream sundae without too much analysis, got home, fixed a cup of tea and retreated to my room.

I sat alone in my squeaky rocker close to midnight. I wasn't reading or formally praying anything, I was just thinking about *acceptance*, and accepted that I was different from most of the girls my age. I think I always felt different because I was not as pretty or thin or athletic as the other girls. I wasn't boy crazy since sixth grade. The coeds at school now were kind of flighty and wild; some others, like flower children, were protesting the war, and others were getting angry over feminist rights and issues; the serious studious ones were on their way to Law School or Medical School or Rabbinical School; and I lived in the world of books and literature, movies and philosophy and was not really sure what I wanted to be when I grew up.

I accepted that my coming to know and, dare I say, *love* Christ was genuine and was not something *I* did, but something that was *given* to me—it was purely a gift, and, for whatever reason, I was ready to receive it…to *accept* it. Maybe that was a big part of faith—simply accepting what God wants to give, what God has said and revealed about Himself, accepting that God doesn't want to remain anonymous to His creatures. I also knew and accepted that I would probably be plagued at times with doubts and fears, and always wondering if what I was doing was God's will, if there is a God. And I accepted that there must be a God who loves us into life, for by ourselves we make such a mess of it, and can't understand why things happen to people, like Grace Price getting leukemia.

Perhaps I was always an atheist to the world's gods and goddesses. I feared that Ruthie was falling under their spell. The world can be very seductive and God so very distant, or so it seems. Yet the more I read the Gospels, the more I discovered how much God wants to be close to us. The Incarnation, I knew, was for our salvation, but I think it was also so God could be as close to us as humanly and divinely possible.

I knew the time had come to tell my family what I was planning to do—to be baptized in the Catholic Church. Next week I was beginning my formal instructions with Fr. Rayburne at Blessed Sacrament Church, where Ezra had gone, the church where Gracie's funeral would be tomorrow. But I was so lacking in courage and so full of fear. Would anyone in my family be able to accept this? I prayed the

Novena Prayer to Our Mother of Perpetual Help again. I had "borrowed" the pamphlet we had in our pew.

I told Ezra that I would meet him at church and that he should save a seat for me. I wanted to be at the funeral home in the morning to say my final goodbye before they closed the casket. I left before the others did, and walked over to the church. In about the fifth row on the right side was Ezra and a strikingly beautiful woman in a black muu-muu, none other than Lady Gwendolyn. She even had a black lace handkerchief tucked in her bracelet on her right wrist. She had a large, black, floppy hat, with a silk hat band, and a stick pin with a miniature penguin! I had forgotten to get a nice hat—did I even have a nice hat?—so I wore a silk bandanna, one which Gracie always admired. It was a wavy design of muted grays and blues, nothing flashy.

The Funeral Mass was another wonderful turning point for me. I told Ezra afterward that if I had not had a religious conversion months ago, I would have during that Mass. There were a lot of people there, many from television because of Mr. Price, and Gracie's (and my) old high school. I think there was a contingent of students from NYU where Gracie had had only one semester.

Fr. Kelly, the pastor, came out to meet the coffin at the front door of the church. He wore black vestments with gold brocade that matched the funeral pall they placed over the coffin. They processed up the aisle while the small choir sang the Latin *Requiem*. Gracie's family followed; Mrs. Price looking very stoic, but I'm sure she was just holding it all in tightly…some of us learn how to do that quite well.

In his sermon, Fr. Kelly spoke of the Lord's tremendous love for us, stressing that the Lord loves us even more than we do ourselves. He pointed out how the Lord had a special love for the poor and for children. *Let the children come unto me, for to such belongs the Kingdom of Heaven.* He tried to make the point that the Lord loves Gracie more than we do; He is her Creator and her End; the Lord loved her so much He couldn't wait any longer to bring her home to the Beatific Vision of Heaven...and so He called her home.

I don't know what that means for really old people, but I understand what he was trying to say, and I think it was a consolation to Gracie's family. But then, just like he did at Christmas Midnight Mass, he zeroed in on the profound truth of who Jesus Christ is—*a Divine Person who took to himself a human nature, so that our human natures could become divine in Him.* And this begins with baptism. My ears perked up. He said we began Holy Mass by draping the coffin in this black and gold pall praying "that as Grace put on Christ in her baptism may she now be clothed with Him in glory."

It was a beautiful meditation on baptism and Heaven— the final fulfillment of that first sacrament. He also reminded us that we needed to pray for Gracie's soul and for any remnants of sin she may have in need of being purified. The Catholic funeral Mass is certainly sobering and solemn. My heart ached at Communion time for the day when I would be able to receive Him so intimately. Oh, I almost forget to mention, it was the first time I realized that Gwendolyn was a Catholic, and I watched her more than anyone as she knelt at the Communion rail, and when she returned to our pew, she knelt immediately and put her face into her hands and didn't move for probably five minutes. It must be such a wonderful moment, I thought to myself, such a wonderful moment. What a blessing it must be.

The next week Ezra took me to speak with Fr. Rayburne and to get signed up to take instructions. His class would begin on Shrove Tuesday, the evening before Ash Wednesday, and go for the forty days of Lent, plus some. It was only then that I realized there was a schedule conflict with school. The one and only evening class I had was on Tuesday and by time I got here, even by cab, the class would be half over. However, he mentioned that a Dominican priest at St. Vincent's across town offered convert instruction classes on Monday and Thursday evenings. If I would like, he would call him himself and introduce me before sending me over.

"Monday nights would be perfect!" I exclaimed, already planning in my head my course of action. I could pray in St. Vincent's before. And so it was all arranged. Fr. Aquinas Meriwether, O.P., would be instructing ten of us in the large parlor of the Priory beginning at 6:30 p.m. until 8:30. He was not waiting till Lent began, but was beginning immediately; actually, they had already begun, but I could catch up. He also asked to meet me Saturday afternoon for an hour to get acquainted and to have a tour of the church. He said he liked to begin in the church proper and introduce the students to the correct etiquette for entering and leaving the church. I told him I would meet him in the Priory at 2:00 Saturday afternoon and that I had been in St. Vincent's many times already.

Sally was coming up from Philly that Sabbath weekend for some kind of sorority reunion and would be home for Friday night Shabbat supper. I decided that would be as good a time as any to tell everyone. Whenever I said that to myself or Ezra, my stomach did a flip flop. How would they take this news; what if they kicked me out of the house; what would I do; where would I go? All the worst scenarios played in my head till I told myself, "Stop it. You don't know how they will take it, but the Lord will give you the grace."

I knew that, I believed that, but I still got clammy palms when I tried to rehearse how and what I would say. I don't recall anyone in the Feinstein family becoming a Christian. I had a distant cousin in California who became a Buddhist, and nobody seemed to blink an eye at that, so what was to worry?

Friday evening arrived. Mama lit the Shabbat candles and prayed. I silently prayed too, to my *other Mother*. If I ever needed help it was that night! Papa suspected something was up, as he could always read me. He wanted us to remember my friend, Grace Price, after he prayed the blessing for the challah, which was so kind of him.

My cue came when Sally unceremoniously asked across the table, "So, Becky, what's new in your life, what's going on?"

"Oh, I'm taking three courses this semester, including one on Shakespeare; my best friend, Grace Price died a week ago; I lost three pounds this week; and I'm taking instruction to become a Catholic."

If Sally had worn dentures, she would have blown them across the table. Instead she kind of sprayed us with a mouth full of coleslaw. Mama dropped her fork with a great clunk on her plate. Ruthie exclaimed, "I'm right, I'm right, I win! I bet Bridget Murray that you're becoming a Catholic." Papa very quietly quieted her: "Quiet, little one. Please God, it is something you have been thinking about for a long time, and it is not just an aftershock from Grace Price's death and the beautiful Mass for her?" His voice was soothing. He did not appear startled or visibly upset. Mama, on the other hand, was a bit beside herself.

Mama couldn't contain herself: "Such news you drop on this table when we're eating challah? I knew that boy was a bad influence on you, such a schmuck to lead you away like he did."

"Mama, I've been thinking of this since *before* I even met Ezra. He's been a great help in many ways, but the decision is totally my own. Not even Gracie had an influence."

"Well, I think it's ridiculous and disrespectful," spake the coleslaw sprayer. "How do you know your mind at 19 or 20? You're just mesmerized by the art and music in the Catholic Church, but really, Beck, how can you submit yourself to the Pope, and believe that Jesus is God, and all that? I think it's just a phase that will pass; it's those books you're reading. Pass the chicken, please."

"It's not easy for me to articulate all this," I began, "but as circumstance would have it, I have come to know and believe in Jesus Christ as the Son of God. I have always loved my Jewish faith and heritage, and even more now, as I see how it comes to completion in Jesus of Nazareth. I'll have more Mogen David, please." Mama sat still, unable to eat, which I've never seen before. Even when we got the news of Josh's death, she ate. It was Papa who passed the wine after filling his own glass, and telling Mama to drink a little. It was like Mama was incredulous. Sally wouldn't let it rest.

"Well, I know you young people are the generation who are rebelling against the establishment. Just look at the hippies and the drugs and drinking and…"

"Sally, darling," broke in gentle Papa again, "Rebecca is not a hippie or on drugs; she's not rebelling against us or her Jewish heritage, she's thinking about the deeper things of life, and has opened her soul to a relationship with the Almighty, may His Name be blessed, which many young people are *not* doing today. I do not know if I can give my blessing to it," he looked directly at Mama, "but I can give my blessing for the search. If your mother and I have instilled anything in you, I hope it's that you are children of God and free in your souls to pursue the path or paths on which the Almighty leads you. Pass the challah!"

"Thank you, Papa. I would never do anything to disrespect you all. I've been dying to tell you this for months, but was afraid. I'm not so afraid anymore, knowing that I have Papa's blessing to search, as he said." I took a big gulp of wine, grateful for the sweetness and the aftertaste which tickles your nose.

Mama and Sally were silent and picked at their food. Ruthie raised her hand like she was in school: "May I say something now?"

Papa nodded, "Of course you may, Ruthie, this is not a school. But be kind." Ruthie took a ladylike sip of her wine, reminding me of our tea parties at Horn's. "If Becky becomes a Catholic, does she cease being Jewish?"

No one answered her, sheepishly looking at each other. It was Mama who broke the silence: "Of course not, look at Jesus." And we all burst out laughing. After helping with the dishes, Ruthie was off to her girlfriends to, quote unquote, "do homework." Sally was off to see some other sorority sisters, Papa was embedded in the paper, and Mama was quiet, putting some flowers on the table with the candles for Shabbat, lost for a moment in their flames.

I gave Ezra a call to tell him that it all went well, thank God. "They haven't kicked me out yet! I want to celebrate—can you meet me at Tea on Thames? My treat."

It was a bitterly cold night with flurries off and on, but it felt good just to walk over to Broadway and hop on the uptown bus. The cold didn't seem to keep people from going out for dinner, of course. It was Friday night. I got to Tea on Thames and had to wait in the area by the front door till a table was free. Lady Gwendolyn waved from behind the register while two others waited on tables; Columbia students, I figured.

Ezra arrived before a table was clear, but we soon crowded into one along the side wall. We ordered two pots of Earl Grey and a high tea plate, which was a triple deck dish with assorted pastries and cakes. It was like a meal in itself. I dropped a little saccharine pill into my cup before devouring a cream-filled petit four. I recounted the exchange at our dining room table, except for Mama's compliments about him. He was excited to hear it all and even more excited to hear about my classes with Fr. Meriwether.

Her Ladyship stopped by after the crowd thinned out and said, "You two look like you're celebrating something special?" I think she was trying to see if I had a ring on my finger.

"We are," I half whispered. "I begin my instructions to become a Catholic on Monday, and I told my family tonight during supper."

Gwendolyn got all teary eyed: "Well, darlin', I think that's so marvelous. I wondered if and when that would happen, not that I'm eavesdropping over your conversations the last five months!" We laughed. "I thought something was up with you, Miss Feinstein, since Gracie's funeral. I'm a Yorkshire Catholic myself, you know, and I'll tell you it's been the singular grace in all my life. We'll be praying for you, darlin'," and she leaned down and kissed me on the cheek.

The little tea shop became suddenly quiet, as most the people there listened and were probably a little stunned. "It's lovely," announced Gwendolyn in her best Yorkshire accent. "It's lovely."

Eight

IT *WAS* LOVELY; for nearly ten weeks I was immersed in the Catechism and learning about all the lovely sacramentals and practices of the Church. We learned the basic prayers, how to pray the Rosary, and how to follow the Mass in one's missal, although we heard that the Vatican Council would be coming out with a New Order for the Mass, much of which would be prayed now in the vernacular.

It was an exciting time in the Catholic Church. Pope John XXIII was elected Pope to succeed Pope Pius XII, and Pope John had called for an Ecumenical Council. He died during the Council and Pope Paul VI was the present "Holy Father," as we called him. That in itself was such a revelation, I'm almost embarrassed to share my ignorance, and I was nearly 20 years old! I thought that there had been only twelve popes, who were all *pious*. The last one, during my own childhood, was Pope Pius XII. Imagine how stupid I felt when I learned he was only the twelfth one to take the name Pius (not pious), and that actually he was the 261st pope in a direct line from St. Peter the Apostle.

Once I saw that, it helped to make everything else fall into place. It was obvious that the Catholic Church, the one Church still under the "headship" of St. Peter, as it were, was the first and only Church established by Christ Himself. The

Catechism spoke of the true Church in light of all the thousands of Christian denominations in modern times.

It's always something of a mystery to non-Christians interested in Christianity as to why there are so many denominations. Was the Bible, as some claimed, the only source of what Christ taught, and if so, is there not one authority over that, as it seemed like all the different churches were claiming their own interpretation as the true one? There had to be an authority over and above even the Bible, at least the New Testament, since the Church was established years *before* even a word was written.

Once I accepted (there it was again...acceptance) the authority of what they called the "Magisterium of the Church," I was not arguing the different doctrines, but accepting them and seeing them as the fullness of truth coming from Christ and the apostles, developed in some areas, over time, as naturally as other things are developed, but with the truth always there in the seed, in the kernel.

I loved the organic nature of the Church, to use a more common word today than back in 1966. The Church was a living organism which was in reality the Mystical Body of Christ, and all those who were baptized became living members of that body...living stones in this temple, which is the Body of Christ. And a Body has a head, a neck, lungs, hands, a heart. Christ is the Head, and the Head is ascended into Heaven, while Peter (and his successors) would be the visible head on earth; they called him the *Vicar of Christ*... we called him Papa...Pope. I liked that. I could identify with that. I had a wonderful Papa who in his own way was my first and loveliest experience of God the Father. It wasn't a tyrannical authority, but a paternal, loving one.

The Mystical Body was Christ among us. Through His members living by His life, Divine Grace, or what we call "Sanctifying Grace," the work of redemption is accomplished. The hands of Christ are still blessing, healing, teaching; the feet of Christ are still traveling in pilgrimage and in missionary journeys everywhere in the world. But best of all, the Offering of Jesus on the Cross to His Papa and His glorious Resurrection is still happening, as it were…is still made present for us in the Holy Sacrifice of the Mass.

It's enough to blow your mind, as my generation was saying about many other things which seemed to amaze them, even, I'm sorry to say, the psychedelic hallucinations one could experience through drugs like LSD. And for two thousand years, we have had the Body, Blood, Soul, and Divinity of Christ still loving us and joining us to His act of love on the Cross.

I am so grateful to Fr. Meriwether for the time he took to show us that. It was fascinating how much of my Jewishness, especially our holidays and observances, were carried over into the Church's liturgy, especially the Mass, which is the new Passover Seder, celebrated and eaten, not just once a year or once a week, but really every day. I think every Christian should become Jewish, at least for a year, to see how Christ has fulfilled everything in Himself in such a marvelous way.

I was unable, of course, to share all this with my family, but I became friends with a couple of the other inquirers, and of course there was Ezra and my newly discovered

Catholic girlfriend, Gwendolyn, who actually envisioned her little Tea on Thames business as a kind of apostolate. Gwendolyn belonged to Corpus Christi Parish and was an active member of their Altar Rosary Society. She also belonged to a Marian Sodality, but I think the most powerful influence she'd had was what she called a *Cursillo*. It was a weekend retreat with 50 to 75 other women in a Church gymnasium, which blew *her* mind. She was in weekly contact with her own group that went through the weekend together, and she participated in other weekends for first-timers.

Isn't it funny: I never knew any of these things about her when I first started going to Tea on Thames. She was also a naturalized American citizen and a widow since she was 32. She had only a son who was her pride and joy. He was killed by a drunk driver at the Jersey Shore five years ago. His name was Christopher; he was thirteen years old and riding his bike. He collected penguins.

Gwendolyn said it was mainly getting through that time that she turned to her faith, which, she said, used to be rather wishy-washy…more wishing going on than washing. She calls herself the "merry widow" now at age 40.

Around three weeks into our instructions, I was again distraught, not with doubt and fear this time, but a kind of sadness that is difficult to explain. I knew that being baptized would change my whole life, and that I wasn't *giving up* my Jewish faith as much as I was *fulfilling* it, but nonetheless, I cried a lot, for about a week. Mama wasn't the same around me; Sally wouldn't speak to me; and David, well, David is a whole story unto himself. He who prided himself on being an intellectual agnostic, bordering on atheist, suddenly became an expert in Jewish Law and Custom. He accused me of betraying the heritage of our whole family and of the great rabbinical tradition we inherited from Austria. He told me I was being foolish, and selfish, and worst of all, that I was being disobedient to my parents and causing them humiliation and embarrassment among their Jewish friends. He even said that all that the Zionist movement was doing to establish a Jewish state in Israel was being belittled by my myopic vision of life; that I didn't even know what life was about; and why would I want to restrict my freedom by the restrictions and moral code of a Church?

Wow! I didn't know my converting to Christianity had international repercussions! I also didn't know my brother was so passionate about the State of Israel. Only in retrospect many years later, do I think the real issue was more the restriction of one's freedom by a morality which curtailed one's subjective moral choices or contradicted them. It was almost ironic to lambaste the Catholic Church for her moral code when the entire Mosaic Covenant is built on Law. Nonetheless, I was terribly wounded by David's insinuations and couldn't or wouldn't argue with him.

And so I'd sit alone in my rocker at night and cry. Maybe it was all a mistake; maybe David was right; maybe I was living in a world of delusion. The whole "Jesus-thing," as David would refer to it, was perhaps the crux of it, more than any rules or moral codes. Jesus Himself asks the apostles one night the most important question in the New Testament: "Who do you say that I am?"

I can picture them around a campfire where they had pitched their tent for the night, back together again after having been sent out in pairs to preach. They've cooked their dinner, the stars are out and there's a definite chill in the air, and they're sitting around the fire talking about the people they had met and talked to. They're enjoying the delicious date-and-nut cakes one of the women in town gave one of them in gratitude to Jesus for healing her son who was one of those lepers. And Jesus sits down in the middle of them, square in the middle of their lives—"*Who do people say that I am?*" That was an easy enough debate; they loved telling the stories of what they've been hearing over the months.

I had a course at Barnard that treated the New Testament as literature, among other classical works, and one would think that this Jesus of two thousand years ago, this Jewish rabbi from an insignificant town in Palestine, was just one among many interesting people who said some wise things and had a following. That's all He is for my sister Sally. But then Jesus brings it home: "*And you, who do you say that I am?*"

It was actually Fr. Meriwether who said it was the most important question in the New Testament, and I think he was right. He, Fr. Meriwether, also said in response to people like Sally, that Jesus wasn't really a wise man if what He said about Himself is not true; then He's actually a disillusioned liar, or some kind of egomaniacal teacher with a messiah-complex. He thought He was God, for Heaven's sake! Fr. Meriwether used to almost jump out of his chair when he'd talk that way.

That is *the* question, though. I don't know exactly when I knew, if "knew" is even the right word. But I said it out loud, not around a campfire with others, not in our Monday night class, not over tea and biscuits with Ezra and Gwendolyn, but in my squeaky rocker, alone in my room. *"You are the Lord."* It wasn't quite as Simon Peter said, or Thomas the Apostle the week after Easter Sunday night, but maybe like my Jewish friend, St. Paul, who had to be knocked off his high horse... *You are the Lord.* And more than anything else, I knew that He loved me. I had "passed over" from being a Jew to being a Christian, at least by baptism of desire.

The first day of Passover fell on April 5...I was to be baptized in May. This was before RCIA and baptisms during the Paschal Vigil became popular. I was so hoping to be baptized before Easter, but Fr. Meriwether was very thorough and wanted us to cover everything in his lessons, drawn from the *Baltimore Catechism*, but also incorporating documents from Vatican II. Most people in the class were "becoming Catholics" because they were marrying a Catholic, and I suppose Father wanted to make sure they were also doing it for themselves.

I was the youngest person in the class. There was another man around my age who was a student at NYU; he and his fiancée were getting married at St. Vincent's in June. My best friend from the class, however, was Greta Phillips. She was an attractive woman, in her early fifties, with a sweep of blonde hair streaked with white and gray pulled back into a French twist. She was a widow, and her deceased husband had been a Lutheran pastor in north Jersey. She moved into the City after his death principally for work reasons, but she also loved New York. She was an assistant librarian for the New York Public Library on Fifth Avenue, fluent in four languages besides English. She had spent nearly twenty years in Mozambique, Africa, with her husband, Pastor Phillips, where she literally set up an entire library in a mission school, sponsored by the Church of the Nazarene. So she knew her Christianity very well and loved to talk about books.

Greta introduced me to the writings of Dietrich Bonhoeffer, a German Lutheran pastor who spoke out against the Nazis and was imprisoned and died at the age of thirty-nine on April 9, 1945. The book that meant the most to her, and became a favorite of mine as well, was *The Cost of Discipleship*. It was an interesting and useful concept, I thought. He would speak of "cheap grace" and grace that cost you something, not in money, of course, but in "losing oneself," as the Lord would put it, "in dying to self and following Him." It was a marvelous morsel to meditate on as I knew more and more what the interior and familiar cost of my becoming a disciple meant. It would also be a reminder for me all my life, when I forget what discipleship means. The first disciples even spoke about the "cost"...*what about us, Lord, who have left everything to follow You?* And He gently leads us to a kind of purification. This happens more than once, of course, and is always in God's time and His choosing.

It was no small matter for this lovely widow of a noted Lutheran pastor to become a Catholic; her social standing was all couched in the Lutheran circuit. One Monday night at a coffee shop after class, she told me that there were two things principally that drew her to the Catholic Church, even before her husband died. First, the authority entrusted to the Pope; it made perfect sense to her and without it everything was "up for grabs." And secondly, the Catholic devotion to the Blessed Virgin Mary. She and her husband had actually visited Lourdes in France one summer. "I was shook to my poor Lutheran bones," she said, rubbing her arms together. She said she had an experience of the Church at Lourdes, especially in the evening candle light procession, that she never had in the Lutheran Church.

"Do you have a devotion to the Blessed Virgin?" Greta asked me with the same nonchalance that she might ask me if I had ever been to the Statue of Liberty.

"Oh, yes, indeed I do," I answered almost as nonchalantly. "I think of her as my *other Mother*."

"How charming," was her reply, not with even a hint of sarcasm, more of envy, if we catechumens could express such capital vices while learning about the virtues. I laughed.

"Oh, I don't know how charming it is. The mother I have from birth is quite a wonderful lady to know, and I'm afraid I've gone and dismayed her, or disappointed her, or failed her by my becoming a Christian. While my mother, her name is Hannah, is not overly religious by any means, she's very spiritual in her own way, and very Jewish. My brother says I am betraying both her and my father by this lame-brain infatuation with Catholicism." My cheerfulness had turned rather sullen in my thoughts about my mother.

Greta was silent for a moment, letting me be lost in my thoughts, and she in hers. "Your mother is only reacting as any mother would because she loves you; give her time, she'll come around when she sees and knows you're happy."

"I hope so…I've put that all into the hands of my 'other Mother,' Our Mother of Perpetual Help." And I told Greta about my friend, Gracie, and our praying the Rosary together last New Year's Eve. I put my hand into my jacket pocket, no longer for a Milky Way, but for Gracie's pearl rosary. Greta held it in her hand like it was a relic. "It's very beautiful," she said. "My special rosary is the one I bought at Lourdes several years ago. There's something about the Mother of God that I haven't found anywhere in all my searching and reading and travels. And yet, she is the most obvious of mothers and friends, given to us by the Lord Himself, and she was the first disciple, really, and more than anyone else ever, she knew the 'cost of discipleship,' didn't she?"

I liked Greta. Her years of experience, in which I was lacking—at least as far as Christianity—gave her a built-in maturity which made chatting with her such a delight. Being a librarian didn't tarnish her reputation with me either; somebody I could talk to about books! She promised she would bring a copy of *The Cost of Discipleship*, not from the library, but for keeps. And she added a bit wistfully, to quote Lady Cordelia Marchmain: *There is no real holiness without suffering.*

At twenty, of course, well, I suppose at any age, that sounds rather pietistic and is always filtered through one's subjective lenses. I don't remember if I responded, but I remember remembering that when I was rocking in my room that night. *There is no real holiness without suffering.* I didn't even know who Lady Cordelia was—I thought it was a friend of hers, and I was an English Lit major—but I thought about my own suffering and wondered if it would apply.

Thanks to Ruthie from our tea parties years ago, I remembered Edith Stein, and decided that I should read about her a little more now. She certainly knew what suffering was. Some say that Jews know better than any other people what suffering is. The Passover was an exodus from slavery and all the suffering that entails to a new freedom in a promised land. Fr. Meriwether drew the parallel of Christ being the new Moses and His death being the Passover from the slavery of sin to the freedom of the children of God and that Heaven is the new Promised Land. I couldn't believe how rich and profound the Catholic Faith is.

April 5th was Tuesday of Holy Week and the first night of Passover. We had had class on Monday evening, and Fr. Meriwether went through all the parallels. And I knew that the next night's Passover would be my last Seder with my family. No one really spoke about it in those terms. David would be there. Sally was unable to come up from Philly due to work, she said. Or she just wasn't able to be around me.

I don't know why she was so opposed to my becoming a Catholic, but she was. David and Mama were too, of course, and I knew it was killing Papa, but he never tried to argue or persuade me not to. Ruthie thought it was all very dramatic, and I think she loved the potential discord in the house; she was her own little rebel, but that wouldn't show its true colors till some years later.

David, the evangelistic agnostic, had exhausted his protests and had become more quiet about it, as had Mama. I was able to get over to St. Vincent's late in the morning after helping Mama with some of the preparations to spend an hour praying before the tabernacle, within glancing distance of my favorite statue of the Sacred Heart, Jesus the Priest.

I don't remember much of what I prayed about, but I was aware that what I was doing *was* a kind of suffering to me, in my own passover from the faith of my family, my childhood, my whole life, really, to Christ. It was a suffering in a different way for my family, certainly, and there was nothing I could do to change that. Oh, I could not become a Catholic or I could wait till Mama and Papa were dead and buried, but I knew I couldn't...I couldn't wait to be united to Christ...to be joined to that Sacred Heart which drew me to Himself the first time I walked into that Church. And so I prayed simply for the grace to surrender to God's Holy Will and to have the courage to bear whatever suffering came my way. I felt very much alone at that moment, but I also knew that I wasn't, that He was with me, His Mother was with me; indeed, the whole Court of Heaven in the Communion of Saints was with me.

And a gratitude to God passed over me for Papa and Mama, for all my family...for Gracie and Josh, for Ezra and Gwendolyn, for Fr. Kelly and Fr. Meriwether, for Greta Phillips and my other classmates, and for the silent and anonymous people I saw every time I went into church, praying in the pews, lighting candles, mumbling over their beads, gazing at the tabernacle where the Lord was filling me with *shalom.*

Nine

TWO WEEKS BEFORE I was to be baptized, the Sabbath began at sunset, May 13. I had missed a few of our Friday evenings over the months, and Mama asked me especially to be there on the 13th. I noticed immediately that the high holy day china was out of storage along with the finest linens and silverware. Perhaps this was Mama's way of celebrating for me.

The table was set most beautifully. In the middle was an exquisite bouquet of lilacs in full bloom filling the room with their aroma. On either side were the traditional Shabbat candles. Banked around the candlesticks were little colored wrappings of candy and mints. Lilac-colored linen napkins, neatly pressed, gave added color to the table. There were also several extra places set, and I had no idea who the company might be, but apparently my captors did.

One of the "guests" was David, who usually didn't come for Shabbat, so I thought maybe the other one was for Sally who was going to surprise me with a visit from Philly, but Sally hadn't been talking to me since I dropped my Catholic bomb on the table after New Year's. But it was not Sally. Twenty minutes before sunset, the doorman announced that our visitor was on his way up the elevator. Mama, engrossed in matzo ball soup, hollered for me to get the door.

I opened the door, and there smiling from ear to ear was Rabbi Liebermann. I tried not to act surprised but fumbled

around with my welcome, asking him whether Mrs. Liebermann was coming…glancing down the hall toward the
elevators.

"Oh no, Rebecca, she's having Shabbat with her sister's
family in Brooklyn; they've just returned from Miami Beach
for the summer. Your father was kind enough to invite me
to join all of you."

My father? I thought to myself. My father never invited
the rabbi from across the street to join us for dinner. I
began to see the scheme they had laid. No one of my family
acknowledged that I was going to be baptized in two weeks,
but this was, no doubt, their last-ditch effort to persuade me
to come to my senses. I brought Rabbi Liebermann into the
front parlor and told him I would let my father know he had
arrived. I passed my father in the hallway. "Your rabbinical
guest is here." Papa only smiled.

To add to the drama, Mama asked me if I would light the
Shabbat candles. I think I had done that only once in my
whole life, when Mama was too sick and Sally was away and
it fell to me as the eldest daughter present. I smiled and told
Mama that it would be an honor. And the family, with our
rabbi present, gathered around the table, and I prayed the
Baruch Atah with a soft but clear voice. My eyes, of course,
were closed, and I drew the light to my face and opened my
eyes on the Sabbath. "Good Shabbat," I said to the rabbi.
"Good Shabbat, Papa…Good Shabbat, Mama," I said and
kissed them both on the cheek. "I am touched that you have
asked me to welcome Shabbat. I hope you will always know
that I am your daughter and that I love you and thank the
Lord every day for the blessings He has given me in being

your daughter," and turning to David and Ruthie, I added, "and your sister."

I could see that Mama was already becoming a bit weepy. She wiped her hands on her apron, and came over to embrace me. "I wish you weren't doing what you're doing..." she managed to get out.

"I know, Mama, I know." And I held her close to me. Papa took it as his cue, and gestured for the rabbi, and David to sit down at the dining room table; Ruthie made her exit "stage left," into the kitchen, to help carry out the festive dinner. Papa blessed the challah and David poured the wine, and everyone relaxed...for a while. I was quiet and always polite. I did not have it in me to argue and hoped that it wouldn't come to that. I knew that when I was confirmed and received the fullness of the gifts of the Holy Spirit, I would be a "soldier for Christ" and would have the grace to bear witness to the Faith. Still, I had imagined that would be on the college campus or in the Belgian Congo, not around my dinner table on West 79th Street.

I dissolved for a moment into the soft warmth of the challah, and thought of Mary, the Mother of Jesus, who baked the challah for Shabbat and lit the Shabbat candles every Friday evening, like I had tonight. And I silently pictured her in my mind, like the icon of Our Mother of Perpetual Help, and again prayed silently for her help. And I thought of Edith Stein and wondered if she ever was in a similar predicament; of course, she would have had the philosophical vocabulary to match anyone at her table. I didn't.

Not a word was said about my forthcoming apostasy till dessert and coffee. Rabbi Liebermann began innocently enough, asking me how my year at Barnard went and what courses I would be taking next year. "I understand you have been friends with a Jewish man who has become a Christian?"

I simply acknowledged that: "That's right, Ezra Goldman from Buffalo. Mama and Papa know him; he and his aunt came for Thanksgiving."

"Ah, yes, I think your father told me that. A fine young man, I understand…are you thinking of marrying this Ezra?"

"Oh no, Rabbi, he's not my boyfriend, just a friend…" and before the rabbi could proceed with his premeditated interrogation, I said, "It was most providential, I suppose, as I had been thinking of becoming a Christian since last summer, and didn't know that Ezra had become a Catholic about six months before. He saw me coming out of Corpus Christi Church one morning and followed me to a little tea shop near school and introduced himself to me there. He didn't have any influence on my becoming a Catholic, however. If anything, he shared with me how difficult it is for the family."

Rabbi Liebermann didn't say anything for a moment, but I knew David would be adding his two cents before long. "Tell her, Rabbi, how foolish she is; tell her how the Christians have not only been living in a terrible delusion, but have been the cause of our being persecuted for nearly two thousand years. She's going to subject herself to the Pope of Rome, for heaven's sake, and lose her ability to think on her own and make her own decisions; she's betraying her family and her people, and she's…"

"Enough, David." My father interjected, stopping David's tirade. "We've been down this path before. What do you think, Rabbi?"

Everyone suddenly stopped eating the rhubarb pie Mama had slaved over all morning to make from scratch. All eyes were on the man they had hoped would save me from making a terrible mistake.

Rabbi Liebermann slowly took a sip of his wine, which he seemed to prefer to coffee, and stroked his beard like men do when they are thinking. He looked off into the distance like there were people there we couldn't see.

"My grandfather, may he rest in peace, like your grandfathers, came to this country after the First World War, maybe even before. Perhaps they already surmised the rumblings of a further war in Europe that would not favor them, but they came here to make a new life for themselves. What a blessing. *(We all nodded in agreement.)* In this country, and in our beloved New York, we have found a home where we can keep Torah and observe Shabbat and our holy days, where we can raise our families in freedom and all the blessings the Almighty has continued to give us. This is the Jewish stock your Rebecca has come from, and the family which has been a blessing—there is much to be grateful for.

"I don't think your Rebecca intends to betray her Jewish heritage or to dishonor her mother and father. She is a daughter of the Commandment to have no other God before the God of Israel, the God of Abraham, Isaac, and Jacob. And she is young. Would that I were twenty again! *(We all laughed on cue.)* Her womanhood is coming of age; her mind is awakened and her heart is becoming the heart

of a woman. *(Ruthie laughed, and stopped abruptly.)* I know
she has mourned deeply the loss of her brother, Joshua, may
he rest in peace. *(He was speaking to Mama and Papa like I
was absent or something!)* And perhaps in her grief she has
found some consolation in the prayers and solemnities of
Catholicism…it happens. Nothing I will say to the contrary
will move her heart at this moment," and he turned his gaze
to me, "but, Rebecca, darling, wait on the Lord. You are too
young to make such a drastic change…wait for a few years;
think of it like one of your classes: you're learning, you're
seeing how other people live; but Judaism is your people; we
are your flesh and blood. Wait for a few years, finish school,
get a good job, and learn what it is to make a living on your
own. The Lord has touched your soul, but that doesn't mean
you have to change. Let your Jewishness become deeper; it is
God's blessing to you. You are a lovely girl, a blessing to your
family. We don't want you to act precipitously, you know.
We think things through, we search the Talmud, we obey
the mitzvahs. Wait, that is all we are asking."

There was a dead silence. Ruthie broke the silence as
only she could. "May I have some more wine, please?" Papa
poured her a full glass without saying a word, and himself
and the rabbi another glass. Nobody was drinking their
coffee.

After what seemed an interminable silence, I spoke:
"Thank you, Rabbi, for your kind words, and for caring
enough to come tonight. I know you must leave soon for
Friday night services, and I think David and my father will
join you." (I didn't dare glance over at David.) "I will sin-
cerely think about what you have said, as I have been all

these silent months. I have been, more than any of you real-ize." (I was proud of myself that my voice did not crack or even quiver, but stayed calm and soft, but firm.) "I don't think I can put into words what has been going on in my soul this past year; I don't believe I am reacting to my grief for Josh or for my friend, Grace Price, or to anything I happened upon in my studies. It is something else…something, or perhaps I should say, Someone, who has been given to me. And I know in my heart of hearts that it is real…and that it is good…and that it is of God. Such a blessing, that it should come to one so young and undeserving of such… such…love. Thank you, Rabbi, for your kindness to me and my family. Mama, Papa, if you will excuse me, I'd like to go to my room." I folded my lilac linen napkin, took one last swallow of wine and stood up.

And it was Papa again…he smiled the smile he once blessed me with that snowy afternoon at Wolfie's near Rockefeller Plaza. "Go, my darling Raf." I kissed him on the top of the head and went to my room. I sat in my rocker and cried quietly for a bit, but I think I was all cried out by that time. I also knew that I was comforted in that moment of letting go…*Comforter of the Afflicted…pray for me.*

***

And now it is time to speak of my day. It dawned warm and sunny. I was up before anyone else. I had bathed the night before and only needed to take out the huge rollers in my hair and fuss for a bit over it all, knowing it would be washed in baptismal water in a few hours. I suspected that Mama and Papa would purposely sleep in till I left, and I had let them know that I would be going to my friend Greta's, who was received into the Church last week. She had bought me a lovely beige-white dress which we picked out together at Bloomingdale's, and a beige floppy hat with a shocking red headband for Pentecost. Gwendolyn gave me one of her beige and red handbags which went perfectly with the dress. No penguin. I was to change at Greta's and meet everyone else at the church before ten o'clock.

Being baptized as an adult did not mean that I couldn't have a godmother and godfather; they were referred to as my sponsors, but I called them my godfather and god-mother. And so my godmother was Lady Gwendolyn, who had become very dear to me, and rather more big-sisterly than godmotherly. I suppose she was old enough to be my mother, but she was much more like a sister. My own older sister was not even speaking to me.

There was of course only one choice for my godfather, and Ezra Anthony Goldman fit the bill. Fr. Meriwether would be doing the baptism in the lovely baptistery off to the right when you come into the church. I never really noticed it till that Saturday before my first Monday night class when Father gave me a little tour of the church. It is set in its own room to the far right when you enter the back of the church. It is actually an octagon with six seats each in their own niche, and each with a fabric-covered cushion. The baptismal font, also an octagon, is in the middle, held up by four angels. Each angel is holding a symbol of the new life of grace flowing from the font of life. The floor itself is designed like waves of water or grace flowing from the font.

Fr. Meriwether explained that the octagon stands for a new creation: the day Christ rose from the dead was the eighth day, the first day of the week, the day the Lord has made. On one side wall was a statue of John the Baptist and on the opposite wall a stained-glass window of the Baptism of the Lord. The rear wall displayed a gorgeous painting of the Pieta by Bartolomeo Caporali.

One could spend hours just in the baptistery meditating on the significance of everything. The stone font itself has an inscription surrounding the eight sides:

> Teach ye all nations, baptizing them in the name of the Father and the Son and the Holy Ghost, teaching them to observe all things whatsoever I have commanded you, and behold, I am with you all days even to the consummation of the world.

I didn't remember that from the day itself, but have often gone into the baptistery to pray and meditate on everything. The Lord's words, *I am with you all days,* have come back to me often. It's a consolation when we most need to remember, like when we're feeling especially lonely or nothing around us is making any sense. But I was not alone on that wonderful day.

Going back an hour, before arriving at the church, I went to Greta's apartment. She was so sweet and kind to me. She was really the motherly type, although she wasn't much older than Gwendolyn. She had a pot of Earl Grey steeping on the counter when I arrived and a piece of very thin toast, which was hardly enough to sustain me, but I had to eat something before the three hour Eucharistic fast (a couple bagels with peanut butter and honey would have been very nice, but I didn't want to complain). As it was, the morsel of toast was plenty, and we dashed out of the building by 9:40 and grabbed a cab. Gwendolyn and Ezra were already there, along with Stephen and Michael, Ezra's roommates, and a young woman wearing a long mantilla, who was Michael's girlfriend, Constance. Greta greeted one of her friends, Russell, who was also a convert from the Lutheran Church. Three of my friends from college came too, perhaps more out of curiosity than the sincerity of wishing me blessings in my new life. A very nice surprise was to see Mr. and Mrs. Price there. Of course, no one from my family was there. I thought maybe, just maybe, Papa would come to see this thing that was happening, but he didn't. It was a bit crowded in the octagon, but everyone was very quiet and reverent; the room draws it out of you!

Fr. Meriwether came in wearing a gold and white cope over his Dominican habit and a surplice and stole. He was very happy that I had asked him to baptize me. St. Vincent's is not in my parish boundary, but I had definitely wanted to be baptized there.

Having renounced Satan and all his pomp and works, having professed the Trinitarian Faith, having assented to everything he asked in the rite, I approached the baptismal font bareheaded and leaned over it. I heard the words in Latin, and felt the warm water being poured on my head: "*I baptize you Rebecca Abigail Grace, in the Name of the Father, and of the Son, and of the Holy Ghost.*"

The joy of that moment erased any fears, doubts, or wanderings in my poor soul. How can one ever express the inexpressible in human words? On Pentecost Sunday, May 29, 1966, I was baptized, and the Holy Spirit flooded my soul to dwell in me and I in Him.

How can one express the change that happens in one's very being by sanctifying grace? My *inner space* was remade anew and filled with God. The profound spiritual, dare I say, mystical, reality of that moment cannot be fully expressed in words, only surrendered to and contemplated in silence...a silence which embraces the whole of the Mystery, like Pentecost itself, a pouring forth of the Holy Spirit and a Holy Communion in the Body of Christ, the Risen God-Man.

The eleven o'clock High Mass would begin about a half-hour after my baptism. Fr. Meriwether brought me and all my guests into the priory just a couple doorways from the baptistery. Everyone was hugging me and congratulating me. I could hardly say anything I was so moved.

That was very kind of Fr. Meriwether, but I'm glad it didn't last more than ten minutes, as we all went back into the church. Ezra, Gwendolyn, Greta and I went into the pew near the front, in direct line with the statue of Our Lady, whom the Dominicans called the *Porta Caeli,* the Gate of Heaven, because she was located between the nave of the church and the friars' choir, leading to the sanctuary. It is a lovely statue in a stone niche with a stone shelf beneath her feet that is ideal for flowers. And that day there was a beautiful bouquet of white and red roses there; I think there were three dozen in all. The small notice in the parish bulletin read, *The flowers at the statue of Our Lady are given in thanksgiving for the Baptism and First Holy Communion of*

Rebecca Grace Feinstein, by the Price Family: Arthur, Caroline, William, and Grace.

There was a beautiful organ prelude, the name of which escapes me now, but I remember just closing my eyes and letting it all soak in. Who would have ever thought that Saturday morning when I came into this church to light a candle for Grace Price, that less than a year later I would be sitting here a Catholic, waiting to receive my First Holy Communion? Ezra nudged me in the side and handed me his handkerchief; the tears were coming down silently. God counts the tears of women, but this time it was tears of joy. It was the parish's Pentecost Sunday Solemn High Mass with a professional choir and an incredible organist. The choir processed in red choir robes and white surplices, and the priest's vestments were red, and the Holy Spirit was liturgically poured out upon us. This is true at every single Mass, but for me this Mass, on this day, was the most splendid Mass I had ever attended because I felt like it was all for me.

I never experienced what I've heard so many women and the other sisters talk about as their First Holy Communion Day with a white dress and veil and white patent leather shoes and a white rosary and a First Communion Prayer Book with a mother-of-pearl cover. There was not a whole class and lots of attention. But I had my new friends, and all my new family in the Communion of Saints. Fr. Ryan, the pastor, preached from the magnificent high pulpit which is a sermon in itself, but I don't remember a word he said. I could hardly wait to kneel at the marble communion rail and receive the Body of Christ for the first time.

Now I knew why so many Catholics return silently and quickly to their pews and, kneeling, bury their faces in their hands. It is the most intimate moment with God this side of Heaven. In that First Holy Intimacy, I thanked the Lord with all my heart and gave my whole life to Him to do with me whatever He wills, just never ever let me be separated from Him.

I would remember this prayer, and renew it many times and meditate on it and ponder it and how the Lord was taking me at my word. We say things in the most poignant moments of love. I knew that, and I was only twenty, and living in the middle of a decade that was going wild and seemed to know no bounds. I had never expected to be there and, if I may sound religiously romantic, so much in love.

After Mass we went to Greta's apartment on East 79th between Second and Third Avenue. She and Gwendolyn had planned a little party for their new Catholic, and I was utterly surprised by their joy, not to mention all the wonderful cards and gifts they gave me. The dress and hat were Greta's gift, plus the party, which included pink champagne—pink for Pentecost! There were finger sandwiches from Tea on Thames, followed by platters of cold cuts and cheese and five kinds of rolls and bread.

Greta also gave me a first edition copy of the writings of Edith Stein, a treasure which I still have, along with my original copy of *The Cost of Discipleship*. Gwendolyn gave me a lovely statue of Our Lady of Grace, the image on the miraculous medal, with the Blessed Mother crushing the serpent's head, her arms opened in a gesture of prayer and welcome… the Mother of all grace. It meant so much coming from her.

There was another statue-shaped box among my gifts. The second one was from Ezra. It was a wooden carved statue of the Sacred Heart of Jesus, not in the priestly vestments as my favorite statue in St. Vincent's has, but the gesture of the hand leading the beholder to His heart was the same. The Prices, who were not at this little party, nonetheless left a gift in addition to the roses in the church. It was easy to guess as I was unwrapping it—a beautiful framed icon of Our Mother of Perpetual Help. And from Ezra's roommates, Michael and Stephen, a leather-bound Roman Missal with Latin and English on alternate pages.

After my party, the plan was to schlep everything home to my apartment and to meet Ezra for supper uptown near school, at a new Thai restaurant we were dying to try, and then to have dessert at Tea on Thames.

I didn't know what to expect when I got home, especially with all my Catholic stuff in tow, but to my surprise nobody was there. I took everything to my bedroom and went into the kitchen to put the kettle on. There, propped up on the salt shaker on the kitchen table was an envelope addressed to me. It was Mama's handwriting. I sat down and read:

> My dearest Rebecca,
>
> Please forgive us all for our hasty departure. Sally has invited us to Philadelphia for the week; she has rented a small house at the Jersey shore, at Seaside Heights. We're all going, except for David, of course, who can't get away. Your father and I thought you might prefer to have the apartment to yourself for a week to begin your summer vacation. We thought, your father and I,

that you might look to find an apartment for yourself
where you will be more comfortable. We will miss you
at the shore, such a summer this seems to be. Ruthie
sends her love, as does your father, such a blessing. We
love you. Mama.

I sat at the table, stunned and at the same time relieved.
The whistling of the kettle brought me back to earth, and I
fixed a large mug of tea and went to my room. I had a couple
hours before meeting Ezra, so I sat in my rocker to drink my
tea, and picked up *The Cost of Discipleship* to read as a disciple for the first time. I didn't unpack my gifts.

Ten

I DON'T KNOW IF I was hurt or shocked or simply numbed by Mama's letter. After months of near silence on the matter, except for inviting the rabbi for dinner and the last visits of my elder siblings, it came down to a letter. I suppose I was really surprised, and also a bit disappointed, that they had to resort to such passive-aggressive methods. I would've preferred to talk it all out. I am partly to blame too; I was always too afraid to bring it up; I didn't want them to be angry or disappointed in me. I didn't want to hurt my parents and put them to shame, as David kept referring to it. I couldn't have or shouldn't have expected that they would support me, let alone rejoice or want to have any part in my day…my glorious day.

It *was* one of the two happiest days in my life, and even this little bomb on the kitchen table did not spoil it. It was the catalyst I needed to be less passive-aggressive myself and to grow up and take responsibility for my life. My girlfriends from school who were leaning more towards the hippies, at least by way of drinking wine, smoking pot and singing folk songs, seemed caught in a pre-adult rebellious kind of mode. There were some who were angrier and more aggressive, and their weapons were the pen, the electric typewriter, and perhaps a protest march.

The less intellectual group was more nonchalant and in your face about things my parents' generation would never speak of in public, and probably not in private among themselves! There were some turning to a kind of spiritual experience, but it was often linked to drug experimentation, an infiltrating Eastern style of meditation, and yoga which came with its own philosophies of reincarnation, karma, and Chinese acupuncture. I flirted myself with the writings of Alan Watts, a former Anglican minister who became a Zen Buddhist, mixed in with Hinduism. *Grist for the Mill* and the poems of Allen Ginsberg were even interesting except for the likes of my sister Ruthie who still read *Archie* comics and travel magazines. Her interests were not yet piqued to high fashion or sports, which mine never were either. Ruthie and I usually acted out our quarrels or disagreements, which often helped to demote them. But Mama's letter was different.

Naturally I shared the letter with Ezra, who wasn't surprised with it and tried to point out the more positive things I could be grateful for. I wasn't rejected, disowned, or declared dead in their hearts and in their lives. I had to accept that they were who they were, and that they were good and proud parents who tried their very best to raise their children. There was more good in them than even they could understand. He advised me to sleep on it, pray on it (an expression I'd never heard him use before) and decide what to do tomorrow. We would meet at Blessed Sacrament for the 8:00 Mass...my Second Holy Communion...and have breakfast afterwards.

When I took stock of my situation, I decided I could not return to Barnard for my final year, at least not as a full-time student. It would be unfair to ask them to pay for my college any more than they did. I would get a job and my own apartment and take an evening course or two. If I had written all that down it would have looked good on paper, but so overwhelming to begin.

As it turned out, Greta came to my rescue. There was an opening at the New York Public Library for an assistant librarian. The hours were good; the beginning salary was not much, but I really had no resume; and I knew that I would love the atmosphere of working in a library. Greta also had a spare room which served as a guest room when needed, and a study for herself when not needed. She welcomed me to move in for a few months, till I got settled and could find a place on my own, and afford it. She also welcomed the company. The best part was that I would be close to St. Vincent's. It would be my parish. Greta and I became daily communicants, the single most powerful grace of my life.

I had cleared out my room over a few days with lots of help from Ezra, Michael, Constance, Stephen, and a few of their friends, one with a small truck which proved to be a godsend. I was able to arrange for a late afternoon class and one evening course which met twice a week. I could handle that. I also got the job, but then, I had Greta's recommendation.

I was at home on West 79th Street when Mama, Papa, and Ruthie returned from the Jersey Shore. I gave them my new address and would be letting them know my phone number once my own phone was installed. Till then, they could reach me at Greta's number. We hugged sadly and said goodbye for now, and I promised I would be over for dinner one night during the week. I did that for a few months.

The frequency got less and less as the weather changed and winter was upon us again. It left an empty place in my heart and at times a great heaviness, but I was also terribly happy that first year, that first winter and Christmas. Greta and I got along so well, our common factors being that we were both converts and loved the Church, and that we were both librarians at the same library. It made it quite convenient to go to early Mass and have a quick breakfast somewhere near St. Vincent's, usually the Starlight Café. It was there that I had my first bacon and eggs. I had often smelled bacon in coffee shops like the Starlight, but never ate any pork, ever. It was quite delicious, a little saltier than I expected, and much too greasy. I liked it, but I don't think I ate pork again for many years! Some things never change.

Living and working on the East Side was nice, although it made my trips to Tea on Thames less frequent, but I had established a nice friendship with Gwendolyn outside of the tea shop, and she would come to our place often for supper and was always a good one to run off with to a movie. I was seeing less of Ezra too, but we always met at Tea on Thames after my Wednesday night class. He was finishing up his last year at Columbia and had to decide what to do from there. He had visited the Passionist Retreat House a couple times more, as well as a Benedictine Monastery near Elmira, New York. He liked it very much. He said they had him up at four o'clock in the morning milking cows. He said it was all very romantic to him, till one bitterly cold morning he got slapped smack in the face by a cow's wet tail. He wasn't sure if he had a monastic vocation after that, he'd jokingly say.

But I knew beneath the joking, he was thinking of a vocation. *It was brewing in him*, as Greta once put it.

I wasn't sure at first what I thought about that and/or how I *felt* about it. Intellectually I knew it was a wonderful thing, and it made complete sense to me, knowing Ezra as I did. He would make a wonderful monk or priest. He was on fire with the writings of the mystics and saints, and talked about them like he knew them firsthand. Most of them were just new acquaintances to me: St. Paul of the Cross; John of the Cross; the Curé of Ars; Frances de Sales. It took a little longer for me to feel good about him having a vocation, and I had to look at my own relationship with him, which seemed to be the personal factor affecting my take on it all. Greta was very quiet and philosophical about things. Gwendolyn was more down to earth and upfront. "Maybe you're falling in love with him, and the two of you should get married and have a dozen little Catholic Goldmans," she once said, adding her typical humor to what she was saying.

What amazed me more was that both of them, Greta and Gwendolyn, saw something going on there before I could see it. I also think people are apt to project their own hopes and dreams onto someone else's life and thus misinterpret what's really going on. I knew I loved Ezra, but I was not *in love* with him. At least I didn't think I was. What did I know at twenty-one years old?

Ezra and I never dated, but we went out a lot together, usually to a school or church thing, or maybe I should say, *always* to school or church things, not counting Tea on Thames or some new restaurant in the neighborhood. I wasn't all too comfortable with the vocation thing. It was all very new and strange to me. I only knew a few priests and had never met a monk or a nun, at least not a cloistered nun.

Ezra was going to the Passionists in West Springfield, Massachusetts, for Thanksgiving weekend, and invited me to go with him and to stay at a monastery of cloistered Dominican nuns, also in West Springfield, if they had a free guest room. I was excited about that and was all set to go when I was told I would be expected to work on the Friday and Saturday after Thanksgiving; I was low on the librarian totem pole. Greta had off, but was going out of town for Thanksgiving weekend to be with old friends of her and her husband. They were retired missionaries living in Braintree, Massachusetts.

I was invited home for Thanksgiving and decided I should go, although David refused to come if I did. Maybe he would at least stop in for dessert. Ruthie was probably the most enthused about my coming to Thanksgiving dinner as I think she missed me the most. So I went and had a lovely time. Even Sally was there, and while she would not speak directly to me, she wasn't inhibited in speaking about everything else to the family. She was actually anticipating a relocation to Chicago and seemed to talk about nothing else.

Mama was happy we were both home—her three girls, *such a blessing to have three*, she would say every time we were together. I couldn't help but recall the Thanksgiving the year before with Ezra and his Aunt Sarah. Mama never once asked about him. I think she still blamed him for taking me away from Judaism. She could never really get it in her head that I was thinking about that before I even knew Ezra.

Papa looked tired to me, and he seemed to have lost weight, but he was his gentle self, and did ask me about Ezra.

I didn't say anything about his thinking about being a priest, not that they should care, but I figured they wouldn't understand. Papa also asked how my job was going and seemed genuinely interested. He wanted to know if I was the one to put the huge wreaths around the stone lions in front of the grand entrance on Fifth Avenue? Ruthie asked about Greta and our apartment and whether we had a dog or cat, which I didn't understand why, except that she was hoping for one for Chanukah.

It was a pleasant enough evening, but I missed Ezra terribly, especially when it was all over, and we would have met at Tea on Thames to hash it all over again. Tea on Thames was closed for Thanksgiving, and Gwendolyn was having dinner out with a girlfriend over from England for the week.

I went back to the apartment, and was rather content, as I recall, to be alone, happy actually. I had the whole apartment and the whole weekend to myself. I would go to Mass in the morning and go to work and then come home and cuddle up with a book. I was fascinated by that time with the life of Edith Stein, and wondered whether there might be a Carmel near Manhattan that maybe I could visit someday…and run off for a retreat, like Ezra did.

That was Thanksgiving 1966. That Christmas I was given a lovely leather-bound blank book, a gift from Greta, who told me I should begin to keep a journal of important moments and changes because it all would move along very quickly. It was my first Christmas as a Christian and my first Holy Communion at a Midnight Mass. St. Vincent's couldn't have been more beautiful. It had been a wonderful year when New Year's came and one thought back on all that had happened since the new year, a year ago. The country seemed to be in so much unrest; the Middle East too, as Papa followed closely the developments in Israel. My favorite professor at Barnard was all agog over Truman Capote's latest book, *In Cold Blood*, and said it would change the style of novel writing. Ruthie was still crazy over the Beatles and the Rolling Stones, and now wanted to look like Twiggy, a model I never aspired to emulate.

***

A year later, Thanksgiving 1967, was memorable because it was my first time not having Thanksgiving with my family. Greta and I were cooking the turkey on our own as a kind of special gift and farewell to Ezra. I was still at Greta's. I never made enough money that I could afford to both pay for school and rent my own apartment. I was able to pay part of Greta's rent and share in the groceries and other little things, and we were good companions for each other. I had received several raises at the Library and was becoming more and more confident in my work, which I loved.

I had also discovered two monasteries in Brooklyn. A small Carmel had been there for over seventy-five years, and there was a Dominican Monastery in Brooklyn Heights. I had also visited the Mother of God Monastery in West Springfield, Massachusetts. I discovered that there were three Dominican monasteries in north Jersey, one in the south Bronx, and one near Mt. Savior, and the Benedictine monastery near Elmira, New York. I never visited there, nor had I been to the Dominican Monastery in the Bronx. There was also a monastery in Connecticut which I had hoped to visit in '68. I was surrounded by them!

There were Carmelite, Dominican, and Franciscan monasteries of nuns all over the country which I had never had any idea of before. I thought cloisters were either a museum, like in Yonkers, or something you'd only find in Europe. We all loved Julie Andrews in *The Sound of Music;* she had won the Academy Award last year for Best Actress, but who knew that monasteries like that still existed, let alone in America! I liked visiting them, not because I was thinking of being a nun—Lord have mercy on me—but because I loved the peace and quiet and listening to the nuns chant. I was a daughter of the Psalms, of course; they are our Jewish songs and poetry, and it was glorious to hear them chanted in ancient Gregorian tones. I envied those who lived near such monasteries and could be a part of their prayer life every day, but East 79th Street was not quite a cloister, although I could find some nooks and crannies in the stacks at the library or down in the archives.

Now Ezra. He graduated from Columbia and immediately began teaching high school to keep himself out of the draft. Vietnam was still tearing us apart politically, and there were all kinds of other scandals and politics which I couldn't get interested in. During the year, however, Ezra applied to enter the Passionist Novitiate, and he was accepted. He was to enter the first Sunday of Advent. So Thanksgiving was really our formal "Last Supper." We invited Aunt Sarah, of course, and his roommates, Michael and Stephen, who were beginning a Catholic Religious Articles and Book Store in the Village. There were lots of Catholic Action Groups forming and rumors of dramatic changes coming. There were lots of changes taking place, not just in the Church, but in our culture and society in general.

The menu didn't change that year, however. It was a good old-fashioned American Thanksgiving Day Dinner with all the trimmings. Gwendolyn brought three homemade pies: mincemeat, apple, and pumpkin (which she always called squash). We teased her that the mincemeat was probably penguin meat, but she didn't find that as funny as we did. Greta actually did the bird and made her own stuffing recipe which I think was originally "Lutheran stuff," we teased, and it was the first time I had had chicken livers and pork sausage in the stuffing. I did the butternut squash and mashed potatoes, which were both kosher.

We had little gifts for Ezra because he couldn't take much with him anyway. I gave him a beautiful black Mont Blanc fountain pen from Cartier's which set me back a week's wages, but I knew he would use it. Greta gave him a lovely blank book journal, which I thought was a wonderful complement to my pen. And Gwendolyn gave him a little glass penguin for his desk, if he had a desk, to remind him of us. Aunt Sarah gave him a framed picture of herself standing in front of her apartment building, so he wouldn't forget her or New York.

Aunt Sarah was a remarkable woman. She didn't understand at all why he was running off to join a group of men called Passionists. "Can't you find your passion right here in New York?" She was half teasing and half serious. She had had great hopes that he would be a lawyer, and blamed the whole Catholic thing on spoiling that, but she didn't rub it in. She accepted and let things be.

I don't think my own family ever got to her level of acceptance. Our relationship became cooler with the passage of years. Papa always hugged me tight and still called me Raf, and still delighted to go out for walks with me, my arm linked in his, strolling down the Avenue. David, Sally, and less so, Mama, never really accepted that I became a Catholic, and I think they secretly hoped it was just a phase I was passing through, and that I would meet a nice Jewish man, get married, and forget this Christian silliness. Little Ruthie, who was quickly growing up, missed having her big sister around and couldn't understand it all, but took it all in stride. She was too busy with her own plans, I think, to get hung up over mine. We would go off to Tea on Thames once in a while, and Gwendolyn always put on a show for her, pretending she was being visited by a member of the royal family. The little girl in Ruthie loved it all!

So Ezra went off to be a Passionist. And a new year began with a wonderful blizzard and change in the air. I decided that holiday to make a retreat between Christmas and New Year's, as I was able to get those days off now from work; Greta would be away herself, and Gwendolyn was busy at the tea shop. So it was Christmas of '68 and the New Year '69 that I went to the Dominican Monastery of Mary, Queen of Hope, in Brooklyn Heights. I had wanted to go to the Carmel in Brooklyn, as I really liked Edith Stein, and had read several times now, the Autobiography of St. Thérèse of Lisieux. It was the autobiography of St. Teresa of Jesus, that is, St. Teresa of Avila, that converted Edith Stein who was much more Jewish and much more intelligent than I. I had not yet read Teresa of Avila's autobiography and asked Santa for a copy for Christmas. Santa gave me a hardbound edition from her own collection…good old "Greta-Claus." However, the Carmel didn't have any guest rooms available. I called the Dominican nuns, and by luck, someone had cancelled their reservation that very morning, and a very nice room with a view towards the Manhattan sky line was open.

I had only been there a couple times, and that was only to pray in the public chapel. It was a very prayerful chapel, like that of the Carmelites, with a beautiful high altar of marble. Unlike the Carmelite chapel, which was L-shaped with the nuns on the side, separated by a curtain and grate, the Dominican chapel was a single nave with a wrought iron grille behind the high altar separating the sanctuary and the public chapel from the nuns' choir, which was their chapel. Over the tabernacle was a wooden carved crucifix, and about a half-foot above that was an inlaid ledge on which was placed a beautiful sunburst monstrance holding the Blessed Sacrament. The nuns had Perpetual Adoration all night and all day, which was the first time I really experienced that awesomeness of having the Lord always seen and adored in the chapel. The public chapel doors were locked after Vespers, but guests, like myself, had complete access to the chapel twenty-four hours a day. On both the nuns' side of the grille and the extern side, beneath the monstrance were six large sanctuary lamps always burning…twelve in all.

The chapel was decorated for Christmas with plenty of red poinsettias and white and red carnations and roses. The side altars were lovely too, Our Lady of the Rosary on the

left, and St. Joseph on the right. Inside the nuns' choir, there
were statues of Our Lady, St. Joseph, St. Catherine of Siena,
and St. Dominic. My friend, St. Vincent Ferrer, wasn't there!
But they did have a Sr. Mary Vincent, who was the guest
mistress and what they called an *extern sister*. She lived on
the outside, above the sacristy actually, along with two other
extern sisters: Sr. Grace Mary, which thrilled me to no end—
her name, I mean—and Sr. Hyacinth Marie who was the
eldest of the three and spent hours—literally hours— praying her Rosary in the presence of the Blessed Sacrament.

The guest quarters were off to one side, with a separate
entrance to the chapel, a little kitchenette, and six guest
rooms. They were small, but cozy, with a single bed, a small
wooden desk at the window, a small dresser with three drawers only, and to my greatest delight, a rocking chair with
a floor lamp. Each guest room was named for a Dominican saint. I was in Bl. Jordan's room. I had no idea who
he was, but he had a nice taste in rockers. This one didn't
even squeak. Off from the small kitchen was a larger room
with a large round dining table. It had a plain green linen
table cover on it with a huge poinsettia in the middle, which
blocked the view of the person across from you. There was
also a serving table, and a tape recorder which would play
tapes of conferences given to the nuns at various times. We
didn't speak while we had our meal, but listened to these
taped conferences. The main meal was served at noon, and a
light meal for the evening. Breakfast was on our own. There
were no radios or televisions, of course, and with the windows closed tightly, it was very quiet in the guest wing.

There were three sisters from one of the Dominican motherhouses on retreat and two other young women like myself. We were not confined in quarters during the day and could go out for a walk. We could not go into the nuns' part of their back yard, which was behind a high stone wall, but we had our own little enclosed garden with a shrine of Our Lady of Lourdes in the far corner. It also had a bank of poinsettias, artificial ones, but quite pretty, and a rack of votive candles which burned all year round. One was asked to keep silence in the guest garden too, but one could also go outside to the street and walk around Brooklyn Heights, which I discovered was much prettier than I ever imagined.

I think it was on my third day that I ventured out and decided to walk to the Promenade, which flanked the Hudson and East Rivers and gave one a spectacular view of lower Manhattan. It was there that I ran into one of the other young women in the guest quarters. Her name was Joanne Meyers. She was from Boston, Massachusetts, and was what she called "discerning her vocation." She had been with the Daughters of St. Paul for a brief time, and felt drawn to a more contemplative life, although, as she put it, "I love books." She had visited the Roxbury Carmel and decided they didn't read much, and that's when her spiritual director told her about the Dominicans.

She had been to several, as I had. Greta was sent to a Librarians and Archivists Convention in Niagara Falls, and she invited me to go with her. We took the train and arrived in Buffalo eight hours later. While Greta was at the hotel, I stayed at the Dominican Monastery of Our Lady of the Rosary. It was so beautiful. Over the altar they have a magnificent mural of Our Lady giving the Rosary to St. Dominic, and on both sides, twenty Dominican saints and blesseds. They are a large community, according to Sister Mary Rita of Jesus Thorn-crowned, they were forty-two nuns. I hoped to be able to go back and make a retreat there someday. It was more grand to me than Niagara Falls, which Greta and I visited and took the Maid of the Mist boat ride. It was most exciting!

Joanne had never been there, but said that she liked Brooklyn Heights the best because it was small and close to the City, which afforded them excellent lecturers and retreat masters, and they also *loved books*. I wasn't exactly sure how she knew that, but I took her on her word. This was her last visit before being admitted inside as an aspirant, which she hoped would begin soon into the new year. She was a sweet and lively person, I thought. Her eyes kind of sparkled when she talked about "the life," meaning the contemplative life. I ventured forth and asked her what she was reading, since she loved books so much. And she said "*The Sign of Jonas* by Thomas Merton. It was the perfect follow-up to *The Seven Storey Mountain.*"

"Oh yeah, Thomas Merton, Merton…" I knew I had heard of him, just recently too. She pointed out to me that he had died by an electric shock when he touched a live wire in an electric fan. That was just this month, on December 10th. He had been taking a shower before an evening conference he was giving. Joanne said his autobiography was a gem and that it should be read in every refectory. I had heard of that book; I think it was even Greta who had brought up his name a couple times. I knew I would enjoy reading him just listening to Joanne when she spoke of him.

Eleven

I LEARNED THREE NEW things that cold December day in 1968… first, that one *discerned* a vocation, one didn't just discover it and that was that. Second, that one might do well to have a spiritual director if one was to discern a vocation. And third, that Thomas Merton was a monk who kept a journal. Little did I know then that I would be about all three in the new year.

The following year I found myself back at the Dominican monastery in Brooklyn Heights between Christmas and New Year's. I was able to reserve two rooms six months in advance. The second room was my Christmas gift to Greta, who had never really made a week's retreat. She was very grateful to have the time and the peace and quiet. It's incredible when you can literally spend hours in the presence of the Lord in the Blessed Sacrament. Greta was in Bl. Jordan's room. I was in St. Albert's, who I learned was St. Thomas Aquinas's teacher…how great is that?!

What a difference a year makes. That past year I had acquired a spiritual director, Fr. Meriwether, who was very willing to serve in this role. I met with him once a month for about an hour. It was comfortable because I knew him from my instructions three years ago. I think I was spiritually attracted to him because he seemed to have the gift of holding in reverence every human soul. He spoke more

147

about the life of the soul, the life of Divine grace, than about other worldly things. Everything else flowed out from one's spiritual life or spiritual condition. He was a tremendous help in guiding me through a way to do an examination of conscience and making a good confession. I was able to begin to see ingrained patterns, as he called them, of venial sin which I took for granted but which were really little roadblocks along the way. His approach to eradicating sins was acquiring virtues. He talked a lot about grace and the virtues. I liked this better than the hell-fire and brimstone some of the Christian preachers had.

Fr. Meriwether also knew what I was going through with my family, and, along with that, I think he knew how much I loved the Lord, loved His holy Catholic Church, loved the Blessed Sacrament, and loved St. Vincent Ferrer Church. Fr. Meriwether said I was practicing the virtue of fortitude very well, and cautioned me that the Lord allows us to become strong in certain virtues because of a share in His Cross later on. He didn't say that with an air of impending doom, but, I think, out of his own experience.

We were now at the beginning of a new year, and a new decade: 1970. And I was trying to discern what God's plan or calling was for me. The Sixties certainly proved to be a turning point in many ways: the Vietnam War, and the hippy movement, and the blossoming of the drug culture. There was the civil rights movement; the election and assassination of the first Catholic president; Vatican II and all that would bring to the Church; a kind of cultural revolution in the Women's Movement, especially with the invention of the birth-control pill; the era of Rock and Roll evolved from the Fifties into the Beatles; the movies and the movements of the Sixties. I remember Ruthie and me doing the cha-cha to Diana Ross and the Supremes.

But most striking for me, of course, it was the decade that changed the direction of my life. There was the sudden and shocking death of my brother, Joshua, and the slow and expected death of Gracie. But for me the most important event was my becoming a Christian. Little Becky Feinstein became a Roman Catholic in 1966. It had been a wonderful adventure in grace, and not without its crosses. I used to wonder why Christians, and Catholics in particular, made such a fuss over the Cross. Catholics even began and ended their prayers tracing the Cross over themselves, but one soon realizes how much the Cross is woven into the very fabric of our lives. My Jewish ancestors certainly knew this, but would never call it "the Cross," let alone see it as redemptive and transforming. Transforming—that's a good word for it. Fr. Meriwether once gave a homily in which he played on the *forming* words: "We are in*form*ed by the Word of God in order to con*form* to Christ crucified and be trans*form*ed by the Holy Spirit. And each year we enter into periods to re*form* our lives and get back on track."

And now in 1970 and a new decade, there was being formed in my soul the desire to give myself completely to the Lord in a life of separation from the world. I was beginning to know and feel the effects of silence, prayer, and penance. The seeds, planted ever so quietly, were now beginning to grow. It somehow overwhelmed me and amazed me, and certainly stirred up an almost anguished feeling of unworthiness and humility. I dared not breathe a word of this to

anyone except Fr. Meriwether and Greta. I would even say
that Greta was like a secondary or honorary spiritual director. Her life experience, now coming through the Catholic filter, as it were, was beautiful to behold and amazing at
times in its wisdom. She and Fr. Meriwether were both gifts
I found at St. Vincent's.

My family. Sally was living in Chicago, near the Lake,
around 3800 North, and worked for the *Chicago Sun-Times*.
She lived with a roommate in a condo with a balcony over-
looking Lake Michigan. She was doing alright for herself,
Papa would say. She came home only for Thanksgiving and
had to work during the other holidays. Mama suspected
there was a boyfriend in the picture, whom Sally wasn't telling us about yet. "She's nearly thirty, she should settle down,"
Mama would say. I don't think Sally intended to settle down
at all, not even at the *Chicago Sun-Times*; I'm sure she had
her eye on the *Tribune*. I discovered that Sally's middle name
was Ambition, something which I didn't feel driving me like
it seemed to drive so many women my age. We were in the
renaissance of the Women's Movement. I often wondered
where Gracie would be with all of it had she lived.

David was a resident at Cornell Medical by the East River
and rarely made it across the park to see the family. Mama
would have liked to show him off more, and maybe he knew
that and stayed away. But what did I know? By that New
Year's Eve of 1970, he hadn't spoken to me in almost four
years. It remained a mystery to me, as he was not a devout
Jew by any means. If anything, he was an agnostic secular Jew who was devoted to science, taking care of people,
and making money, not necessarily in that order. He was

ambitious, too, but in a different way than Sally. He would become what I'd later learn by the title a *hedonist*...a secular hedonist whose passion is a way of having the good and the beautiful, but for David this meant the best and the most expensive.

Ruthie was a senior in high school and applying to various colleges and universities. She wanted to be an actress or a nurse, go figure! The two extremes, I guess, were like our theatrical masks of comedy and tragedy. She was also very cute, and knew it. She never had a weight problem, unlike Sally and me, but neither was she Twiggy or Cher, her favorite female icons. And she was a bit too boy crazy in my poor estimation, but again, what did I know? I hadn't been on a date since before Gracie's illness, and what a significance that was going to play in my life.

I'm still amazed at how God sketches out each of our lives even without our knowing we are being painted! Ruthie was still the little sister, though, and we could laugh together over the silliest things and still play make-believe. She was better at it than I. She was trying to perfect her various foreign accents and would try them out in public. I could play along but was best in British English and French...she could do a Norwegian or Swede, Russian, and Spaniard... and get away with it.

Papa. Dear Papa was working hard, following the news, and seemingly proud of all of us, including me. He followed with much interest the social news, probably more than sports. In 1968, there had been the assassinations of Martin Luther King and Bobby Kennedy; this past year, Neil Armstrong walked on the moon. It was on July 21st, and

Papa was glued to the television. We all watched, even at the Library, in the new lunch room lounge.

Papa always asked me what I was reading, and I would tell him, and he still seemed genuinely interested. Sadly, however, neither he nor my mother ever brought up the fact of my being a Catholic. It would be four years in May. So it was also four years since I had moved out at their behest, although we never spoke of Mama's letter, and in the retelling it would have seemed that moving out was my idea. But it didn't matter. That I was still welcomed at home meant a lot, and I tried to tell them that.

Mama. Mama was less cold towards me but always just a little reserved. I could see the difference in the way she interacted with Ruthie and me. Probably three times each year she'd bring up the subject of "love and marriage." Once I remember she actually had *Sunrise, Sunset* playing when I arrived for dinner. I had yet to finish my degree and may never get around to it, and that would come up about three times a year too. But never a mention of Mr. Goldman!

Speaking of Mr. Goldman, he was now Brother Matthew. He had completed his novitiate and had taken temporary vows just after Advent. I thought maybe they would let him keep Ezra, it's such a beautiful Old Testament name, but they didn't ask me. I had not seen him since he left, except for my one visit to West Springfield with Fr. Meriwether. He would be coming up for perpetual vows in another year, if all went well.

Gwendolyn was still Gwendolyn and a good friend to have. She didn't know a thing of my discerning a vocation or having a spiritual director. I think she always presumed

I would get married, and, at that stage, who knew? I wasn't dating anyone, however, and was not looking to. I wasn't hanging out at the discos or clubs my classmates were crazy about. There were a few men who frequented the Library who turned my head, but it never went any further than that. That I was not really interested in dating and finding a husband was of particular interest to Fr. Meriwether.

So Greta and I began the new year in style—monastic style! Our first night at the monastery was lovely, and I couldn't see anyone except Sr. Mary Vincent and Sr. Grace Mary. The next morning, however, I noticed that there was a postulant and a white-veiled novice. Sr. Mary Vincent told me, upon inquiry, that the novice was Sr. Thomas Mary of the Annunciation and the postulant was Sr. Joanne. "Sr. Joanne?" I inquired.

"Yes, ah…you would remember her from last year. Joanne Meyers."

So there she was. I had lost contact with her over the year, but apparently she had discerned herself right into the monastery. Later in the chapel I sat back, half kneeling and half sitting, on my pew and was lost in thought for a moment. I was so happy for Joanne and even a bit envious. How marvelous it must be to be a nun, I thought, and how scary. Greta touched my arm lightly. "Are you okay?" she whispered so softly that only Jesus and I could hear her. It was then that I realized there were tears running down my cheek.

"Oh yes," I whispered, "I'm just happy to be here."

I couldn't say the new year came in with a bang, even though it was a change of decade, and Times Square, just over the bridge and uptown a bit, was mobbed with millions of people. There were fireworks here in Brooklyn Heights while we were all in the chapel. The nuns had all gone to bed early, after Compline. Greta and I stayed up drinking tea and reading in our rooms, I presume. But we were all in the chapel for the Midnight Office when 1970 came in. We could hear the noise outside: car horns blowing, noisemakers and the boom of fireworks...while the nuns were singing the psalms of the Solemnity of the Mother of God. I caught myself thinking: how happy and grateful I am to be here, and not *out there*, whatever that meant.

Fr. Meriwether had given me a few Scripture passages he wanted me to meditate on during my retreat, especially in the presence of the Blessed Sacrament, and to write down my reflections, however simple they might be. He also gave me a project for the new year. He wanted me to copy and write out in longhand the Gospel of John. The notebook could be just any old spiral notebook that you'd get at a college bookstore, or even a supermarket. They should be separate notebooks, that's all.

It wasn't till that New Year's Eve that I looked at the last Scripture passage he had given me. It was Hosea, Chapter Two:

> So I will allure her;
>> I will lead her into the desert
>> and speak to her heart.
> From there I will give her the vineyards she
>> had...

> She shall respond there as in the days of her
> youth,
> when she came up from the land of Egypt...
> I will espouse you to me forever; I will espouse
> you in right and in justice, in love and in
> mercy; I will espouse you in fidelity, and you
> shall know the Lord.

The Scriptures Father had given me previous to this one were about vocation, too. There was the call of the disciples: *Come and see...follow me, and I will make you fishers of men*; the specific call to Matthew the tax collector; the call of the rich young man who went away sad because he couldn't let go of his riches. These were all powerful passages to meditate on—they still are! They were directly from the Gospels, too, and Fr. Meriwether taught me to listen to the words of the Lord as if they were being spoken directly to me, which, in a real way, they were. But on the eve of the new year, I heard the voice of the Lord from the Hebrew Scriptures and the prophet Hosea, and He was alluring me into the desert and wanted to espouse me to Himself.

This was romantic and scary at the same time. It touched something in me that I recognized as having been touched before...in the deep inner space within me where I would often take refuge, even as a child, and the desire to be all His which touched my soul that chilly Saturday morning when I first went into St. Vincent's. I had my eyes closed in the chapel, pondering these words quietly, and the image of the Sacred Heart statue came to my mind. And I saw the Lord, not just pointing to His Sacred Heart, but gesturing me to

"*Come to me…come here. This is the desert where I will espouse you and speak to you and you will know my love.*" I don't know how long I sat there, perhaps forty-five minutes, but I knew that that was all that really mattered…to be allured into the desert of His Heart. I realized too that this allurement had begun years ago, and perhaps I first only felt it or knew it that Saturday morning on my way to see Gracie. I wondered what Rabbi Liebermann would have said about that!

I didn't fight such thoughts, which I had done in the past. Fr. Meriwether, again, was helping me to watch my thoughts, as he put it, as one watches an aquarium of tropical fish. Not to be afraid, but to remain peaceful, and in an attitude of listening. I was reminded of the wonderful words of Samuel sleeping in the temple: *Speak, Lord, your servant is listening.*

And so I tried to just listen. To be aware that one is in the presence of the Lord both within and without. *I will espouse you in love and mercy*…there was Our Lady at the Annunciation, being espoused in love and mercy by the Lord, and her response was, "*Fiat.*" *Be it done unto me according to Your word.*

That was the meditation that carried me through New Year's Eve day and evening and into the night. And when the Night Office began, and the fireworks and car horns were sounding off outside all around us, I interiorly surrendered in my inner space—my soul—*Behold, the handmaid of the Lord, be it done unto me.*

New Year's Day was glorious. It was cold and snowy, and the monastery seemed to be wrapped in a new peacefulness. I was feeling a little more sober, and I hadn't had anything to drink at all! I had to take stock of my situation. You'd think I would be singing "Climb Every Mountain" like Peggy Wood in *The Sound of Music,* but I was humming Ron Moody's song as Fagin in *Oliver:* "Oh, I'm reviewing the situation…" I could almost see him dancing out of his den of thieves with his treasure box under his arm. He had been nominated for an Academy Award for that role a year before, in 1968 actually. He didn't get it, but did win the Golden Globe Award.

So on New Year's Day in the chapel of the Dominican Monastery, I was reviewing the situation, and came to the cold and sober conclusion that it was absolutely impossible that I become a cloistered nun, and I should not fantasize about it anymore. My eyes were getting very heavy, and I could hardly keep them open…I'm too young and had my whole life ahead of me, I heard me say to myself…I was meant to get married…

And I guess I fell sound asleep right there in the chapel, planning my wedding…Greta was the matron of honor wearing a very un-matronly matron of honor dress, checking out books as she walked down the aisle, pencils sticking out of her hair, her glasses down on the tip of her nose. Gwendolyn appeared looking like a fat penguin waddling down the aisle in short flat steps with a teapot in her hand, smiling at and nodding to everyone on both sides of the aisle. Ruthie was there looking like an emaciated Twiggy with a Beatles' haircut, wandering down the aisle, her eyes glazed over from just smoking a joint in the priory. And sitting in the front pew were Mama and Papa, looking like Tevye and Golda from *Fiddler on the Roof* in overalls and babushka. I ran out the side door and looked up, and there was Joshua playing a violin on the roof, showing me his violin and laughing. Standing at the Communion rail was Fr. Matthew Ezra with a long beard, waving at me coming down the aisle…next to him was a rabbi in tallis and yarmulke…David, looking angry because there was no canopy.

I glanced over to the Sacred Heart Statue, and there was Gracie lighting a candle for me, and I wanted to cry, but I held it back because her mother was there glaring at me from the pew. Sitting next to her was Sally, taking copious notes and not even looking at me, and behind her I heard Mrs. Melbourne say, "She's the brightest of the Feinstein girls." She was holding a package of leaking lamb chops. I got to the Communion rail by myself, and the groom turned to look at me; he was wearing a tuxedo with tails and a white bow-tie, and he had long hair and a beard, and piercing blue eyes…it was the…

I suddenly jumped a foot in the air, and woke up, realizing this was all a crazy dream. Sr. Mary Vincent was next to me with her kind smile, stroking my arm and whispering, "Are you alright, Rebecca dear?" I assured her that I was, that I had just fallen asleep. "I *know*, dear. You were hollering out loud."

I apologized as profusely as I could, and then I dared to ask what I had hollered. Sr. Mary Vincent didn't understand it, but Greta, who had been on the other side of the chapel, had heard it; she said that I hollered, "I don't want to be an orphan; I don't want to be an orphan." They both looked at me, puzzled and waiting for an explanation, and I told them that I had been daydreaming about *Oliver Twist* when I must've fallen asleep. Sr. Mary Vincent smiled and said,

"That's nice, dear. One shouldn't eat too many olives." And she toddled off. Greta and I looked at each other and could hardly keep from bursting out loud laughing.

We scurried off to the kitchenette lest we disturb the poor nun keeping her guard, as they called their time of prayer before the Blessed Sacrament. Greta put on the tea kettle, and I mused, "Sister thought I was eating olives! We should be so lucky, to have a couple martinis with them." And we both laughed. Greta and I loved a martini or two after a long day at the old library.

I told her I was kind of reviewing the situation and the past year, and thinking of Fagin's song in *Oliver*, and must've fallen asleep. She astutely pointed out that I was not Fagin in my dream, but Oliver, the orphan boy. I didn't tell her about my wedding dream or her awful dress or Gwendolyn or anyone, not even the groom. But I thought about it all. Maybe I *was* feeling like an orphan, and becoming a nun would… would what? I didn't know.

I wrote in my journal that evening about the dream, and told myself to snap out of it. I tried to reason it all out very clearly and sensibly. It would be nice to have a lovely apartment on the Upper East Side, be one of the head librarians or archivists at the New York Public Library, and marry a devout Catholic man who was also rich and handsome (well, it was *my* fantasy!). We would have a lovely duplex around East 65th Street and Second Avenue, in walking distance to St. Vincent's, where we would be married, have all our children baptized, and we'd be patrons of the arts, and travel to Europe every other summer while the governesses looked after the children until they were old enough to travel and not embarrass us.

I couldn't get old Fagin's song out of my head: *Oh I'm reviewing the situation...* Maybe my becoming a Catholic was a way of becoming an orphan. My family was better than most Jewish families, I figured, they didn't literally dis-own me, ah...but if I became a nun, especially a cloistered nun, they would, I feared. I would certainly have brought *orphanhood* upon myself. It was bad enough that I should cause them to suffer from my being a Catholic, although it didn't seem like they were really suffering at all. Sally and David were mostly embarrassed and angry; Ruthie could care less; Papa seemed to be accepting, if I was happy... and Mama, well...Mama maybe suffered a little, but was it because she felt that she had failed in her being a mother; or was she suffering embarrassment whenever she was with her Hadassah friends and they'd whisper about me, or so she thought? Had I let her down because I wouldn't be marrying a *mensch* under a canopy and giving her grandchildren to spoil and overfeed? Who was suffering here?

Those were the sentiments I left the monastery pondering that January 2nd. I had one semester left at Barnard and thought about graduate school in library science. Gwendo-lyn was always at me to become a lawyer, but none of it excited me as much as being at the monastery in Brooklyn Heights. Yet despite that, I was in complete denial that I could ever possibly have a vocation. Good for Joanne Mey-ers, but not for me. Amen.

I meet Ruthie at Tea on Thames the day after we got back; she was pretending to be the youngest daughter of a Lady in Waiting for Queen Elizabeth and talked about the rooms at Buckingham Palace where she had grown up. It was all made up, of course, and her accent was rather charming; she sounded a lot like Julie Andrews, and I was expecting her to break into "These Are a Few of My Favorite Things" when Lady Gwendolyn placed a plate of almond biscuits (cookies, for us Yanks) in front of her. Gwendolyn, of course, would put on a serving girl's Cockney accent and curtsy to her ladyship. Even the other patrons in the shop were enjoying the show. Gwendolyn wanted to hear all about my retreat, and of course Ruthie was all ears and full of questions. She promised she wouldn't breathe a word to "Mummy" (as she put it), as she (Mummy) thought it was very peculiar to be going to spend the holidays at a convent of nuns, and had said so more than once.

Ruthie also filled me in on the family news, which wasn't anything too interesting, except that David was there for dinner on New Year's Day with a cute little thing from New York-Cornell Hospital. It's the first time that David ever brought someone home for dinner. "Mama was all aflutter, as you can imagine. And the girl was very nice; very well spoken and intelligent. I think she may be a doctor, too, or a medical student—I missed the beginning," announced Ruthie, while digging into the almond biscuits.

We both devoured a cookie or two in silence. I took a big gulp of my tea, and said, "So, was she Jewish?"

Ruthie almost spit out her cookie when she blurted out, "No, she's Irish Catholic! Her name is Kathleen O'Hara from County Galway," (this with a bit of an Irish brogue).

"I just made up the County Galway part; I think she's from New Haven."

Ruthie had left to meet a girlfriend before David and Kathleen O'Hara left, so she didn't get the immediate post trauma reaction from Mama and Papa when they left. All I said was, "Maybe David will think better of Catholics a little now."

And Ruthie just said, "Probably," and she was off gabbing about *school stuff,* as she called it.

My monthly meeting with Fr. Meriwether was postponed for a week, as he was away somewhere. He never told me where he went whenever he was away, which wasn't very often. I saw him finally the second week of January and kept the conversation light and superficial. He sat quietly and patiently until he told me that he wasn't here to listen to my chatter about the monastic menu. He told me I was holding something back, probably because of fear, as most of us do, but I'd better come clean with him. I had never heard him so stern and yet so perceptive.

And so I told him about my envy of Sr. Joanne and about my crazy dream and how foolish it was of me to think that I could possibly have a vocation. The Scripture passages he gave me to meditate on were very beautiful and about the sacrament of marriage, right?

He leaned forward in his chair and told me that I was afraid that the Lord was calling me to be a nun, and from what he could see over the past year, I may very well have a vocation, and if that was so, what was I going to do about it?

I stood up and told him I did not have a vocation. He was wrong, and perhaps I should stop coming to see him and get on with my life. I didn't wait for an answer, I turned and walked out of the room, threw my coat on quickly, and went out the front door, walking past the front of the church without any acknowledgement of who or what was inside. I was so angry at Fr. Meriwether for being so presumptive. I turned down 72nd Street and went east to Third Avenue, and on 73rd and Third passed a quiet little bistro that looked very warm and inviting. I darted inside, sat at a table, and ordered a gin martini—straight up with three olives, *thank you very much.*

Twelve

THE MORNING AFTER, I felt wretched. I don't think I had ever really known what too many olives could do! I sat brooding over a large mug of coffee made by Greta, who in her sweet, gentle way did not say anything. After a time she softly told me that she was off to Mass and would be back afterwards if I wanted anything. "Yeah, can you go to confession for me?" We laughed.

"Of course not, silly, but I can light a candle for you by the Sacred Heart...bye." Greta. She knew just what to say.

Well, I felt wretched, not because I had too many olives, but because of the way I stomped off in a huff like a ten-year-old schoolgirl, leaving Fr. Meriwether. I was upset and angry at him, but that was all my own ego not getting its way. I wanted him to agree with me and talk me out of any vocation foolishness. Certainly he could see better than anyone that this nice Catholic girl from the West Side was talented, intelligent, religious, and would make some Catholic guy a wonderful and devoted wife and mother of many children. This was the second half of the twentieth century; this was the age of women coming into their own; I couldn't bury myself in a cloistered monastery. I loved life too much; I was a New Yorker, for Heaven's sake. I drank smart Manhattan martinis, even if my sophisticated head was presently achy and feeling full of cobwebs.

What a way to start the new year. And it was first Saturday, and I had wanted to do the Five First Saturdays requested by Our Lady at Fatima. It *was* Saturday, however, so I could go to a Mass at noon, maybe at St. Catherine's over on East 68th between First and York. It was another Dominican parish with its own interior charm and lovely brickwork, but really no match for St. Vincent's. St. John the Martyr on 72nd Street was even closer, and I liked its smallness. It was kind of Catholic cozy. But for the next thirty minutes, alone with my coffee from Grace's Market, I allowed myself to review the situation again. Besides all those reasons I just gave, something was gnawing at me which came across as fear. What was I afraid of?

I was afraid of the repercussions from my family; it was one thing to swallow the Catholic pill, it was something else to "commit suicide"…and that's how the Feinstein Clan would see it. At this point, though, I didn't much care what David or Sally or Ruthie thought—it was Papa I didn't want to hurt, or lose my right to be his daughter. And I really didn't want to cause Mama more suffering than I already had, although again, she didn't seem to be any worse for the wear given the circumstances.

So it must be more than familial fear. I think the idea of living in a cloister for the rest of one's life is quite fearful. Day after day, and year after year, they do the same thing nearly every day. The ingredients would vary with the seasons, both natural and liturgical, but I had a career to think about. Anyway, I had too many faults and imperfections to ever be a nun. I liked Milky Way candy bars and olives. I liked Broadway musicals and shopping all day at Macy's. I loved my independence more and more since I moved out of my family's apartment. I could come and go as I pleased. I loved midnight walks along the East River with the lights of Roosevelt Island and Lower Manhattan glistening on the East River and wrapped around me like a cape of lights.

I liked to walk around Central Park on Sunday afternoon or to lay in the living room with the *Sunday Times* spread out around me, eating bagels and lox. I was no fashion model, that's for sure, but I loved new clothes and hats and handbags, even penguin earrings and high heels. *Raindrops on roses and whiskers on kittens...*I began to sing and laugh at myself.

What did any of this mean? I also knew I loved the Lord and thanked Him every day for the gift of faith and the gift of The Faith. His Church has been likened to many things, but I really loved the idea that His Church is His Bride. And Fr. Meriwether's Scripture passage came back and hit me right between the eyes, like a spiritual boomerang I had thrown out on New Year's Eve and had returned a week later: *I will espouse you to me in justice and truth, and you shall know the Lord.* We are all called by the Lord to be living members of His Mystical Body, the Church, which is so joined to Him that He calls it a marriage...His Church (all of us) are espoused to Him, and that is how we truly come to know the Lord.

This was too much on a floppy stomach and black coffee. I went into the kitchen and began to make a three-egg omelet with Swiss cheese and finely chopped jalapeño peppers; a toasted English muffin; sliced tomatoes; and a fresh pot of coffee. I was feeling remarkably better already. The thought of actually being a nun, like the Dominican nuns in Brooklyn Heights, wasn't as frightening as before, or as incredible, but really not probable, I kept saying to myself. I did like the idea of praying the Rosary during the Night Guard, and chanting the Divine Office. The habit was also one of the most beautiful habits of all the different Orders, not that I had seen very many. Some active Orders were modifying the habit with a little hair showing, a shorter shirt, and no wimple, but I thought the one they had in Brooklyn Heights right now was feminine and most pleasing to look at.

The Sisters of Charity are always quite visible, at least here in New York. Gwendolyn told me people call them "God's Geese." I think the head gear, called a coronet, is really quite lovely, and they are a riot on a crowded subway. But I've noticed how readily people respect the habit. St. Vincent's has Dominican sisters whose motherhouse, I think, is in Columbus, Ohio. Their habit is really beautiful too, although the veil seems stiffer than the nuns' in Brooklyn Heights. Greta told me once, when I was raving about how beautiful a habit was, that "the habit does not make the nun." I don't know where she comes up with these sayings of hers. Of course the habit doesn't make the nun any more than anyone's clothes make the person. The bathing suit does not make the swimmer. But there's something to be said for the uniform helping the person wearing it to remind him or her of what they are striving to be or do.

I remember Fr. Meriwether in one of his classes talking about the accidents belonging to a substance, according to Aristotle. And one of the accidents is *habitus*, or clothes. It's interesting that only human beings clothe themselves;

and like cooking, we've refined making clothes into a fine art. Clothes are also used by us humans to symbolize other aspects of ourselves or what we do, so clothes become in themselves a way of praising God, who made us the way we are.

Such thoughts while nursing a mild hangover! Maybe it was the jalapeño peppers in the omelet. At any rate, the breakfast and coffee gave me the energy I needed to get my face together for the Noon Mass. I went to St. John Martyr on 72nd Street; it was closest and coziest. I needed the small space with lots of candles burning.

Greta had given me a new leather-bound blank book again; it was becoming an annual affair. I had not been entirely faithful about writing in last year's. But a new year lends itself to such resolutions.

Anyway, the point is, that I opened up my brand-new journal while sitting alone in my pew in a rear corner. Just a few people remained after Mass. My own soul was at peace since Holy Communion, and I didn't want to analyze any of it, but simply to be. It's a wonderful moment, letting go and allowing God's presence to calm one's anger, confusion, resentments, anxiety, whatever one is carrying. *Come to me all you who find life burdensome, and I will refresh you.* I knew that refreshment deep in my soul, in that inner space where I could commune with God. And so it was here, in this mind-set that I opened my journal. I wrote:

> Dear Lord, behold your poor child sitting here in your Holy Presence. I am still living in the intimacy of Holy Communion in You fifteen minutes ago. Thank

you, Lord, for this gift of Yourself. The Blessed Sacrament is beyond my comprehension, but help me to surrender to You without understanding. I believe, Lord, I believe, help Thou my unbelief. Lord, you know me better than I know myself. You know my sins and weaknesses, and so I depend entirely on Your Mercy and Forgiveness. My own will is so strong at times, Lord, that I fear it will always be my downfall. Never let my will separate me from You, dear Lord, even when everything or everyone seems contrary to my knowing and willing. Forgive me for being such a huffy little girl in front of Fr. Meriwether. I ask you, Lord, to send Your blessing on him and help him to forgive me. Give me the courage and wisdom to know how to ask him in person.

And Lord, thank you for the week at the Dominican Monastery; and for all the sisters there who serve You by their prayer, penance, and work . I can hardly believe, Lord, that You would want me to be a nun like one of them, but Lord, all I want is to do Your Holy Will. I have no idea what that is and how it will be accomplished, but I trust in You, Lord, and know you will draw me to Yourself despite myself. All I ask, Lord, is that You *give me a sign*, something that I recognize or consent to which I have the ability to do. Do you understand what I mean, Lord? It must all be Your work. It always is, isn't it, Lord? It always is— Your work.

I added a few extra thoughts about the people in my life, closed the book, and closed my eyes. I was at peace. Maybe I would come back at four o'clock when they had confession or go over to St. Catherine's. I liked the Dominicans there, although I didn't know any of them personally. They had a very nice Shrine dedicated to St. Jude, the patron saint of hopeless cases. It always had a good number of candles burning in front of his statue. It was an appropriate shrine to have across the street from Sloan Kettering Cancer Hospital.

I left St. John Martyr and headed east on 72nd Street, deciding to visit St. Catherine's to light a candle. It felt like a good day to go over to Gwendolyn's, and I suddenly missed Ezra and Gracie. Maybe Ruthie would like to go, but I hadn't spoken with any of my family since I had called them from the monastery on New Year's Day. On the corner of Second Avenue, I stopped and bought a soft pretzel, crispy hot from the hot plate, and loaded with salt…I think it was even kosher salt, but probably not. I chuckled to myself. I loved New York pretzels. *Did you get that, Lord, that's another reason I could never bury myself in a cloister: there were no pretzel vendors at any of the corners.*

St. Catherine's was a welcome refuge from the cold. There is something clean and masculine about the red brick and dark pews. St. Jude was there basking in the warmth of all those candles. There was an old man in baggy clothes asleep in the back pew and several people scattered in the pews, lost in their prayers. There was already a woman lighting a candle, bundled up in a woolen coat with an artificial fur collar and trim. She looked over at me, and hesitated. "Becky Feinstein?" she said.

"Yes," I said looking at her intently, "Mrs. Levine?"

"What?" Mrs. Levine smiled. She was one of my mother's best friends from Hadassah.

"How are you, dahling? You look good for your age..."

"I'm fine, Mrs. Levine...for my age. I didn't know you were a fan of St. Jude."

Mrs. Levine got very serious, and leaned into me, talking under my chin. "It's for my friend, Mrs. Melbourne; you remember her, don't you, from the old neighborhood?" She said all this like one would speak of the old country. But I remembered Mrs. Melbourne and her sister, and their lamb chops; she was in my dream for heaven's sake. "She's got cancer of the pancreas and isn't expected to live; she's over there at Sloan Kettering. She's a Catholic, you know, so I thought I'd light a candle for her; what's to hurt?"

"That's very kind of you, Mrs. Levine. I did that a few years ago for my friend Grace Price who had leukemia. She was very grateful."

"That's right, Becky, what's to hurt? Happy New Year, dahling." And she scurried off. I lit a few candles that afternoon. One for myself and my dilemma; one for Fr. Meriwether and his intentions, and one for Mrs. Melbourne, who would soon see the Lord face to face, and probably tell him that my sister Sally was the smartest Feinstein girl. I think I almost saw St. Jude smile at me. Don't you love the Communion of Saints!

Pocket poor by this time, I only had enough to buy a carton of coffee on the corner and walk home up First Avenue. Maybe Greta would be home now; maybe she would like to eat out tonight and go see *Funny Girl,* the movie I was dying to see. Ruthie had seen it twice so far. Her new name is probably Barbra, spelled like Barbra Streisand spells it.

Greta was not only at home, she was in the middle of cleaning the place. I forgot we usually did that on Saturday afternoons. So I threw myself into scouring the bathroom, which was very good therapy. Someone should write a doctorate about it. To my delight, Greta was thinking of *Funny Girl* too, and had already checked the paper and saw where it was also playing uptown on the West Side, and thought we could have a late, high tea at Tea on Thames, and go to the movies. A perfect plan.

The next day Greta was going off to Jersey to see old friends, which meant I had the place to myself…also a perfect plan. We'd go to Mass at St. Vincent's, she'd take a cab to Port Authority afterwards, and I'd pick up *The Sunday Times* and a half-dozen bagels, and have a lazy afternoon without any plans at all. Perfect.

Gwendolyn was happy to see us and would have loved to have joined us for the movie, but she had to work. We got to the movie theater and had to wait in line, but got in for the five o'clock show. Of course, we both loved it, and went through several handkerchiefs at the end, when she sang "My Man." It's always fun to see a movie made after the Broadway show. I was fortunate enough to see Barbra do Fanny Brice on Broadway.

I went over to St. Jean's for Mass on Sunday because I wanted to hear their choir, but it was probably more to avoid running into Fr. Meriwether. They also had Eucharistic adoration after the last Mass for all of Sunday afternoon, ending with Benediction at 5:00. St. Jean's also has a nice side chapel devoted to St. Anne, with a statue of St. Anne and the Blessed Mother as a young girl. St. Anne is teaching her to read, perhaps, and one wonders what they are reading. For sure, it wasn't the *Sunday Times*, which I picked up on the corner of 79th and Third and schlepped home along with my bag of bagels and a container of blended cream cheese.

At three o'clock I lay on the living room rug. I was playing my *Sound of Music* album, having exhausted *Funny Girl*, when the doorbell rang. Who in the world could it be? We were not expecting anyone; no one had called. I got myself up and looked through the peephole. It was Papa! I was so surprised and delighted, and flung open the door. Papa had never ever been here, and for a minute my heart also sank to the ground. Something was wrong; somebody died?

"Papa, what is it?" I was taking his heavy overcoat and scarf from him, and waved at the *Sunday Times*. "Sit down, Papa, don't mind the mess." I must've been as white as a sheet, as Papa immediately assured me that nothing was wrong; he was in the neighborhood and thought he might surprise me and wish me a Happy New Year. "Your roommate, she's not here?"

"No, Papa, she's in New Jersey for the day; we've got the whole place to ourselves. Let me put the kettle on…or would you like a drink, Papa?"

"A drink? My little princess is serving me drinks?" He smiled. "I'd love a little brandy to warm my old bones, if you have some." And we did. Greta had nice friends and a fine-tuned gift of hospitality. We had a well-stocked bar, hidden behind a wood carved armoire that you'd think was a

library for precious books or a private desk. It probably was
at one time, but Greta turned it into the bar. She said it gave
a whole new meaning to studying for the bar.

I decided I'd better not have my usual with olives, but I
would have a little brandy too; besides, I loved the glasses.
I swooped up the newspaper and threw it on an empty easy
chair and brought us each a snifter of Danty X.O. Brandy.
I didn't know if it was good, but I loved the bottle. "Mazel
Tov," said Papa, and I repeated, "Mazel Tov," and we clinked
glasses, and I was filled with such emotion.

"How's Mama?" I said while escaping for a minute into
the kitchen to get something to nosh. What goes with
brandy? Where was Greta when you needed her? I grabbed
an unopened box of petit fours, which someone from the
library had given me for Christmas. The little cakes would
be perfect with brandy, so I arranged them quickly on a
Steuben crystal candy dish. *Schmaltzy*, I thought. I turned
down the hi-fi, which was telling Sr. Maria to "climb every
mountain."

"Don't turn it down too much; I've come to talk to you
about the movie." I repeated this to him, as I wasn't sure I
had heard right.

"Did you see *The Sound of Music*?" He had. It was playing
at one of those theaters downtown that brought back the old
movies...old being only a couple years. Remember this was
before the day of VHS tapes and Academy Award movies on
television.

"I had an appointment on West 23rd Street near the 23rd
Street Y, and when I got there, learned that it had been postponed for four-and-a-half hours. I could've gone back up

to my office, or I could've walked around downtown, and killed time, which I decided to do. I still had a little holiday shopping, and I passed a movie theater where *The Sound of Music* was playing, and beginning in 15 minutes. I knew it had won the Academy Award and that it was filmed in Austria. You remember, our family was from the Austrian Feinsteins…"

"I know, Papa." I wanted to put three petit fours in my mouth at once, but just smiled. He went on. "Well, as you know, I've always wanted to take your mother to Austria, but she would never go till they built a bridge, she'd say, but I thought maybe I could entice her by the scenery in the movie. The posters looked beautiful. So I went in by myself to see it first."

"This is what you've come to tell me? That you went to a goyim movie because it was filmed in Austria?" I hoped I didn't sound too cynical.

Waiting to swallow his petit fours and washing it down with Danty X.O., he continued, "Oy, it was such a beautiful film, but it wasn't just the scenery that moved me to tears. It was those nuns. I didn't know there were people around like that. From the very beginning when they were singing 'How do you solve a problem like Maria?' to when they were so happy to dress her for the wedding day—and what a wedding!—I was a little sorry she didn't stay with the nuns," Papa giggled in the little guttural way he did. "I remembered that Peggy Wood, when she was Mama on *I Remember Mama* on television. She was such a down-to-earth and holy lady, you know, right to the end when they were helping the von Trapps to escape. And I remembered my great uncle was just a boy then in Austria, and it was a monastery of nuns who hid him from the Nazis." I could see Papa getting just a little teary-eyed, and so I poured him just a wee bit more of the brandy.

"I sat there in the theater unable to move while the credits were being shown, and I realized that my Becky is a Catholic and a brave and wonderful woman too, and I would be so proud of her if she became a nun." He was half crying and half gurgling his giggle. I sat stunned. The tears rolled down my cheeks without any inhibition.

"Oh, Papa, you've made me so happy! You are my sign… my sign." And I began to sob quite unabashedly.

Papa came over and took me in his arms. "It's okay, my little Raf, I understand." Papa took out a clean, neatly pressed and folded white handkerchief from his inside pocket and handed it to me. "It wasn't just the scenery I wanted to see. I wanted to see you, little one, and I had a little Christmas gift to give you, but I didn't know where you were. You never answered the phone; they told me you were off for the week from the library; I even came over here, and no one was home. So I asked Ruthie if she knew where you'd be for the holiday. I knew she would see you once in a while. And she said she had no idea, but maybe your friend Gwendolyn who owned the tea shop would know. Good idea. This tea shop I wasn't sure where it was exactly, so I took Ruthie for a winter walk, like we'd do, and she knew right where it was, and this Gwendolyn knew her and was so friendly to me— you'd thought I was from the royal family. And that tea shop, oy, did you know she has a whole flock of penguins at the nativity set?" Papa laughed, and I laughed but still couldn't say anything, the lump in my throat was so big.

"She even came and sat down with us and had a cup of tea. She gave me a penguin tea cup which she said was her favorite. Well, to make a long story short, she told us you were spending the whole week at a Dominican monastery of nuns in Brooklyn Heights, named Mary Queen of Hope. Both you and your roommate were there, even over New Year's Eve. Such a place, I thought. It must be something for you to give up even New Year's Eve in New York to be in a monastery of nuns. Gwendolyn said you went there quite often. And then she leaned forward, and almost in a whisper, looking over the top of her glasses, she said, 'I wouldn't be surprised, Mr. Feinstein, if Becky was thinking of being a nun, but don't tell her I said so.'"

Papa said that Ruthie sat there with her eyes almost popping out of her head. "Mama would have a cat if she heard that." I don't know where Ruthie got that expression, but he didn't like it. Staring straight into Ruthie's eyes, Papa said, "Mama will not hear a word of it."

"Of course not, Papa..."

And so Papa explained that that was the main reason he went to see the movie, to get some firsthand ammunition, and wound up loving the nuns more than the von Trapp Family. We sat in silence for a few minutes; the album had started over again and was playing "How Do You Solve a Problem Like Maria?"

"No, as a matter of fact, she and Ruthie are on a train right now heading for Chicago to see Sally. I made excuses to stay home because I wanted to see you and just to let you know we love you." That nearly started Niagara Falls again, but I got a hold of myself.

"Well, I think you should let your second daughter take you out for dinner." And Papa said he would be delighted, that he hadn't been taken out for dinner since, well, he'd never been taken out for dinner, come to think of it. And we laughed. I told him to help himself to more brandy while I freshened up and changed into something more suitable for the royal Feinstein Family Singers.

I went to my room and knelt down at my bed, and I sighed a sigh of relief that I hadn't realized I was holding in. I went easily to my hiding place inside, and thanked the Lord for answering my prayer so dramatically and so quickly. How could I ever doubt that He hears our prayers and answers them? And there and then I made a little surrender on my knees to whatever God wanted. I had no idea how it would work out, but I trusted that it would.

And tonight I was taking my Reuben Sandwich out for dinner and I knew the perfect place. A half hour later we were out on Third Avenue and Papa waved down a taxi… we climbed into the back seat, and I leaned forward and told the driver, "Brooklyn Heights, please."

Thirteen

I HAD PROBABLY NEVER had a more memorable evening with my father than that night. There was a wonderful, family-run, Italian restaurant two blocks away from the monastery, where we ate spaghetti and meatballs and devoured a whole loaf of garlic bread and a bottle of Taylor's rosé wine. We talked of many things, and Papa allowed me to share about my life of faith the past four years, and he never expressed judgment or tried to argue with me. He listened and seemed at times quite fascinated by it all. He said that although he couldn't understand a lot of the religious beliefs, he could see what it did to me, how it influenced the way I lived. He said that I was never given to the superficial banalities many young people seem so attracted to, that I was always more serious about life and thought about things. He said he could understand why I would be attracted to a life with others who pondered things deeply and were given to prayer.

I couldn't believe my ears. It was almost as if Papa knew I wanted to be a nun before I did, and that I could actually be happy being a nun. I didn't know if he realized what being a cloistered nun meant, but he was viewing it all through the nuns in *The Sound of Music*, and they were cloistered.

When we drifted off the subject of me, Papa shared some things I've never heard him speak of. He was proud of his first born son, David, and proud that he was a doctor, but

he saw a *lust for money* (Papa's words) which didn't sit well
with Papa. He was worried that David would wear himself
out, and not always for the right reasons. Sally, his eldest
born daughter, was full of ambition. (I could have told him
that years ago.) She was always good to the family, and came
home as often as she could, but (Papa said) her political
views were a little too far left for his comfort. David had a
new girlfriend every six months and couldn't settle down,
while Sally was married to her career, and had become a
feminist of sorts. Papa hesitated saying it, and quickly covered it up with a mouthful of garlic bread. "And our Ruthie,
well, you know our Ruthie. She wants to change her major
to Dramatic Arts, and is taking tap and modern dance; she's
obsessed with her diet, and, frankly, she dresses a little too
immodest for your mother and me, and she (Ruthie) flies off
the handle if I say anything and threatens to *run away like
Becky did.*"

It was my turn to listen and let Papa get it all off his chest.
"Your mother, God bless her, is a very superficial woman…
appearance is what matters, and she has a stubborn streak
that I haven't been able to break through in thirty-two years.
She's been a good wife, don't get me wrong, and I love her
dearly, but she can't hear or see my concerns over our children. You, of course, are the black sheep of the family, and
I don't know if she can ever open her mind and heart to try
to understand."

I still didn't say a word, but took Papa's hand across the
table. "I know, Papa, I know…and I don't hold it against
Mama that she can't accept me. I think it has been the most
difficult cross I've been given to bear, after thinking that

you didn't accept me either." I stopped before I got too choked up.

"Ah, my little angel, I have accepted you and am more proud of you than you will ever know." Now Papa was getting choked up. "I have always wanted for you to be happy and to be free to be yourself. That's all I want for all my children, but *you, you* are the only one that doesn't cause me worry and anxiety. I think you will make a beautiful nun…" and the words caught in his throat.

We changed the subject and talked about the dessert menu and how the meatballs were a little too spicy, but good. We talked about *The Sound of Music* and *Oliver* and *Funny Girl*, the one movie Mama went to and loved. After a while of easy small-talk banter, Papa got serious again. "You must not tell your mother about your plans, but leave it to me. Actually, leave it to me to tell her, and Ruthie, and David, and Sally—in their own time. Can you imagine!" And we both laughed.

"Nothing is decided yet, Papa. It's not like I can knock on the door and say 'Here I am' and that's it. There's a discernment period, (*thank you, Joanne Meyers*), but till tonight I was unwilling to even begin that."

"And now?"

"Now, I'm ready to begin. I feel so light and happy, like a ton of bricks has been lifted from me. It's almost five o'clock; would you like to sneak into the back of the monastery chapel and hear the nuns sing Vespers? They're not quite up to the Salzburg Music Festival, but they're good."

I paid the waiter, leaving a more than generous tip, and walked the two blocks with my arm linked in Papa's, just like the old days. We slid into the pew near the front, just as Mother was intoning "*Deus in adjutorium meum intende.*" Papa sat enthralled for a half hour with his eyes closed much of the time, thinking about Austria, no doubt, or his family, or maybe, just maybe, thinking about God.

Sr. Mary Vincent came over almost immediately after Vespers, and I was happy to introduce her to my father. She didn't look at all like her, but it could have been Peggy Wood, Papa was so humbled to meet her. Sister was the epitome of discretion, a special grace given to extern sisters, but I caught the twinkle in her eye as she gave me a little hug goodbye. "We'll be seeing you again soon, I hope…you bundle up now, dear, and take care of your father." And she disappeared behind a doorway.

We took a cab back to West 79th Street. It cost more than the dinner, but I could see Papa was tired and had a lot to process. He invited me in, but I said I couldn't, and promised I would come by and cook dinner for him tomorrow night when I got off work. He thought that would be splendid, and said I should bring my roommate.

I took the cab further up town and got out at Tea on Thames, thinking I would surprise Gwendolyn and thank her for being…well, for just being herself really. I walked through the front door, and I was the one to get the big surprise! There sat Ezra Goldman and our old friend, the Earl of Grey.

I had to get used to calling him Br. Matthew. He looked marvelous, not at all the old man with the long white beard from my dream. He was dressed in "civvies," and his hair was all buzzed off, which made him look younger than ever, but his broad smile hadn't changed in the years since I'd seen him. Gwendolyn was at the table in an instant to celebrate the happy reunion, with an entire devil's food cake in the shape of a penguin lying on a plate of coconut snowflakes.

We had so much to talk about we didn't know where to begin. So we let Br. Matthew take the lead. He was on a Christmas "*quies,*" as he called it, a Latin word for rest. I suspect our English word quiet comes from it. He was only in the City for two nights and would go back to West Springfield by train. He was expecting to take his final vows in four months, sometime in May, and hoped that we would all be there. He was doing very well, and would be going to the seminary in Boston in the fall. He was staying at his Aunt Sarah's while here, and hoped we could have dinner tomorrow night. I told him that was perfect, because my father was alone for a couple days, and I was to cook supper there tomorrow night; they could all come. Even Gwendolyn could come, as she often took Monday nights off and let her niece manage the place.

While Ezra and Gwendolyn solved the world's problems for a few minutes, I called Greta at home. She was grateful and wondered where I was; it looked like I had been abducted in the middle of reading the *Sunday Times*. I told her that I had been, and that I was being held hostage at Tea on Thames. Then, all I told her was that my father was alone for a couple days, I was going to cook supper for him tomorrow night, and he had invited her—could she come? I had forgotten Monday night was her "Bridge Night," but it had been cancelled for the holidays and wouldn't resume till February...so she could and would be delighted. She'd bring a Bavarian pastry for dessert. I didn't tell her who else would be there.

We sat at the table for a couple hours; poor Gwendolyn wasn't making any profits from our patronage. She said she would bring the wine—red or white? I hadn't even thought about what I wanted to cook. Br. Matthew suggested pasta with anchovies and chunks of chicken…he'd help. I didn't say anything about God's giving me a sign; it was too awesome to throw out on the table amidst the half-eaten penguin and Earl Grey. It could wait.

It was close to ten o'clock when I sunk into my rocker and was reviewing the situation. How incredibly ordinary and miraculously God works in our lives. I sat in that rocker with a different mindset than I ever had before. I also still felt bad about Fr. Meriwether. Although I'd been to confession and did my penance, I felt like I needed to make it up to him personally. So I hoped he had the seven o'clock Mass tomorrow, but I'd write a note just in case he didn't. I had shared the afternoon's events with Greta when I got home, and she was awestruck and happy for me. I asked her, "Greta, do you think it would be an awful thing if I became a Dominican nun?" She came over and took me by the shoulders.

"My dear Becky, I think it would be an awful thing if you didn't." And she hugged me.

And that's how the old ball got rolling. Greta and I went to Mass on Monday morning on our way to work, as usual. Fr. Gleason had the seven o'clock. Br. Albert was always hanging around the vestibule in the morning, greeting people. I gave him my note for Fr. Meriwether and he said he would see that he got it. It was primarily a note of apology, but it also asked for another appointment before our monthly appointment, as he had given me much to ponder.

There was a whole other side to Fr. Meriwether which I don't think most people knew or saw. And I don't know if I did till this little incident. He called me at work that very morning and made an appointment for Tuesday after work. He was so full of kindness and gentleness. In other words, he was very fatherly…paternal in the best sense of that word. He may come across as academic and even scholarly when he teaches class or preaches, and a bit direct and unbending in some things, but beneath all that he's very gentle.

While I was afraid that he would reprimand me for being so rude, which I was, he didn't even mention it when we met on Tuesday. He let me do all the talking at first, and blubber over how sorry I was for speaking to him the way I did and walking out all in a huff. He only smiled and said, "You see, even after baptism, confirmation, and hundreds of Holy Communions, there's still some of the 'old girl' left."

The "old girl" was his way of saying St. Paul's "old man." There was a stubborn, self-willed, independent old girl left in me. I hadn't realized how belligerent she could also be!

He was delighted to hear my tale regarding my father and how that whole incident happened when it happened, and how I wouldn't have been in a frame of mind to grasp it had he, Fr. Meriwether, not said what he said. This was Tuesday, the night after our dinner at my father's apartment with Greta, Gwendolyn, and Br. Matthew. I told him I wish he could've been there and met my father, and perhaps one day he would.

It was a bit intense for poor Papa, I told Fr. Meriwether, being surrounded by four Catholics, three of whom were converts. But Papa handled it in a gentlemanly way. Of course he already had met Br. Matthew several years ago, and found that whole thing interesting, Ezra now being a Passionist Brother. Aunt Sarah was also there, so Papa wasn't the only practicing Jew in the house! A good time was had by all.

"And now," I told Fr. Meriwether, "I need your direction as to how to go about 'discerning' if I have a vocation, this time, accepting the fact that I may, and that I even hope I do." I remember feeling that saying it was all a bit over-whelming, even a little surreal!

Fr. Meriwether is very spiritual but also has a gift of being very down to earth—of keeping it real, and sometimes I need to *get real*, as they say today. He said that on a practical level, it's very simple: you ask to see the vocation directress, who is usually the subprioress, or even the novice mistress or assistant novice mistress.

"They already know you, so that part is easy. If there are no impediments, they will probably ask you do an aspirancy inside the cloister." The word *impediments* frightened me, and I couldn't imagine what impediments there were, and figured I probably had at least two. Fr. Meriwether could tell already by my expression that I had sunken into a dark hole, just in my thoughts and fears.

"Being Jewish is probably an impediment, right? Or hav-ing a Jewish mother who disapproves of your being a nun, and two siblings who don't speak to you?"

"Rebecca!" Fr. Meriwether's gentle sternness brought me back to earth. "Being Jewish is not an impediment if you're also a baptized and confirmed Catholic! Jesus and the first Thirteen Apostles were all Jewish!"

That, of course, made me laugh, and his throwing in the thirteenth apostle was so "Meriwetherian." I knew he meant St. Matthias who took Judas's place.

"'Impediments,' Rebecca, have to do with one's freedom: you are not married, and are therefore free to enter the monastery; your age, and your physical and mental health are normal and sane; and no one is forcing you against your will to do this. You are practicing the faith—more than most, I might add—and you have a prayerful and peaceful disposition. All of those things are *expedients*, not *impediments*."

Well, that was a relief. I didn't quite know what he meant about mental health; some people would think I'm crazy, and sometimes I wonder if they aren't right! He also knew my soul pretty well and knew I wasn't living a life of habitual sin; I was chaste, but I also knew that I had a lot of venial sins, and probably a lot of habitual venial sins, which may be impediments.

"Heavens to Betsy!" the priest exclaimed. "We don't come into religious life as saints ready for canonization. There's always going to be a struggle with certain sins perhaps, and the life is not free of sin or suffering. One needs to be able to let go of a lot of good and ordinary things, but all that is discovered in the 'discernment process' and over time. You won't be taking your vows the week after you enter," he added with his usual grin.

After a minute or two when we both sat silent in our thoughts, he said, "What I think you should do right now is to pray about all this, and to make a retreat somewhere other than Brooklyn Heights (meaning, the monastery there) and then let the prioress or even the guest mistress, who knows you, let them know what you're thinking. Are you able to get any time off from work?" And of course, I could. I had accumulated sick days, and we had enough assistant librarians on the staff that we often covered for each other so we could take some days off. He also had something—some place—in mind, but would have to get back to me on that.

"For now, continue doing what you're doing. Try to go to daily Mass and pray the Rosary every day, and do spiritual reading…oh, and if you're dating or planning to date, now would be a good time to let it fizzle out." *Fizzle out*—those were his exact words, I've never forgotten them. I would learn over time, that that's just what we have to do with a lot of *impediments* in our spiritual life—let them fizzle out.

This was his plan. He was scheduled to go to the Dominican nuns' monastery in West Springfield, Massachusetts, to give a series of lectures for five days on the Theological Virtues in St. Thomas Aquinas. He had been there before to preach their retreat, and he knew that they had three or four rooms for women guests. He had called the prioress and asked if he brought two young women with him would they be able to stay in the women's guest quarters and make a private retreat? The rooms were available. We would drive there from New York, stopping at the Dominican Priory in New Haven, Connecticut, on the Yale campus for lunch, and would arrive at the monastery in mid-afternoon. This was all pending on the weather, as the lectures were scheduled for the last week in January. This gave me time to arrange for someone to cover for me for a few days, plus three sick days I could use.

The other young woman was also from the parish. I had seen her on occasion in church, but didn't really know her. Her name was Barbara Parker, and she was discerning a vocation as well. There was also another Dominican Brother, Br. Jerome, whom I didn't know either, who was going to visit his sister, who was in the community. Br. Jerome was probably in his sixties and had lived for many years at the House of Studies in Washington, D.C.

West Springfield…of course. That's where the Passionist Monastery and Retreat House was, and where Br. Matthew presently was. Fr. Meriwether promised to drive me there one afternoon and surprise him. He liked Ezra and wished he had become a Dominican.

Barbara and I sat in the back seat the whole way and enjoyed the view. It seemed like it was expressways and interstate highways the whole way, but quite lovely, especially going through Connecticut.

St. Mary's Priory was very impressive, and the church was really beautiful. The friars welcomed us to a casual pick-up lunch in their beautiful refectory, very masculine-looking with a dark wood dining table under an elegant, early American chandelier. Their front parlors were also as exquisite as St. Vincent's, and I told Fr. Meriwether that I'd be happy just to stay there for my retreat. But I was also excited to visit another monastery. We were not far from another Dominican monastery in North Guilford, but didn't have the time to visit there, perhaps on the way back. It was also threatening to snow.

We arrived in West Springfield close to four o'clock. The drive up their entrance road is so wonderful with the monastery at the top of the hill. There are acres and acres of land, covered in snow. The enclosure wall on the side is hidden by huge hedges. Unlike Brooklyn Heights, there were no immediate neighbors; this was almost like farmland except for the commercial businesses going on across the street. But still, the monastery itself is far enough away and up a large hill that one doesn't even hear the traffic passing by. So different from the sights and sounds of Brooklyn, New York, going on outside one's window!

We visited the chapel before letting the nuns know we had arrived. The chapel was so beautiful, larger than Brooklyn Heights, but, like Brooklyn, had the monstrance in the middle of the large wrought iron grille. The nuns' part of the chapel (the choir) seemed very plain from what I could see, devoid even of statues except for one (Our Lady of Grace, I believe, but she can't really be seen from the public chapel). The stained glass windows depicted the mysteries of the Rosary and, high above them, various Dominican saints and blesseds. The pews were a light blonde stain, which made the chapel seem brighter, and the floors—all marble—were clean and shiny. There was a marble communion rail separating the nave from the sanctuary.

The community was also quite large, probably twice as big as Brooklyn. They sang most of their Office in English, which was new and different, and quite lovely. They have an impressive pipe organ inside the choir with real pipes over the back entrance to the choir.

I didn't know if Fr. Meriwether had intended this to bring on a crisis or a greater or lesser degree of surety. I had only really known the monasteries in Brooklyn Heights and Buffalo, plus little visits to Corpus Christi in the Bronx, and once to Summit, New Jersey.

Our rooms were small and very plain with tiny windows looking out on the front drive. By the time the bell rang for Vespers, it was snowing outside, which blanketed everything in the most wonderful silence and in turn made the nuns' singing even more angelic. We had lots of time to pray in the chapel and read. Fr. Meriwether gave his lectures in the nuns' community room/Chapter room, and Barbara and I weren't invited. We got to know each other during the five days, however, and every afternoon we bundled up and went for a walk up and down the entrance driveway.

It was nice having a new friend about my age, maybe a year or two younger, who was thinking of doing something so radical as entering the cloister. She was intimidated by the stress on study and the intellectual life of the Dominicans, and was more drawn to the Carmelites or maybe the Poor Clares. She seemed a little rigid about some things, or maybe just shy. She was a pretty young woman who didn't appear to be aware of her beauty. Maybe it's just a foible of us slightly overweight maidens to think skinny girls are prettier or have it more together.

She also made a fuss over the difference in the Carmelite and Dominican habits, something I had not really paid much attention to. We both noticed, however, that some of the active orders of sisters were wearing what they called "modified" habits, and we wondered where all that was leading. There was a spirit of renewal in the air since the close of the Vatican Council, and we were all rather swept up in it.

I remember Fr. Meriwether being very cautious about it all, and perhaps his caution rubbed off on me, too. After all, I was the daughter of Tevye and Golda Fiddler, who held fast to tradition. It was a traumatic enough event to embrace Catholicism, but it was also something very solid, stable, and an unshakeable rock like Peter, the rock on whom the Lord founded the Church.

On the third day of our retreat, Fr. Meriwether told us that after his morning conference we would take a ride over to the Passionist Monastery. He had called ahead and arranged to meet with Br. Mathew, who didn't know who would be hiding under Father's cappa. It was only a ten-minute ride to the Passionists, located on Monastery Road.

The retreat house and grounds were most impressive, especially when blanketed in snow. The house where the priests and brothers lived was warm and cozy; there was even a fireplace in the parlor, which was nicely alight with birch logs. The porter led us in and called Br. Matthew, who came bounding into the room a few minutes later, totally surprised and delighted to see us. Of course, he had never met Barbara, but knew Fr. Meriwether fairly well.

We sat on sofas facing each other near the fire, and Br. Matthew talked excitedly about the work of the house, about his making final vows in a few months, and about the marvelous liturgical changes they were incorporating into their retreats now. Active participation, lay readers, and everything being in English were the main points. He was so excited about it all, he didn't seem to grasp why we were there, at the Dominican Monastery, or didn't really put two and two together yet. But that was okay. Sometimes, I think the world revolves around me, and wonder why others, like my friends, don't get that, too.

We left less than an hour later, as we were due back for dinner at noon, and Fr. Meriwether had to look over his afternoon conference, which I presumed meant he wanted to take a nap beforehand. I'm sure he had everything down pat in his head already. I was surprised when Br. Ezra hugged me and gave me a kiss on the cheek, not because he'd never done that before, but it seemed awkward given the place, and I promised I would be there for his final vows, unless I was making my own, but he missed that entirely. He even hugged Barbara, which I found more surprising, and Fr. Meriwether, who always seemed humble and shy at those moments.

The drive back was rather silent, and I was lost in my thoughts, not able to put a finger on something about it all that disturbed me. Maybe it was just the bleakness of the weather.

Fourteen

THE MORNING WE left West Springfield, it was frigid cold
in a way I was told that only New England knows, but it
was also sunny, and the roads were clear. Father had invited
Barbara and me to join him the evening before in the Large
Parlor, where we met the community and were able to say
thank you. I don't think I was in a major crisis, but it was
difficult to leave them, as I found them very warm and
charitable, and full of joy. I imagined the nuns in Brooklyn Heights were also charitable and joy-filled, but I hadn't
had a "parlor" with the whole community, and really didn't
know. I was also struck by the largeness of the place and all
the land around them. Mother told us they had 146 acres.
That certainly preserves their solitude and silence in a way
that Brooklyn Heights doesn't have. And yet I recalled that
I was always struck by the silence in the Brooklyn Heights
monastery.

I took three postcards from the display rack in the front
entranceway: one for Greta, one for Gwendolyn, and one
to send to my father. He would appreciate the thought and
probably ponder for a while what the Catholics could ever
mean by calling Mary the Mother of God (Monastery of
the Mother of God is the name for the monastery in West
Springfield).

I guess I was beginning to discern that one was called to a particular monastery, in a particular Order, and that the realization of that was a two-way street. It wasn't just God dropping you down somewhere, but guiding you to where He wanted and letting you know interiorly that "this is the place." Again, it was simply a matter of knowing and doing His Will. How often we pray for that: *Thy Will be done.* That had an added significance to me now as I found myself back in familiar surroundings, in my squeaky little rocker on East 79th Street. Greta, of course, wanted to know everything about everyone, and I tried to describe it all to her, and told her about Barbara, and our going over to see Ezra. She filled me in on all the gossip at work and the new books she'd discovered.

I kept in touch with Barbara, and we went out for dinner a few times. I even took her over to Tea on Thames to meet Gwendolyn, whom I recall was not impressed with her. Perhaps she was a little jealous of my friendship with her, but that never seemed to be a problem with any of my other friends. Gwendolyn actually loved being my godmother and at times would teasingly call me Cinderella, as she saw herself as the fairy godmother and wished she had a magic wand and could change the couple mice that appeared one day in the kitchen into handsome coachmen. Instead she exterminated them. She had no sentimental attachment to mice, and thought that St. Martin de Porres probably had a screw or two loose for talking to them.

Gwendolyn was always a bit irreligious without being offensive. She kept things down to earth. She was a nice balance in my life for Greta, who could keep things stimulated on an intellectual level, which I also twigged to, while Gwendolyn could be more sentimental and even devotional. Not that Greta wasn't a devout woman—she certainly was, and Gwendolyn wasn't a dummy when it came to teaching the faith. They were a good balance for me.

I didn't let many days pass before going to Queen of Hope Monastery in Brooklyn, and had arranged by phone to meet with Sr. Imelda Mary, who was the sub-prioress and the sister in charge of vocations. We met on Saturday morning in the small parlor (sometimes called the Prioress's Parlor), which was used for more private meetings. Sr. Imelda Mary of St. Dominic was a native New Yorker and had been in the monastery for almost 25 years. She had taught school in Brooklyn after graduating from St. Francis College in Brooklyn Heights, and knew of the monastery since college, and used to come here on retreats. She was quite lovely and reminded me of Sr. Benedict in *The Bells of St. Mary's*. That was Ingrid Bergman, who was quite a beautiful actress. I told Sr. Imelda Mary that, and she blushed slightly and said, "I know; people have told me that. No Academy Awards here, my dear."

She laughed in that lovely innocent way only nuns seemed to be able to laugh—at least, I thought so, till I became a nun, and I realized there were different laughters because there were different sisters in different places in the spiritual life. Sr. Imelda Mary's laughter always remained the same and came from a place of peace and contentment. She was the perfect nun to be the face of the nunnery for those discerning a vocation. She was able to put one at ease from the start. Of course, that's all subjective opinion. Maybe I was already more at ease than others because I had been visiting there and had made a couple retreats there.

Sr. Imelda Mary knew me even though she had never met me. And she was delighted with my inquiry into their life and went through a little litany of questions, which I already knew were covering Fr. Meriwether's impediments. She also knew of my conversion from Judaism, which, of course, was not an impediment, and she knew something of my broken relationship with my family because of it. I guess Sr. Vincent was more astute than I figured! That too was not an impediment, Sr. Imelda Mary assured me, but she told me that it may one day be one of the splinters of the cross the Lord was preparing for me. She said that with a naturalness and gentleness that assumed (I presumed) that everyone knew the Lord was preparing a cross for them.

"Remember the three P's, dear. Our life is one of Prayer, Penance, and Peace." She smiled. She asked if I could stay for a couple hours and said that a guest room was available if I wanted to rest, and that we would meet again after None. That was fine with me, and I was happy to be there for the day. I had brought my spiritual reading with me for the subway ride, and looked forward to just being in the chapel alone. No one was on retreat, so I had lunch by myself, served by Sr. Hyacinth Marie, who told me that Sr. Vincent Mary was not feeling well and was resting.

After None, I was surprised that Sr. Imelda Mary had brought two other nuns with her: Sr. Mary of the Trinity, the novice mistress, and Sr. Catherine Agnes of Mercy, the mistress of postulants. I realized then that I was meeting with the Vocation Team, although they would never call themselves that. Sr. Catherine Agnes did most of the talking, and seemed to me somewhat cold and objective about things; she had probably been a business woman, I thought to myself, and was used to doing personnel interviews. She didn't repeat any of the impediment litany Sr. Imelda Mary had run through, but spoke more about practical matters, like my educational background, my work experience, any ambitions I had concerning my career, if and when I would be free to come for an aspirancy, and whether I had any debts.

I did have some school loans which could be paid up quicker than I planned if need be. I talked a little about my work at the Public Library, but I was not ambitious about a career there or anywhere for that matter.

Sr. Mary of the Trinity seemed to like that answer. She was Novice Mistress and told me there were four novices and a postulant at present, along with two temporarily professed sisters who still lived in the novitiate. She had been Novice Mistress, I later learned from Sr. Hyacinth Marie, for a total of nine years. It is most difficult to tell a nun's age, but I guessed her to be about 60. She was actually 70…born in 1900. She was from an old Catholic family in New Hampshire and moved to Manhattan after college, hoping to be an airline stewardess (her words) or an actress. She actually became an assistant cook at St. Rose Home on the Lower East Side run by the Dominican Sisters of Hawthorne. She had entered their novitiate, and it was there that she felt a call to the cloister. Brooklyn Heights was her first and only choice.

She had a warmth about her that was most charming for someone like me, trying to say all the right things, wanting the three of them to like me and accept me before Vespers, if possible. Sr. Mary of the Trinity asked about my prayer life and whether I attended daily Mass. She knew St. Vincent Ferrer Church well and agreed with me that it was the most beautiful church in New York. She was more probing about the interior movement of my soul that drew me to the contemplative life, as opposed to a more active order. All three listened very attentively without comment.

It was Sr. Imelda Mary again who asked if I had plans for the evening and told me that if not, I was welcome to stay for Vespers and supper and she would meet with me again shortly after her supper. That was fine with me. I figured they wanted some time to talk among themselves. I was feeling a little nervous and was most distracted during Vespers rehashing everything I said that day. Maybe they would find me immature, although they didn't know about my tendency to take things too personally; I could be easily hurt, and if I didn't get my way, I would pout like a ten-year-old girl. Maybe I was just too young and maybe saying I didn't have any ambition was the wrong thing to say. Did I love God enough to be locked up behind a grille, in an "enclosure," as they kept calling the cloister? Finally, all I could do was pray that God's will be done. It was also quite interesting (and probably obsessive) for me to observe myself, and in all that distraction I realized that I really wanted this life and was praying that that was indeed God's will.

I still remember supper that night: Campbell's tomato soup and some saltine crackers and peanut butter, if I wanted it. I figured this was the same as what they were having, and I was probably right, as I've had Campbell's tomato soup and saltines with peanut butter more times than I can remember.

After supper, I waited in the parlor for Sr. Imelda. It was also a little escape from Sr. Hyacinth and Sr. Grace Mary, who always came to lock the church doors after Vespers. They were both most cordial and loved to chat. I didn't want to talk to anyone else at that moment. The silence was most welcomed, even if the interior silence was only in bits and pieces. Sr. Imelda Mary came into the room on her side of the grille. She was smiling from ear to ear.

The meeting with the sisters went very well, she told me, and they were all quite positive in their assessment. Usually they would suggest several more visits, but since I had been there on retreat several times, the next step would be an aspirancy inside. They liked a month or more, but knew that was difficult to ask, as most young women today are working. Could I possibly take a month off sometime in the next six months? I told her I was pretty sure that I could and would get back to her about that. I was only a subway ride away, I told her, and if there was room, I would like to come back next weekend for the weekend. She said that would be delightful and we could meet again next Saturday. She shared more about what the aspirancy would include, and I left before Compline and headed for home.

I walked back to the subway a foot off the ground. I was murmuring to myself, "A cloistered nun…a cloistered nun?" I was elated and apprehensive at the same time, a very strange emotional state to be in! There were two Sisters of Charity on the subway car when I got on, and I thought about that…and Sr. Imelda Mary's Three P's…Prayer, Penance, and Peace. The sisters on the subway appeared to have all three, at least Prayer and Peace. One happened to glance at my book, and smiled at me, and I smiled back. I was reading *The Seven Storey Mountain* by Thomas Merton.

Greta was all ears to hear about my day, and was very reassuring that everything would work out well. She suggested I work weekends for a few times and then get others to cover for me for a week, and I had two weeks of vacation which could probably be taken earlier than scheduled, and "play sick for a week if you need to," spake Mrs. Phillips, the widow of a Lutheran minister.

Fr. Meriwether met with me during the week and was most pleased with how it had all went. "No impediments yet," he added, with a smile. There was, of course, my remaining school loans…it had taken years to pay. It was only then that Fr. Meriwether mentioned that there was a Catholic-run program which helped out men and women wanting to enter religious life, by absorbing a debt under $3,000, if everything else was in order.

The personal impediments for me would again be my family, but Papa had assured me that he would handle that. It continued to amaze me how accepting he was, almost as anxious as I was to get it all settled. I went over to their place for supper midweek. It had been almost a month, and the first time since Mama and Ruthie had been to Chicago to see Sally. Mama was like her publicist talking about how wonderful her apartment was, and the fancy restaurants she and her roommate, Bobbie, took them to, and shopping on Michigan Avenue, how lovely her wardrobe was, and on and on.

Ruthie wasn't as enthralled by it all, nor too impressed with Bobbie. She said that Bobbie didn't know who any of the theater people were, not even movie stars. The only thing Ruthie liked was that Bobbie was a cop and looked neat in her uniform. Mama couldn't understand why women would want to be cops, but the city paid her well.

Ruthie wanted to talk more about the school play she was rehearsing and what her costumes would be like, and would I come to opening night? I noticed a little of what Papa had spoken about regarding her flippancy towards our parents. She also told me all about Anthony Bevelaqua, her latest boyfriend whom she was hoping would be her senior prom date. She seemed to want to make it a point to tell me he was a Catholic, so I would like him…this was during supper, which obviously didn't help with Mama's indigestion. Papa had wine with the meal, which wasn't the usual practice during the week, but he was happy I was with them, so it was in my honor. I noticed Ruthie was drinking it a little too fast, or so it seemed, and got louder and more belligerent.

No news from David. Mama said perhaps he would drop in later, but I knew he wouldn't if he knew I was going to be there. Sally asked about me, according to Mama, but Sally never wrote or called, not even for my birthday or Christmas…well, you wouldn't expect a Christmas card, I know.

I told them about my trip to West Springfield with Barbara Parker, and that we saw Ezra there, and that he had inquired after them. Mama could only shake her head and say under her breath, but loud enough for me to hear, of course, "That poor boy, such a schlemiel." Mama did ask about my work and was happy to hear it was going well and said again how she hoped to go down to the New York Public Library and let me show her the place. She had been saying that for over three years. I knew it was her way of showing interest. Only when we were alone in the kitchen doing the dishes did she ask in her old familiar way, "So any love interests in your exciting life at the Library? Any romance novels?"

"No, Mama. I think I'll probably be the old maid of the family."

"Not on your life, Becky Feinstein," she teased, "you've got a very pretty face that men could die for, if you let them in a little." That was Mama's compliment and backhanded comment about my not-so-girlish figure.

Papa liked to read the evening paper and watch the news on TV at the same time. But he put the paper down when I joined him in the front parlor. I told him quietly that I had been to Brooklyn Heights for the day and started the ball rolling. They invited me to make an aspirancy for a month as soon as I could get the time off from work. I told him a little about the sisters who interviewed me, and he found that all very curious and businesslike. And I assured him it was also very spiritual…they never asked me at the Public Library how my prayer life was!

Curiously he asked about the regulations (his word) on seeing me; could the family come to visit, and could I ever come visit them? This cloistered thing had no exceptions? I didn't know what the regulations were, and told him I'd be seeing Sr. Imelda Mary again on Saturday and would ask her.

I was excited when Friday came, and I rushed home from work, threw some clothes in a bag, my few toiletries, a couple books and took off for Brooklyn; I'd be there for two nights till Sunday evening.

When I met with Sr. Imelda Mary on Saturday morning she went over their *horarium*—their schedule for the day, which I already knew fairly well from being there on retreat and attending all the hours of the Divine Office, including the Night Office. I asked her about the visiting rules and times, if ever, they the nuns could leave the enclosure. I was surprised to know that they never really left; they never had home visits or vacation days; they didn't even leave for their parents' or siblings' funerals. She mentioned this was beginning to be discussed in Chapter, as it was now being left up to individual monasteries. So far Brooklyn Heights held to the stricter observance. They would also go out if need be to the doctor and of course, to the hospital. The other exterior works—shopping, driving sisters, picking up guests at the airports—these were all done by the extern sisters. I thought about all that for about a minute and decided it was all just and right and that once I was inside I would never want to go out again. Wrapping one's mind around that, as they say today, was not really as easy as all that. It was near impossible to imagine that one would spend the rest of one's life in a single place. But it was all for the Lord; why else would one do something so.....bizarre?

Sr. Imelda Mary said the grille was often shocking to parents and people who had never seen one before. It was also difficult because they could not hug or kiss their daughter. Family could visit twice a year, except for the first year of novitiate, when one did not receive visitors. Correspondence was unrestricted, but all letters were mailed without being sealed, and both outgoing and incoming mail were read by the sub-prioress or prioress. There was no mail sent or received during Advent and Lent.

Sr. Imelda Mary was very kind and unrushed about everything. She said the vocation was not easy, nor was it common. It proved in the end to be rather laborious but peaceful, if one gave herself to the life. It was a life of sacrifice and the Cross, but when borne with love, it was a most precious gift. She also said that the Lord will always provide the graces we need, and that what brought us or drew us to the cloistered life would probably not be what keeps us here. And she smiled as if I understood what she meant, and, of course, I couldn't begin to comprehend all that, but pretended that I did—like they were my own sentiments.

She told me my interviews were very favorable, and they would like me to clear up my financial responsibilities, and to submit two letters of recommendation— one from my pastor, and another from someone of my own choosing (it could be another priest or spiritual director)—and along with these, a copy of my baptismal and confirmation certificates. She also kindly said that perhaps Lent would *not* be a good time to make an aspirancy inside, as the life was more austere and would not give a clear picture of the rest of the year, but I would be welcome at any time to spend a day or two in the guest quarters. It was only then that I learned they had an aspirant's room always set aside and in a different location from the regular guest rooms.

That was all on Saturday morning and a short time in the afternoon. The rest of the evening I had to myself. I had brought several books and my journal along but wound up sitting in the chapel the hour before Compline and for an hour after Compline. The Lord in the Blessed Sacrament took on a special beauty in the darkness and quiet of the night. There were moments when I felt myself being "absorbed," for lack of a better word, by the Lord's real presence.

I was grateful the nuns had Perpetual Adoration, and knew that it would always be my greatest joy. In His presence in the Sacred Host, all my worries and fears and projections about everything would dissolve and nothing mattered except that God be loved and adored. How wonderful this Sacrament. I loved to pray over and over the now familiar prayer:

> O Sacrament Most Holy, O Sacrament Divine,
> all praise and all thanksgiving, be every moment
> thine.

Feelings of unworthiness, and worse, fears of delusion and disapproval could be dissolved by gratitude...*all thanksgiving, be every moment thine.*

It was those quiet hours alone in the chapel which lingered in my memory during the week. I could close my eyes on a jammed subway car at 8:30 in the morning, with all the smells and human herding, and be at peace.

I was able to schedule twelve hours of overtime for the next several weeks, and worked for several people on my days off. I paid off a good piece of my remaining debt, and applied for an earlier vacation, which I got without a hitch. I was planning, tentatively, to make my aspirancy in the month of June. Fr. Meriwether and Fr. Norbert Georges, O.P., agreed to write letters for me. I had become a member of the Martin de Porres Guild, of which Fr. Georges was the director. He didn't know me as well as Fr. Meriwether, but I knew he was well known and respected by the nuns.

The only thing left was telling my family and friends. *O God, come to my assistance, O Lord, make haste to help me!*

Fifteen

PASSOVER 1970 CAME late; the first night wasn't till Tuesday, April 21st. Fortunately, Papa and I had talked several times since February. Unbeknownst to anyone in my family, including Mama, Papa paid off my school debt and only requested one thing: that I be present one last time with the family for Passover Seder on April 21st. He also suggested that I do my month at the monastery before then, so that by then I would know what my definitive plans were. He would tell Mama and Ruthie that I was off on a month's retreat, something those Catholics try to do every ten years, or something! He's so wise, my father!

Easter Sunday was March 29th. Sr. Imelda Mary and the powers that be agreed that I could enter to begin my month's aspirancy two days before Palm Sunday, on March 20th. Then I would have all of Holy Week and three weeks of the Easter Season. This also worked out perfectly fine at work, although my supervisor was not really happy with my missing a whole month—but what would it matter to me if I returned to enter for good? So I frankly didn't care what they thought at work. If I lost my job over this, I'd find another one. After all, this was New York and the Seventies!

And so it happened. I arrived mid-morning, having attended Mass at St. Vincent's with Greta. I took a cab to Brooklyn Heights as Greta insisted I do, giving me money for it. I tried to keep to what they told me to bring and what not to bring. I was allowed some personal books, a Bible, journals, quiet black shoes, work shoes, undergarments, two nightgowns, a bathrobe, a jacket, and some work clothes (I didn't quite know what that meant). They would provide a black jumper, white blouse, and a short modified veil that I would wear in choir and refectory.

Sr. Vincent and Sr. Grace Mary welcomed me and took me to the enclosure door, which is at the far left end of the entrance hallway when one comes into the monastery. There is no door knob on the extern side of the door. There was no ceremony, as I was only coming in as an aspirant, but nonetheless, I waited for five minutes, and then the door opened from the inside by Sr. Catherine Agnes, the Mistress of Postulants—and apparently the mistress of aspirants, too.

"Welcome, Rebecca, let us bless the Lord in His works."

And I knew my response was to be "Blessed be God now and forever." I was also to learn that when we entered into a room where we would speak to one of the nuns, we were to say, "*Laudetur Jesus Christus*" (Praised be Jesus Christ), and the other person would say, "*In aeternum*" (Forever and ever).

Sr. Catherine Agnes was always a bit stern looking, but had a heart of gold, I'm sure. I used to think to myself, "Tarnished gold, tarnished!" She walked very upright and close to the right hand wall, her hands hidden under her scapular, her eyes cast down and slightly ahead. We turned left and down a small corridor which led to the novitiate wing. Sister did not speak till we arrived at "our cell" (we were not to refer to anything as "mine"). I was near the middle, in a cell named Queen of Martyrs. All the cells had titles of Our Lady over the lintel. I hoped that it was not too significant that I be given Queen of Martyrs, but in many ways it is appropriate to the life, and certainly appropriate for Holy Week. It also made me think of Edith Stein, but I don't think they thought of that.

***

Pre-Holy Week Journal March 20, 1970
Queen of Hope Monastery Brooklyn Heights, New York

Sister has left me alone in "our cell" to unpack, to put on my jumper and blouse. I have done that, and am waiting for the next thing to happen, which, according to the schedule on my little desk, is Sext at 11:50 followed by the Particular Exam, the Angelus, and dinner.

Here I am nearly 25 years old, and I'm feeling like a schoolgirl on her first day. It's all a little surreal; a little bit spooky; a little exciting and nerve-wracking; but also a little romantic, in a spiritual sense.

Fr. Meriwether told me not to shun the spiritual romance when it comes, for it will also go and leave me cold and alone. I think I'm feeling some of that spiritual romance right now, like I'm on a date with the Lord, and we're at a place we've never been before, but which I've been wanting to come to, and now here I am, waiting for Him to arrive. I'm sure I will be less nervous once I go through everything at least one time, like where I'm to be in the choir and in the refectory.

"Our cell" is very small compared to my bedrooms, both at home and at Greta's. I shall miss my rocking chair this month. There is not even a chair in here except this wooden bench at this small desk, which only has one drawer in the middle. There is a wooden crucifix over my bed with a wooden carved corpus, all in a blonde kind of wood. There are two pictures on the wall: The Sacred Heart and the Immaculate Heart. They are over a small bookcase next to the desk, which is only waist high, with two shelves for books. There is no wardrobe or chest of drawers, but a plain niche-like closet without a door. It has five shelves, like square boxes stacked on top of each other; there's enough room to hang up my bathrobe and skirt and blouse. Next to this is a very small mirror, I would guess five by seven inches; I suppose that's so I'll get my little veil on straight. No way to tell if my slip is showing. The veil is not the most comfortable, with an elastic band which goes behind my ears; it's a bit tight on me, but I suppose I'll stretch it.

The regulation jumper is a little too big, but at least it's not too tight. The bed is low; way lower than my bed at home which I almost climb into compared to this, which I will go down onto. The thin mattress is on a wooden platform, and it is remarkably comfortable, at least to sit on. I'll see if I can write that tomorrow! There is a thin foam rubber pillow, which I'm sure did NOT come from Bloomingdale's.

Well, here I am, Lord. Be with me today and each day of this special month; reveal Your Holy Will to me so I may follow it; and keep me close to You when I am afraid. I thank you, Lord. I love you; do not forget me. Your Becky.

***

Sr. Catherine Agnes came for me at 11:30. We went first to the refectory, as it was closer than the church. She showed me my place, already set with a coffee mug, a tea towel, and a spoon and knife. The novices and postulants (and I) were at the far ends of an n-style table arrangement. In the center was an oblong table which served as a serving table. Off to the top left of the "n" near the head table was a raised platform with a table and chair and a microphone. This was the Reader's table. On the opposite side and above the head table was another table along the wall, which had bowls of fruit. I learned that after Lent that would also be the dessert table.

The refectory was quite bare. Behind the head table was a rather large crucifix, and on one wall near the entranceway was an icon of Our Lady. There was a shelf under the icon, which would be used for flowers…again, after Lent. There was a small red vigil candle burning there instead.

Following Sister along the right wall in the cloister, we came into the ante-choir, where there were several shelves of books. There was a large bulletin board with a table beneath it. The Mass schedule, intentions, and other liturgical notes were posted there, and several low cut boxes held sheets of music. There was also a row of large hooks, but there was nothing hanging on them. There were also three sturdy padded chairs for infirmed sisters.

We came into the choir from what I used to think of as the back of the choir. One would do a profound bow towards the tabernacle, which was outside the choir area on the other side of the large choir grille. Sister took me to my place in the front row of stalls. I would be next to Sr. Jude Mary, who was a novice and would serve as my choir angel; she would help me navigate through the books and show me the correct choir rubrics. I thought of them as choreography, but wouldn't call them that…yet. I was told to stay there in my place till Sext, which would begin in less than ten minutes.

Maybe that was when I surrendered, in those ten minutes waiting. There was just myself and Sr. Thomas Aquinas praying at the rosary stall before the Blessed Sacrament, and I looked up at the monstrance, and for a very short moment everything around me dissolved, and I was at peace. Before I knew it, sisters were moving into their stalls. Directly across from me was Joanne Meyers, whom I had met last year. I thought maybe she'd remember me and smile, but she never looked over at me.

***

March 20, 1970—Evening

Lord, it's over for the day, and I'm sitting here (as you know) in what looks like my grandmother's nightgown. It's so quiet, even the noise of the city outside is muted, only an occasional car horn is heard. Thank you, Lord, for this day. Vespers this evening was so awesome I could hardly sing. I had heard Vespers from the guests' chapel many times, but hearing it intoned from the inside is so much better. I don't know if writing in this is breaking Great Silence, but I couldn't go to bed without saying "thank you" —may I remember to always be so grateful, regardless of what happens each day, when I sing Magnificat anima mea. Bless my family, Greta, Gwendolyn, Ezra, Fr. Meriwether, and especially Papa. Such a blessing You gave me, Lord, in him…my Reuben sandwich.

***

Sr. Catherine Agnes told me not to get up for the Night Office because I was just learning things, and that I could sleep in till Lauds for a few nights. I didn't tell her that most nights I was still up when they were all going in for the Night Office. I must have dozed off for a couple hours, but I heard a light bell around 11:40, and was wide awake, so thought I would make a good impression and appear at the Night Office. I didn't need a week to adjust to this schedule; I could do it. Joanne Meyers probably needed at least a week to get used to breaking her sleep.

The Night Office was lovely, as I had remembered from my times on retreat here. So I was quite pleased with myself. I shuffled off to bed afterwards, but lay there wide awake for hours, and just dozed off, I think, as a nun knocked on my door and rang her schoolhouse-sounding bell: "*Benedicite,*" she exclaimed. I think I remembered to give the right response. It took a couple seconds to get my bearings. There wasn't much time to get dressed and over to choir; a little cold water on my blood-shot eyes and adjusting that elastic band veil made me almost run down the corridor to be there on time.

Afterwards, Sr. Catherine Agnes, made a sign for me to duck into the small periodical room on the first floor near the Chapter Room. I thought she was going to praise me for my diligence, or recommend a magazine, but instead she reprimanded me for disobeying her wishes. "I told you, Rebecca, not to go to the Night Office. I thought I made myself perfectly clear."

"Yes, Sister, you did, but I was…"

"I don't need to hear an excuse. You are to stay in your cell during the Night Office till Wednesday of Holy Week. And Rebecca, under no circumstances, are we to run or skip down the cloister. Do you understand me?"

"Of course, yes…" And she was off without hearing me out. I stood there alone, dazed. I could feel the tears welling up behind my eyes, and my lip began to quiver. *Get a hold of yourself, Becky Feinstein. Your intentions were good, and you really did misunderstand her. You thought it was a suggestion made in kindness, not a command made with authority.*

I was miserable the rest of the morning, until Mass. The sisters were singing the responsorial psalm in English after the first reading, which was from the prophet Ezekiel:

> I will make with them a covenant of peace…my dwelling shall be with them. I will be their God and they shall be my people.

And then we sang:

The Lord will guard us, like a shepherd guarding
his flock.

And I was at peace again, and actually thanked the Lord
for the little humiliation this morning, and for giving me
something to offer to Him. I was lost in my own thoughts
and don't remember a word that Fr. Antoninus said.

Fr. Antoninus Callen, O.P., was our chaplain. He had his
own quarters on the other side of the chapel, with a private entrance to both his rooms and to the sacristy. I didn't
know him at all. He was probably in his sixties or seventies
and walked with a slight limp. He gave a short homily every
morning, which was always a theological tidbit, as he called
it. Some of his tidbits were very chewable! I learned later on
that he had been a professor at the Angelicum in Rome. But
that first Mass inside, I didn't remember a word.

The day before, Sr. Catherine Agnes had shown me the
turn room, which was just off the enclosure door, close to
a corner of the cloister. It held the large turn, something
like a large built-in lazy susan, where the mail was delivered
from outside the cloister and picked up inside. Off to the
right of the turn were the community mail slots; each sister
had a cubbyhole, arranged alphabetically. Next to these was
a large cabinet with drawers, also giving each sister's name,
first names only. I didn't realize, of course (it was just my
first day), that nuns communicate with each other by leaving notes in the drawers or in an envelope in someone's mail
cubbyhole, and so one should get in the habit of checking
the drawer and mail slot regularly. Since I had just arrived,

and only a few people knew where I was, I didn't think a thing about the Turn Room or my personal drawer.

What I didn't know, because it wasn't on the printed schedule or horarium, was that the novices and postulants met each morning at nine o'clock sharp for the morning work assignments and any other announcements which needed to be made. I didn't know this because I didn't look in my mail drawer where Sr. Catherine Agnes had left a note telling me to go to the upstairs classroom/community room in the novitiate. At seven minutes past nine, a quiet rapping at my door, woke me up; I had fallen asleep on my bed, reading. The rapping at my chamber door was not from the raven (nevermore!)…but from Sr. Rosaria Mary, one of the novices. She had come to fetch me and take me to the community room. Sr. Catherine Agnes was sitting patiently at the head of the table.

"Rebecca, you would do well to check your mail drawer every morning before Mass. Had you done this, you would have known we meet here every morning except Sundays. Now, sit down, and don't be late again." "I'm sorry, Sister, I didn't look in my mail compartment this morning; I didn't think I'd have anything, I just arrived kinda." I tried to sound penitent and humorous, but hated myself for sounding so infantile. "Don't be insolent, child." The response came at me like an arrow shot from the bow of Sr. Catherine Agnes. I was struck dumb and sat down at the table in slow motion. The other novices were all staring at the table in front of them.

"Sisters, this is Rebecca Feinstein, our new aspirant who will be with us for a month. She will help Sr. Thomas Mary in the Laundry three times a week."

I didn't know a thing about laundry work, that was always my mother's job. But I was glad for it after a time. It was mindless work after you got the routine down, and the fresh linen smelled so wonderful. It lent itself to silence, which we were supposed to be practicing even when we worked.

I couldn't speak that first morning anyway. I was still in shock at the harshness with which I was treated. I was nearly 25 years old, and this nun was talking to me like a child, even calling me that, and had the audacity to say that I was *insolent*. She really spoiled any romantic fantasy I was hoping would sweep me off my feet till next month.

My laundry partner was Sr. Thomas Mary, who was actually a black veil novice and was in her second year of temporary vows. She still lived in the novitiate. Only once when we were close by each other folding sheets, did she quietly say, "Don't let Sr. Catherine Agnes get to you. She's a mean old croaker." And just the way she said it made me burst into laughter. Sister went on: "I think she's mean on purpose to test your humility and docility...she's really quite nice underneath all that." And she smiled, as she was still remembering the last sister who had been integrated into the professed quarters.

I thought about it all afternoon and in the quiet half hour before Vespers...*humility* and *docility*, not two of my predominant virtues! I thought at one moment to write Sr. Catherine Agnes a note expressing my dislike for being spoken to as a child, *and stick it in her mail drawer.* But I remembered Greta, who used to say we should have restraint of tongue and pen. "Sleep on everything before you write or speak." I didn't always get along with one of my supervisors at work who failed to acknowledge that there was a life outside the library. I practiced a lot of restraint in her regards, so Sr. Catherine Agnes was a restraint-piece-of-cake.

It wasn't till Tuesday that I was able to speak ever so briefly to Joanne Meyers. We were assigned to work together in the library, re-shelving books. The library was a bit of a mess, and didn't follow the Dewey Decimal System but some monastic or Dominican system which I had to learn. I made a mental note that when I'm professed they would have me redo the entire library system. Joanne remembered me from Thanksgiving. She seemed to be very happy and fitting in. She, too, smiled and told me not to fret over Catherine Agnes. "She hasn't liked me since the day I entered. But here I am; I'm glad you're here."

I told her I was glad she was here, too, and that she was the one who introduced me the expression "discerning a vocation."

"Well, I guess it worked!" And she turned into a library aisle with an arm full of books.

I had these two assurances not to get bent out of shape over Sr. Catherine Agnes. I didn't think of it as Joanne did, that she didn't like me. I wanted her to like me, of course, but I didn't really care if she didn't. She didn't even know me. It was more the disapproving tone in her voice when I did something wrong, and the way she'd talk to me like I was a dumb little girl just learning to walk in high heels or put on mascara, which I actually didn't do.

The month passed swiftly by, and I was less prone to mis-step as the weeks went by. Holy Week and Easter were so peaceful and beautiful till near the end, when we were over-whelmed with flowers, and work, and spring housecleaning. I liked the novices and postulants, and didn't really get to speak with the professed, but I could observe them in choir, the refectory, and in the cloister.

Once a week, Joanne and I would go with Sr. Cather-ine Agnes to the infirmary to visit with the sisters who were there permanently. I grew quite fond of an old Sr. Hyacinth, who was one of the oldest sisters. Her mind was still sharp at age 95, which she said was due to her studying languages, including Arabic and Mandarin Chinese. I could never figure when she had the time to do that. I liked visiting the elderly sisters; the Infirmary gives a different sense to "time." Time seemed to go by very quickly, in or outside the Infirmary.

That night I wrote in my journal:

April 14, 1970

I only have a week remaining and I shall have to come to a decision. I thought the decision would be easy, that I would sail in and sail out without any storms on the sea. I also realize, as I've always known but didn't give it much weight, that the decision-making is a two-way street. "They" will be making a decision, too, and I'm not sure how that will all go. I'm glad that the final word will not be up to Sr. Catherine Agnes, whom I think would be happy to see me out of here and back in Manhattan "tending to my books," as she once referred to my occupation. I had made a very helpful and constructive suggestion about their method of cataloguing their collection of the lives of the Saints. And Sr. Catherine Agnes almost flippantly snarled at me, "You can tend to your books however you want at your library, but here, you do it our way."

My reaction was to become silent and pout, like Ruthie would be when she was little and didn't get her way. If Sr. Catherine Agnes could read minds, I probably wouldn't be sitting here on this backbreaking little bench in this two-byfour of a cell writing this! At least it gave me something concrete to bring to confession. I'm no saint, that's for sure, but sometimes I just can't come up with some very good sins when we have to go to confession. (I once heard Fr. Meriwether say, with a glint in his eye, "There are no 'good sins,' Becky, they're all bad!")

So I confessed that "I had a terribly uncharitable thought about a sister who was flippant to me." Fr. Mel (the extraordinary confessor) asked me if I had forgiven her. I said, "I'm not really sure, Father, she's a pain in the neck and has made my time here very difficult. She talks to me like I'm a schoolgirl, and I'm a professional woman with a responsible job. Nothing I do satisfies her."

"But have you forgiven her?" he repeated. He wasn't being much help, I thought. I wanted him to sympathize with me. He probably knew to whom I was referring because probably everybody has something to say about her.

"Well?" Father broke my train of thought. "Well what?" I hope I didn't say it with too much of an edge in my voice. David used to tell me that I have an edge in my voice when someone doesn't agree with me. And I realized that David was right. I do get that edge. And in that little moment of grace, I was able to forgive Sr. Catherine Agnes. "Yes, I forgive her, or I want to be able to forgive her when she hurts my feelings."

All Fr. Mel said was "Good, and for your penance say three Our Fathers for her." And I did, wondering how many Our Fathers had filled this choir for Sr. Catherine Agnes.

On Monday (in two days) I'm to meet with the "Big Four," as I call them, and they will want to know, I presume, how the month has gone. I don't know if they will tell me to pack my bag and hit the road or what. The novices are very discreet about sharing their experiences. Only Sr. Joanne has been frank, and, I must say, encouraging. She told me that one girl about my age was told that she needed to mature in the faith a little more, and to come back in three years. That could very well be me. Mama would be happy; Papa might actually be disappointed; Greta would be sad and hopeful at the same time; Gwendolyn would be furious and be here in a New York minute to give old Catherine Agnes a piece of her mind.

But you, Rebecca Abigail Feinstein, how would you feel? I would be very disappointed, maybe even crushed. And I can't write about it anymore.

That was a sleepless night, as I recall, except that it showed me that I really wanted to come here, even if Mama would turn her face from me and think of me as one who had died—my photo next to Josh's on her dresser, lined in black. Even if Sr. Catherine Agnes thought I was the worst aspirant they ever had, I knew in that quiet place within me that it was the Lord that mattered, and that if He wanted me here, it would happen; maybe not this year, maybe not while Sr. Catherine Agnes was Postulant Mistress, but it would happen.

The meeting went well. They were all more relaxed, meaning less formal, and we reviewed the month with delight and even some laughs, except for YouKnow-Who; I don't think she cracked a smile. She also didn't bring up her litany of Rebecca-mishaps, which I was grateful for. Maybe three Our Fathers for her a day would help, I thought!

On Friday of that week I was called into the subprioress' office. She told me that all those charged with observing my month were well pleased, and on behalf of Mother John Dominic and the Council, I was invited to enter as a postulant. There it was—no fanfare, no long preface, just a poached egg plopped on my plate.

Ker-plunk!

They said that they would like me to enter on May 31st, the Feast of the Visitation. Sr. Imelda knew that only gave me a month to make arrangements. If all that was amenable to me, I should let Mother John Dominic know in writing as soon as possible.

She told me she knew that my month wasn't up till Sunday, but I was free to go now whenever I liked, and added,

"Oh, Rebecca, one of the nuns suggested that you might lose a few pounds and leave the Jean Naté at home."

Of course that little remark made me eat twice as many cookies that night after supper and be terribly selfconscious wondering who "one of the nuns" could possibly be. Besides, how can one lose weight on a high starch diet? I got through my first week thanks to white bread and peanut butter. But I'd try, eventually. I imagined St. Augustine (or maybe his mother) praying, *"Make me thin, Lord, but not just yet."*

I went from Sister's office directly to the choir, Jean Naté and all; only the Rosary Sister was in the choir—Sr. Regina Mary, close to 90 years old. She was nearly deaf and a bit stooped over, but she had the loveliest smile of all the sisters. I don't think she even heard me come in, although she probably could smell it was Sr. Jean Naté. I just knew it had to be Sr. Catherine Agnes; she always noticed how much peanut butter I ate, or I thought she did.

I went down on the floor, prostrate before our Divine Lord in the Most Blessed Sacrament, and through my tears and the huge lump in my throat, I thanked Him, and all I could think of was our Blessed Lady's words: *Behold the handmaid of the Lord, be it done unto me.*

I knew it was just the beginning, the tiniest second step, but my surrender was huge. It always is, Lord, isn't it? When we look back at things we sometimes think it wasn't such a big deal; but when we're in the middle of it, when it's really happening…it's a big deal. Following the Lord is a big deal.

That afternoon I called Greta at work to tell her my news and that I would be coming home on Saturday afternoon. She was delighted—so delighted that she wanted to come down to the monastery for morning Mass and meet me in the guest parlor when I was "released" and we'd have a big breakfast somewhere with lox and bagels and fresh brewed coffee, and then we'd take a cab home. It all sounded delicious to me!

I also managed to get Joanne alone in the library after supper and told her my news. She was so happy and said she'd be counting the days for my entrance. She then shared with me that her entering the novitiate was up for the vote and she was hoping that it could be on the Feast of the Sacred Heart and hoped that she would get that title with her new name. She wasn't too anxious about the vote, but, like me, was afraid that Sr. Catherine Agnes might put the kibosh on it.

The postulants and novices do everything together, so we would still be together and could fight the Old Battle Axe together, except that she would no longer be under her, but Sr. Mary of the Trinity, the Novice Mistress.

That evening I wrote my formal letter requesting to enter and said I would do so on May 31st...exactly two weeks before my 25th birthday. Blessed be God. Greta advised that I give only a week's notice at the Library, rather than not go back to work at all. The other librarians and library staff would want to throw a little farewell, and this was such an unusual reason. "It will shock them, but not really surprise them, especially after being away for a month in Brooklyn Heights and not the Riviera."

She said that Joe Waterman in the Archives would be especially disappointed, as he'd been building up the nerve to ask me out. I had had no idea, I told Greta. And she informed me, "Oh yes, he's been working at it for over a year."

"Over a year! No wonder he's an archivist. The present moment is too unreal, or too scary, or too something."

"Too soon." We had a good laugh over poor Joe. My heart was not broken; it wasn't even moved! But it made me wonder for a moment what I would have done had he actually asked me out, say, a year ago. All of that is silly speculation. I hadn't really placed myself in the dating mode without being self-conscious about it, although I did think about having children and being a mother, especially when you'd see them in the park or shopping together.

Gwendolyn, my dear godmother, was another story entirely. She only told me then that during my month away, she had made a novena to St. Thomas More that I would change my mind. But she was also delighted with my decision, and said she'd never pray to Sir Thomas More again, definitely the wrong saint if you wanted somebody to change their mind.

In the next breath she was telling me that since she was going to be the godmother of a cloistered nun, she would have to create and name a dessert after me. She thought maybe Abbey Apple Turnovers, till I told her Dominicans don't have abbeys. She'd think about it and make a batch of Whatevers for the monastery on the 31st. I told her to stay away from anything with a penguin in it!

One disappointment: Ezra's profession was moved to the Feast of the Sacred Heart in June, and I would not be there for it. He promised he would do all he could to get down to New York to see me before I entered. "We have to drink a bottle of champagne together and toast Our Lady and The Lord and all the saints, for bringing us to the Faith."

Then there was the Last Passover that I promised Papa I would be home for, and so I was. Two nights before, he called me and wanted to meet me for tea and dessert at Gwendolyn's. Tea on Thames had become Gwendolyn's Place for Papa. I was happy he was so comfortable with her. Apparently, he had become a regular teetotaler during my month away. He even called Gwendolyn "Gwen," and she called him "Ben."

Papa was very happy with my news, but had not yet broken it to Mama or Ruthie. He wanted me to know that he was 110 percent behind me, and prayed that he lived to see me a "full-fledged nun," as he put it. He knew it would take a few years. "But what's a few years when you're twenty-five and in love?"

Papa understood that, better than some of my Catholic friends, I think maybe better than Gwen did.

"Now, my little Catholic angel, I want you to listen to me and not say a thing till I'm through. Agreed?"

"What is it, Papa? Is something wrong?" "Agreed?"

"Of course, Papa," and my stomach dropped to the ground, wondering what he was going to say.

"Your mother loves you, you know that, and you should always remember that. She's also proud of you, but she'd never tell you that...she gets it on all sides from Sally and David and the blue-haired ladies in her Hadassah. They won't let it go that 'your Becky became a Catholic.' But my Hannah knows how I feel about you; she knows how I feel about all our children because I tell her—she's got to be strong, I tell her. Only your mother and David know what I'm going to tell you, and you must promise me that it will not change your plans one iota, agreed?"

I sat nearly paralyzed with fear at what he was going to say. I couldn't even get an "agreed" out of my mouth. I just nodded my head.

"I have inoperable pancreatic cancer. The doctors give me six months to a year. It could be sooner, according to your brother, the doctor...the great optimist." Papa smiled.

I couldn't smile or utter a word.

"I am at peace with God; you, of all my children, have taught me that. You are my child of God who makes me so proud."

Papa's voice cracked. We both took each other's hands and said nothing. We couldn't speak. Gwendolyn saw us and let us be—she even directed some new customers to the other side of the room. "Papa?" I looked over at Gwendolyn.

"Gwen knows. I told her while you were away. I told her I didn't want to tell you yet, that you should go, and not let this keep you from fulfilling your dream. You must go—promise me that."

I couldn't say a thing. I began to sob a little and struggled to get control of myself.

"Gwen convinced me I must tell you, that it would be worse if you learned once you were in the monastery."

Without saying a word, Gwendolyn came to the table with a porcelain white teapot and two clean white cups... all she said, in a whisper, was, "Pretend it's tea, my darlings."

She poured a half cup's worth in each cup, and we sipped some lovely brandy. It was our best medicine from our

British doctor, Gwendolyn. Finally, I managed to get my words together.

"Papa, I can wait for another year, and can even move back home to help Mama take care of you when the time comes. Let me do that for you, Papa? Please."

"Becky, Becky, I want to see you in your beautiful habit and to hear what name they will give you—I want my last months to be filled with that image of you in my mind. Your brother and sisters, or at least Sally, will blame you. Your mother will think you caused it or that God was punishing us by your converting to Christianity. Do not listen to them. You are my pride and joy. When my time comes, and I'm to bear the trial of it, it will be my greatest consolation that you are there in Brooklyn Heights, praying for me. David and your mother will handle the physical part; Sally will keep my mind alert with humor and news; Ruthie is in charge of music—my kind of music, and she will help your mother with food. You, my little angel, are in charge of prayer."

"I should be there too, to help take…"

"Stop, stop." Papa raised his hand. "Your Mama, she will be the nursemaid, God help me, but you should be pursuing your—what do you call it, your *vocation*. And do you know who agrees with me? David does—the agnostic doctor of the family understands that the dying patient needs to have his heart at peace. He told Mama right to her face, 'If Becky stays, Papa would be deprived of his finest dream for her. She should go.' Then it was your mother's turn: 'She should go? Go where? She's gone to the East Side of Manhattan, that's far enough.'"

Papa poured a little more of our special tea and took a big sip, cradling the cup in both hands, his eyes twinkling at me. "David didn't know that Mama didn't know what you were up to. So I told her there and then." Papa grinned, watching for my reaction. "I told her: 'Becky's going to enter the monastery in Brooklyn Heights. Hannah, she's going to be a nun.'"

After we both had another sip of brandy, Papa said, "You could have lit a cherry bomb on her head and it wouldn't have made her move. David moved his hand in front of her face: 'Earth to Mama; earth to Mama…come in, Mama.'

"'I'm going to die next, what's to live for after this?' Your Mama started her lament. 'My son killed in Vietnam, my daughter becomes a Catholic nun, my husband gets cancer. I'm going to die next.'"

Papa smiled, his face a little flushed, pinkish from the strong, sweet "tea." "So I took her in my arms…'You are not going to die, Hannah. Becky is doing a good thing…a *mitzvah*. She's obeying a call from God.'

"'Mitzvah, spitzvah—she's killing me.'"

Just the way Papa said it set me into a fit of laughter. The more I laughed, the more Papa kept it up—sounding just like Mama: "'All my life, all I want is for my Becky to marry a nice Jewish boy, but then she brings home Ezra, the Catholic monk, and now you tell me she's going to marry Jesus?'"

Gwendolyn, by this time, had joined us, bringing her own cup of "tea."

"'All I want are some little Feinsteins running around the apartment to spoil, and you tell me she's going to be a nun? Not even Christian grandchildren am I getting, you.'"

Gwen chimed in, sounding like Peggy Wood: "Climb every mountain…"

Papa joined in: "Ford every stream…" I joined: "Follow every rainbow…"

The whole tea shop was singing: "Till you find your dream." We all laughed and applauded. Only in New York! We started out with the saddest news in my life and ended up with a grand production number, all in a would-be English tea shop.

The night ended with my promise to Papa that I would enter as planned, and he promised that he would be there on my "wedding day." The rest was up to God.

And so it came to our last Passover. It was the first time in years, since my "great apostasy," that the entire family was together. Sally was here from Chicago, without her friend; David from his enclave near New York Hospital; Ruthie in her best Passover frock; and Rebecca, the black sheep.

Ruthie, being the youngest (but trying to look the oldest), asked the age-old ritual question: *Why is this night different from all other nights?* Papa, looking very patriarchal in his navy blue suit and tallis, wearing his Passover yarmulke, gave the ritual answer, reminding us that we keep this night to commemorate the passing over of our people from slavery in Egypt to the new land God would give them. And then he broke with tradition. "Tonight commemorates another Passover. We are here to bid our farewell to our beloved daughter and sister, Rebecca. As you are all very much aware, Becky passed over to Christianity five years ago; she was asked by us her family to leave our home, and she did. But she has never—never—(*he hit the table*) passed out of our hearts. She is still a Feinstein, the daughter of Hannah and Ruben Feinstein. On May 31st, our Rebecca will enter the Dominican cloistered monastery of Mary, Queen of Hope in Brooklyn Heights. She is going into a new land, like Moses and our ancestors, and she goes with my prayers and my blessing."

Papa picked up his wine glass and nodded that everyone do the same, and they did. "To Becky, *Mazel Tov!*"

To my utter surprise everyone, including Mama, David, Sally, and Ruthie toasted me and shouted back, "*Mazel Tov!*"

Almost on cue, Ruthie asked, "*Why do we eat bitter herbs?*" Papa spoke of the bitterness of slavery, and more poignantly, I think, he spoke of the bitterness of families divided by their personal bitterness, ambitions, and greed.

Sally sat mesmerized by Papa's erudition and eloquence, as did we all. Even David didn't show his usual impatience or disdain. Ruthie's eyes were as wide as saucers, I hope from Papa's eloquence and nothing else. And Mama—we caught each other's eyes, and I could see the tears rolling down her cheeks. Hannah of a Thousand Silver Hairs, looked tired and a little lost for words, but she also looked lovely in her blue dress. It was then that I realized that it was her anniversary dress which she wore that night to *Fiddler on the Roof,* when she was so happy to receive the gift from Joshua. I never saw her wear the brooch again until this night, different from all others.

"Our bitterness is changed to joy," Papa went on, "like *charoset* of honey and apples, to see my family around the table again. It may be my last Passover, as you know, and it is our Becky's last with her family. I thank you each for being here. My Hannah and I are happy to wish you each a Blessed Pasach—keep us always in your prayers. Drink with me: To life—to the Feinsteins—to God!"

Perhaps it was divine grace or Papa's prePassover promptings, but David and Sally, and Mama too, spoke to me and actually asked questions about the monastery and life "behind the walls," as Sally put it. I think she had read that dreadful book *The Awful Disclosures of Maria Monk*. It was enough to frighten anyone, and fueled the Catholic bashing agenda. Greta was very good at giving me an education in the library on this new genre. It was fascinating in that it seemed that the world hated Catholics *and* Jews.

I was happy my siblings asked questions, even if it was after five years! It was Ruthie, I thought, who made the most astute observation, albeit in a backhanded kind of way, when she said, "It's rather like having our own Edith Stein in the family."

Not quite, that's for sure, but maybe in my family's mind it was that bad. The brightest of the Feinstein girls and the doctor in the family didn't know who Edith Stein was. Sally pretended she had heard of her— something about the Holocaust…Mama didn't know but pretended she did. Ruthie had written a whole school paper on her which got her an A+, and Papa had read it word for word, as Papa would always do. I'm sure the "plus" came from his spelling and grammatical corrections.

Papa had a phobia against poor English grammar, which we kids seemed to inherit…or some aspect of the *word*. Sally wrote it as a journalist, David studied it and prescribed it as a doctor; Ruthie memorized it and acted it out as a would-be actor, Mama spread it and whispered it in typical Hadassah gossip, and I prayed it and believed it to be a Divine Word, a Divine Person who became man. To my family, my relationship with "words" was the most scandalous, but it has always been a study and love affair most fascinating to me.

David inadvertently confessed his ignorance, and Ruthie picked up the cue and expounded to us, especially David, who Edith Stein was, that she was a Jewess atheist who became Catholic and taught school for ten years with Dominican nuns before becoming a Carmelite nun and later died at Auschwitz for "her people." "That's us," Ruthie underlined, smiling at me.

It was Sally who asked, "Why didn't she become a Dominican like those teachers?" I wasn't really sure of the answer, except that the Dominicans she taught with were not cloistered, and it was the life of Teresa of Avila that had converted her, and she (St. Teresa) was a cloistered Carmelite.

Ruthie, after pondering all this over her wine glass asked, "Will we never be able to see you again, ever?" Mama caught her breath. The idea of cloister never really sunk in.

"Of course you will," it was Papa now. "The nuns can have visitors, especially their families. They meet in a very nice room called a parlor. I've been there; I've seen it."

Mama nearly swallowed her teeth with that revelation. "Ruben Feinstein!" exclaimed the Jewish mother of the house, "You set foot in such a place? Oy vey, what would Rabbi Liebermann think?"

"Rabbi Liebermann? Rabbi Liebermann should think about why his lovely wife is divorcing him and moving to Connecticut; Rabbi Liebermann should think why his son is three times in a rehab for drugs and the police are watching his other son. Rabbi Liebermann should set foot in the monastery and get a little hope in his life."

Mama rebounded: "I never heard of such a thing. My Ruben setting foot in a Catholic monastery!"

"I did, and I'm doing it again on May 31st, with or without you all."

"Oh, Papa, you don't have to do that." I could feel myself already getting choked up over the thought of it; I didn't know if I could handle it.

Almost as if reading my mind, Papa came back: "You can handle it, darling. It's the least I can do for you. Besides, it's all settled with Gwen and Greta."

"Gwen and Greta?" Sally and David chimed in unison. "I guess Rabbi Liebermann has nothing on you," chided David to poor Mama's embarrassment.

"Gwendolyn is Becky's godmother, and Greta is her roommate of the last five years, you ignoramus. You would know that if you spoke to your sister."

Papa calmed down in an instant while everyone silently refilled their wine glasses and broke matzo crackers into bite-sized pieces. "Gwen insists on a limo— her exact words were, 'If you're gonna do it, baby, do it in style.'"

We all laughed, thank God. Thank God for Gwen and the dessert she sent over—"Cloistered Crumb Cake" with English walnuts and dried apricots.

That was my last night with my family on West 79th Street. David left shortly after Cloistered Crumb Cake. Sally was staying in her old room, but went out into the night to wherever she goes. Ruthie promised she'd come and visit me, and could she bring her friends? Everything had become a Broadway production for Ruthie, who still had our Comedy/Tragedy masks on her bedroom wall and our theater money coffee tin.

Papa said he needed to go in and rest awhile, leaving me alone with Mama. She had changed out of her pretty blue dress into an old house dress and apron, her dishwashing clothes, the brooch safely put away near Josh's photo, I suppose.

She washed; I dried.

"Are you really upset that Papa will take me to the monastery, Mama? Maybe you could go with me, too."

"Oh no, I couldn't. I know how your father is— and he's getting very sentimental in his old age. He cries at the movies, can you believe it?"

"I think it's more than old age, Mama."

"I know. I know." She stopped washing and wiped her hands on her apron. I could tell she was gathering her words and breath together. She slowly walked over to the kitchen table and gestured for me to join her. She took two of the newly washed and dried wine glasses and pulled the chilled Mogen David out of the fridge. She poured two glasses almost to the rim. She smelled her glass for a few seconds, lost in her thoughts and in the sweet aroma. I noticed the lines in the face had gotten a little deeper and more spread out from her eyes. Still a very attractive woman, my Mama.

"Papa is dying and we can't do anything to change that. He will do what he will do. Me? I want you to know that I love you too; you are my dearest and only Becky who never gave me a silver hair till, well, you know when. But you are your father's daughter, and you will do what you will do. I know that Papa knows that, and you are his pride and joy." Mama's face seemed to relax a bit from whatever tension she had been wearing. She brushed back the loose locks of hair which kept falling over her eyes. She smiled her old familiar smile and looked into my eyes.

"This becoming a nun, oy, I can't even imagine. But Papa? He is so proud, go figure. So, my darling, I can't go to that place, but here, Becky," she was touching her heart, "here is the cloister you will always be in. Now go, sugar-plum, before I fall to pieces."

Mama and I squeezed each other tight and wept in each other's arms. She held my face in her hands and looked in my eyes and squeezed my cheeks like I was her eight-year-old kid.

"You be a damn good nun, you hear—such a blessing." And she pushed me by the shoulders towards the door and bent over the sink in her private tears. I grabbed my purse and jacket and looked down the hall where I took my first steps and played with my dolls and grew up in this family that I knew tonight, different from all other nights...I knew they loved me.

Sixteen

I STEPPED OUT ONTO West 79th Street and pulled my jacket on as I headed west to Broadway where I planned to get a crosstown bus but changed my mind and headed uptown on Broadway towards Tea on Thames. Looking in the window, I saw two familiar girls wiping down tables—I went in, and there were Gwendolyn and Greta. They said they were there to hold me up or sit me down, or get me drunk—whatever my soon-to-be cloistered heart desired. They figured I'd head there after the Farewell Discourse, and they were right.

Gwendolyn liked to shock Greta with outrageous proposals. Greta finally agreed to the limo, but reneged on the string quartet playing "Climb Every Mountain" by the enclosure door. Gwendolyn had it all planned out. The limo driver would pick her up first, with her two boxes of Cloistered Crumb Cookies, already proving to be a big hit at the café. (They were black and white dough with a nougat center covered in crumb cake with a sticky sweet syrup in the shape of a cross or a Star of David. "Very popular on the Upper West Side," she said). Then they would pick up Papa, and go crosstown to East 79th Street. I learned from them that Ruthie had wanted to go too, but Papa said not this time. I was happy she at least wanted to go.

***

May 31st. Our Lady's Visitation to Elizabeth. Greta and I went to Mass at St. Vincent's, and Fr. Meriwether brought us into the parlor of the priory afterwards. He had coffee and half a bundt cake waiting for us. He seemed very pleased, and both paternal and fraternal, which is hard to explain. He promised he would remain my spiritual director and would visit me bi-monthly, if not more often.

It was almost as difficult to say goodbye to him as to Papa. He was my other father in so many ways, and I wouldn't be doing what I was doing without his having been there for me. His blessing was a great gift (*such a blessing!*), and I remember kissing his hands afterwards, something I had never done before. The hands of a priest…and he was *my* priest. I asked Greta to stay with him for a while longer as I wanted to go back into the church for just a few moments by myself, and I would meet her out front.

I was only going to Brooklyn, but it was a heartache to say goodbye to my dear St. Vincent's Church. How could I ever say goodbye to it? Would I ever see the inside of these walls again? How mysteriously and wonderfully God's grace touches our lives, I thought, as I pushed the heavy doors from the vestibule into the church. The familiar smell of incense and candles brought it all back to me—that Saturday morning when I first stopped in here to light a candle for Gracie.

I went over to the Sacred Heart of Jesus, High Priest, and lit another candle, for me, I guess, and I said a quiet goodbye, but knew that it wasn't really goodbye because He was with me. And I knew the same Lord was waiting for me in the tabernacle and monstrance at the monastery. It made the leaving a little easier, but it was nonetheless sad, mixed with tearful gratitude. After one last glance at the statue of St. Vincent, still preaching, I hesitated, hoping maybe his bell would ring for me, but it didn't…thank goodness!

Greta and I got back to the apartment before the limo arrived. I had only one large suitcase and two boxes of books, and another bag with photos, and my Sacred Heart statue and Perpetual Help icon, not sure if I would be allowed to have them (I purposely didn't ask ahead of time, in case they said no). I also brought bedroom slippers and a six-month supply of Ipana, my favorite toothpaste.

Before we knew it we were zipping down FDR Drive, and our in-limo lingo was light and frivolous. Papa was exaggerating Ruthie's disappointment at not coming with us, making us all laugh. Dear Ruthie, I thought. I would be missing her graduation in three weeks, and her running off to Europe with four other girls for the summer before she started New York University of Dramatic Arts. I don't know how she got Mama to consent to her going to Europe with four girlfriends!

I would also be missing Br. Matthew's profession, and Reba Schooner's wedding (one of the librarians from work). The wedding was going to be at the Public Library Main Reading Room—how weird, but then, Reba was a bit strange. At least she chose the Reading Room, and not the stacks.

Greta was telling Papa and Gwendolyn about her as I watched the blocks of Lower Manhattan whiz by. *Thank you, Lord, for letting me be born and raised in this marvelous city where I came to know You and love You…*

The limo jerked to a stop in front of Mary Queen of Hope, the late morning sun painting the entire east wall of the extern chapel. The stone Gothic façade seemed to be absorbed in peace and quiet, even on the outside. I was pointing out to Papa the frieze of Our Lady of Hope over the entrance, when Sr. Mary Vincent came bursting out the door, as excited as if the Mayor or the Queen of England were arriving. Sr. Grace Mary followed suit, and the cookies and bags all seemed to disappear before we got ourselves inside.

"There's coffee in the guest dining room; Mother wants to meet with Mr. Feinstein in the Prioress's Parlor in five minutes, alone, and then at noon, after the bells for the Angelus have stopped ringing, Rebecca, dear, present yourself at the enclosure door and knock lightly three times, then kneel. Mother will open the door and welcome you, so best to say your goodbyes before." Sister grabbed Papa by the arm and off they went.

Greta, Gwendolyn, and I popped into the chapel to make a visit. Gwendolyn loved the guest chapel because it was small and cozy, like a "cozy" on a teapot. She looked especially cozy herself today in her flower print muumuu and yellow floppy hat. A rose color cotton jacket made it all modest; she sported brown Birkenstock sandals and a straw handbag, which had a vase of spring flowers embroidered on the side. No penguins, till we got to the guest dining room, and a little stuffed penguin with a happy face and yellow feet appeared out of her bag.

"You've got to smuggle Vicky in with you. She's always wanted to be a nun since her husband died."

Greta rose to the occasion and asked, "Dare I ask what Vicky's husband was named?"

"Albert." She spoke as if it were Vicky who was talking. "She's all yours, darlin', so you'll never forget me." Gwendolyn leaned over and gave me a huge hug and kissed the top of my head. "I can't say goodbye, so I'm running down to the Promenade. I'll be back at the limo after the bells stop." And she ran off, leaving me with Greta and Vicky.

Greta, being much more composed, suggested I stick Vicky in my jacket pocket and not *carry* her in, and said that penguins like to burrow under pillows. So I did. She also said she would stay behind when it came time and would take care of Papa. She also told me that she did not intend to rent out my room. *If it didn't all work out,* I had a room waiting for me. She hugged me too and said, "I shall remember you each day at Holy Mass."

"We shall remember each other there. You've been a dear, dear friend, and I've been so blessed to know you. Leaving you and our apartment is a real part of my *cost of discipleship.*" I had never seen Greta Phillips shed a tear till that moment.

It seemed that Papa was a long time alone with Mother John Dominic. He'd spoken to her longer than I had! But finally he came out, delighted with his talk. "Such a fine lady, such a holy woman—you are going to be so blessed, my little Raf."

I knew Papa would like her, and I was secretly grateful he didn't meet with "the other one." Papa saw that Greta and I had been crying, and he tried to make us laugh, God bless him! "Such a happy time to be so sad. You Catholics have no monopoly on that paradox, you know."

Greta added, "You can say that again."

"You Catholics have no monopoly on that paradox." And Papa giggled at his own Vaudeville joke, and Greta giggled. All three of us began to chuckle.

"Such beautiful candles you have in that chapel; your Mama said I should knock you on the head with one and throw you back into the limo." Imitating Mama's voice, he added, "It would be such a blessing." And we burst out laughing.

"You can say that again."

"It would be such a blessing." We roared; Greta was holding her side she was laughing so hard. And then the first bell rang. The Angelus. Greta kissed me quickly: "I love you"… and disappeared into the chapel.

Papa and I went to the enclosure door—my arm in his, and I hung on, and for the first time, didn't want to let go. The bells were ringing and would soon stop. Papa held me close and neither of us could speak. I felt his chest heaving in sobs…the bells stopped…Papa looked into my eyes, tears freely falling from his own.

"May the Lord bless you, my daughter, and keep you. May He make His face to shine upon you, and be gracious to you, and always give you His Peace. *Shalom*, Rebecca Feinstein." He kissed my forehead and moved away.

"I love you, Papa." "I love you, Raf."

I knocked three times and knelt down.

The door opened, and there was Mother John Dominic and all the sisters behind, holding lighted candles and smiling.

"Arise, my daughter, and welcome home." I walked through the door into their smiling faces and never looked back. My heart was full of joy, and there in candlelight, beaming a radiant smile, was Sr. Catherine Agnes, nodding her head in welcome.

The chantress intoned Psalm 121, the Pilgrim Psalm:

> I rejoiced when I heard them say, let us go to
>   God's House,
> and now our feet are standing within your gates,
>   O Jerusalem.

I was indeed home. Shalom.

***

Four months later, on the feast of St. Thérèse, something very special happened. She sent me a bouquet of roses that day in the form of many graces. Mother John Dominic called me and Sr. Catherine Agnes into her office that morning—together. That in itself is unusual; I was sure I had done something grievously klutzy, and Sr. Catherine Agnes was marching me into the principal's office—that's how it felt. But Mother was all smiles and embraced me when I entered. No principal ever did that!

"Sr. Rebecca, the Council met yesterday afternoon and we decided unanimously (Sr. Catherine Agnes smiled) that you are ready, if you so petition, to begin the novitiate. We are thinking of December 8th. You will have completed six months' postulancy, and while our normal time these days is nine months to a year, we do not want to hold you up (*She paused to let this sink in*). There is also, I'm sorry to say, another reason to consider. Your father, dear, has taken a turn in these last weeks. He is still able to move about with help, but the doctors, according to Gwendolyn, do not give him much time beyond the new year." Mother paused again to let me absorb this news little by little. She had crinkly eyes at times like these, and her smile was ever so gentle and reassuring.

"We know what a sacrifice it has been for him to have you enter here—a joy and a sacrifice, that mysterious paradox, to quote your father. He and I have spoken often since your entrance (*I didn't know that!*). And he accepts in such a faith-filled way that you are to be a Bride of Christ. He even uses those words."

"I know, Mother," I broke in, "he's been greatly influenced by *The Sound of Music*."

Mother crinkled. "Yes, I know, dear. He thinks I'm Peggy Wood in person and is afraid I'll ask you to leave to climb every mountain with some Captain von Trapp." We both laughed, except for old Sr. Catherine Agnes, who didn't get the allusion.

"He's quite endearing, as you no doubt know, and I know your dear mother does not share his joy at your 'nuptials,' shall we say? But we both want his remaining weeks and days to be full of hope." (I didn't know if *we* meant my mother and her, or she and I, and I didn't ask.) Mother shifted slightly in her chair and leaned forward towards me, like she was going to tell me a nunnery secret.

"As you know, the custom of wearing bridal gowns at the clothing ceremony has been discontinued since just before Vatican II. We haven't done it now for almost ten years. But Sr. Catherine Agnes has suggested that we might make an exception in your case since all your father can speak about is your *wedding day*. It's quite moving, I'd say, since he's not even of the Faith. So what do you think of that?"

I couldn't tell her my immediate reaction was one of shock that it was Sr. Catherine Agnes who came up with the idea. I think I looked at her with a softer emotion from that moment on. I collected my thoughts for a moment and then told Mother and Sr. Catherine Agnes that I was very touched by their consideration of my father, and it would bring great happiness both for him and for me.

Sr. Catherine Agnes actually smiled, and seemed very pleased with my approval of her idea. Who were these women, and what depths of soul lived hidden beneath that veil and wimple? I knew it was an experience of God's love for me in such a real and familial way.

As it turned out, Papa's condition became much worse in the next weeks. The doctors now did not think he would see Thanksgiving. It's difficult to explain what happens to one in the face of such a dooming future and a newly found sense of powerlessness in helping. This whole monastic structure and dynamic, I learned so early on, was held together by common agreement, much of it written down, following established precedents or establishing new policy or rule. I wanted to love my new life and to give myself to it fully. It killed me not to be at home with Papa, and yet I knew he wanted me to be right where I was and to be a part of it.

That awful disease was making it all impossible, and I didn't know what to do.

Mother John Dominic was not a woman to be outdone by the powers of death. Nor was she a nun to be blinded by observances which were meant to *transform* our lives, not *paralyze* them. She had authority to serve the needs of those under her charge, and she would do all she could to let the Sister experience life at its most poignant moments within the exigencies of our life. I say all that in retrospect of course. I only knew how devastated, confused, and powerless I was feeling at the time, only a beginner in the life here.

Mother contacted the Bishop immediately and requested a canonical dispensation for "time"—counting my previous visits, if necessary. And she got it. I was to receive the habit on All Saints' Day, November 1st. It was to be a quiet affair: my family and a few close friends. I told Mother that my family would not attend, to which she informed me, "Your father and Ruth will be here." She always seemed to know more than I did about things!

I invited the obvious friends: Gwendolyn, Greta, and Br. Matthew, who couldn't come. I also invited the Prices, including Gracie's brother, William. Fr. Meriwether would be here with our chaplain, Fr. Antoninus, and that was better than having the Bishop.

So that's how I got the hand-me-down 18 and a half wedding gown and pillbox veil. A platform was placed by the grille for my father's geri-chair. He was thin and very pale, but quite alert. He insisted on being dressed in a suit and tie—his old tuxedo was too big on him now. He was propped up on pillows and well attended by Gwendolyn and Ruthie.

The chapel was so beautiful that morning, with two dozen white roses by Our Lady's statue, a gift from the Price Family. I could see Papa and Ruthie by the grille. Ruthie gave a short excited wave when she saw me. It was her first time here, and she looked lovelier then I remembered. I think she had her hair done and was wearing mascara…the ex-European drama student from NYU.

I don't know if Papa had ever attended an entire Mass before—perhaps a wedding or funeral at one time or another—but he was most attentive, and only dozed off a little by the *Agnus Dei* (or so I'm told). To my great delight, Fr. Meriwether preached the sermon, which we're now calling the homily.

After the homily, I came forward to a chair set beside the grille and knelt before Mother John Dominic. It was Mother who gave me my new name, but Fr. Meriwether who announced to me and all present, that Rebecca Abigail Feinstein would be known in religion as Sr. Mary Baruch of the Advent Heart. I was surprised and pleased, and just a little disappointed.

After Mass, I met with Papa, Ruthie, Gwendolyn, Greta, and William Price in the large parlor. They were all thrilled to see me, as if it had been years! And I think they were even a little awestruck at seeing me in the Dominican habit, with its full sleeves and soft white veil over the coiffure that covered even my neck. Gwendolyn said I looked "holy, and ten years younger," and where could she get one in powder blue?

Ruthie was amazed by it all and had a thousand questions, and more than once said that "Mama should've seen this." She put a small box on the parlor turn, and said, "It's from Mama." It was a lace and linen handkerchief embroidered with tiny blue flowers and a Star of David. I recognized it immediately. It was Mama's from her wedding day. It was the best gift I ever received, next to Papa being there in his navy blue suit.

"Sister Mary Baruch Feinstein," Papa said, as if he were trying it on for size. "Baruch is a fine name for a Feinstein." He gave his old endearing giggle.

I remarked immediately, "*Ruben* would have pleased me more, but I'm happy because Mother John Dominic chose Baruch for me."

Ruthie got into the name game: "Does it have to be a man's name?" She was no doubt thinking of Sr. Vincent and Mother John Dominic.

"No, not at all, it can be either a man or a woman's name, as long as they are a saint or an Old Covenant holy man, or woman, like Ruth!" I thought that would please her. I could see her thinking ahead of me speaking…

"I would want to be Sr. Laurence," she announced.

"After St. Lawrence?" I was almost astounded at her hidden knowledge.

"No," Ruthie proclaimed, "after Sir Laurence Olivier."

Gwendolyn actually got in the last punch: "Well, that's better, my dear, than Lawrence Welk!"

Greta thought Ruthie's wanting to be named after Laurence Olivier was the funniest thing she'd heard in a long time, and she and Ruthie struck it off from then on. Ruthie

and Gwendolyn, of course, had been friends for years. But
Greta had actually read a biography of Laurence Olivier and
knew all about him.

Not to change the subject, which Ruthie was fond of
doing, she said, "I saw that handsome monk friend of yours
at Gwen's place."

"Ezra? Really? How is he?"

"I think he was with his girlfriend." Gwendolyn quickly
jumped in.

"That's not his girlfriend, silly. She's just a friend; she's a
friend of Becky's, I mean, Sr. Mary Baruch's too."

"Who could that be?" I was wracking my brain thinking
of the friends from Barnard whom Ezra would have known
too…

"You know, the woman from St. Vincent's who went to
Massachusetts with you."

"Oh, Barbara Parker, I didn't realize they had become
friends." I think I had just a twinge of jealousy, not because
I thought of Ezra—Br. Matthew—in a romantic way, but
because I was his friend who had tea at Tea on Thames with
him. It was where we had first met.

Poor Papa didn't have much of a chance to get a word in,
but he sat contented to listen to us and to kind of gaze at
me, in amazement. Our parlor visit wasn't very long, as the
Angelus was ringing and calling me to the refectory. I could
have had a couple hours in the afternoon, but Papa was
really tired. We touched fingers through the grille, and told
each other we loved each other. I told him to "kiss Mama for
me, and tell her I'll cherish her gift forever."

It was the last time I saw him.

***

Being a novice, I was now under Sr. Mary Trinity, the Mistress of Novices. I also got to see Joanne more, who was Sr. Anna Maria of the Sacred Heart. There were two others ahead of us, Sr. Thomas Mary, and Sr. Rosaria Mary. We made a lively little group; it didn't seem like I was a little schoolgirl anymore, more like a university sorority sister— just without drinking, smoking, boys, or hours on the phone! We were given more responsibility while still learning all the different ways we did things and the monastic vocabulary.

I suppose one learns an esoteric vocabulary in every profession. Just learning how to put on the cap, bandeau, and two veils, using only that silly postcard-sized mirror, often made for giggles when we'd arrive in choir for Lauds. More than a few times, my bandeau was down below my eyebrows, and if I sneezed I was afraid it would slip down and cover my eyes. One also got used to puncturing one's head with these huge straight pins—ours had white tips on them which helped, as they were not always straight or holding things together. One learned not to turn one's head too fast, lest you wound up staring at the side of that coiffure that we thought didn't turn with you. Our fifteen-decade rosaries in those days were all chain and beads, unlike our quieter ones now, made with linen cords and wooden beads. I don't know how I managed it, but I was forever getting mine tangled in knots or caught on something like door knobs and choir stall folding seats. Sr. Rosaria once caught hers in the seat and the chain broke and the beads went flying all over the floor. She uttered a little word of exasperation, and the

novices were all horrified, but the older sisters took it all in
stride without missing a beat in the psalm tone.

Poor Sister Rosaria was mortified and had to kneel out in
the refectory. We teased her for a while after the incident,
calling her Sr. Broken-Rosaria, but she didn't think it was
very funny. I guess it hurt her feelings. I was always extra
careful after that to make sure my scapular was wrapped
around my rosary whenever I sat down.

Our scapulars were to be spotless and folded and ironed
to make six "rectangular squares." How can you have rectangular squares? I learned early on it didn't help to question such things; just do it. Learning to iron my habit was a
major project for me to begin with. I hated to iron anything
because I had never really had to do it; my mother did it,
Greta did it, or I had it dry-cleaned and pressed. I prayed not
to be given that charge.

Of course, one has to learn how to eat all over again when
you're all in white and dreading a dribble of tomato sauce.
Sleeves were a special challenge, as was maneuvering on the
refectory bench with a full skirted tunic, an under-slip, a
scapular, and a rosary. Our refectory benches are just that,
benches, without any backs. Sr. Catherine Agnes was forever
giving us postulants a signal to "sit up straight." No resting
the old elbows on the table either, something I was grateful
Mama had formed us not to do in since childhood.

Being a novice, I was grateful not to be under the eye of
Sr. Catherine Agnes, whose full attention was now devoted
to intimidating two aspirants who arrived the week after my
clothing. They were to be here till after the new year. I don't
know how they managed that, but we weren't allowed to ask.

I became guardian angel to the second arrival, named Rosita. She was Puerto Rican and didn't speak English very well, although she had lived here in Brooklyn for four years. And I didn't know Spanish and was just getting to know how to pronounce Latin when sung—so Rosita was my challenge. It also meant Sr. Catherine Agnes had one eye on me...still.

Funny, isn't it! I got to like Scar (Sr. Anna Maria and my secret name for Sr. Catherine Agnes Russell)...it turned out that she really liked me and believed in my vocation, and so she had intentionally made it difficult. It turned out—years later—that I found her to be one of the funniest and kindest sisters in community.

Sr. Anna Maria had a terrible time being a guardian angel. Her aspirant was, according to Sr. Anna Maria, either dense, dumb, or plain belligerent. She didn't want help arranging her books in choir, but then Anna Maria got in trouble for all the confusion and distraction that caused, page-flopping, which raised Scar's blood pressure! Her name was Elsa, Elsa from Yonkers, who we decided (Sr. Anna Maria and I) was spoiled most of her life and used to doing things her way. One is not supposed to argue with your guardian angel; she is there to help you do it right and avoid the wrath of Scar. Not Elsa—her way was better, quicker, more practical, less trouble, what have you. "It's not practical," was her mantra.

Her breaking point came when Scar gave her a toothbrush and a pan of warm water and a can of Clorox to scrub the corners of the tiles in the refectory. A good old-fashioned rag-mop could've done it in five minutes; the toothbrush method, which also required one to be on hands and knees, took an hour! I'm sure there were other problems, but after the afternoon with the toothbrush, Elsa went elsewhere. Sr. Anna Maria was not disappointed and rejoiced to brush the tiles herself all afternoon.

My Rosita, on the other hand, was generous and hard-working, but also overly pious. She was given the chore to dust the choir stalls and dust mop the floors in choir. She would spend fifteen minutes dusting the Blessed Mother's statue like a Lady's Maid getting her mistress ready to go out for the evening. She would talk quietly in Spanish to Mary, who never blinked an eye. She loved dusting all the statues, which was not in her job description (just the stalls and the floors).

She was very sweet and sensitive, and cried easily, especially if Scar reprimanded her (she was supposed to dry mop the choir floor, not lie prostrate for ten minutes to say a decade of the Rosary!). Poor Rosita became stressed out over the choir books after several weeks, and one evening, in the middle of Vespers, she couldn't find the Common of Martyrs and threw the book on the floor and ran off to her cell.

That was the last time I saw Rosita. We never received any information about who, why, or when anyone was leaving. Their napkin and cup were gone from their place in the refectory and life went on. Anna Maria and I were both happy to be relieved of guardian angel duty for awhile.

There was also lots of laughter and simple joys at recreation. We recreated separately from the professed, but once a week or on big feasts we were invited to join the professed sisters, like for Mother's Feast Day. We went into pre-production casting for the MPP: Monastic Production Players.

It was great fun. Most of us, being New Yorkers, knew how to put on a show!

Four of the solemnly professed sisters had a barbershop quartet; they called themselves the Sister Mary Adelines and would sing popular barbershop songs, sometimes with new made-up lyrics. They were very clever, even wearing costumes, like brown derby hats and clip-on moustaches and striped jackets with arm garters. They were my favorite. I always hoped Ruthie would get to hear them, but they were very much "inside the actors' studio."

Correction! I would have to say they were my favorite *group*. My very favorite single performer was Sr. Gertrude of the Sacred Heart. She must've been in her fifties or early sixties—I could never guess their ages, and a novice would never ask. She was a tap dancer, and an actual old hoofer in her younger days. Before entering the monastery, her big dream had been to be in a show on Broadway; something like *Forty-Second Street*, with lots of tap dancing. She knew Tommy Tune, who visited her once in the parlor. She never made it to the lights of Broadway. As she puts it, "The Lord of the Dance asked for my dance card," and she's been dancing with Him ever since.

She told me that at the first recreation I went to with the professed after receiving the habit. I'll always remember her telling me, "Let Him lead, regardless of the beat, whether rhythm or blues."

So you can imagine my surprise and joy when Mother's Feast Day Show, the following June, premiered in the community room, and the novices were invited. The lights went off except for a single spot (we actually had a theater spotlight), and the tape began: "Give my regards to Broad-way"…and out came Sr. Gertrude in full habit, hiked up to her shins, wearing a top hat, gloves, and swinging a cane. She had on her own real tap shoes, hoofing it across the community floor.

The sisters all exploded into instant applause, which gave her all the extra energy she needed to keep going. Then, a small chorus of six sisters, also wearing top hats and carrying black canes with white tips, came in behind her singing:

> Give my regards to Mother; A Happy Feast Day
> from us all.
> Tell all the nuns above in Heaven, that we'll be
> there ere long.
> Whisper a prayer of yearning, to meet St. John
> and all the saints;
> Give our regards to Mother John Dom, and
> thank the Lord for all our sakes.

Hats off, arms extended…and Sr. Gert would "break." I think I held my breath that she would get through it, and she did. The grand audience, of course, went wild! Sr. Gertrude and the Backup Girls took their well-deserved bows.

I've been to more than a few Broadway shows, but never have I seen an audience so with it. There were (and still are) several beautiful singers among us, and they would always have a number or two prepared.

Sr. William Mary and Sr. Beatrice came out with hobo jackets on and sticks with a bundle on the end. Sr. William wore a sign: "Mother John Dominic," and Sr. Beatrice, a sign: "Sr. Beatrice, Bursar," (which she was) and they began to sing:

> We ain't got a barrel of money, maybe we're
> ragged and funny, but we'll travel along,
> singing our song, side by side.

They sang the whole song through, accompanied by Sr. Sarah at the piano. I was amazed how the lyrics fit the monastic life so perfectly—at least in my 13 months' experience of it.

Sr. Mary Bruna was our "poet laureate." She always had an original poem to recite, which over the years I came to appreciate, even if the meter was somewhat, shall we say, original.

Mother's Feast Day Show ended as it began, with Sr. Gertrude, who had had plenty of time now to catch her breath, soft-shoeing to "Me and my shadow, strolling down the Cloister Walk."

We ended with "Now Thank We All Our God," which everyone sang together, and Mother was given a bouquet of flowers and made a speech. Such a blessing, I thought, as Mama would've said, to have her as my first prioress. Papa knew that the day of my entrance. Such a blessing.

I needed that first Feast Day show more than Mother, I think. My first year as a novice was so happy and so sad. It was a joy each day, and many times a trial. It wasn't all Broadway lights, but more like the single light that is left on the stage in Broadway theaters when all the other lights are out, and the house is empty. I can remember lying on the low, hard bed in our cell at night, staring at the wall and

thinking my Comedy/Tragedy masks would fit very well on
that wall. How mysteriously the Lord's love is forged through
it all, without our knowing it, and even sometimes with our
resisting it. To believe I am loved by God…a haunting meditation that has been with me through all my years.

The joy of my wedding day, as Papa loved to refer to it,
was so full because I felt like I had really given myself to
Christ, whom I had learned to love beyond anything I ever
imagined. I knew more and more what St. Thérèse meant
when she said, "All is grace." I didn't do anything extraordinary to come to know the Lord except go to daily Mass, of
course, and receive Him every day in Holy Communion. I
loved reading the Mass readings in my new *St. Joseph's Daily
Missal.* Working at the library and having Greta to talk to
and share books with was so enriching too, but the Lord
filled me with a deep sense of His abiding presence. I wanted
everybody to know Him, and wondered at times, like St.
Thérèse did, whether I should maybe be a missionary or a
teacher. Those thoughts would come and go for some time,
even after entering, and especially at night, staring at the
wall. At least I knew that when I was going through a difficult time and I would think I should be in Africa or South
America, or teaching in a Catholic school in Manhattan,
of course, that it was my escape hatch from not accepting
something going on—almost always dealing with my own
willfulness.

When I accepted the situation, those thoughts kind of
disappeared and I wanted nothing more than to be a cloistered nun. I couldn't believe how good God was to call me
to such a unique and intimate hidden place with Him. If I

could have, I would have written St. Thérèse's words in huge block letters on the wall of our cell: **I WILL BE LOVE IN THE HEART OF MY MOTHER, THE CHURCH.** Of course, that would've gotten me the next subway to Manhattan, so I wrote them inside of me, in my quiet hidden place.

Thanksgiving was coming the third week after my clothing, and I was feeling not homesick, but left out. I could be terribly distracted thinking about Thanksgivings past, and the drama which ensued every year in Mama's kitchen. I was also left out on any news about Papa. We weren't permitted to receive phone calls or to make them without permission. The week after my receiving the habit, I asked Sr. Mary Trinity for permission to call my father just to see how he was doing—or at least to call Gwendolyn, whom I knew was keeping an eye on him for me. And Sister said, "No. It's not necessary. If anything happens you will be told."

That was one night when I had my whole itinerary planned for opening a mission school in the Congo…or Greenwich Village. This life was inhuman and infantile. I was twenty-six years old and had used my own phone in my room, by my bed, and at work, for years. And now I couldn't have permission to call someone! It was difficult after that to get in the swing of making table decorations for Thanksgiving. We novices spent our entire morning making turkeys out of apples, toothpicks, and colored construction paper.

But on Thanksgiving Day, the refectory was a glorious sight to behold! In the center of the room, on a table, was a huge wicker cornucopia spilling forth colored Indian corn, yams, and bumpy gourds which I had never seen in my life.

It was lovely and looked like it could've come from a window display at Bloomingdale's or Lord and Taylor.

The tables were covered with real linen tablecloths with matching napkins. Each table also had an autumn arrangement in wicker baskets, with dried flowers and autumn leaves and sprigs of wheat. Several real pressed autumn leaves surrounded the base of the wicker basket holders. And the final, eloquent touch— candles of various autumn colors.

Our apple-bodied turkeys stood at each sister's place, guarding her napkin and a yellow paper cup of Planters Mixed Cocktail Nuts, without the cocktails. We did have a small wine glass, and a sister came by serving a dry Chablis for those who wanted a glass. I missed my Mogen David!

We sang our grace to the melody of "Praise God From Whom All Blessings Flow." The decorations were an apt setting for the meal that followed: a truly all-American turkey dinner with stuffing, sweet potatoes, wild rice, and homemade bread.

The weekly reader read the gospel of the day, and then we dined in silence with the New York Philharmonic playing a medley of Americana, with full orchestrations over our refectory PA system. It was magnificent!

My lousy mood was easily dissipated in the luxury of such beauty and warmth. The elderly nuns seemed to appear almost youthful in the glow of candles and with "O Shenandoah" filling the room. Not talking is not a burden, even when we're feasting. One can wander off in one's memories of holidays in years past, and I wondered, "What's going at the Feinsteins' on West 79th Street, and who's there? Where are Greta and Gwendolyn today?" And my thoughts naturally turned to Papa, but not in a sad or homesick way. I wondered if he was wondering about me and trying to imagine what our Thanksgiving dinner was like, and did we watch the Macy's Parade and the football games (the answer to both of which was no).

We did have coffee and dessert in the community room, and were free to chat with each other. Sr. Grace Mary and I gabbed our heads off over pumpkin and mincemeat pies (a sliver of each, thank you very much). The downer of course was all the cleanup and dishes, of which there seemed to be twice as many as usual. The novices were allowed one phone call each in the afternoon, and I called home, of course. David answered and was pleasant enough and said Papa was not well. He was home, but resting in his room. They were arranging for nursing care. Mama was in the kitchen with Ruthie, and he called to them.

Mama sounded tired and sad, but said they missed me. Sally hadn't made it either (as if I were free to come for dinner if I so chose) and was going to Paris for Christmas with Bobbie. There was no special emotion in Mama's voice about that, and I didn't inquire more about it. Ruthie got on and made the most fuss that I wasn't there, and wanted to know if we had turkey and who cooked it? She seemed almost manic, but she was young and excitable and loving school. She had also baked her first pumpkin pie, and was sad I wasn't there to eat it.

I didn't get to talk to Papa, but Ruthie and Mama promised to give him my love. That night we had turkey soup and bread and cheese, and Sister read a Thanksgiving message from President Nixon.

'Twas a lovely day, as Gwendolyn would say. Compline is always very peaceful and perhaps my favorite hour of the Office, but that night it seemed even more peace-filled, and a quiet gratitude settled into my poor heart.

The next Sunday would be Christ the King, and then Advent would begin the following Sunday, and we wouldn't be able to write or receive any letters till Christmas. I was prepared for that emotionally, but I was still expecting that an exception would be made in my case, regarding my father. But it wasn't. I had to trust that the powers that be would let me know of any developments. All I could do was pray, and so I did. I dedicated my first Advent to praying for my father.

I knew St. Joseph was the patron of a happy death. I think Greta actually taught me that. I didn't really have a devotion to St. Joseph; I can say now that I had no devotion to St. Joseph at all. I decided to do a novena for Papa beginning on Christ the King. St. Joseph was Jesus' Jewish, albeit foster, papa. Realizing that warmed me to St. Joseph. A holy death...what does that mean? We have a lovely statue of St. Joseph in the choir and also in the cloister, in what is called St. Joseph's corner. At the base of the statue is carved: *Ite ad Joseph.* And so I did. Advent is my favorite season of the Liturgical

Year, maybe because in every Jewish heart there is a longing for the coming of the Messiah, but also it marks the transition from autumn to winter. There was a real chill in the air now, and it was dark at Vespers. Brooklyn Heights seemed to get quieter in Advent. It may also simply be because Mother John Dominic gave me the title *of the Advent Heart.*

This was certainly the Jewish heart, and the heart of every Christian watching for and yearning for the coming of Christ, and for me, it includes all human beings searching for God, however that manifests itself in each one's life. Of course, this magnanimous heart wasn't reflected on that first First Sunday of Advent…we have to give our hearts time to expand or shrivel up, get softer or harder.

I was still a toddler in the Faith. It would take a few sunrises and sunsets to realize that we wake up each morning with Advent Hearts before the day unfolds, and in a sense, we go to bed each night waiting for the Lord to come again tomorrow. The Advent Heart is Blessed Mary's Heart, as she carried the Incarnate Word within her and pondered on all that had happened to her. It was the Heart of Mary, Queen of Hope.

And in a unique way, the Jewish People are the Advent Heart awaiting the coming of the Messiah and the redemption of Israel. And is not all of life a waiting for the Lord to come at our Passover to Eternal Life? So I've always been grateful to Mother John Dominic for this title. And thus, my very first Advent in the monastery was filled with this kind of meditation and thoughts of Papa and how much my vocation was realized by him. He had an insight into it which many Christians never arrive at. He had an Advent Heart although he probably never said those words in reference to himself. I could do nothing for him now, but I placed him in the Immaculate Heart of Mary…*take him, dear Mother of God, as your own little Ruben.*

Seventeen

THE SECOND SUNDAY of Advent began with a light sprinkling of snow; one could see it falling in the light of the street lamp outside the dormitory windows when we rose for the Night Office. Papa always loved the snow, as I do, and delighted in its blanketing New York. It changes the pace of life and brings about its own peacefulness. My thoughts were laden with Papa all morning.

I suppose I wasn't surprised when Sr. Mary Trinity pulled me aside after Mass and told me that my sister Ruth was in the parlor. "Go to her," was all Sister said, and I knew. From the ante-choir to the parlor one passes St. Joseph's corner. I looked at him and smiled. I knew why Ruthie was here, and I was most grateful she came.

When I went into my side of the parlor, she was standing by the window and staring out. She turned when she heard the parlor door open. "Oh, Becky, it's Papa."

"I know," I said, and came close to the grille so our fingers could touch. "Thank you for coming down to tell me in person. How's Mama doing?"

"Mama wanted me to call you, and I said, 'No, I'll go down myself. Papa would want that…and I've been there before, I know where it is.'"

She went on, sitting down quietly in one of the wooden chairs near the grille. "He struggled all night, it seemed, but around 4:30 this morning the nurse came and woke up Mama and me. Mama held his hand for maybe ten minutes, and he opened his eyes quite wide like he saw something, and he smiled, and Mama swears she heard him say: 'Mama,' and he closed his eyes and died. It was so peaceful."

Ruthie could just about manage to get it all out. She looked miserable, I thought, her eyes were puffy and bloodshot.

"The funeral is tomorrow morning and then we'll be sitting Shiva. Sally is flying in this afternoon—can't you come out for one night? It would mean so much to Mama."

"I know it would," and I paused for a few moments lost in thought. "She would probably freak out if I walked in." And in our grief, we got the giggles. And I went on after a minute.

"Mother John Dominic is very fond of Papa; she moved my clothing day up, you know, so Papa could be here and see me…can you wait for a half hour more? I will go tell her about Papa."

I guess I had anticipated this moment so much with great emotion, that when it actually happened, I was filled with peace and a quiet grief. Ruthie didn't know that much about our life, and our observance of enclosure, or the chain of command. I went first to Sr. Mary Trinity and obtained permission to tell Mother that Papa had passed away. I wanted to tell her myself, not Sr. Mary Trinity.

Mother was in her office, and Sr. Mary Trinity went with me, having called Mother first on an intercom to see if she was free. Sister went to Mother's office door with me and knocked, but let me go in alone. Mother seemed to have known, perhaps she had given permission for me to see

Ruthie. She stood up immediately and came around her desk to embrace me.

"Papa passed away this morning," I blurted out quietly.

"Blessed be God; he is now out of his misery and suffering—and on this Second Sunday of Advent. Shall we pray for him?" And with that we turned to the crucifix on the wall on the side of Mother's desk, and prayed an Our Father, Hail Mary, and Glory be. *Eternal rest grant unto him, O Lord, and let perpetual light shine upon him.*

"We shall send flowers," Mother added after a silent pause. "Do you think that would be appropriate?"

I knew that was an opening. "Not really, Mother. Jews don't usually send flowers, but you could send me, Mother, just for a couple hours this afternoon."

I'll always remember Mother John Dominic's expression then. It was kindness, compassion, love, and firmness all wrapped into one. "No, Sister, that wouldn't be possible. We don't go out—even to our families' funerals."

Of course I knew that, but it never sank in as much as that December morning. "I know, Mother, and I accept that, but I told Ruthie that I would ask."

Mother's voice remained very soothing. "Give Ruthie our deepest condolences to take to your mother and family, and assure them of our prayers for your dear father, and for them."

"Thank you, Mother, I will." I turned to go. "Not 'Thank you,' Sister. '*Blessed be God.*'"

Ruthie didn't really understand and thought it was mean and unfeeling and a few other unkind adjectives I don't recall. But when she left, she promised she would visit, and would call Gwendolyn and Greta, as I requested. I went to the chapel directly from the parlor and silently wept for Papa and for our loss and felt for the first time like an orphan. It was the eighth day of my novena, and I thanked St. Joseph and Our Lady for his peaceful death. I'm convinced that his whispered "Mama" was not Hannah Feinstein or his mother, Sarah, but Our Lady. She came for him. And so her words again became my own: *Fiat*...my *amen* coming forth from an Advent Heart.

Only after living with a few prioresses can I see in retrospect how extraordinary Mother John Dominic was in being both observant and flexible. Love and compassion seemed to be the criteria she lived by, which were applicable when she would say "no" as well as "yes." And so I'm sure she bent the rules for me one more time on the Tuesday of the Third Week of Advent when Ruthie again came back. Perhaps Ruthie was smarter than I thought. She never called to ask if she could come to see me; she just showed up. And she knew the line of command, as she politely asked Sr. Vincent to ask Sr. Mary Trinity to ask Mother if she may see me in the parlor. She had also brought Mother and me an obituary of Papa's death, in case we didn't read the newspaper during Advent. She told me afterwards that she had rehearsed that line so it wouldn't come out sarcastically, and of course, Ruthie *was* an acting student at NYU.

Sr. Mary Trinity told me it was "highly irregular," but I could visit with my sister for ninety minutes that afternoon, and to explain to her that I wouldn't be able to have visitors till after Christmas. I also knew that Sr. Mary Trinity *meant* ninety minutes when she said ninety minutes, and

I wondered if monasteries in other countries were as strict about and keeping to time by the minute.

Ruthie looked a little disheveled; her eyes were bloodshot, but that could have been from the cold outside and the wind coming off the river. She told me all about who came to pay Shiva and who didn't.

She said Gwendolyn came looking like the Merry Widow, all decked out in black, with a black floppy hat and a black net veil over her face. "Mama had never met her, but knew who she was, and I think she secretly was enjoying the reaction and looks of those who didn't know who the lady in black was. It was so nice of her to come; I went by the tea shop yesterday to thank her and to tell her I was coming down to see you, and she said to ask you why you haven't responded to her letter and cards?"

I had to explain that I hadn't received the letter and cards yet. Ruthie thought it was all "most peculiar" and "weird," but then again Gwendolyn had a nativity set in the shop with a flock of penguins around the crib rather than sheep.

"Do they really have penguins in Israel? Or was that one of your miracles?" She asked again without a hint of sarcasm…I wondered if she had rehearsed that line too.

"No, that is a tradition peculiar to Gwendolyn." "Oh, quite!" Ruthie responded in her best British accent, giving us a sisterly giggle to warm things up. David and Sally had had many unkind things to say about my "incarceration" in "the nunnery," as they called it, thinking they were sounding very Shakespearean, I suppose.

"Did you tell them you would be visiting Sr. Ophelia in Brooklyn?" That was almost enough to set Ruthie off doing a soliloquy from *Hamlet*, but she refrained, choosing instead to feign a Swedish accent.

"Greta Phillips stopped off to pay her respects; Mama also got a card from 'Becky's Ezra,' which she thought was kind of him. His Aunt Sarah paid her respects, but guess who made the biggest guest appearance?" She didn't give me chance to guess. "Father Meriwether! He walked in all decked out in his black suit and priest's collar…looking like an older version of Spencer Tracy… (*Ruthie was off on a roll.*) Mama was impressed. 'Such friends, your Papa had! The Catholic priest can come to pay his respects and your sister won't?'"

I just let it go. Instead I just said, almost like thinking out loud, "Papa was respected by many people; he had a good heart and wanted to learn from each person. That's humility because most should have gone to Papa to learn!"

"I know." Ruthie got suddenly quiet and sad. "It won't be the same without him; I hate Chanukah this year."

"Oh, Ruthie, Papa would want you to light all the candles of the menorah and decorate our famous 'Chanukah Tree.' Eat plentifully and enjoy your little gifts. He's come into the Light now."

Ruthie stared at me. "I don't know what light you're talking about, but it's not on West 79th Street this year. Sometimes it all just seems so meaningless, strutting our time on this stage of life."

She was slipping into her own Shakespearean tragedy mode. But that's what grief and loss can do, especially without True Light which became a man and dwelt among us. I was thrilled to think that Fr. Meriwether went to pay Shiva and told him so when he came to visit me on the third day of Christmas.

It was Ruthie who announced to me that our time was nearly up, and she made herself ready to leave. She promised she would kiss Mama for me and thank Greta and Gwendolyn. I knew Gwendolyn was probably very sad; she had a great fondness for our father.

"She has a stuffed penguin in the window with a Santa hat on, and a sign: "Ruben the Penguin says 'Happy Holidays—stop in for tea.'"

I was so grateful Ruthie came to see me; no one else in my family said a word to me. It was only then that I broke down in front of her, trying to thank her, and she put her fingers over mine in the little metal squares of the grille.

"Papa loved you best, you know…" and she couldn't say any more.

"He loved each of us, Ruthie, to the fullest. You know that. You were his baby; he used to say that you were the best youngest in the whole family."

God let us cry together for the few minutes that remained. "I'm gonna get salt stains all over my new habit," I mumbled enough for Ruthie to chuckle.

"Merry Christmas, Becky," she said and turned quickly, grabbed her coat from the chair and fled through the door. I looked at the short obituary from *The New York Times*, which I later placed in my prayer book. I remembered Papa now every time we remembered the dead at Mass and especially in our daily prayers. I was able to somehow "let go," and found that I felt closer to Papa now than ever before

I was able to fall back into Advent and the silence of the sisters and that special peacefulness that fills the house at this time of year. I thought about the people hustling and bustling, doing Christmas shopping and attending office Christmas parties; the stores were all in full decoration now, the tree at Radio City lit behind Prometheus, and fancy ice skaters looping around the small rink in front of him. The grand lions in front of the New York Public Library had their large wreaths around their necks, and Gwendolyn had penguins with Santa hats decorating the shelves of Tea on Thames, and one named "Ruben" for my father. There was the luscious and comforting smell of English tea and sugar cookies. I missed them all, but I was content to be right where I was. It happens every Advent.

***

December 18, 1970

I'm having a hermit day, which is so wonderful and peaceful. I'm praying it will snow all morning; we had flurries early in the morning, before the sun came up, enough for the novices to get out and shovel the path from the cloister back door to the garage, and from the side door to the gate where milk and other things will be delivered.

We are certainly busy these days; I never realized how active the contemplative life can be! I'm being facetious, Lord, You know. It will be the Fourth Sunday of Advent in two days and we'll have the week with the Annunciation and Visitation gospels. The professed sisters have been making oranges with cloves stuck in them as part of the little gifts we get and give. We novices are doing Christmas decorations for the refectory, our own little tree in the novitiate, and then something in the choir and church. The poor sacristan, Sr. Sebastian Mary, has so much to do. We're helping with the cleaning, which has never been my forte. So I'm trying to remember to offer it up for Papa's repose. House cleaning! I rather liked the Greta Phillips approach to house cleaning: if you can pay someone else to do it, do it. We actually had an all-male team of apartment cleaners come in once a week and wash, vacuum, dust, and do floors, windows, and bathrooms—all in two and a half hours. There were four of them. My contribution was only $50.00, and well worth it.

Now I'm washing, vacuuming, dusting, waxing and polishing, and I ain't getting paid a nickel! Only joking, Lord. You know I love doing it for You. As a matter of fact, if it wasn't for You, I wouldn't be doing it at all!

We also have community chant practice every day this week, which I know is very important even if it can be so tedious at times. We're singing the Dominican Introit, Puer Natus Est, at Midnight Mass. I never realized how much goes into singing the chant well. I guess I took it all for granted at St. Vincent's and let the choir or the friars do it.

Sr. Mary Trinity keeps telling us to be silent and recollected during these days, and I'm trying to be, but my head is sometimes full of distractions, especially when we're supposed to be silent and do silent prayer or meditation, or, as one sister calls it, "mental prayer." Sr. Mary Trinity sometimes calls it contemplation, but I don't think I'm there yet. I'm distracted just thinking about what to call it. We have a quiet half hour from the end of Vespers till supper, and it's very peaceful in choir, so I stay there. When we were postulants, Sr. Catherine Agnes made us stay, but it formed a nice habit. I feel sorry for the sisters who have to go prepare the refectory and help in the kitchen. Others serve in the Refectory for the Infirm, which is really in the main refectory, but separated by a wall. There is a speaker in there so the infirm can hear the reading clearly. They also have meat served more often.

Just when I am beginning to get into the profound silence in the choir, the heat comes on, and clangs and bangs in stereophonics; or the sister behind me is sniffing every 20 seconds, and I find myself counting the seconds instead of meditating on the points given in my meditation book. It also used to get very warm in the choir the first week the heater came on, and I thought I'll never last the winter here; it's too hot. One should not be perspiring in choir in the middle of December. That got adjusted after a Chapter meeting which we in the novitiate did not attend. It's easier to stay awake now.

Sr. Mary Trinity wants us to meditate on the antiphons for Advent, especially the Magnificat Antiphon. We're to read it over several times in Latin, then translate it, then think about it. It's been difficult for me; I drift off thinking about Papa, about Ruthie's visits, about Mama and our Chanukah Tree, and what's going on outside these walls. The city is all dressed up for Christmas...and then, I start singing, silently of course, "City sidewalks, busy sidewalks, dressed in holiday style... It's Christmas time in the City." I can get a little homesick for New York even while living in it! The bell is ringing for Vespers...Advent Bells.

***

Thank goodness for my journal, as I would forget how that first Advent and Christmas was. I must say there is nothing so wonderful as Advent and Christmas in the monastery; they remain my favorite time of the year. I always loved Christmas, even as a nice Jewish girl who got to mix it in with Chanukah; I thought Chanukah was better because we got gifts every night for seven nights. But after becoming a Catholic, Advent and Christmas became the color of the City in a way a non-believer cannot experience. It's all because *Puer Natus Est*, isn't it?

One soon loses a certain sense of time here. The days seem to fly by so quickly, and the seasons of the year are really marked by the Church's feasts and liturgical seasons. We kept Advent almost to the end, and only decorated for Christmas two days before. There is a wonderful spirit in the house, so different from what one is used to in the world. Just celebrating Christmas was new for me in the world, but here one really prepares and celebrates in a deeper way.

Being the youngest novice in religion, although not chronologically, I was given the honor of carrying the baby Jesus to the communion window at the start of Midnight Mass and handing Him over to the priest celebrating the Mass, who places the Baby Jesus in the manger in the crèche set up in the sanctuary. I was hoping it would be Fr. Meriwether, but no such luck. The Midnight Mass was beautiful, and I was swept up in the quieting effect the chant has on the soul. We were also able to receive Holy Communion twice on the Solemnity of the Nativity.

Perhaps the loveliest time in the monastery in the whole year is the Octave of Christmas, from Christmas to the Solemnity of the Mother of God, which used to be called the Feast of the Circumcision. The Christmas antiphons are so wonderful for St. Stephen, St. John, and the Holy Innocents.

I almost forgot to mention, as it's changed now like many of the old customs, that on Christmas morning in the refectory there was a bright orange at each one's place, along with their Advent mail. We weren't to open them then and there, but to take them to our cells afterwards. My pile of letters and cards was much smaller than the other novices.

Many of my family and family's friends did not really want to acknowledge where I was or what I had become. I was amused to find a delightful Christmas card from Ruthie; it was a humorous card, as opposed to a religious one. I had several cards from Gwendolyn, a lovely card from Greta, and a Christmas note from Br. Matthew. And, bless her heart, a Chanukah card from Ezra's Aunt Sarah. She wrote very beautifully of my father's passing. Nothing from Mama,

David, or Sally, but then I wasn't expecting anything, nor was I able to send them cards.

I was happy for 1970 to end and for a new year to begin. I prayed only for the grace of perseverance. This way of life was certainly not of this world. I knew there would be other crosses to bear down the road, but I knew with Whom and for Whom I carried them, and that made all the difference in the world. How could I ever live with these same women in this same place for the rest of my life? It seemed like a most impossible scenario. I was able to speak that way with Fr. Meriwether, who came to visit me on the third day of Christmas. He looked rather tired, no doubt from the clerical workout the poor priests go through over the high holy days. But he was delighted to see me, and we spoke about Papa, and how he found my family when he went to the wake. We spoke of different parishioners I had been friends with at St. Vincent's, and the wonderful decorations that transform the interior of the church into a medieval-looking cathedral. There was a huge holly wreath with red berries on each of the pillars going up the center aisle. I think he said each wreath cost something like $300, but each was given by benefactors who wanted to do that every year. There were maybe a hundred poinsettias on the principal altar and side altars, and six real balsam evergreen trees banking the high altar and on the far end of the friars' choir stalls. The trees were flooded with tiny Italian white lights.

And then he told me that he had a Christmas gift for me, but I must promise him that it would be top secret between us. I could not tell anyone of my family or friends. I agreed immediately, dying of curiosity, but half dreading that he was going to tell me that he was being transferred to Pakistan or Peru or one of those square states west of the Mississippi. But it was none of the above; it wasn't about him at all.

And on the third day of Christmas I received the most wonderful gift I have ever received. He told me that he had received my father into the Faith privately, two months before he died. Papa specifically requested—more like demanded—that no one be told, and that only I could be told upon his passing. Fr. Meriwether told me that Papa had come to see him several times after I had entered. His mobility became worse and worse, and he knew he wouldn't be able to keep coming on his own. He had read the New Testament that he found in my room; he went through it several times. He came to believe that Jesus was indeed the Messiah and Savior, but he could not bring himself to embrace the Faith publicly; it would break Mama's heart. Fr. Meriwether told me that Papa would live with Mama as brother and sister, which they had been doing for a long time already, so there was no need to have his marriage blessed. He also told me that Papa was very moved by a private conversation he had had with Mother John Dominic, but would not share with him what the context of that was. To my great delight and utter shock, he told me that Mother John Dominic had been present at Papa's baptism and is in the registry as his only witness; she is, in effect, Papa's godmother.

I could feel the flood of tears rising behind my eyes and causing that painful knot in my throat. It had happened on the evening of the Solemnity of the Assumption. The church was locked, and nothing was going on in the Priory or the hall. Mother arrived by cab, alone. Papa, she, and

Fr. Meriwether met in the Priory and went into the church from the priory entrance, which leads directly to the baptistery. Fr. Meriwether had received delegation from the Cardinal to also administer the sacrament of confirmation, although Papa was not yet *in articulo mortis*. After the baptism they walked together up the right side aisle, and Papa lit a candle at the statue of Christ the Priest, the Sacred Heart statue which had melted my own heart the very first time I walked down that same aisle. Mother John Dominic and Papa sat in the friars' stalls in the Friars' Chapel, and Father celebrated Mass on the altar there, and Papa received his first Holy Communion.

And my gift, besides this wonderful revelation, was a photograph of Papa and Fr. Meriwether in front of the statue of Our Lady, the *Porta Caeli*, at the entrance to the sanctuary. Mother took the photo with Father's camera. She would not allow herself to be photographed, and Fr. Meriwether didn't press it. On the back, in Papa's own hand, was written, *To our dear daughter, from your two Fathers, with our Heavenly Mama. Shalom, my little angel. Pray for me.*

Eighteen

As I've ALREADY mentioned, it was almost natural for me to accept the Communion of Saints, ever since I made my way around St. Vincent's and met St. Thérèse of Lisieux on the crosstown bus. Perhaps every ethnic group has their own unique experience of family, and this would be universally experienced, even stretching into the animal kingdom with those who live in lairs, nests, prides, and packs. There is certainly a strong adherence to family in Judaism, and this is one of the tragedies of those who break with their families. The truly conservative Jewish families consider one as dead when they leave the family—or the family faith. This was the rift I caused in my family when I became a Christian: not that they denounced me as dead, but apostate and somehow lost. I know this isn't unique to Judaism, but it was one of the wounds of my heart, or as I learned early on from Greta and her Lutheran Pastor Bonhoeffer, the cost of discipleship.

In more recent times, it's not uncommon for a candidate to our life to come from a totally secular family where no religious practice was lived except the religion (so to speak) of Secular Humanism. And to become a Catholic and enter a cloistered monastery is really to be an apostate to the Secular religion, and secular, worldly families feel betrayed. So one way or another, most people today feel the separation from their families, and I suppose this has always been true.

Even the Apostles felt it. *What about us, Lord, who have left family, wife, children, and home to follow You?*

I remember the first time I learned about St. Thomas Aquinas's family, who kidnapped him from the Dominicans and held him prisoner in a family tower, like a 13th-century intervention. And how wonderful, really, when a family believes and are awestruck that their daughter and sister has the desire to give her life to the Lord in a consecrated way. I had my friends, of course, but no one in my family to be happy for me.

And so the extraordinary gift Fr. Meriwether gave me on the third day of Christmas became a soothing remedy to my wounded heart. Knowing that Papa gave his blessing to my decisions years ago saved me a lot of anguish, and may have even saved me in the faith. His acceptance and encouragement, and even pride in my becoming a nun, made it all possible. It could have unfolded as God's Providence unfolded anyway, but I'm forever grateful to God for giving me this grace. *It's all grace*, as St. Thérèse said, and Papa's embracing the Faith was such a grace for *me*, one that got me through the more difficult moments of my novitiate.

I had a sense of Papa's intercession and watching over me. It was a familial experience of the Communion of Saints, which I hope others also have. I never asked anyone, even Fr. Meriwether, whether praying to our deceased relatives and friends was included in the teaching of the Communion of Saints; I just did it.

I also never had a problem with the teaching on Purgatory. It, too, made great sense to me, as I intuitively knew that almost everyone would be in need of purification before possessing the fullness of the Beatific Vision of God. Even the Lord says so in Matthew's Beatitudes: *Blessed are the pure of heart, for they shall see God.* If we don't die with perfectly pure hearts (and who does, pray tell?) then God will purify our hearts in an experience of His Mercy and Love. Again, being Jewish gave me an ingrained sense of being kosher. Kosher is simply *clean* or *pure*, approved and blessed by the rabbis. Purgatory is just the Kosher Kitchen where we are purified before going into the Dining Room for the Eternal Banquet. Maybe that's a little too "cute," and I really don't like cute theology, but I remember Mama wiping our hands and faces with a dampened washcloth before we were allowed to even sit at the kitchen table and eat a sandwich. "Wash your hands" was a Jewish mantra I knew all too well.

Maybe our Kosher Kitchen also has our Heavenly Mama scrubbing the dirt off our faces and hands. I just hope she doesn't imitate my earthly Mama while sticking that wet washcloth in my ears and telling me that they are "so dirty you could grow potatoes in them."

So I decided I would pray for Papa's soul for 90 days, like a 90-day novena. I made up my own booklet of Catholic Kaddish which included the Psalms from Lauds and Vespers of the Office of the Dead, and I added the Litany of Our Lady and a Prayer to St. Joseph. I also included all my friends in Heaven who knew Papa, especially Josh and Gracie, and I invoked the intercession of St. Vincent Ferrer, St. Thérèse, and St. Dominic. I also asked St. Thérèse to send me a rose as a sign that Papa was now released from Purgatory and had entered into the glory of Heaven. I had never done that before but knew a woman named Margaret from St. Vincent's who had told me she did it all the time and that her bedroom wall was covered with paper roses she had received by way of cards. I didn't like putting conditions on the saints' intercession any more than putting a price on someone's prayers on earth. So it wasn't a solemn condition or even a firm conviction that St. Thérèse had time in her busy schedule to arrange for a special delivery rose, but I asked, and kind of forgot about it.

I think it was that time after Papa's death that instilled in me a devotion to all the Poor Souls which naturally became a part of my spiritual life. I love our Dominican devotion to the Poor Souls too, and am happy to know I will be prayed for by the Order after my death…I suspect I'll be in the Kosher Kitchen for a long time!

I was concerned, but not devastated, about how Mama was managing without Papa. It was just her and Ruthie at home now, and I suspect Ruthie was a handful and a half. Ruthie would visit me and caught on to the regulations in that regard. We do not receive any visitors, letters, or phone calls during Advent and Lent. Ruthie thought it was crazy and didn't apply to her, but she learned that first Lent after Papa's death, when she arrived and asked for me, and was told that I was fine and could not go to the parlor. When she saw me that first week after Easter, she was taken aback by the weight I had lost, something like 25 pounds. It was great because I wasn't even trying and wasn't on a diet like I would do every New Year's since I was twelve! I told her it was the monastic fast, and Lent, of course, but she thought they were starving me on purpose.

Ruthie herself didn't look so well, but she never blamed it on anything except hard work at school and putting up with Mama. She was also full of news about Broadway and the most recent movies, forgetting that I never went to either of them, nor did we get papers or magazines about them. She wanted to subscribe me to *Variety*, but I talked her out of it.

It got better as the years went by. I guess we always get used to things. Ruthie was really my only source of news about everyone else in the family, as Sally and David never visited me, nor Mama, of course. Mama had begun going to Boca Raton with three of her girl friends who were also widows. They were hoping to buy or rent a condo for the winter, and Mama was talking about giving up our apartment on West 79th Street. The building was going co-op, and Mama didn't want to buy our apartment; but as long as it remained rent-controlled she would keep it.

David was back in school and was going to be a psychiatrist. His Irish Catholic girlfriend had flown the coop, as Ruthie put it, and he was dating a Japanese woman who was a pediatrician. Ruthie didn't know what her religious affiliation was, and I wondered how David was dealing with all that. Was he ranting about Buddhism as he did Catholicism?

Sally was still in Chicago, while traveling a lot for the paper. She liked that, and would send postcards to Mama from her various trips. She had come for Thanksgiving the November after Papa's death, bringing a new roommate with her, who according to Ruthie, was very attractive, had short cropped hair, and wore pant suits. Her name was Charlene, but everyone called her Charley. Apparently she was a photographer, not with the *Chicago Tribune* but with her own studio off Rush Street. Ruthie said that Charley loved her face and wanted to photograph it, and that she had let her. She also said that Sally always asked about me and told Charley that I was the sister who ran off to a nunnery.

I also had regular visits from Gwendolyn and Greta, both of whom were always doing well. Greta had turned my room into a studio, guest room, and sewing room, but never sewed in it. She also had in "my room" now a treadmill and a small television. My rocker had moved to the master bedroom and still squeaked. How I missed that rocker! Gwendolyn missed me the most, she said, and Tea on Thames was not the same without me. Br. Mathew would always stop in when he was in town.

I was the third of the three novices making up the novitiate now, which also included postulants, and whenever an aspirant was visiting on the inside, she stayed in the novitiate. We had classes three days a week in the morning, and work every afternoon. I was the chief duster and floor-mopper for the choir and antechoir (Rosita's downfall). It was rather menial work and, I soon realized, not very big on drawing applause and affirmation. I don't think anyone noticed that I had dusted the choir stalls and swept the floor; sometimes *I* couldn't even tell that I had.

There was always a sister at the rosary stall, so I had to mop around her, which was not a good idea when Sr. Mary Mercy of God was that sister. She didn't like any disturbances while she was praying her Rosary, and would scowl at me when I got near her. Once she literally yelled at me, "Get out of here, Sister, I'm praying!" and I scurried off to do the ante-choir, hoping no one was in the exterior chapel and heard that. Sr. Mary Mercy of God never seemed very happy to me, not just when I disturbed her in choir, but all the time. Sr. Anna Maria and I used to call her Sr. Misery of God. She belonged to the Order of Sisters of Perpetual Frown.

We would make fun of her and make up silly stories about her like we were in junior high. I mentioned it once to Fr. Davidson, our confessor, who reprimanded me for being uncharitable, and then I was hurt and resentful towards Fr. Davidson, till I realized he was right. I never realized how our childish humor could be hurtful and really a sin against charity. I saw that making fun of people was a habit in me which I brought into the monastery with me. Ruthie and I were accomplished at it.

So then I just stopped dry mopping the choir when Sr. Mercy of God was in there praying and worried if that was a sin of disobedience because mopping the floor was my charge and I wanted to be the most obedient novice there was, or at least more obedient than Sr. Anna Maria and Sr. Rosaria Mary, the other two, older, novices. And Fr. Davidson told me that was a sin of pride. I was quite beside myself; the life of virtue was getting me all tied up in knots. The icing on the cake came when Sr. Mercy of God accused me in Chapter of Faults of not keeping the rosary stall dusted. I wanted to bop her over the head with the broom handle, but instead I got sarcastic and pouted for days whenever she was near me.

So the next time, I went in and dry mopped as noisily as one can with a dry mop, and shook out the mop head right behind her kneeling in the rosary stall, hoping the dust would make her sneeze. And I was struck then and there with the realization of how vindictive I could be and how lacking in charity. I went close to Sr. Mercy of God to tell her I was sorry, and I startled her; she jumped, and yelled, "*Don't touch me, you insolent little Jew!*"

I was shocked. I dropped the mop and ran out of the choir to my cell and cried. That was the first time anyone called me that. There was anti-Semitism right in my own house, and that's when I decided I didn't have a vocation, and that I would leave that night, maybe right away. Sr. Mercy of God would really feel sorry then that she made me lose my vocation. I started to collect my things in my cell to pack, and that's when I held the photo of Papa and Fr. Meriwether at St. Vincent's. And I think I cried out loud to Papa, "Oh Papa, what should I do?" And I knew what I should do. I should go to Mother and tell her everything. I knew that was the right thing although it was also not the proper way we did things. I should go to Sr. Trinity to ask permission to see Mother, and she might not give it to me. So I chucked monastic protocol and marched myself down to Mother's office and knocked on her door.

It was almost as if Mother was expecting me. She opened the door herself and invited me in; she had her usual calming smile, and that put me at ease. And she let me cry for a few minutes while she sat patiently behind her desk, fingering her beads. When I got hold of myself, I explained the whole situation and told her what Sr. Mercy of God had said. Mother John Dominic didn't seem shocked by the remark, but shared very quietly with me something of Sr. Mercy of God's background.

Her father, an immigrant from Poland, worked for a Jewish man in Manhattan who was in the diamond business.

Her father worked there for many years and was a rather trusted employee. Unbeknownst to anyone, except Sister's mother, her father had a rather progressive gambling problem, and he got himself into a great deal of debt. In a panic or out of desperation, her father "borrowed" a couple diamond watches worth about $10,000. When he was found out, he was both fired and wound up in prison. His poor mother blamed the Jewish jewelers. When the father was released on parole, he was broken and bitter, and his bitterness spilled over into prejudice. Prejudice is an awful thing, Mother explained, and can seep into a child's subconscious.

That certainly put things in a perspective, but it didn't help much. Mother went on to explain to me that Sr. Mercy of God was very sick. She had been carrying around a death sentence for over a year. She was given the option to undergo chemotherapy and all its miserable side effects, or to let nature take its course. The professed community only was aware of this, but "Sister is a bit of a gambler herself," Mother told me. "She chose to let nature take its course. She only has about six months to live, and while it weighs on her greatly, she has given all her free time to prayer. That is why she's in the choir so much. The doctor said that the cancer would affect her emotions and she might become erratic until it progresses beyond even that. She has cancer of the brain, Sister."

I was both stunned and mortified by my own behavior. Mother sat quietly and let it all sink in till she gently added, "You see, Sister, we never really know the whole story of what someone else is going through or why they act the way they do. I'm sure Sr. Mary Mercy feels terrible for what she said, if she even realizes it. Sometimes we just have to let things go, and forgive and, well," she paused, "show her a little mercy these last few months."

I thanked Mother for sharing all that with me and promised I would keep it a secret, which I did. As I was leaving, Mother asked me if I had gotten permission from Sr. Trinity to see her. When I said that I had not, she told me to inform Sr. Trinity of this and to ask for a penance. There was no need to explain why. I don't remember my exact words, but they were words to this effect: "Oh, Mother, I feel so wretched, like I can't do anything right. I feel so immature and childish, weeping over a Sister's sharp remark...I'm in my mid-twenties, and I'm acting like a fourth grader. Maybe this life isn't meant for me." There it was. I had lowered the boom.

Mother smiled and came out from behind her desk and put her arm around my shoulder. "My dear daughter, you are right where you are supposed to be. You have just begun on the monastic path and are learning that it is one of sacrifice and letting go of our self-willed egos. That's the spiritual battle we're engaged in, and it will bring many more tears than you have shed tonight, but God will give you the grace and the joy to balance the affliction. So pray tonight for the grace of perseverance for yourself and for Sr. Mary Mercy of God, okay? Pray for her every day, will you do that?"

"Yes, Mother, of course, I will."

Mother's final words to me nearly did me in: "Don't worry about crying, Sister, it gets us through, and God counts the tears of women." Those were once Papa's words to me. I knew Papa was still here with me, and it gave me courage that night to mentally unpack my bag and stay another day! And it also gave me the courage to fess up to Sr. Trinity, who gave me a kind penance…I had to dry mop the choir floor tomorrow at the same time.

"Yes, Sister." It was the monastic way!

A greater penance, which she didn't know of course, would have been to make me cook supper more than once a week. As it was, we novices each had to cook supper one night a week. At first I panicked at the prospect. I always believed only superiors should do the cooking, like mothers and older sisters, or buy it already cooked at the deli and have it delivered. I learned that one meal a week was relatively easy. We often only had cereal for supper or a simple soup with bread. That was my favorite when someone else was doing it: homemade soup, with homemade bread, and real peanut butter. I got pretty skilled at making oatmeal and tapioca pudding for supper.

As the year went on, we advanced in our skills, and added responsibilities were given. It was decided that the novices should spend an afternoon work period visiting the sisters in the infirmary. Our youth and energy would invigorate them, and their holiness and serenity would inspire us…or so it was thought. I think the infirmed sisters were just happy to have somebody else to gab to. I thought that for cloistered nuns, these girls loved to talk. And they loved to tell stories about their early years and when they were novices, letting us know how much more difficult it was to live the life then without all our modern conveniences. I guess Teflon and Velcro made a big impact on monastic life!

After a month or so of this, I was told by the Sister Infirmarian to go fetch Sr. Mary Mercy of God from the chapel
and wheel her back to the infirmary. I did this and was surprised that Sister didn't object or yell at me when I went to
get her. She was almost pleasant. I whispered to her, "Let's
go the long way around, and stop at the bulletin board."
She was delighted with this because it was being a little
ornery, and because she missed reading the board. The General Community Bulletin Board had letters, instructions,
changes in the horarium, and notes from Mother. Sr. Mercy
of God read them all out loud and made a few choice comments...the "old girl" was not totally transformed yet! But
this time, I was able to laugh at her comments, and the more
I would laugh, the more she would keep it up, till we were
both laughing. I think she probably forgot that I was the
insolent Jew who made lumpy non-kosher tapioca.

Other than food, prayer, and work, a lot of our mental
energy in the novitiate was aimed at making first profession.
The study of the history of the Order, the lives of Dominican
saints, and things like Latin, chant, and house customs are
all good, but the classes on the vows reminds one constantly
that that day is just a few months or weeks or days ahead!

I think a certain emphasis has changed over the years.
Years ago, which the senior Sisters would have gone through,
they saw the life as really beginning with the novitiate. The
postulancy was perhaps still a time of discernment on both
sides, but once you were clothed in the habit, you were
truly a member of the Order, and if you died during the
novitiate you would be buried in the monastic cemetery.
It evolved into thinking that the novitiate is still a time of

discernment. In some of our monasteries, the novitiate is two years, and there may even be an extension of temporary profession. Maybe this discernment emphasis changed over time because of the number of women who would make profession and then, when a crisis hits a few years later, up and leave.

***

I looked forward to profession and to receiving the black veil. It felt like you belonged even more. I was even looking forward to "integration" into the Professed side two or more years after first profession. First profession came rather quickly, given all I had been through my first year, and happily, all three of us became professed. One is also given more responsibility. First profession was done privately, within the enclosure, in the Chapter Room, witnessed only by the sisters.

I was sure first profession would promote me to the library, which I was looking forward to revamping, but the most that I got was re-shelving books about once every two weeks. Greta was still at the New York Public Library and advancing in her career. She was also very generous to us and always brought a bag or two of books for our library when she visited. Among them was a new edition and new English translation of St. Thérèse's *The Story of a Soul*. Greta knew of my friendship with the Little Flower ever since we met on the crosstown bus.

When we get new books, they are quickly catalogued and given cards and put on display in the reading room for about a week, and one can sign out a book for when the display ended. Some had a list of prospective readers, and others had none and probably spent their whole book-life on the shelf without ever having its back cracked or somebody to carry it around for weeks, looking inside it whenever there was a free ten minutes. I loved that most of the Dominican nuns loved books; we were a bookish clan, and the book in the refectory was often the best entertainment of the day.

I signed out *The Story of a Soul*, and thought it would be a wonderful way to prepare for St. Thérèse's feast day, October 1, which was coming up in a couple weeks. The change of season, especially from summer to fall, prompts one to settle in with a couple good books. It's like we're settling in for the winter.

I hadn't read St. Thérèse's autobiography in years, and this was the first time reading it as a nun myself. I loved every page! I had identified with her years ago because of her closeness to her father, but now we were really like blood sisters. I loved the stress on silence and the joy of enclosure which the Carmelites seemed to exude. I envied them the two hours of silent meditation and their devotion to "Holy Mother," St. Teresa of Avila. I began to wonder if maybe I didn't really have a Carmelite vocation. And this, of course, threw my Dominican life into a tailspin. I also didn't want to tell a soul *my* story, not even Sr. Anna Maria, and certainly not Sr. Trinity or Mother John Dominic.

I remember reading some years ago, *The Sign of Jonas* by Thomas Merton, his journal begun when he was preparing for solemn vows. He wrestled with the desire to be a Carthusian. We had an article read in the refectory about Mother Teresa of Calcutta, the foundress of the Missionaries of Charity, and how she began as a Sister of Loreto and then left and started her own congregation. Why, even Sr. Lucia of Fatima had begun as a Sister of St. Dorothy and then became a Carmelite. Maybe the Lord only wanted me to begin here as a Dominican in Brooklyn as a stepping stone to Carmel. Maybe I was supposed to be a modern Edith Stein (without Auschwitz, please). Or a modern Thérèse of Lisieux...Baruch of Brooklyn had a nice alliterative ring to it, like buying bagels at Baruch Brothers Bakery in Brooklyn. That became a distracting fantasy which took up all my meditation time one afternoon after Vespers, and I thought, I'd never have such distractions if I were a Carmelite. I would really have the time to pray and meditate and not have so many recreations and all the talking we do.

Mind you, I had never set foot in a Carmelite monastery in my life, but I thought I knew all about them. Their silence, prayer, enclosure, and strictness were all much more authentic than ours. After all, I thought, how many Dominican nuns have been beatified or canonized in the last hundred years? I couldn't think of one. Where was our Teresa of the Andes, Blessed Elizabeth of the Trinity, and Sr. Teresa Benedicta of the Cross? The Carmelite way must be holier and more religious. Maybe I should just ask for a transfer; we even had a Carmel right here in Brooklyn.

This debate went on within me for a few weeks, at different intensities. Every time I noticed how lax a particular sister was, or how I wasn't getting my way, like more time for reading and prayer, I thought I should be a Carmelite... all the nuns there are probably really much holier than here.

At the beginning of Lent, I decided to read *The Interior Castle* by St. Teresa of Avila for my Lenten reading, and without my knowing this at all, Mother John Dominic announced in Chapter that we would have a five-day workshop during Lent by Fr. Daniel Kitchens, O.P., on St. Teresa of Avila's *Interior Castle*. I couldn't believe my ears. I almost broke out into a sweat, which I hardly ever allowed myself to do, thanks to the intercession of Gracie Price. I thought this must be a sign from God.

I began fantasizing myself in the Carmelite habit, and receiving my new name, Sr. Elijah Thérèse of the Flame of Divine Love. The title was negotiable. I didn't really want to be Elijah Thérèse of the Cross because everyone who had that title seemed to be made to live up to it. I was a little too sophisticated and modern to suffer in that way. My way would be the way of love, the little way of St. Thérèse, without the T.B.

I was anticipating Fr. Kitchens' talks with every passing day. One of the older sisters mentioned that he was an expert in Carmelite spirituality and had a doctorate from the Teresianum in Rome. Wow. Maybe I would be able to go there to study and become a doctor of the Church; all of my intellectual gifts were being wasted here at Queen of Hope, where I had no hope of ever advancing, even in the library. They obviously were oblivious to my God-given talents. And, of course, Carmel would pick them up right away because…I wasn't sure why…maybe because they prayed more?

Finally the day came when Fr. Kitchens arrived. We would have two conferences a day, which would eliminate one of our recreations, which we didn't have every day anyway in

Lent. He was a rather rotund priest, I thought. Maybe that's what St. Thomas Aquinas looked like. He had long, naturally curly hair which kind of bounced when he walked or when he bounced into the room himself. The community room was converted into a classroom, and was set up with a large movable blackboard, and we all sat behind tables facing Fr. Kitchens, who, Sr. Anna Maria whispered to me, looked like he spent lots of time in the kitchen.

His conferences were wonderful, and he took us step by step into the seven mansions of the interior castle. I realized how much I love things being laid out in steps or a schema. I wished I had read St. Teresa of Avila in earnest sooner than now, and I was already exploring the library on other works by her and St. John of the Cross. Some of it I realized was really over my head, especially John of the Cross, but it gave me something to chew on.

Fr. Kitchens was also a Thomist, and his Carmelite spirituality was filtered through "the basic theology of our brother Thomas," as he would say. I knew that if I wanted to really plumb the spiritual writings of the mystics, I would need to know St. Thomas better too. And I almost laughed at myself when I realized that St. Teresa of Avila was leading me to study St. Thomas.

I got so wrapped up in the material Father gave that I forgot about actually being a Carmelite for a few days. And I'll always remember a passing remark Fr. Kitchens made—isn't it interesting how we sometimes get more out of a spontaneous comment then the prepared lecture! Fr. Kitchen casually mentioned that he would love to present these conferences at a certain Carmel, but they weren't given to study or outside conferences, especially non-Carmelites.

It was then that I glimpsed something of our Dominican charism which was always there, but which I must've taken for granted. It was the Dominican love for study and philosophy and theology, and having conferences, and reading noted theological periodicals, and even the books which we were reading in the refectory, and that I would not have this same opportunity or dynamism in the Carmelites. The pursuit of truth, which had always haunted me and made me somehow different from other girls, was a deeply ingrained gift that God had given me, and He knew better than I ever would what atmosphere and environment I should be in to seek Him in Truth. There it was represented all over the monastery in carved stone capitals or wooden shields: *Veritas.*

Study and reading would always hopefully be a part of my life. It didn't matter that I wasn't working in the library cataloguing books; it was more important that I read and ponder and pray using words.

I was amazed at how God knew exactly what to do with me—to plop me in the middle of a Dominican Monastery in Brooklyn Heights, New York, with sisters who also loved books and reading and conferences and study and discussion.

We all share a little in each other's spirituality, and there can be a Carmelite or Benedictine or Franciscan strand in our Dominican souls, because the Dominican soul encompasses the spirituality of the Church, and not only studies it and ponders it and prays it in the Rosary, but celebrates it in the Divine Office and especially in Holy Mass. I went to bed that night content to put my head on my Dominican pillow and rest my weary head...sometimes I *think* too much, but somehow that's very Dominican...and I felt at home.

Nineteen

INTEGRATION. I*T'S* A word which had political clout outside the walls of our small enclosure, especially in the Seventies. But for us inside the walls, it meant a nun would move from the novitiate, where she had lived her entire monastic life up till now—usually four years—to the Professed side of the house. This may not seem like a big deal to anyone on the outside; they'd probably view it as a job promotion or graduation, but for us it marked the beginning of the lifetime commitment to the monastery. One was getting close to solemn vows, and before that final surrender on the marble floor of the sanctuary before the altar of sacrifice, one was weaned from the nursery, as it were, and moved in with the grown ups.

The irony of it was that if you had been truly formed in the four years before, you would know it was just a beginning. The growing up was just beginning, but now one would belong to the community until death. So while it was exhilarating to arrive at integration, it was also a little frightening.

My integration day was the Solemnity of All Saints in November of 1973. That meant the date for solemn profession would probably be All Saints' the following year. Sr. Anna Maria had been integrated six months previously and would hopefully be making her solemn profession on the feast of the Visitation, next May. I missed her the most, as once you were integrated to the Professed side, your contact with the novices and the other temporarily professed was nearly nil. Anna Maria had been my partner in crime since before we entered. Over four years ago, when we were both on retreat at the monastery and had really just met, and Joanne Meyers introduced the concept of discerning a vocation, we raided the guest refrigerator freezer and ate two bowls of chocolate ice cream with chocolate syrup after the midnight office, alone in the guest dining room. I remember we were being super quiet, as any of the other guests or an extern sister might hear us. That, of course, added to the drama of it, which made us giggle over our ice cream, like teenage girls drinking a beer at a pajama party. Maybe that's why I felt especially close to Sr. Anna Maria, because we snuck into the kitchen and ate forbidden ice cream after the Night Office. The night before Sister was going to be integrated, meaning the last night she'd sleep in the novitiate, we made a pact to meet in the kitchen 20 minutes after the Night Office, which was extra long because of St. Dominic, and we'd have a farewell ice cream.

We were careful not to break open the special Rocky Road which had been donated by a kind benefactor who thought we never had ice cream. That would be served after dinner; we ate plain old vanilla with some caramel topping, and I told her about Ruthie and me discovering the "caramelites" at Horn's. I also told her about my Carmelite temptations my first year in temporary vows, and Sister started imitating Fr. Kitchens, and we got hysterical laughing, while trying to suppress any noise, of course. All we needed was for

Sr. Catherine Agnes or Sr. Mercy of God to stroll in for a glass of prune juice or something. But nobody came in and our little party went off without a hitch.

Now it was my integration, and I didn't have anyone to sneak ice cream with, but I was looking forward to being with Sr. Anna Maria again. Our other novice, Sr. Rosaria Mary, had been integrated over a year before and solemnly professed on September 8, so she was already an old timer, but I was looking forward to being with her again too. Sr. Rosaria almost didn't pass the scrutiny one goes through before each advancement. She was not the brightest light on the tree, but she had a way of endearing herself to everyone. She was rather clumsy and given to breaking things, which kept her from being assistant sacristan, I think, although her career in the kitchen was often shattering. One afternoon she was carrying a bowl of boiled white potatoes to the serving table. They were steaming hot, and she didn't have a potholder or dish towel, and let the bowl slip from her hands, and it came crashing down right next to old Sr. Regina Mary, who was sitting quietly with her eyes closed. Sister must've jumped a foot in the air out of her seat and let out a yelp, thinking a bomb had gone off in the refectory. The crash made Sr. Bertrand spill water all over her coiffure as she was quietly taking a vitamin pill before the meal began right when the bowl hit the floor.

Poor Sr. Rosaria was mortified as ever, and cried while picking up the pieces and cut her finger on the broken glass to add blood to the rolling potatoes. But afterwards, she gave no thought to herself, and went to apologize to Sr. Bertrand

and Sr. Regina Mary, who in her nineties thought the whole experience was a riot and couldn't stop laughing.

Sr. Rosaria wanted to learn to play the organ. She had had a couple years of piano, and so she could read notes, but couldn't sight-read if there were too many notes or too many chords; she also couldn't coordinate her feet and her hands. She practiced for weeks just to play the hymn and psalm tone for the little hours. She made her organ debut at Sext one Wednesday in Ordinary Time, as we were now calling the time after Pentecost.

Poor Sister broke out in a cold sweat sitting on the bench and got so nervous she couldn't get through the hymn without hitting dissonant chords which threw everyone off and made everyone nervous. Sr. Sophia, the regular organist, came to her rescue without any fuss and took over for the psalmody, but again, Sister was humiliated and couldn't look at anyone till Vespers. She kept at it though, for which I give credit to Sr. Trinity, who insisted she get back on the horse, or the organ bench in this case. She practiced the hymn so much she could play it with her eyes closed. The second attempt was a complete success, and we were restrained from applauding her in the choir, but she could tell from our faces how proud we all were that her fingers got through it without a mishap.

Sr. Rosaria was made assistant Infirmarian after she was integrated. She was not allowed to do anything with medications, but she was a great comfort to the infirmed sisters, and had a way of making them all smile. The Infirmary at the time had a hand puppet dog named Torch, and Sr. Rosaria became the personality of the pooch, visiting the old nuns and making them laugh and sometimes scream, when Torch would nibble at their hands or feet. She developed a marvelous baritone bark which Torch would emit whenever someone else came into the room and interrupted them.

Sr. Rosaria was also very prayerful and would sign up for the Night Guard in the hours following the Night Office when most of us were running back to our pillows and woolen blankets.

Coming up behind me were two white veil novices and a postulant. And there always seemed to be someone on retreat, observing us from the other side of the grille.

When All Saints' Day arrived, I was ready. I had been allowed to move things over to our new cell during the week before, but not the day before. So I only really had a small bag and a few books. Sr. Trinity accompanied me like a chaperone taking her charge to a sock hop, and to my surprise our cell door was decorated with a lovely picture of Our Lady with all the Dominican Saints under her mantle. Angels, flowers, and even candy were all on the door as well. A banner stretched across the lintels: *Welcome Sister & Mazel Tov*. I was almost moved to tears.

Sister seemed to disappear rather quickly, and I was left alone in our cell. I was flooded for the moment with a remembrance of when I was taken to our cell as a postulant, and how frightening and strange it all was. Here I was not frightened, and everything looked as usual, but there was a nice feeling of having grown up and become a full-fledged member of the community, as I hopefully would in another year. I went to bed that night feeling very content and grateful for my vocation, always marveling at how it all happened. I would have been happy to have taken my final vows that same night.

In the new year, 1974, on January 12th, we were to have an election for a new prioress. Mother John Dominic's terms were complete, and according to the new Constitution of the Nuns she was not eligible for a third term. I didn't realize how serious this all was till I was on the other side. There was no outward campaigning at all—that's much too pedestrian for this house— but there were rumblings and whispering going on. I was going to miss the opportunity to vote by ten and a half months, but I was beginning to realize how different life may be when we had to "integrate" a new prioress.

I was beginning to feel somewhat depressed or blue; it was getting more difficult each morning to get up, to go to chant practice, to do anything with the realization that Mother John Dominic would not be Mother anymore. My whole monastic life had been under her; she had gotten me through the roughest times and had even been a big part of my father's coming into the Faith. How could anyone take her place? I was secretly plotting that if Sr. So and So got elected, I would leave. I just couldn't abide by it. How could I ever promise obedience to someone I didn't like?

Some of the names floating around the laundry room were Sr. Mary Trinity, the Novice Mistress, whose thumb I was just getting out from under with integration. She was very strict on the rules and customs, and rather matter-of-fact. I didn't really appreciate her style in the beginning, but grew to see the wisdom in laying down the law. It did help me transcend my personal emotions and feelings at times and simply do what was being asked of me. I used to hate

that, I think, as I was used to getting my own way, or at least
to doing things a certain way. Some of that gets burned out
during postulancy, but it flares up again to a greater degree
when a novice and when simply professed. Sr. Trinity was
good on practicing what she preached, however, and I think
she taught more by example than in her classes. She would
be a strict prioress, probably, but faithful and dependable,
which are not bad qualities for a prioress. Greta was like
that, except with a little more human warmth mixed in.

Sr. Imelda Mary of St. Dominic was the sub-prioress, and
she had the experience of leading the prayers and taking care
of a lot of business details which Mother couldn't be both-
ered with. Sr. Imelda loved that kind of work. I think she
was happier with figures, papers, invoices, and sales orders
than with people. No doubt she would be an excellent
administrator, probably even more efficient than Mother
John Dominic. I didn't know Sr. Imelda much beyond her
subbing for Mother, which wasn't very often. She was often
late for the Office, if that meant anything.

Then, there was (are you ready?) Sr. Catherine Agnes of
Mercy. Lord have mercy on us. Scar. She was officially the
Mistress of Postulants and Vocation Directress, and in charge
of preparing sisters to lector, something brand new since the
renewal of the liturgy. Sr. Anna Maria whispered to me one
afternoon when we were folding white muslin sheets, "I'm
running scared it will be Scar."

And I'd say, "Don't be scared of Scar." But really, so was I,
but I'm not sure why. Maybe I always just felt that she didn't
like me, that she didn't really believe in my vocation and was

always watching me, or (as I thought in sisterly paranoia) she was out to get me.

My candidate would have been Sr. Mary Vincent, but externs can't be elected to an Office. Like Mother John Dominic, she had a heart of gold, loved the life, loved the Order, and genuinely loved the sisters. She was outgoing. I never noticed a swing in her mood, and never saw her get angry. There was a lot of depth to that woman, I used to think to myself when I was a laywoman on retreat. And I still believe that. Her hospitality was ideal for being outside to welcome guests and fuss over them a little and make them feel welcome. That's a little of what I believe the prioress's job is: to welcome sisters and make them feel at home in this community of women, and to be able to overlook the foibles of others, the elderly and younger sisters as well. What wonderful qualities for any prioress to have. Maybe it would be a complete surprise and be somebody we'd never expect, but I still didn't know if I could go on without Mother John Dominic at the helm. Sr. Anna Maria would not get to vote, but she was leaning towards Sr. Imelda Mary. This would be the first prioress election for Sr. Rosaria, Sr. Michael Marie, and Sr. Sophia of Divine Wisdom, but I couldn't squeeze anything out of them.

I was fretting a little too much over the whole thing one afternoon when Sr. Anna Maria and I went for a walk outside. It was winter in New York again, and I loved being outdoors. I would jokingly stand on my tippy toes, breathe deeply through my nose, and tell Anna Maria that I could smell the soft pretzels in Times Square. "If Scar becomes the prioress," I announced to her, "I'm moving back to Manhattan, the soft pretzel capital of the world."

"I think Philadelphia is the soft pretzel capital. Anyway, you shouldn't discern your vocation according to who's prioress," she officiously told me. She was really big into this discerning stuff. "Besides, we have a votive Mass of the Holy Spirit in the morning, following three days of praying to the Holy Spirit. So what if the Holy Spirit wants Scar to be prioress?"

"How could He? Why, I'd move back to Manhattan and become Jewish." And that would get her to laugh. I loved to get her to laugh. She was always so serious, it seemed. Maybe that was a side effect of discerning so much, but when she laughed her whole face and disposition changed. Her eyes got all crinkly and nearly closed, and she'd stomp her foot on the ground if it was something really funny. My becoming Jewish was usually a foot-stomper.

January 12th arrived. It was a snowy day, and I woke up feeling very anxious. The Bishop was here and would celebrate the Mass and then preside over the election. The non-voters were not even invited into the Chapter Room, but were asked to pray either in our cells or in the choir. I wanted to raid the refrigerator with Sr. Anna Maria and eat a gallon of ice-cream, but Sister didn't think it was a good idea…I guess she *discerned* that gluttony was not something to do while the future mother of the monastery was being decided. If and when there was a prioress elected, the bell would ring, and we would gather in the cloister and process into choir where she would be installed, and we would sing the *Te Deum*, and then process into the Chapter Room and renew our vow of obedience.

That morning I couldn't eat anything sweet for breakfast. I was sacrificing the cinnamon raisin Danishes and only had a hunk of whole wheat bread with peanut butter. I usually slathered it all with honey, but I sacrificed the honey too, and offered it up, hoping against hope that Mother John Dominic would be postulated for another term.

The election process began at 10:00 a.m., and veteran sisters were saying it would all be over by 11:00 at the latest. The clock in the ante-choir struck 11:30, and there was no sign of the new prioress. I was all prayed out by 11:00 and decided to just sit and be anxious. I'd throw in a *Memorare* every once in a while.

The professed sisters all processed into choir at 11:45, but no bell was rung. There had not been an election. They were to pray, eat, and go back to the Chapter Room at 1:00. No siesta today. Everyone looked rather grim, like the opening scene in *Oliver Twist*. I thought you could cut the tension with a butter knife, but Anna Maria used to say that was just my hyper-sensitivity. I never knew how in the world she discerned that absurd piece of pop psychology. I knew about these things. For one thing, I was Jewish, and we know when there's tension in the air, and besides, I went to Barnard during the late Sixties.

Poor Mother John Dominic looked tired and distressed. Maybe that was a good sign, I thought. Maybe they're nearing a hung election and will have to postulate her for another three years. *Please Lord, please, please, please.* I called on all the big guns in Heaven as well: St. Joseph, St. Thérèse,

St. Catherine, my father, Gracie, and Josh, whom I was sure was there and understood it all now.

At 1:45 p.m. I was awakened by the bell ringing. I was not in our cell, as I normally would have been, enjoying a siesta. I was sitting in my choir stall, my chin down to my waist, it seemed. My hand rosary was on the floor where I had dropped it, and for an instant I didn't know where I was or what was happening. I didn't know if it was 1:45 in the afternoon or 1:45 in the morning, as I would sometimes doze off during the Night Office and jump awake around 12:45!

I scurried out and into the cloister as the sisters came processing down from the Chapter Room. We would process together into the choir, and the new prioress would be "installed" in the prioress's stall. I was dying to see who it was. I saw Sr. Michael Marie looking at me, all smiles. I saw Mother John Dominic now in her place in religion with the other sisters, and I knew it wasn't her. There were several of the sisters clumped together around the bishop. One would be the new prioress, but I wouldn't know yet till we were in the choir. I think I felt a little perspiration in the back of my head. *"O Lord, don't let me sweat, and please, Lord, don't let me pass out."*

I watched with almost incredulous eyes as the new prioress was escorted to her stall, and the chantress intoned the *Te Deum*. It was a total, total surprise. I didn't know whether to laugh or to cry. It was Sr. Jane Mary of St. Dominic.

I didn't really know Mother Jane Mary of St. Dominic. She was very quiet; she never had anything to say at Chapter. Of course, in those days, most of the sisters had very little to say; they weren't used to sharing or expressing opinions.

Mother Jane Mary was the bursar, which is one of the biggest responsibilities in the whole monastery, but one which I didn't give much thought to or just took it for granted. She had a small office on the second floor without much of a view, I presume. I don't think I had ever actually been in her office.

I learned in the days ahead that Mother Jane Mary was sixty-two years old and had been born in Toronto, Canada. She was the middle child of nine children. She had been married to a French Canadian and lived for a time in Montreal where she had a baby, a son, named Jean-Pierre. When he was eight years old, he and his father had gone ice-fishing. It was the dead of winter, and they were both killed in an automobile accident involving a semi-truck.

Her name in the world was Adeline Garnier; that was her married name. I don't know what her maiden name was. Adeline had always been a devout child, and as tragic as the accident was, it was her faith which sustained her and to which she gave over her life. When she was in her mid-thirties she tried her vocation at the Dominican monastery in Quebec Province, but didn't persevere. She began working for a bank in Toronto, where she had returned, and after several years applied for a transfer within the same bank to New York City.

It was not long before she discovered she was surrounded by Dominican monasteries. When she entered here, she was in her forties, and entered as an extern, but changed her status to the cloistered nuns during temporary vows. Apparently she had hoped to receive Elizabeth Ann Seton as her name, she being a widow too. But she was named for St.

Dominic's mother, Jane of Aza, which also made her happy. She served for years in the vestment department and was in charge of maintenance after her solemn profession, and from there became bursar. Finally her financial expertise was paying off.

Well, it was certainly different having a new prioress. The life goes on as usual, of course, but each prioress and her council contribute their own flavor to the spirit of the house.

In my first interview with Mother Jane Mary, she seemed "cool as a cucumber," as Papa would say…cordial, interested, and more loquacious than I ever knew when she was *Sister* Jane Mary. What was hiding in there all these years? She certainly seemed to know more about me than I knew about her. And I'll always remember that first meeting because she asked me if I was happy.

"The Lord wants us to carry our cross, but that doesn't mean we should be miserable."

I agreed, like an expert in the spiritual life. And I assured her that I was very happy, or at least I thought I was. I had only been a Dominican for about three and a half years and I was already parsing over the meaning of our words. I knew St. Thomas says that "Happiness" is the end of all human life; I learned that years ago in Fr. Meriwether's parlor.

"Well, that's good, Sister," Mother quickly inserted, "I'm glad to hear that, because you don't always look very happy."

Boom. Mother didn't ease into lowering it, that's for sure. I was taken aback and didn't know what to say. "Uh…I did lose my father a couple years ago, and sometimes I get sad if I get thinking about him…or my mother and wondering how she's coping."

"Yes, I know," (sounding very motherly and comforting… trying to soften the "boom") "but one needs to let go of the mourning state and move on." She paused and scrutinized my face, like Anna Maria would do when discerning something major, like whether she should make lentil soup or split pea, something I could never discern very objectively, although I think I favored lentil. And I caught myself wandering off in my distraction. I hope Mother didn't catch it.

"You're coming up for solemn vows in less than a year, and we'll be watching to see if the life is…is making you happy." She looked down at a notepad opened on her desk. I wondered who the "we" were, but didn't dare ask.

"Thank you, Mother, and I'll be watching you, I mean, you—all of you—the community." Darn it, that slipped out before I could think. I just hope it didn't sound flippant. Papa used to point out my flippancy when I was nervous or anxious. I had to be on guard that it didn't spill over to cynicism, something I could easily fall into. I grew up in a cynical age. Even here we were being told to get in touch with our feelings, in the spirit of Vatican II, to "name them, claim them, and call them your own," as one lecturer told us.

I told Sr. Trinity that I didn't like some of my feelings and didn't want to make them my own; I wanted to get rid of them. She used to laugh at me and tell me to just keep praying. I knew she wasn't buying all the psychological jargon being thrown at us. But I wasn't too sure if Mother Jane Mary thought it was all hogwash too, or if she had bought into it all. It was good in many ways and respected the human element in us and our weaknesses, but it seemed to drive a lot

of religious right out the door. The Catholic papers were full
of stories now of priests and religious leaving.

"Now, Sister," her tone was becoming more officious,
and I could feel the forbidden moisture straining to break
out behind my neck. "I've decided to appoint you to the
Professed library. It needs some renovating, weeding, and
expansion. You've had library experience in the world, I
believe, so you're ideally suited to the task."

"Oh, thank you, Mother," I was truly elated. "I worked
for the…"

"Yes, yes, I know. Well, we're not they, and don't pretend
we are. We're a monastery, not the Library of Congress."

"Yes, Mother." Holding my tongue. Cynicism is not the
monopoly of novices and the simply professed, I see. I was
tempted to blurt out, "New York Public Library," but I held
back, and just smiled. I giggled just enough to make her
think I caught her humor.

"I love books." Now it was Mother's turn to laugh.

"Well, indeed you do, don't we all? It's a Dominican blessing or a curse."

"A blessing, Mother, it's a blessing to love books, and reading," I blurted out, sounding a bit school-girlish. Mother
peered over her horn-rimmed glasses at me:

"Yes, it's very Jewish."

Boom—a second boom. I didn't know what to say. I
didn't know what that meant. I just stared at her and smiled,
hoping that the tears I was feeling behind my eyes stayed
there. I didn't say anything. That was what they called good
old fashioned repression. Some of us were better at it than
others, and I was learning it was also an acquired ability

which was somehow linked to obedience, at least in the beginning, when obedience was either romantic or military. It flashed through my mind in a blink, that Mother John Dominic made obedience romantic and Mother Jane Mary was going to make it military, but I knew at the same time that it was neither one of these. Sometimes holding one's tongue is virtuous…the fruit of prudence. Be that as it may, I didn't think that loving books was intrinsically Jewish. Fr. Meriwether never said that, and he was big on words like intrinsic, efficacious, and substantial. So I just gave Mother a big Jewish smile.

She added, "Now, know you can always come to me if you're having problems." (*Ha*, I thought, *that's not an intrinsic possibility*.) "Try to do some outside work in the afternoons; I don't want you in the library all day, and I'll be naming you as one of the regular chantresses, along with Sr. Rosaria." (*Oh great, more chant practices!*)

I thought the interview was over. I hoped it was over before she went any further. "Thank you, Mother."

"Blessed be God, Sr. Baruch, blessed be God." "Sorry, Mother. Blessed be God." (*Blessed be God this interview is over.*)

"Do you have any questions for me, Sister?" Mother asked in a formally routine, but kind, way. No one here had ever asked me that before either. It's a new day, I thought to myself, not sure if I was happy or apprehensive about that. I'm supposed to be happy. I can ask questions, be a chantress, and re-work the library.

"No, Mother, Blessed be God."

"You may go, then, and wait till next week to begin anything in the library, after I've posted all the new charges. Oh, I almost forgot, you have an extra night to prepare supper, too, and you'll have the 3:00 a.m. Guard two nights a week. Blessed be God."

And that was that. I was "happy" about everything really, except the extra supper; I'd rather eat it than prepare it. I'd even rather wash up afterwards, but we all do that anyway. I'd never had the Guard at that odd hour either and wondered how I would manage my sleeping, but I knew the Lord would take care of it all.

I made my way to the choir, which had its own unique light flooding in through the windows at different times of the day. Mid-morning was one time I was not familiar with, and it was nice to kneel there. The only other nun in the choir was the sister keeping guard, Sr. Gertrude, and she may have been dozing off lightly. There was even a certain smell in the choir of candle wax and lingering incense.

I looked up at the monstrance, always there in such humility and silence, and a deep peace came over me which I hadn't had for weeks, ever since integration maybe. The Lord would indeed take care of me, and I was all His, regardless of where I was, who I was, or what I did. He had integrated me into His Sacred Heart, like a heart beat, and that's all that mattered. All thoughts and emotions, all fears and anxieties were suspended for a brief moment, and I knew I was being held by Jesus, My Beloved Bridegroom. That made me happy…it was intrinsic.

Dear Sr. Gertrude dropped her rosary, and the light clank was enough to wake her up, and it woke me up too; I wasn't exactly asleep, but I was resting, and when the dropped rosary woke me up, I wasn't sure for a second again, like on election day, where I was, and whether it was 9:30 in the morning or 9:30 at night, till I realized the sun was lapping in through the eastern side window and making the floor look shiny and clean in places. I loved that floor and my stall, the wooden hue of which almost matched the hardwood. I had dusted, cleaned, and polished them every day for six months.

I sat down and prepared my breviary for Sext and reviewed my little breviary collection of holy cards, reminding me of people to pray for. My most cherished card was the photo of Papa and Fr. Meriwether in St. Vincent's the day he was baptized, confirmed, and made his First Holy Communion. And I prayed for Mama and her secret ailments and ambitions, and prayed to Papa to coax Mama into coming to see me. It would be almost five years since I looked into her face and delighted in those azure eyes which didn't seem to dull with age.

And I thought of the wonderful flow in our life with the changes of prioresses and others, and those that come and go, and the charges that get moved around, and the rhythm of the liturgy and liturgical seasons which always seems so much more deliberate in the monastery. I looked around and got momentarily choked up, thinking this was home now, and I'm home and enclosed for the Lord. What a fantastic vocation. I had stopped trying to figure out "Why me, Lord?"

Ten years ago I thought that I was going to make a name for myself on the Broadway stage, or writing about it.

Rebecca Feinstein, Chief Critic for the *New York Times*, said this or that. People would trip over themselves to make sure I had the center orchestra seats reserved for VIPs, and there would be a table reserved for me at Sardi's. But here I sat in a nuns' chilly choir in a stone monastery in Brooklyn Heights, surrounded by fourteen acres of some of the most expensive property in Brooklyn, learning what it means to be vowed to obedience. It's such a profound and deep mystery which must reveal itself over the years in happy/sad, painful/joyful, exhilarating/confusing ways.

The clock struck 10:00, and I remembered that I was supposed to be helping out in the kitchen. I liked being a scullery maid, as I called myself; I liked doing those menial jobs, maybe because I never really did them in the world. It was like hands-on humility. I loved to make things smell clean. I missed the early days when I was a postulant and worked in the laundry folding room, when the sheets would come out of the dryer warm and smelling like Mama's linen closet. But I also liked the smell of books and the smell of a library after years of housing books on shelves. And I liked the quiet, unlike the silence anywhere else, different from the choir and the cloister. There's something awesome about being surrounded by books…Greta taught me that.

Quite recovered from my interview with the new prioress, I couldn't wait now to talk to Sr. Anna Maria to tell her about my new charge and to hear how her initial interview went. She was hoping, I know, to work in the altar breads department, although they were eliminating the actual baking and going to be the distributor for a non-monastic, factory-style, altar bread company. Sister would tell me, "Larger whole wheat hosts are the future." This was totally out of context to what we were kibitzing about.

She often did that; she could be looking right at you and her mind would be off somewhere else. She had been an administrative assistant before, involved in marketing, so she was always coming up with marketing schemes and ideas for "selling" the contemplative life. It was quite beyond me. How could you sell something intrinsically spiritual? Of course, my mind was probably one track too, on books. Come to think of it, Thomas Merton seemed to do a good job of selling the contemplative life, at least up until the Council. Now there seemed to be a "reverse trend," another expression of Sr. Anna Maria.

I wasn't sure how repackaging whole wheat hosts was going to solve the reversal, but Anna Maria was gung-ho. As it turned out, Mother gave her the laundry, full time. It was a big charge, including folding, ironing, and keeping the wardrobe up to date, which wasn't too taxing, given we wore the same outfit every day! Ruthie once called it my "thirteenth century couture."

Sr. Anna Maria became Laundress Extraordinaire, treating it like a big business, and was questioning her purchasing power and whether she was the supervisor of the elderly nuns charged with folding. She wasn't impressed with Mother's lack of interest or lack of insight into the efficiency of newer industrialized dryers. Sister said Mother was curt and officious and kept referring to her notes. We both agreed she wasn't the warm, intuitive, caring prioress we had known and loved in Mother John Dominic.

For being simply professed, we certainly thought we were experts on the life. And all the time we were both naïve and curious about the inner politics of the community, although they would never call it that.

The politics here revolved around how one interpreted the life, which was something relatively new, not the life, but the expressing of one's opinion. There were no political parties, of course, but an unwritten dividing people into progressives or traditionalists, or maybe even open or closed. Most of the nuns, I'd say, were traditionalists, and serious and solid in their religious beliefs or theology, and in living the life. But some were more permissive about the rules, of which there seemed to be one for every aspect of one's life. One doesn't just swing their arms and go skipping down the cloister, even if you feel like it. Maybe that's why our monastic theater productions are so much fun and exploding with hidden talent.

It was an interesting time to be living through…looking back at it all. There were lots of changes going on, both in the Church and in the Order. There were monasteries talking about doing away with the grilles. There were some active sisters, including Dominicans, who had modernized the habit and were talking with a new vocabulary. We'd hear it in articles which were read in the refectory. I can remember listening to an article on the renewal of religious life, and when it was finished, I had no idea what had been read. And sometimes we'd all get a great laugh over things, even things a bit shocking. What was the world coming to? The older sisters would shake their heads, and pass each other the Maalox.

Even Fr. Meriwether commented to me that there was an upheaval causing lots of turmoil and that lots of new things were being experimented with, especially in the Mass, which we now called the liturgy. For the most part it didn't seem to affect us as much, but we were hearing and reading about it. So it wasn't easy to be a prioress, we simply professed experts concluded when we'd talk about it all at recreation. Of course, maybe it never was easy, but it was certainly a challenging, exciting, and shaky time.

One day, Sr. Paula of the Cross wasn't in choir for Lauds, wasn't in the refectory, wasn't in the infirmary, *and* wasn't in her cell. She wasn't anywhere to be found. We learned later that she had left. She was dispensed of her vows, and went back to "the world." I felt sad that she had left, and sad that we didn't get a chance to say goodbye. I didn't know Sr. Paula very well—I didn't really know her at all—but I missed seeing her sitting in a folding chair in the east cloister every morning, reading; she'd always smile at me and wave, which wasn't really permitted, as it was still Grand Silence, but she'd wiggle her fingers at me anyway. I've often wondered whatever happened to her.

Only with some hindsight have I seen that Mother Jane Mary was just what we needed in the mid-Seventies. She was strict and unbending in ways that Mother John Dominic was not. I would say that, in "the spirit of the renewal" (a new catchphrase we were reading all the time) or the "spirit of Vatican II," those among us who were excited about all the changes didn't like Mother Jane Mary, and those who were leery of change and even a little scared of any change didn't like her either. And she bore it all quite bravely. As she once told me, many years later, she learned that she really didn't have any friends and that that was a luxury a prioress didn't have. That can make for a very lonely life.

Mother was more cautious than Mother John Dominic, and that was good, I think. Who could have ever imagined the changes we sailed through! Mother John Dominic was a wonderful prioress, and when her terms were up—and she had several—she was a wonderful sister in community. She would become my exemplar for relating to power and authority. She was Mother Jane Mary's most faithful and obedient sister. Only many years later did I come to learn that she disagreed with much of what Mother Jane Mary did and believed, but never spoke an uncharitable word against her, at least not to me or around me. I don't know how Mother John Dominic was among her own cronies, if she had any.

So life went along very nicely from my corner of the cloister. I was happy with the new prioress mainly, I think, because I was happy with my new charge, Librarian Extraordinaire! I didn't think there would be a conflict with my making solemn profession. That beautiful winter night in Brooklyn's haven of peace, I didn't know what lay ahead...as we traveled along, singing our song, side by side.

Twenty

SOMETHING HAPPENED THAT spring, which was a really big first for our monastery. Sr. Trinity's brother was ordained a priest for the Archdiocese of New York, and Sister and a companion were permitted to go to the ordination at St. Patrick's Cathedral. That was really quite extraordinary! Her brother, Fr. Jablonski, came to the monastery for a Mass of Thanksgiving, and gave us all his first priestly blessing, and then we all had a recreation with him in the large parlor. Sister was so proud of him. Mother's letting her go to his ordination had changed her opinion of Mother, which before wasn't always so sweet. Sr. Trinity had not been reappointed Novice Mistress, but had been put in charge of maintenance, which was a huge responsibility but which Sr. Trinity thought was a demotion...she once called it "going from white-veiled novices to broken-down boilers and stubborn handymen."

Sr. Catherine Agnes was now Novice Mistress. Sr. Anna Maria couldn't refrain from rolling her eyes every time I'd mention it. Sr. Anna Maria and I figured that Sr. Trinity must've been in the running for prioress, or should have been, and maybe that put her in a negative disposition towards the new prioress. Again, who knows? I'm embarrassed to think of all the wasted time and energy, not to mention uncharitableness, we engaged in over such things. Sr. Trinity never said anything about it all, at least not to me

or Sr. Anna Maria, and one couldn't always read her face, so
it was all cloistered speculation. But going to the ordination
of her brother seemed to change her disposition toward the
Prioress.

When I received in my Easter mail an engraved invitation
to attend the ordination of Rev. Brother Matthew Goldman
at the Cathedral in Springfield, Massachusetts...I wanted to
go. There was a precedent now, after all, with Sr. Trinity and
her brother. I was immediately distracted by my own fantasy
of the whole thing. The really sad and stupid thing about
my fantasies is that I am always the star. I was picturing
myself coming down the aisle of the cathedral and greeting Gwendolyn and Greta and all the Goldman family, who
were in awe of my being there. Even the bishop stopped in
the procession to give a nod to me and thank me for being
there, and of course, Ezra was overjoyed at my being there.
I must've played with that fantasy in my head for a good
ten minutes, and when I came back to earth, I thought, *I've
just got to be able to go. Sr. Trinity went, so there's a precedent;
we do that sort of thing now...in the spirit of Vatican II.* I had
to chuckle to myself, as I had more than once criticized a
Sister for invoking Vatican II to advance her own agenda.
"It can all be very subjective and manipulative," I whined
to Fr. Meriwether about a few little changes that I didn't
particularly like.

Before running off to Mother's office, however, I waited
till my Easter visit the next day with Fr. Meriwether, and
told him I had gotten an invitation, and there was a precedent for going to ordinations, and what did he think? He
was my spiritual director, after all, and I wouldn't want to

do anything that was really really against what he thought, but I knew he usually thought along the same lines as I did. Obedience was really at the heart of our life, the one vow we profess, and I "love it" except when it goes against my will.

And to my utter delight, Fr. Meriwether was very supportive and told me that he and Fr. Rayburne from Blessed Sacrament were both going. They were driving up and taking Ezra's Aunt Sarah from the Upper West Side with them, and if Mother gave permission, there would be room in the back seat for me.

"And what about a companion? We only go out with a companion..."

"Well, it's a large back seat, there would be room for all three of you." (I was already secretly praying that Sr. Anna Maria could be my companion.) Father thought out loud, saying that he could pick me up at the monastery, and as he and Fr. Rayburne were staying at the Dominican Nuns' Monastery in West Springfield, my companion and I would naturally stay there too, in the enclosure, and he would be driving to and from the cathedral, so we wouldn't have to inconvenience anyone. He used to think about those things.

It was perfect. I was so excited in my head that I don't remember anything else that we talked about in that visit. I was thinking about Aunt Sarah, whom I hadn't seen in years, and I knew that Gwendolyn was planning to go according to her Easter card where she wrote that she would take pictures for me. She would be thrilled to know that I was going—presumably—and would probably be making something special and delicious for the occasion...probably a Penguin Priest Cake.

When Fr. Meriwether left, it was nearly time for Vespers, but I wrote a quick note asking to see Mother Jane Mary in the morning. I hardly slept that night as all I could do was think about the grand reunion with Ezra, Aunt Sarah, Gwendolyn, and hopefully Greta; I bet Ezra's old roommates would be there too. And it would really be neat going back to the monastery in West Springfield this time as "one of them" and being welcomed inside. I also thought about how marvelous God's Divine Providence had been in my meeting Ezra at Tea on Thames. I might not even *be here* had we not met and become friends. He was there for me when I broke the news to my folks, when I was baptized, confirmed, and received my Holy Communion. He was my godfather, after all. This would be a wonderful fulfillment of God's Providence; I would be at his ordination, and he will be at my solemn profession.

I was grateful for the three o'clock guard, as I couldn't sleep anyway, but my meditation was hardly on the Joyful Mysteries, except my own anticipated joyful ones. After Holy Mass, I found a note in my box in Mother's handwriting:

Dear Sister Mary Baruch,

I cannot meet with you this morning as I must go out for a doctor's appointment, and of course, my afternoons are very full. I shall meet with you on Thursday, fifteen minutes after Mass. If this is a medical crisis, you should see Sister Subprioress. Blessed be God.
Mother Jane Mary

Thursday! And this was only Tuesday. Oh well, that gave me two more days to plan what I should take; and could I make something special for Ezra, I mean, Brother Matthew? Two days was also a nice length to obsess over it! I was glad it was the Easter Season and we had lots of candy available on the dessert table and even in the community room. People are so generous to us and probably think that we never even eat candy. A lot of the time we don't, especially not Godiva Chocolates. We probably had two dozen five-pound boxes of Whitman's Samplers, which was always Mama's favorite.

So I obsessed about it all, even during my prayer time, and work time, and time in between. I couldn't keep it from Sr. Anna Maria and showed her the invitation, and told her that I hoped Mother would send her as my companion.

The two days finally passed, and I was on my way to Mother's office, hoping my face wasn't breaking out from too much chocolate. My guimpe was feeling a little tight and I was comfortable with my belt a notch looser. Mother's door was open. She was sitting behind her desk, already working on something. She politely put down her pen and waited for my greeting: "Laudetur Jesus Christus."

"Now and forever," she smiled with a broad smile. (*Ah, thank you, Lord, she's in a good mood.*)

"Sr. Mary Baruch, what is it? You look like the cat that swallowed the canary. Did you discover a first edition of the *Imitation of Christ*?" She put her head back and laughed like it was the funniest thing she ever said.

"No, Mother," I tried to laugh, a little hysterically, realizing I was playing politics! But then I announced my tidings of great joy: "Oh, no, Mother, much much better." And from under my scapular I produced my engraved invitation. "My best friend and godfather, Brother Matthew Goldman, is being ordained next month, in Springfield, Massachusetts; and Fr. Meriwether is going and has said he would be happy to pick me up and drive me to the ordination." I had rehearsed it three dozen times since the Night Office. Ruthie couldn't have done a more enthusiastic and authentic performance. I stressed again that Fr. Meriwether thought it would be a wonderful gesture for me to be there. "And…." Mother was no longer smiling. "And, I'm asking your permission to go."

Without a moment's thoughtful consideration, Mother said, "No! It is not our practice to go to ordinations."

You could have hit me with a boulder. It took every ounce of Feinstein composure to remain cool, calm, and collected as a kosher cucumber. "But Mother, Sr. Trinity just went to her brother's ordination and…"

"Sr. Trinity's brother was ordained for New York, just across the river. She was there and back in four hours. She's also a solemnly professed nun. Why, what would the nuns in West Springfield think if they ever heard of such a thing?"

"Fr. Meriwether said I could stay there with them. I've been there before, Mother, when I was discerning."

"Well, it's out of the question, Sister. Fr. Meriwether should have known better than to presume you could go and to get your hopes up. Of all people, he would know you needed to obtain permission first."

I was sunk and speechless. I could feel the anger or hurt, mixed together, rising from my neck to my forehead. My face felt hot and red; I could feel the tears building up behind my eyes and a constriction in my neck. I had heard about "blind rage" but never experienced it till this moment. It's like I stopped breathing and went into a conscious coma. I don't really remember leaving Mother's office, and vaguely remember falling into my stall in choir and silently weeping. My stomach was all in knots and I felt so utterly alone.

I came around when I felt a gentle hand on my arm. "Sister?" A soft voice roused me. "Sister? Are you alright, dear?" It was Sr. Catherine Agnes...Scar.

"Yes, Sister, I'm sorry. Was I making a disturbance?"

Sr. Catherine Agnes whispered, "No, Sister, it's only the Lord and I here at the moment. Can I get you anything? You look wretched." (That was her bedside manner, and it almost made me smile.)

"No, Sister, I'm okay...thanks." My voice cracked. "I'm just very disappointed over something."

"I see." Scar stared off into the distance for a second, remembering something. "You stay here for a few minutes with the Lord, will you? I need to go out for a moment." And she handed me a clean handkerchief and quietly left the choir.

I was so upset I couldn't think straight, and at the same time I was so moved by Scar's kindness. She didn't probe into why I "looked so wretched" or correct me for weeping out loud. She was so kind to give me her handkerchief; I wouldn't dare blow my nose in it.

I looked up at the grille, and there in utter silence and hiddenness was the Lord in our beautiful sunburst monstrance...the same Lord who touched my heart ten years ago that autumn morning at St. Vincent's. The Lord of the Golden Tabernacle...the Lord whom Ezra and I visited in

all the churches we could visit in Manhattan…the Lord who
called me to Himself and to whom I said, "Yes, Lord, I will
be obedient." And I smiled and breathed in a deep breath of
acceptance.

"So be it, Lord. I offer it all for Ezra; it's my gift, in gratitude, Lord, for all You have done for me through him, and
all you have done for him. Make him to be a happy and
holy priest. And Lord, please don't let Mother be mad at
Fr. Meriwether." I closed my eyes and let myself go to my
inner space where I always knew peace, and a gentle peace
seemed to settle over me and over the choir. Oddly enough,
I thought of Mama and remembered how she closed her eyes
and prayed the prayer welcoming the Sabbath, praying for
all her children and her husband. I could almost hear her
voice murmuring the prayer.

I may have dozed off a bit, but before I knew it, the sisters were coming in one by one and preparing their books
for Sext. I likewise fixed my book and stood for a moment
facing the monstrance as sisters passed to get to their places
before Mother knocked and we knelt for the *O Sacred Banquet*, which we were now praying in English. I liked that
little change. "*The soul is filled with grace,*" and so, I realized,
we were…all of us at that moment, filled with His grace in
His holy presence.

Looking back, I have to say it was all a miracle, that morning. It was an action of grace, for I had never felt so disappointed or angry at "the life" since I had entered. My normal
reaction would have been to hold on to the grudge for days
or angrily try to change Mother's mind; at worst, of course,
I would have packed my bag and left to show her how sorry

she would be not to have let me go to the ordination. But I didn't do any of those. The miracle was that God gave me the grace to accept it without resentment or revenge, as if I were even capable of that! I was also happy just to be here, with these sisters, schlepping into choir like they do… and perhaps the biggest miracle of all…I had found a new friend…Scar.

***

It had been a very hot and humid summer that year. I was proposing air conditioning for the library, for the sake of the books, which were beginning to smell musty, especially those in the dank corners where nobody seemed to go. There were books which had never left the shelf; never had their binding broken or their contents read by an interested reader. They were not popular. Many of the books on philosophy and theology were not touched either; they looked impressive on the shelf, but no one seemed enthralled enough to read them. The popular shelves were biographies and "spiritual reading books," books on prayer and meditation and a few on religious life and the vows. Under Mother John Dominic we had begun a section of mystery novels and secular biographies, as opposed to the lives of the saints. These were very popular too, and seemed to be a pleasant enough "escape" for some.

We were also getting, thanks to my suggestion, audiobooks. These were mostly for the elderly sisters who couldn't read the small-print books anymore. They could listen to a book, with earphones on, making it as loud as they needed. We also had a whole closet, almost like a little room, with a huge collection of tapes. I think we had every retreat, every conference, every word spoken by a lecturing Dominican priest since the invention of magnetic tape! Sometimes we listened to former conferences in the refectory, at supper mostly. Cataloguing them was a huge project which I had begun but had to stop when the hot weather stifled me too much. It's nice winter weather work.

One tends to perspire in the habit during the long humid days of summer, but we never complain. Interestingly, Advent and Lent, the penitential seasons, are both in cool climates, even snow. But summer perspiration is a great penance for me...perspiration at any time is a penance for me. Humidity is worse than humility, but without the lasting effects. I don't know why I have an aversion towards perspiring. Somewhere in my youth and childhood I must've been told it was unladylike for a girl to sweat. I'm not complaining now, but reflective about the irony of it and hope that I've helped many souls in Purgatory with each saturated bandeau and wet hair under my veil of tears.

The summer of 1974, however, was unique in the perspiration department. By July 4th, I was to present my letter requesting solemn profession. I thought of the irony of that too...the day we celebrate our independence, I requested to be allowed to be dependent until death. Of course it's wonderful dependence. It's a dependence on God's mercy, and that of the community. I knew more and more that that's exactly what it has been—God's mercy and theirs. There were a few times over the past five years when I wanted to pack my bags and throw in the towel.

There were a few times that I was being observed with greater scrutiny than I realized. One big scrutiny followed my request to go to Ezra's ordination and my reaction to Mother's refusal to let me go. Mother Jane Mary was not happy with either my request or my reaction. It could easily have been the straw to break the camel's back about whether I would be accepted for solemn profession or not. Mother was concerned about my lack of docility and whether this was indicative of a psychological hostility to authority. And that raised a question in her mind as to whether I could live under holy obedience for the rest of my life. There was an independent streak in me that was both a blessing and a curse.

This would all be discussed discreetly at the Council Meeting which would make or break my fate, in a way. One is voted on by the entire Chapter after one first passes the positive vote of the Council. One is never privy, of course, to the deliberations of the Council. And needless to say, I was very nervous. I knew they could also tell me that they didn't think I was ready yet and that I should renew my temporary profession for a year or more. That would be fine, I thought to myself. But what if they simply said I didn't have a vocation and should leave immediately? I couldn't defend myself very well regarding my maturity or lack of docility or whether I could be obedient forever, so I didn't know what I would do, if that were the case. All I knew was that I had learned over those few years to trust in the Lord's Providence and to be resigned to whatever happened as God's will. It was all out of my control. I had learned from Sr. Anna Maria that that day I was upset and weeping in the choir, when Sr. Catherine Agnes spoke to me, and then left me there alone, that she went to see Sr. Anna Maria, and asked her what the trouble was. Anna Maria didn't know, of course, and only mentioned that I had received an invitation to Ezra's ordination and was asking Mother's permission to go, hoping that she, Sr. Anna Maria, could go with me. All Scar said was, "I see," and left.

I learned much later that Scar had gone to Mother to suggest that I might be permitted to go to the ordination, since there was a precedent, and since I had no real family supporting me all these years, and Br. Matthew was like a brother to me. Mother was unmoved by Sr. Catherine Agnes's pleas and rather displeased that she would interfere in the situation, and blamed me for going to her (Sr. Catherine Agnes) to beg her case.

"Sr. Mary Baruch has no idea I am here. I have left her alone and weeping in the choir. She is one of our finest young sisters on the cusp...on the cusp, Mother...of solemn profession. I would hate to see her leave on this account."

Mother mellowed a little, I'm told. "I respect your concern, Sister, and share your good sentiments about Sister; I would not want to see her leave us either. One does not come to this life, as you know, to carve out a career for oneself, or to have one's will catered to. We have embraced the Cross, and it comes to each of us in a unique way. Will Sr. Mary Baruch surrender her will or will she resist?"

Sr. Catherine Agnes did not answer that question. Only later in the day when she passed me in the cloister, normally a place of profound silence, she took me by the arm and whispered, "Trust in the Lord, Sister, and embrace His holy

Will as cheerfully as you can." And she smiled at me with a warmth I never knew she had.

"I have, Sister, I have…at least, I hope I have." And I smiled back and squeezed her hand still holding onto my arm. "Thank you, Sister, thank you more than you'll ever know."

The Council and Chapter both accepted me for solemn profession on November 1st, All Saints' Day. However, the Bishop was unable to come because of the Holy Day and his obligations at the Cathedral.

Mother Jane Mary announced at Chapter that the bishop would not be coming. However, she had been able to get a priest to come as principal celebrant. Celebrating my Profession Mass would be Fr. Matthew Goldman.

I closed my eyes, lest anyone see the tears waiting to roll down my cheeks. I was so happy, and in my joy I remembered my Sacred Heart statue of Jesus in priestly vestments… like Ezra would be.

**

The Chapter Reading that evening was from our Constitutions, read at the request of Sr. John Dominic:

> Called by God, like Mary, to sit at the feet of Jesus and listen to his words they are converted to the Lord, withdrawing from the empty preoccupations and illusions of the world. Forgetting what lies behind and reaching out for what lies ahead they are consecrated to God by public vows through profession of the evangelical counsels of chastity, poverty, and obedience. In

purity and humility of heart, in loving and assiduous contemplation, they love Christ, who is close to the Father's heart.

When I went to our cell after Compline, someone had left a single rose at my door. I still have it pressed in my old New Testament.

I went to bed that night full of joy and gratitude and anticipation.

Oh, Lord, will it really happen? Will it all come to pass? Is this really Your will for me? Mother of God, be my Mother now and obtain for me the grace to say yes. Solemn profession as a cloistered Dominican Nun…such a blessing. Amen.